For those who love without condition.

HEATHER McCORKLE

TEMPERED
& TURNED

CHILDREN OF FENRIR BOOK TWO

CITY OWL
PRESS

TEMPERED & TURNED
Children of Fenrir, Book 2

CITY OWL PRESS
www.cityowlpress.com

Cover Design by Tina Moss. All stock photos licensed appropriately.

Edited by Yelena Casale.

For information on subsidiary rights, please contact the publisher at info@cityowlpress.com.

Print Edition ISBN: 978-1-64898-046-6

Digital Edition ISBN: 978-1-64898-045-9

Printed in the United States of America

PRAISE FOR HEATHER McCORKLE

"Kickass women, Icelandic warriors, and plenty of action!"
— *Kait Ballinger, Bestselling Author of The Execution Underground Series*

"The characters have lots of depth to them and are strong, sexy and fun. A fabulous story line full of magic and danger that I was pulled into from the first page. I can't wait to read more of this series. I loved it."
— *Petula Winmill, Book Reviewer*

"Holy werewolves, Batman! What did I just read!! A winning combination of romance and heat, action, and drama, not to mention plenty of Norse lore and mythology to make a paranormal lover combust! This story was unique and quite different from the shifter stories we've come to know and love. Ms. McCorkle did a marvelous job with weaving her story and I am so looking forward to what's coming next."
— *Katrina Berry, Book Reviewer*

"Excellent book!! Not your average shifter book. I really like the Norse bent to the storyline. Couldn't put it down and anxiously awaiting book 2 of the series."
— *Susan Hall, Book Reviewer*

"What a great story this is! One of the best things about it is that I can't think of a book to compare it too. The reason why I love that, is because the story is just so unique. Which is why I kept turning the page!
Loved it!"
— *Ali Cross, USA Today Bestselling Author of Young Adult Fantasy*

"There's trouble in the Dragon Empire, the kind that could start a war between dragons and the races of people...For those who love fantasy, dragons and a sweet love story, this book is definitely a must read for you!"
— *Geeky Book Gal*

"Channeler's Choice is definitely my choice for a fantastic story. Heather McCorkle turns the heat up in her second novel of the Channeler series... McCorkle is an outstanding storyteller, and she totally blew me away again."
– I Heart YA Books

CHILDREN OF FENRIR

RECOMMENDED READING ORDER

CHAPTER ONE

VIDAR

Vidar

Being chosen wasn't an option. It was necessary, essential, vital. I had to get back to her. For every *uppskera*—reaper—there has always been a *verndari* monk from the Order of the *Verndari* at their side. I had to be that *verndari* for Ayra. I forced myself to go faster, until my legs were no more than a blur as they flew over the forest floor. Pine needles and twigs tickled at my bare feet, feathery boughs brushed at my arms. The wonderful, sweet, heady scents of the forest poured down my throat, but something else came right behind them—the musky odor of my rivals. Their feet brushed the ground behind me, and their breath touched my shoulders.

The rocky terrain grew steeper. Fighting the instinct to slow, I forced myself faster through the ferns and brush clinging to the mountainside. From somewhere nearby, the clean, fresh scent of a waterfall carried to me. The trees thinned the closer I drew to the top, letting the afternoon sun break through in large, warm patches, too warm on my sweaty, ebony skin. I concentrated on trying to outrun the light itself.

I reached the top of the plateau I'd been ascending and launched across it. A hundred feet away stood three raised stone-encircled platforms, the fighting rings. The slightly salty scent of the sun-warmed sand within them drifted to me. Close to a dozen men and women clothed in simple linen uniforms stood at attention in an arc on another raised area around the platforms.

I went straight for the highest ring. My feet slapped on the stairs in a few heartbeats. Sand gave way beneath my feet, a welcome relief after an hour of running barefoot on rock and dirt. The brows of a few of those waiting rose, but otherwise, they didn't react.

The smaller ring would be the most challenging of the three. Three winners would emerge at the end, and the waiting priests would choose one of us based off how well we performed and how much risk we took.

I would take every risk I had to for her.

Chest pumping like a bellows as I regained my air, I turned to see who else would make it. I found my calm center and sank deep into it. My breathing slowed. Clarity filled me, followed by determination. One by one, my muscles relaxed as I willed them to. Power hummed beneath my feet, and the ground vibrated slightly. That power tugged at my own, encouraging it to rise and rejuvenate me. The Order had chosen this place for the trials specifically because of that power. It ran deep through the earth and fed our kind as surely as the air that filled our lungs.

The others soon burst up over the edge of the plateau, men and women all eager to be chosen, eager for the wrong reasons. To them it was an honor, one that would bring them fame and renown. I saw it in their wide eyes, smelled it on their sweating skin.

My fangs sprouted from my top and bottom jaws, and a growl forced my lips apart.

In only running shorts—and sport bras in the women's cases—the strengths and weaknesses of each were on display. One ran with a limp, another sucked air so hard his chest looked in danger of collapsing, and another bled from a gash across her abdominals. They all glared at me with a ferocity that made my hackles rise.

I bared my fangs at them out of instinct.

The first four went to the other two rings without hesitation. Out of the corner of my eye, I watched as they rested, some bending over to put their elbows on their knees, others collapsing onto the sand. Only one remained standing, and she looked as though she may fall over at any moment. Despite our training, not one of them calmed themselves or drew on the power of this place to replenish their energy.

Fools.

They weren't worthy of her.

At last, the sixth and seventh candidates burst over the plateau edge, both tall, broad, blond men native to the Icelandic soil we stood on. But then, so was I. It made no difference that my ancestors had been stolen from English slave traders and brought here over a thousand years ago. I was just as native as these lot were. Some didn't see it that way, these two included. Even now their expressions tightened with judgment. My ancestry, coupled with the fact that I wasn't born in Iceland, rubbed their fur all kinds of wrong ways.

One of the final two took one look at me, hung his head, and collapsed on the rocky soil. For once, my reputation served me well. Or rather, it served Ayra well. She deserved someone far more determined to protect her than that man. They were good monks, each one of them, but that didn't mean they were what she needed. I smiled, enjoying the furious snarl of the remaining man that strode to my ring.

Mat Matheson.

Despite his swagger, the reluctance in his eyes and stiffness in his gait made it clear he would have rather gone to any ring but mine. For that alone I would have to beat him. He sauntered up the steps at a leisurely pace. Clearly, he meant for me to think he was confident he'd win, but I could see right through the ruse. Each slow step gave him more time to suck in air and recover a little. Fine by me. I wanted him at his best, or as close as he could get.

No wounds covered his pale skin. He didn't limp or favor any part of his muscled body as he moved. Sweat plastered locks of his shoulder-length hair to his glistening skin. He rolled his neck as he climbed the steps. Slipping into a fighting stance, he swung his arms out and around to loosen them, then flexed his pectorals until each bounced in rhythm. One of my brows rose as I swallowed a humorous quip.

A man and a woman leaped onto the outer rock ring that surrounded my fighting pit, two of the monks who had been waiting for us. They walked to opposite sides of the circle and stood at attention, waiting to serve as judges. From the raised arc surrounding the three rings came the voice of the High Priestess.

"Welcome. Congratulations on being the top six to complete the second round of the physical trials. The very fact that you have made it here means you are favored by the Gods."

Keeping Mat in my peripheral vision, I gave the priestess my attention, as was proper. Back straight, muscled arms behind her, blond hair woven into a single, massive plait that trailed over one breast and down to her waist, she looked every bit the priestess of Frigg and Odin. The knotwork tattoos on her bare upper arms and trailing down her neck into her cleavage completed the image. Still, she was nothing compared to Ayra.

The remaining competitors began to climb—and in some cases, crawl —their way up onto the plateau. They sat on the rocky ground around the three rings, eager spectators for an event that would go down in our kind's history books.

The priestess went on. "There can be only three potentials. You will fight by the old rules until a winner is declared. Judges, ready?"

Six collective affirmatives shouted out.

"Begin!" the priestess announced.

Out of the corner of my eye, I saw Mat move. Fists rising, I shadowed him. We danced back and forth, around and around for several moments. Kicks, punches, jabs, and more flew as we blocked, spun, and sidestepped in an attempt to gauge one another's skill. With the blinding speed that only our kind can manage, Mat kicked for my abdomen. That one move signaled the dance's end and the fight's beginning. The kick was fast enough it was going to hurt, but I didn't block it. Instead, I raised my hands to block the second kick that I knew would come for my face.

Sure enough, the first had been only a good fake, and the second one, even faster, came at my jaw. I caught it easily, cupping my hand to grasp his heel and throw Mat's leg back at him. Rather than let the motion jam his own leg into him, Mat used the momentum to backflip away. When he landed on all fours, it was as a brown wolf. Almost before his paws touched the ground, he lunged with teeth snapping.

Instead of sidestepping, I crouched and grabbed his furred throat, holding those sharp teeth at a distance. Continuing with Mat's momentum,

I rolled onto my back and placed my foot in his chest to throw him past. As I turned to face him again, I saw him skidding to a stop in human form, teetering on the edge of the circle.

His display had blown his running shorts to pieces. Bits of them fluttered down to the sand. Most wouldn't have thought to try shifting back to catch themselves from falling over the edge, or even been fast enough. Stepping or being thrown out of a circle meant losing.

His ability to shift in mid-fight meant he had the power of an alpha's *verndari*, or possibly even an alpha. I hadn't expected that. I smiled as our eyes locked again, and this time Mat bared his fangs at me. That look told me he knew I had underestimated him. But I wouldn't do it again. We paced around each other to the sound of a cheering crowd.

Then we were on one another in a flurry of kicks, blocks, and strikes, too fast to see. I had to feel, instead, to open myself up to instinct. I kicked for Mat's chest. He sidestepped and caught my leg, locking an arm around it. Unable to pull it back, I pushed against him and jumped into the air, twisting and kicking. He let go, but too late. By the time he ducked, I shifted into my hybrid form—half man, half wolf—and the different angle of my leg allowed me to land the kick solidly into his back. He collapsed, the air forced from his lungs with a loud grunt. He rolled to the right, escaping my second blow and getting closer to the center of the circle.

The crowd gasped and cheered louder. The hybrid form wasn't something many of our kind could do. Even those that could had to practice long and hard to pull it off, something I did daily. I was lucky to have a father who could also shift into the hybrid form, and he had taught me well.

I leaped for Mat, my hybrid form giving me the extra reach I needed to grab him by the shoulders with my black furred arms. I spun him around, and with deadly four-inch claws, marked him across the chest with shallow gashes. Mat's eyes shot open in shock as blood trickled down his chest. I had moved far too swiftly for him to even begin to block. Speed was another thing I worked on incessantly.

The crowd fell silent as we straightened and stood looking at one another. All knew I could have opened Mat's chest and torn out his heart. The fight was over. No judge could challenge that. But I remained ready, just in case they did, or Mat got any ideas to keep fighting.

"Match!" both of our ring judges called at once.

Mat fell to one knee and bowed his head nearly to the ground. Sweat and blood dripped into the dirt. With a thought, my body flowed back into that of a man.

The judges turned their backs to us. As they deliberated silently with hand signals, the other fights to our left and right slowly came to an end. Mat rose but kept his head bowed and his eyes averted. It was no less of a submission. The stench of defeat—a mixture of a sour, sweaty smell and tangy rot—hung heavy on him. Our judges approached us at the same time the others approached their fighters. Mat's gaze finally lifted to mine. Respect shone in the depths of his blue eyes, and his shoulders slowly drew up. We smiled at each other.

Just because I was the clear winner physically didn't mean the judges would pick me. The match was won by skill, creativeness, and passion. He had fought well and earned my respect. There was a good chance he had earned the judges' favor as well.

The winds of anxiety and doubt attempted to blow me out of my calm center. Controlled breaths and years of discipline helped me stand fast.

One judge took hold of my left hand while the other took hold of Mat's. My breath caught in my throat, making it feel as if my chest was about to collapse.

"Judges, choose your winners," the priestess commanded. The judge holding my hand thrust it high into the air. A triumphant howl rose from me before I could stop it. The howls of the other two winners soon joined mine, reminding me this wasn't over yet.

After the howls died down, the priestess said, "Winners approach."

Quelling the urge to keep howling, I found my calm center again and gathered my wits. I bowed deep to both the judges and my opponent. The new respect in Mat's eyes as he bowed in turn heartened me. I leaped down from the fighting ring and approached the base of the steps where the priestess stood. The other two winners, a man and a woman whom I knew to be excellent fighters, joined me. The woman smiled and nodded while the man glared with a ferocity that tried to call both my anger and my power up. Being sure to retract my fangs, I grinned at him. He glared all the harder.

Tall and broad as I was, these two were not diminished in the slightest standing beside me, not even the woman. At less than three inches shorter than me, she possessed the muscular build of a big-boned Norse woman who dedicated her days to the gym. The other male finalist was cut to the point that he probably possessed zero body fat. All well and good if it were a bodyguard Ayra needed. But she needed much more than that. Her body wouldn't be the only thing in danger.

The judges joined the priestess on the raised platform before us. Their solemn gazes weighed heavy on each of us in turn. Snowcapped peaks of jagged mountaintops rose behind them in an arc that hugged the horizon. As it so often did, the beauty of this place added to the poignancy of the moment. One way or another, I'd be leaving tomorrow, and I'd miss this magnificent island deeply. It had a way of digging deep down into one's soul and nesting there. But I had to go. Whether it would be as the chosen, or as only a friend, I had to return to Ayra. Not even my love of this island could keep me from her. Four years away was too long.

Behind me, I felt the press of the other competitors' power as they gathered to witness. My fighter's instincts didn't like them at my back, but I couldn't turn away from the council in front of me. I didn't need to see the other competitors anyway. Their defeat and acceptance of it weighed heavy in their power.

The priestess stepped forward, her glacial gaze sweeping over me and the other two winners with an impartial air. To my left, the other potential fidgeted as if disturbed by that gaze. It comforted me. Impartiality meant she would choose based on logic, not favoritism. I could only hope the other six would do the same. The priestess's gaze settled on the woman to my right.

"Why do you want to be the *uppskera's verndari?*" she asked her.

The reaper's protector. The very phrase seemed an oxymoron. The reaper of those *varúlfur*—werewolves—who'd gone mad and started killing people. My Ayra, my childhood best friend, had become the thing all monsters fear. But the *uppskera's verndari* was only an oxymoron to those who didn't understand why the reaper needed a protector. Sadly, many of today's competitors didn't. That knowledge was lost to the ages in which we didn't have an *uppskera*. But I had found it, I knew. These competitors just wanted to be her *verndari* for the glory it would bring their family, their pack. Which was part of why it had to be me. Ayra was more than just the *uppskera* to me. So much more. "To honor Odin and his plan for our kind," the woman said.

Giving no reaction whatsoever, the priestess turned her head to me. "Why do you want to be the *uppskera's verndari?*"

I swallowed to wet my throat and loosen my words. "To ensure both the *uppskera's* physical and mental health." Not a grandiose answer, but it was mine nonetheless. Raw honesty was always my policy.

The priestess asked the man to my left the same question. He puffed his bare chest out. "To help protect our kind from both discovery and persecution." His overconfident tone made him sound like a student who knew he had the right answer.

Each time one of us answered, the council of six would scribble in the small notebooks they removed from their belts. I tried desperately to discern what those notes might be by the sound of the writing. Who was to know, though, if less or more scratching was good or bad? Their power weighed heavy on us. It crawled across my skin like a prickling breeze, searching, feeling, judging. With practiced control, I kept my own power from flaring up in reaction. The others didn't do quite as well. Whether mine or theirs was the proper reaction was hard to say. But I found comfort in my discipline, so I was sticking with it.

Still looking at the man, the priestess asked, "Would you kill for the *uppskera?*"

"Yes," he answered far too eager for my liking.

Both myself and the woman answered yes when the priestess asked us. For the third question, the priestess looked to me first. "Would you die for the *uppskera?*"

"Absolutely," I said without hesitation. Now who was too eager? Dammit. I hadn't meant to jump on the question like that.

The priestess's eyes widened just a touch, the only reaction I'd seen her give so far. She moved on with the same removed air she had possessed before, making me wonder if I'd imagined the look. She asked the others the same question. They both answered yes, but slower, and with a touch of hesitation in the man's case. A powerful protective instinct rose in me at his reaction. If they chose him, I wasn't sure I'd be able to walk away from here without another fight.

The seven turned away from us to gather and compare notebooks, not saying a word. As *varúlfur*, we possessed the sharp hearing of a canine, so to speak would be to give away results. Tension started to build up a terrible pressure in my chest. The last four years of training and learning came down to this moment. If I wasn't chosen, all that time away from Ayra would be wasted. True, I had learned about what she was becoming and what I needed to do to help her, but if I wasn't chosen, what good was it? If that happened, leaving her four years ago would feel like I'd abandoned her when she needed me most. My power became a steam kettle threatening to explode, or at the least make me scream.

Just when I feared I couldn't take it anymore, the six turned around and took their places before us. Their stoic expressions gave away nothing. The priestess's gaze settled on me, and my heart felt like it stopped.

"Vidar Balderson, you have earned the right of First Impression. You will have one moon to impress the *uppskera*. If she does not choose you as her *verndari* by the new moon, Birna will have the second opportunity to impress her. If Birna fails, Seth will have the third opportunity of Impression," she announced.

The relief that coursed through me made my knees weak. I bowed low, grateful the motion hid my reaction and gave me the opportunity to draw in a few deep breaths. It wouldn't be good for the council to see the depth of my emotion.

"Thank you, honored council. I will not let you down," I said in a voice far steadier than I felt.

The priestess gave a very slight shake of her head. "Our opinion is inconsequential. It's the *uppskera* you can't let down. May you go with the speed and blessing of the Allfather," she said.

It was all the dismissal I needed. I bowed low to the council, turned, and ran for the edge of the plateau. If I hurried, I might be able to catch an earlier flight out. Every moment counted. Already, I hadn't been there when her power awoke. For that I would never forgive myself. But I'd had to come to Iceland. I'd had to learn everything I could about her ability and the history of those like her. Now that I was armed with the knowledge, I would help her survive this. I had to. Whether I survived or not remained to be seen, but mattered far less.

I leaped from the plateau and plunged headlong over the edge into an uncertain future.

CHAPTER TWO

AYRA

I reap the wrongs others have sown,
so that our kind may remain unknown.
-Uppskera Journals

T he sweet, cloying scent of hay forced me to breathe through my mouth, resulting in the taste coating my tongue. But my mouth was dry for more reasons than just that. My hands trembled a little as I ascended the ladder into the hayloft. Not from fear, but from the anger growing inside me like a tornado coming to life, devouring everything in its wake. Calder never allowed me up here, so I knew it was the one place I had to look. In all his cockiness, my arrogant prick of a brother wouldn't expect me to have the guts to come here. I was not the same woman I was before the awakening, though, and therein lay my advantage over him.

When he had kidnapped me and exposed me to the seeker, Sonya Michaelson, to awaken my power, I'd still been afraid of him. I had been the frail woman he beat up whenever the mood struck him, which was often. The awakening had burned the fear away, replacing it with a rage so powerful it frightened me almost more than being the reaper did. The scared little girl in me had turned into something else that night.

At the top of the stairs a small cobweb-infested landing awaited me. The scents of dust, moldy straw, and untreated wood teased my nose. Above those, Calder's musky scent trails lingered, but it was an old scent. Two days or more had aged his most recent trail. Choosing my footing carefully on the loose bits of straw that remained scattered across the worn wood floor, I walked to the door. The knob resisted my efforts, but I snapped the lock with ease. With no more than a little push, the door swung open, revealing a small, dark room beyond. It figured. Calder was so confident that I would stay away out of fear of him that he didn't bother with a deadbolt. My dear brother had a lot to learn about the woman I was becoming. Just inside, I found a light switch.

The bare bulb buzzed to life, throwing muted yellow light across a desk and backless chair. A collage of images covering all three walls in my immediate view drew my attention to the reason I had come here. Newspaper clippings, both from actual newspapers and from online news sites that had been printed out, papered the walls from floor to about the seven-foot-high level. Only after peering into every shadowy corner and up into the rafters did I finally cross the small room. Cocky or not, I didn't trust my brother not to have left an unpleasant surprise like a bear trap or something equally painful. It wouldn't have been the first time. Anger tried to swirl again at the memory, but I kept it down to a brisk wind. I didn't have time for it right now.

Aside from a bit of dust and grime on the floor, nothing unpleasant awaited me on my way across the room. Grisly images of crime scenes and startling headlines of murder and maulings dominated the clippings. The dates of the articles on the wall to my left started twenty years ago, ascending as they went from one wall to the next, and the next, up until only a few weeks ago. Not a clean space of wall beneath seven feet of the roof remained. There were thousands of clippings from all across the upper United States and the lower territories of Canada. Chills traveled through me, raising bumps along my arms and chest as they went. Every one of them looked like an animal attack, a wolf attack specifically.

Varúlfur didn't do this, at least not those that had been properly brought into a pack. The only ones that would do this were those bitten in against their will.

I knew there had to be some over the years, those in need of either guidance or putting down. It was the reason the *uppskera* had awakened within me. Never had I imagined there were so many, and going back so far.

My mouth dried out again, but this time it had nothing to do with the air quality. Dread made my steps slow and heavy, but I managed to force myself over to the desk. Save for a few office supplies, the wooden surface was bare of anything but scratches and dings. Locked drawers offered me more resistance than the door to the room had. Despite my strength, they wouldn't budge, which meant the wood had to be reinforced and the locks were of something akin to titanium. Regardless, it couldn't hold up to my efforts. The wood snapped and splintered, all but exploding beneath my clawed hands.

Within the ruined mess of wood sat a metal lock box. "Damn you, Calder," I hissed through my fangs.

The creak of stairs snapped my attention back to the door I had left open. Moving on the balls of my feet, I crossed the room light as a ghost and twice as fast. The newfound speed that came with being the reaper still left me a little dizzy, forcing me to place a hand on the wall to steady myself. I cringed at the image of an eviscerated torso beneath my fingers but didn't move. If I did, I risked the paper crinkling, or worse, me stumbling. Heavy steps moved across the landing, nearly silent by most standards, but clear as a bell to my ears. Someone of Calder's build easily from the sound of it, but possessing less grace, if that were possible.

I knew who it was before I smelled them.

My lips pulled back as my fangs extended. A shock of white-blond hair exactly the shade of my own preceded the hulking form of the only other man on this planet that I loathed as much as my brother.

"Father, what are you doing here?" I demanded. Sperm donor was more like it, but habits that had been beaten into one died hard.

A blue-eyed gaze as cold and unfeeling as glaciers stabbed at me, trying to pin me in place. I returned his stare, letting the contempt I felt for the man fill my eyes. He looked away first.

"I didn't come to argue. I must say, though, this is literally the last place I could think of to look for you. I'm impressed you were brave enough to come here." His snide tone made me twitch. He couldn't even give me a compliment properly.

"That would be a first."

Ignoring my jibe, he went on. "I came to let you know your mother and I support you, and we...love you. As does the Arnoddr pack. They are your family as much as we are, and you can have the highest of ranks among them, above even the alpha. It is your rightful place."

The way he stuttered over the word "love," like it was a foreign thing that tasted bad on his tongue, made me bare my fangs again.

"Really? Have you asked Isak how he feels about that? Because I'm not sure your alpha would enjoy giving up his place at the top of the pack."

My father's pale brows came together in a bundle of deep wrinkles. "Of course he would. He'd be honored. You've received his invitation to join the pack, haven't you?" Ah, so he was fishing for information. That explained the rare visit. I had received the invitation from Isak, and from the other two pack alphas in Hemlock Hollow. "If that were your business, you wouldn't have to ask," I said.

His size thirteens shook the wooden floorboards as he stormed across the loft. Sliding into a subtle fighting stance, I held my ground and returned his fierce glare. This time he didn't look away. But neither did I for once. Less than a foot remained between us when he stopped, forcing me to look up to hold his glare. I had to open my fists as my claws started to grow. Not noticing, he grabbed me by the biceps, fingers digging deep enough into the muscles to hurt. But I was used to the pain.

"You are my daughter. Everything you do is my business. You have a responsibility to your family, to your pack, to honor us. I came to make sure you do exactly that," he said in a voice that rumbled with the beginnings of a growl.

I smiled, exposing my fangs. His fingers dug even deeper into my arms. No claws sprang from them because he didn't have that kind of control. I brought my hands together, thrust up between his arms, and to the outside of them, breaking his hold on me with ease. Pulling my claws in just a bit, I grabbed hold of his arms like he had mine. I let him feel the prick of my claws, but just barely.

"I don't owe you, or the Arnoddr pack. They are not my pack, and you are not my family," I said in a steady voice.

His face turned bright red. Using his strength, he yanked free of my grasp and struck me across the face hard enough to make me stagger. I hadn't expected it, or the strike never would have connected. He hadn't hit me in over two years, but that was mostly because I had left home the day I turned eighteen. The blood warming my fingers told me he hadn't escaped unharmed. The pain of the slap was minute compared to what I'd been through during my childhood. I had spent it learning to fight, endure pain, hunt, and kill. All because I was of the *uppskera* bloodline, and they'd hoped the power would awaken in me.

Very slowly, he raised his hands up beside his head, fingers splayed. "I didn't come here to fight, and I didn't come here to stop you from going after your brother."

"Then why are you here?" I snapped.

He lowered his arms and motioned to my hand with a thrust of his head. "To remind you that you have a wedding in two months that you had better be back for. And if you don't return out of a sense of duty to the Arnoddr pack, do it for Elí."

I forced my claws back in and closed my hands into fists. Of course he would use that against me, the bastard. If didn't go through with the engagement, not only would I dishonor myself and my entire family, but I would dishonor Elí, and none of this was his fault. He was a pawn as much as I was. Unlike me, though, he was an innocent. While we shared no love between us, I respected him and his pack. And I was an honorable person, dammit. Even if I was a monster. My father knew that and wasn't above using it against me.

Fury boiled so hot in me that I had to look away. If I didn't, I was going to return every slap he had ever dealt me, and there had been many. I took several slow, measured breaths like my *glíma* instructor had taught me. The anger started to recede like a slow tide.

My father took a step closer, bringing the wave of anger right back onto shore. "When you find your brother, just remember, everything Calder did was to make you stronger so you not only survive being the *uppskera*, but so you'll be the greatest one history has ever seen," he said.

I poured all my anger into one growl that resembled a word. "Leave." Power rolled off me and slammed into him, shoving him toward the door. In a barely controlled rush, he stumbled to it. His hands slapped hard against the wood.

He stepped out the door. "All right, all right. I'm going. But don't forget what I said. You have responsibilities. Elí is a part of them. Turning your back on that would only show how weak and afraid you are. You'll understand soon. Make the right choice." With that, he thundered down the steps.

Roaring, I grabbed a metal ballpoint pen from the desk, spun around, and threw it at the door. It sank into the wood up to the gel finger rest. Daddy dearest was lucky he moved fast. I turned back to the desk and gripped the edge of it. My claws dug in, splintering the wood with a satisfying crack. Steps sounded on the stairs again. The fool couldn't actually be coming back for more, could he?

"Ayra?" came a deep, familiar, masculine voice that vibrated along my bones. The last time I had heard it, it hadn't sounded quite this…mature.

That voice had occupied my dreams for the last four years, bringing me comfort when nothing else could. But they had been only dreams. When he left, I had been a girl with a crush, and now my entire world was different. He stepped into the doorway, and my heart began to pound hard enough to remind me that not everything had changed. "Vidar?" I asked, afraid to believe it. That kind of hope was dangerous.

The yellow light of the bare bulb made his ebony skin look golden. Swirls of black knotwork tattoos peeked out from beneath the straining arms of his vintage comic book Thor T-shirt. Both the irony of that and the fact that he clearly still loved comic book heroes almost made me smile. The tattoos had to be the markings of the monks. I wanted so badly to lift his sleeve and look, to caress those arms. At the same time, I wanted to scream at him, or slap him. He had been the one friend I had. And he'd all but disappeared four years ago. Vague letters had come once a month at first, but in the last two years, they had dropped off to special occasions.

Green eyes mixed with yellow that shot out from his pupils like solar flares regarded me with a tenderness I did not want or deserve, not considering what I had become. Something else lay in those eyes too. Was it regret? Longing? His black hair was cropped short. I missed the tight curls. And Gods, he had filled out, a lot, to perfection really. The pictures he sometimes sent me of him at the temple in his uniform had not done him justice. He had always been tall, but now he towered at least a foot over me, and at five-five, I wasn't exactly short.

Those magnetic eyes wouldn't look away from me, almost as if they couldn't. His power pulsed and crackled like a growing fire, one that wanted desperately to reach out and combine with my own power. Impossible. He'd never felt that way about me. This had to be a dream.

"Vidar, is that really you?"

The big smile that flashed ultra-white teeth at me was unmistakable. A mixture of childlike joy, repressed desire, and repressed anger spun me into a whirlwind that made my heart pound like a Viking drum. Was that moisture in his eyes?

"Yes, White Wolf, it's me. By the Gods, you look amazing!" Giggles of pure happiness bubbled from me quicker than I could stop them. I couldn't help it. I'd waited so very long for this moment.

"As do you!"

In two great strides, he closed the distance between us and swept me up into his arms, enveloping me completely. He felt so warm, familiar, and safe that I couldn't help but relax into him. The tight vise of his arms took my breath away. But that was all right. I didn't want to breathe. I wanted Vidar. He was all I had wanted for the last four years. For a moment, I was the teenage girl he'd left behind again, happy, full of hope and dreams, not yet a monster, not yet engaged to someone else.

But I was a monster now. The anger over him leaving me behind returned in a rush that left me a bit dizzy. Drawing on it, I went against every instinct and desire in me and pulled away from him. The anger gave me strength. In it, I found an old comfort.

"What are you doing here, Vidar?" I demanded. For him to see me now, as the *uppskera*, and not the woman, it was too much. All I'd ever wanted was for him to see me as a woman. Now he never would because I could never be just a woman again. In the back of my mind stuck the idea that if he hadn't left, I might not have been forced to become the *uppskera*. And I certainly wouldn't have been forced into an arranged engagement with Elí.

Pain and regret flashed in his eyes as his hands slid slowly from my arms. "I've come back for you. I meant to come before your awakening, but a ceremony delayed me. I'm so sorry."

"That's right, the ceremony you mentioned at the *Verndari* Temple." He never did tell me what the ceremony was about. But then, his infrequent letters had never talked much about the temple. What he had told me, I wasn't exactly thrilled about. Like how he'd taken a vow of celibacy. At first it had been a comfort to know he wasn't bedding some Icelandic woman. But it also meant he wouldn't ever be bedding me either. Not that it was an option now. It was far too late for that. In fact, with each moment the shock of seeing him again turned more and more into anger.

"It wasn't like you'd have been able to stop me becoming the *uppskera*. Destiny and all that," I said in a harsh tone that sounded completely unconvincing.

He looked down at his shoes. "Doesn't matter. I should have been here."

Hell yeah, he should have. I had to clamp my jaw shut to keep those words in. I wanted to say it, and more. I wanted to hurt him like he'd hurt me. But that only made me feel more like a monster. Another part of me wanted to reach out to him, but I couldn't. I wouldn't. He had left me in my own private Muspelheimr.

"You weren't my keeper," I said instead.

Wrinkles formed in the dark skin between his brows. "No, but I am your friend." He swallowed hard after the soft words. "I ran into your father in the barn. Looks like you put him in his place." He smiled a bit at the last part. The pride in his eyes made me tingle down to my toes. But sadness quickly replaced it. "Did I hear him right, that you're engaged?"

Why would he be sad? He'd never thought of me that way. He'd left me.

I lifted my head. "Yes, Elí Gabrielson."

"Isn't that a nephew of Isak's?" he asked, tone guarded.

"Yes. It surprises you that I'm engaged to a nephew of the alpha of the Arnoddr pack?"

A flustered look came over him, and his mouth worked a bit before words came out. "Yes. I mean no. But, yeah. You said you never wanted to get married. Was this your choice?"

I moved some papers around the desk, needing to look at anything but him as I answered. "Elí and I were friends throughout our senior year. My parents convinced Isak we would be a good match, and they made the arrangements."

Vidar swallowed so hard I heard it. The sound was both satisfying and heartbreaking. "When is the wedding?"

"In August, when he gets back from visiting his parents in Quebec.

He's been studying molecular biology at UCLA." I tried to sound proud, because I was, really. But it came out sounding a bit petulant.

He tried to move around the desk to catch my eye. "Do you love him?" he asked in a soft voice that cut deep into me.

I lifted my chin and looked him right in the eyes. "Vidar, you don't get to come back here after four years of near silence and ask me that." I wasn't going to tell him how agreeing to the marriage had gotten my parents to finally allow me to move out. Or how it had stopped my brother from beating me up on a daily basis. And I certainly wasn't going to tell him that those had been the main reasons I'd agreed to it. He didn't deserve to know that.

Vidar flinched as if I'd slapped him. "Fair enough," he whispered. "You're still going through with it, even though you're the *uppskera* now?"

"Of course I am." I had to. It was the honorable thing to do, and being honorable meant more to me than just about anything. Honor was all I had that separated me from my horrible family. Besides, I wouldn't want to disrespect Elí or Isak by backing out.

"How will that work? Being married and being the *uppskera?*"

I waved a hand in a dismissive gesture. "Don't know. I'll figure it out as I go."

Upper lip curled in distaste, Vidar looked around. "I thought you hated this old barn." The abrupt and obvious change of subject would have made me smile if it weren't so sad.

To hide the chill that danced over me, I turned my back to him and returned to the lock box. Just looking at him was almost harder than I could handle. Time and distance had made me want him more, and here he was in the flesh—really hot, hard flesh at that. My mind was pissed at him for leaving me for so long, but my heart was glad he was back. It should have felt like a betrayal to Elí, but it didn't. While he wrote to me every week and sent me gifts all the time, only one of us was in love, and it wasn't me.

"I do hate this place, but I have to find out more about what Calder was up to. Hopefully something in here will lead me to him. You heard what happened, I take it." It had to be why he was here. He had only just received his bachelor's degree, and I knew he wanted to go for his master's. He'd left not only the temple, but the university, and all because of this damn *uppskera* thing. If I hadn't become the *uppskera*, would he have even come back? Doubtful.

Footsteps almost too light for such a big man crunched across the dirty floor. Clearly the temple had been good for his ninja skills. That thought made my lips turn up. The boy I had known had loved not only comic book superheroes, but also the ninjas in Japanese manga.

"You think he had more to do with this than just ensuring your power awoke?" His voice—deeper than I remembered—vibrated along my skin.

I had to give myself a mental shake to stop picturing him sprawled on his bed reading comics. He had been cute then. Now he was downright sexy. I did not want to see him that way. Not after he had abandoned me.

"I'm fairly certain he did." *Did I sound breathy? Shit, I think I did.*

I picked the lock box up and set it on the desktop. It had to weigh at least fifty pounds, though it was no more than the size of a shoebox. While that posed no issue for my werewolf strength in lifting it, it might for opening it. Claws extending, I picked at the seams. The metal didn't even dimple. Leave it to my brother to find something hard enough to resist werewolf claws. I halted my efforts as I felt Vidar hovering over my shoulder.

"I'm so sorry, Ayra. I saw Dustin at Crescent Coffee. He told me how bad Calder became after I left. If I'd known, I would have come back and put that dog in his place. I wish you would have mentioned it in your letters. I should have been here." His voice rumbled so close behind me that I could feel it against my back.

Oh, how I wanted to lean into all that hard muscle and lose myself. I shoved the stupid thought aside and started picking at the box again. One, Vidar had only ever seen me as the young girl I had been, his best friend, but one he had left behind. Two, the day he left my brother started "training me to fight," which translated as daily beatings in the guise of sparring matches. I couldn't even begin to tell Vidar how bad Calder had gotten after he'd left.

"Stop apologizing. I'm not a delicate princess who needed to be rescued. And besides, you were accepted into the *verndari* temple in Iceland, the highest form of *lögreglu* training for our kind, *and* Reykjavik University. You couldn't pass those opportunities up. Now you can be a *lögreglu* with a science degree like you always wanted. Fighting crime one tornado at a time." The words both sounded and tasted bitter. I wanted to yell and scream instead, but my good girl programming was hard to override.

A *lögreglu*—the Icelandic werewolf version of a cop—with a master's in sustainability science and renewable energy were a combination I had always teased him good-naturedly about, partly because I figured he only wanted the master's because he wanted to help me with my lightning channeling problem. Always wanting to help, that was Vidar. But it was more than that. He wanted to be like the superheroes he read about. It had to be why he was back, to achieve glory through me. It was what everyone wanted, after all.

"I didn't mean..." A look of pain came over him as he struggled to find the right words and failed.

I ground my teeth against what I really wanted to say until I had my anger under control. "Don't, Vidar. I can stand up for myself. I'm not the girl you left behind," I finished, as if my last encounter with my brother hadn't left me cowering.

But that was before. I was stronger now. Now, I would stand up to him. I had to. By biting in the unwilling, he risked exposing our kind. He also risked drawing the attention of other shifters and races that wouldn't want a light shone on the things that went bump in the night. If that happened, it would be the Salem Witch Trials all over again, only with werewolves burning at the stake. The violence and fear in this world was already reaching a crescendo. All it needed was a focus. Our kind would be that focus if we were outed.

I wanted to cling to the rage within, but it was hard to do so with Vidar so close. I had waited so long to see him again. But not now, not like this. There could be no future for us now that I was the reaper and engaged. Not that there could have been before. Some part of me had always known my dreams of chasing storms with him were just that—schoolgirl dreams that would never be.

"Here, this should help," his deep voice broke into my ruminating.

A key dangling from Vidar's hand appeared over my shoulder. I snatched it up and slid it into the lock. It fit and turned.

"Where did you find this?" I asked.

"I know where Calder used to hide his important stuff. Apparently, that hasn't changed."

The box held only one thing: a small black book. I sat it on top of the box and opened it. Names with dates and locations next to them filled the page. The dates began thirty years ago. My eyes strayed to the clippings on the walls. With shaking hands, I picked the book up and carried it to the earliest of the clippings. The names in the book didn't match the names of the victims, and the dates were days, sometimes weeks off the clippings. I flipped through the pages. More of the same filled them.

"This doesn't make any sense," I muttered to myself.

Behind me, Vidar walked the room, cursing softly in Icelandic as he perused the gruesome wallpaper. It took every ounce of control I had to focus on the book instead of watching him. Oh Odin, I had missed him. The asshole. Finally, about halfway through the book I came to a page filled with writing instead of just a list of names and dates. This was more of a diary entry dated about twenty-one years ago.

Despite my efforts, the power still hasn't awakened in me. It doesn't make sense. I've made plenty of rogue varúlfur *in need of being put down. I am of the* uppskera *bloodline, the power should have awakened in me by now.*

The next entry sent chills shooting through me.

My sister was born today. It turns out the mark doesn't appear after the awakening, one is born with it. She will be the next uppskera. *Not me. Her. After all I did to make sure the power awakened. How could I have been so stupid?*

"Oh, Odin. How could he have...?"

The book fell from my hands, sending up a puff of dust as it hit the ground. Such cruelty was extreme even for my brother, or so I had thought. To bite in so many against their will and leave them to deal with the becoming on their own, knowing full well they would go mad or kill, it was tyrannical. Vidar was suddenly at my side, bending to pick up the book, and I hadn't even heard him move. I was starting to think ninjas had nothing on *verndari* trained at the Icelandic temple. He was silent for a moment as he read.

"That son of Loki. I never would have thought he was capable of this," Vidar whispered.

I swallowed hard. "Me neither. I suspected he had bitten in at least one person against their will, but this, this is..." The lump in my throat wouldn't allow me to finish.

The tenderness toward a man who detested me and bullied me my entire life, the weakness, I hated it. Anger rose in me and devoured that tenderness as if it were kindling.

"I have to find him. He has to answer for what he's done," I said through gritted fangs.

"Yes, he must."

"But where do I start? Where would he have gone?"

I flipped through the journal a bit more. A page toward the end caught my attention. Calder's handwriting on these last pages was a messy, passionate scrawl.

If we are condemned to exile on this world, we might as well rule it. And who better to sit on that throne than me? My sister may be the uppskera, *but I will be the one who leads our kind into the light. Mine will be the greater destiny in the end.*

The first step to that is coming out as a species. The second is war. I must continue to bite in the worst of the worst, build an army of them, and then activate our sleeper agents in the governments.

First attack: July.

"He's insane. Our kind will be slaughtered in droves," I murmured.

Vidar cursed in Icelandic and nodded. "He is, and that's the problem. He'll leave a trail of bodies for us to find him by."

Keeping my face as emotionless as possible, I turned to him. "Us? No. The *uppskera* works alone."

Slowly, as if trying not to startle me, he took one of my hands in his. As much as his touch thrilled me, I did not like being handled like a porcelain doll. I was the reaper, for the Gods' sakes. I could hardly blame him, though. When he had left, I had been an insecure teenager nearly at the bottom of the pack. It would take him time to get used to the fact that I was now more powerful than most alphas. Helheimr, it would take me time to get used to that. But the bottom line was that he had no right to handle me at all. He'd lost that right the moment he left me behind.

"The *leitar* has her *kennari*, and the *uppskera* has their *verndari*," he said.

I laughed, the sound coming out bitter. "Vidar, the *uppskera* doesn't need a protector."

He shook his head and gripped my hand when I tried to pull away. "You misunderstand. The *uppskera's verndari* isn't to protect them from others, but from themselves. Reaping takes a toll, Ayra. You'll need someone with you."

It wasn't just the line of an old, concerned friend who felt guilty for leaving me. Part of me wished it were. The old *uppskera* journals I had been reading since childhood mentioned such issues. Some *uppskera* lost themselves in the reaping, others went insane. Not all, but enough to scare me sleepless as a child. None mentioned the reaper having a protector, though. I twisted my hand free of his grasp and took a step away. The pain etching lines into his face almost made me regret my actions. Almost.

"Please, just let me travel with you, help you find Calder, for the sake of our kind if nothing else. Then we can go from there. There's still a lot we have to talk about," he urged.

I tried not to read into what he meant by "go from there." That was a dangerous road to travel. But I couldn't deny that I wanted and needed help fighting Calder. The thought of facing off with him still sent a shot of fear through me.

Nodding, I met his gaze and held it. "Fine."

One corner of his full lips lifted to expose the two upper fangs to the right of his incisors. "Good, I have a score to settle with that dog."

"Not before I do. When can you be ready to leave?"

No matter the cost, I would protect our kind from exposure. And I would kill those who had forced this on me, my brother included. Hel hath no fury like mine. Maybe that's because I'm a creature of it now. Or maybe I always was. I would make the people that forced it on me pay.

Starting now.

The fact that one of them was my own brother made a deeper, darker fury fester in me. He had to die. And if I had to take Vidar with me to accomplish that, so be it.

CHAPTER THREE

AYRA

Neither alpha, pack, nor Council stands above the uppskera. Only the Aesir themselves may govern the chosen of Odin.
-Uppskera Journals

The town of Hemlock Hollow had always been a refuge for me. It had been my escape from my cruel family. From its thirty-acre round park in the center of town, to its library with an extensive section on storms and weather, it was the perfect getaway. A unique main street—or Aðal Street to us locals—that wrapped around the huge, circular park like the world's biggest roundabout, ensured visitors drove in, around, and right back out. The great restaurants and ski shops sprinkled throughout the green spaces made it feel more like something that should be nestled in the hills of California or Colorado instead of Montana. But it wasn't the shops, parks, or even the library that kept me coming back; it was the people.

I closed my brother's journal and tucked it under my arm. So far I hadn't found anything more about the war or his plans for an attack in July. I had no idea where to turn or which way to go. It frustrated the hell out of me to have a ticking time bomb over my head and no direction.

The towering pines and bushy aspens crowding the road gave way to Mike's Malt Shop. Beneath its extensive covered patio a score of high school students sat enjoying summer break, eating burgers and milkshakes. Seeing them stung. My time in high school hadn't been like that. The blond waitress with enviable curves who skated her way through the patrons called out a hello and waved at me with the hand not balancing a tray.

"Hey, Ofelia," I called back as I strode down the sidewalk.

On another day I would have stopped in for a shake and an update on the town talk. Not only did I have places to go, but I *was* the gossip. The heavy gazes of a score of high schoolers lifted as I passed several tall spruce trees growing up out of the wide green space between the sidewalk and street. After a jeweler and an art store, I took a left on Hemlock Street, which ended in a roundabout a few yards down. A massive wrought iron gate stood at the entrance to a seven-foot-high rock wall that stretched behind all the businesses on Aðal Street.

Down by one of the ski shops I spotted a news van. A reporter primped in the mirror before turning to her cameraman. She fluffed her hair, pasted on a concerned look, and gave him the nod. Though they were forty feet away, my *varúlfur* hearing picked up her words clearly as if she stood beside me.

"We're here in Hemlock Hollow, the town nestled between forest and a massive wolf preserve. There have been no reports of wolf attacks anywhere near Hemlock Hollow, which is odd considering the rash of attacks all across the rest of Montana and into parts of Idaho."

She went on, but I turned away. I'd heard more than enough, and didn't want her getting wind of me and deciding I looked like a good person to interview. The police chief would redirect her out of town soon enough. My teeth ground together. Poor wolves, getting a bad rap because of half-mad werewolves bitten in and abandoned to go through the change alone. For now, the new werewolves were only killing livestock, but they would move on to more challenging prey if they weren't brought under control. Sonya had her work cut out for her, but so did I. If I didn't stop Calder from biting in new wolves, she'd never be able to keep up with saving them.

At the wrought iron gate, a press of a finger on the DNA-detecting keypad told it I was local. Well-oiled hinges hummed as the gate slid open. The moment I was through, it closed behind me. Here, the businesses turned a bit more practical. Just past the hardware store I saw the sign for my destination. Tension began to lift from my shoulders when I pushed open the door to Nitro Moto.

No bell rang to announce my arrival, and an old metal band wailed through the speakers throughout the part-filled shop. Regardless, the man behind the counter looked up at me. He may be getting on in age, but he still possessed the outstanding hearing and sense of smell of our kind. Crow's feet pulled at the corners of his eyes as he smiled at me. "Ayra, perfect timing. Those new tires arrived yesterday, and I just got them put on for you. Come on back." He waved a hand as he opened the back door.

I vaulted over the counter and caught up before he could disappear into the shop. The scents of oil, gasoline, and half a dozen other vehicle-related liquids mingled into a pungent concoction that stung my nose. A black, souped-up '78 Corvette perched on a lift dripped oil into a pan. Along the opposite side of the room sat three motorcycles: a Sportster, a Kawasaki, and my BMW with its shiny new tires. To be accurate, they didn't exactly shine, but they looked pretty sharp considering the brand new tread.

The rest of the bike really did shine, though. The pearl-white paint job reflected my image as if it had been freshly washed and waxed. Anything chrome left on the bike that I hadn't gotten around to getting powder-coated yet caught the overhead lights and sent them bouncing in every direction. If it weren't for the hard bags on the side and back of my bike, it would have looked every bit the speed machine it was meant to be. While speed was vital to me, function would be just as vital where I was headed. Who knew how far I'd have to go or how long I'd be gone. Some gear would be necessary and the bags would give me all the room I needed. My closed face helmet hung on the left handlebar.

"Looks good, Olaf. Thanks for getting them done so quickly," I said as I dug my tiny wallet out of my front pocket. "How much do I owe you?"

Olaf waved his hands in the air. "Don't you worry about that."

I hoped he didn't mean what I thought he meant. "I don't know how long I'll be gone, so I want to square things up before I go."

He patted my shoulder as he walked past. "We're square."

Grinding my teeth against any further protest, I started counting bills out. It ended up being a good-size bundle of twenties and tens. I felt bad having to give him so many smaller bills, but my seasonal job at the forest service never put anything larger in my pocket. When I held the money out, Olaf shook his head.

"You're off to hunt the condemned. Charging you wouldn't be right," he said with far more reverence than I was comfortable with.

"The tires cost you money, and it took up your time putting them on, not to mention the wash and wax job. Not paying you wouldn't be right," I insisted.

He retrieved my keys from a pegboard on the wall above one of his workbenches. The star-struck look he gave me as he handed them over made me want to vomit. But he didn't seem to notice. "You are the *uppskera*. Your mission is sacred, and the fact that I got to work on your motorcycle is payment enough."

I wanted to scream at him, slap him, anything to make him listen. But I knew it wouldn't work. Everyone had become like this toward me since my awakening. To them, Ayra was gone. Now I was just this *thing*.

I stuffed the money back in my pocket and took the keys from him. Grinning like an idiot with no clue about my inner turmoil—despite the fact that it bubbled through my power—he pressed the garage door button. Sunlight spilled into the dim shop, forcing me to squint. Power crackling with aggression rolled in on the afternoon breeze. My own power tried to flare up in response, but I held it down. *Never let them see you sweat.* That mantra had saved me from a lot of beatings at my brother's hand. Once a werewolf knew they got you riled up, they pounced. And this was definitely a werewolf. Three of them, in fact. They stood on the opposite side of Olaf's huge parking lot, just near the thick fir trees. That they were in human form didn't much reduce the hostility that hung in the air around them.

Olaf glanced from me to them and began to chew on his bottom lip. "Sorry about them. They've been coming by, asking about you every day since you dropped your bike off. Don't pay them any mind. They're just foolish kids."

"What's their deal?" I asked.

Olaf waved a dismissive hand. "They think they can challenge the *uppskera* and gain your power if they defeat you."

I was relatively certain it didn't work that way. If it did, my brother would have challenged me the moment my power awoke. Wouldn't he have? The "what if" ate at me. Could there be a chance for me to pass this power onto someone else? The thrill of hope that shot into my heart was almost too much to bear. It would have to be a good, legitimate fight, of that I was sure. I wouldn't be able to hold back. Odin would accept no less. But that was fine. I really didn't know how this new power worked yet, so winning wasn't guaranteed.

While Olaf made a rude gesture toward the three men, I tucked the money for my new tires beneath a wrench on his bench and put my helmet on. I didn't know if I could beat these guys. Years of training in various fighting techniques could only get one so far. And the clear skies above meant I couldn't hope lightning might strike me, lending me its power. Then again, no one besides Vidar knew I could do that, and I didn't really want to expose the secret. A few weeks ago, many had seen Sonya—the seeker—and I get hit by lightning, but they didn't know that she had attracted it and I had channeled it and turned it into a force to heal her. From the rumors, they just thought Odin had used divine intervention to heal the seeker.

As far as I knew, that healing trick, channeling lightning, and detecting the condemned were the only extra powers an *uppskera* had. And the lightning thing seemed to be unique to me and Sonya because the *uppskera* journals didn't say a thing about it.

Even that didn't compare to an alpha's ability to suppress, or even draw out, their packs' power to the point where they could force them to shift. What good was the ability to channel lightning when I had to rely on a storm?

"Get lost, you fools! You can't beat Odin's chosen," Olaf shouted. Like any red-blooded werewolf, he sounded excited by the prospect of them trying.

I fired up the bike and drowned out the trio's snarky replies. I left some of my new rubber behind on the floor of Olaf's shop as I tore out of it. The BMW hit forty-five before I whipped it into a hairpin turn to pull in the next driveway down and over from Olaf's. I killed the bike's ignition beneath the arched entrance sign of the Hemlock Street Park and coasted to a stop in one of the parking spots along the expansive lawn. This place would do nicely. Being behind the seven-foot-high rock wall that surrounded the circular public part of town, no outsiders would see what happened here. I climbed from the bike and turned around just as the three jogged up the drive. Crossing my arms beneath my B-cup breasts, I waited.

They were older than me, but not by much. Each one was tall and built. They wore traditional Norse hairstyles, long on the top and shaved on the sides, the long bits braided back in different fashions. So they thought they were badass Vikings of old then. Fine by me. That would make this interesting.

"Ayra Valdisdóttir, the tiny albino is the *uppskera*," the middle one said with a shake of his head.

I recognized him from high school, a member of the Arnoddr pack. He'd been almost as bad of a bully as my brother. And a redundant idiot on more than one level.

I lowered my arms. "Yeah, I am, Corey. I hear you think you can do the job better."

He thrust his chin up. "Damn straight I can." He swept his arms out to his companions.

Now that they were close enough, I recognized them too, Claude and Leif from the Reinhard pack. Leif was a friend of Raul Anderson's—the man who had bitten in the Seeker without her permission. The prickly fingers of fear poked at my innards. Corey and Claude had been among those that had tormented me through middle school and half of high school. Memories flooded in and I was helpless to stop them: the boys pulling my hair while they made fun of how much closer to white than blond it was, of them piling extra food on my lunch tray as they walked past while teasing me about being a runt, the nasty notes left on my locker.

A seed of anger sprouted inside that fear. My left foot slid back, and I settled into a fighting stance. Lifting my chin, I beckoned to him.

"Then prove it," I said in a voice so steady it surprised even me.

It was stupid, I knew, challenging three guys who had played college ball at Montana State. If I died, then I was right and Odin had made a mistake in choosing me. A more worthy *uppskera* would rise. If I was wrong, then these bullies would finally get what was coming to them. Either way, I was good with the outcome.

The assholes came at me all at once. So much for honor.

Corey lunged straight for me with a front kick so fast his leg was just a blur. But I knew it was coming. His power gave it away. A steady pressure built in his legs before he even moved into position. I dodged with time to spare as Claude and Leif flanked me. One threw a sidekick, the other moved in to grab me. One huge step back took me out of their range. They collided with a thud. Leif fell toward me, and I slammed my foot into his jaw. Blood flew and he sprawled back onto the grass.

Claude let out a roar and rushed me. Instead of moving, I grabbed his shirt and rolled backwards, pulling him with me. Knees to my chest, I placed my feet against his abdomen. I extended my claws, right into his pecs. A girlish scream came from him. It wouldn't kill him, but one would think so with the racket he made. As we rolled back, I kicked out, throwing him past me with his own momentum more than my strength.

A booted foot flew at my face. I grabbed it and yanked it toward me. Corey growled as he hit the ground. His muscles flexed and his power flared, giving away the kick his other foot was about to attempt. Keeping hold of his foot, I rolled away. He rolled with me rather than let me dislocate it. Damn. I let go and continued to roll. I jumped up just in time for the other two to come at me again.

Anger flared, raising my power with it. The strength of it scared me. Teeth gritted to hold the anger back, I threw a sidekick into Claude's chest. He grunted and stumbled back several feet. The surprise in his eyes made me smile. From behind me I felt the press of Leif's power as he advanced. I thrust a leg back and connected my foot with his jaw at a high rate of speed. The scent of more blood flavored the air. I breathed it in like a delicacy to be savored. With it came a bit of Leif's power. It tingled on the edge of pain and pleasure, a bit like lightning and electricity did.

That was new.

A full feeling, like downing too much water too fast, filled me with an intense pressure. Corey landed a punch in my solar plexus. Pain reverberated throughout my midsection. Ignoring it, I jabbed a fist straight into his stomach. The full sensation slowed my strikes, making them less powerful. I tried to breathe Leif's power out, but it wouldn't leave me.

Corey landed another punch to my right shoulder. Furious, I let out a scream as I punched for his nose.

Power—my own and Leif's—flowed down my arm, adding speed and strength to the strike. Blood exploded from Corey's nose as my fist connected with it. The full feeling left me.

He didn't go down, so I breathed in, seeing if I could suck in his power like I had Leif's. I could. It fed my power, which in turn fed my strength and speed. But channeling it wasn't easy. It came and went in bursts, growing weaker when I needed it most and stronger when I couldn't do anything with it. I hit him three more times before he finally went down.

So this was what the *uppskera* of old talked about in their journals. Their references had been vague, as if they didn't want whoever was reading to understand unless they were experiencing it themselves. I got it now. Couldn't have the packs knowing this was the reaper's true power. Not even alphas could use others' power like this. They simply attracted or repelled it like a magnet, not absorbed it. If only it were easier to control and use.

My attackers kept coming. They were every bit as strong as they looked, and fast, and well trained in various fighting techniques. Each attempted strike and hit made me madder and madder until red began to tinge the edges of my vision.

As I drew their power, getting stronger and faster, they grew weaker and slower. But I could barely control this new ability. If I could only figure it out, it wouldn't matter that I was a buck-ten soaking wet.

Maybe, just maybe, the Allfather hadn't made a mistake in choosing me after all, *if* I could figure this out. I almost believed that as I beat them back again and again. They landed a fair amount of blows on me, but I landed more. I could take it. I'd grown up taking it.

A fist slammed into my jaw. Rage erupted from me in the form of a vicious growl. With it went the power I'd just stolen from one of them, right into my kicks, punches, and swipes of my clawed hands. Two of the men went down, and stayed down. They moved, so they were still a threat, but I focused on the one standing for now. When he didn't attack, I stalked toward him.

Deep in Corey's eyes hid a healthy amount of fear. It only enraged me more. He didn't get to be the victim. Not after the way he had tormented me over the years. Claws and fangs bared, I launched myself at him. We ended up on the ground with me on his chest. I started pummeling him. I had the good sense to close my hands into fists rather than slash at him with my claws—but just barely. At first he fought back, bucking beneath me and jabbing at me with his fists. But with each struggle I drank down more of his energy. Soon he couldn't even hold up his hands to block my strikes.

The press of power warned me of Leif and Claude rushing up behind me. I tried to suck in their energy and couldn't, not while I was punching Corey. A fist struck me in the breastbone so hard the air in my lungs vacated in an involuntary rush. Anger scorched away the restraint I'd been clinging to. A furious growl tore from me as I started punching him. His hands fell away. Blood spewed from his mouth, splattering my chest and hands. The smell fed my rage.

"Ayra, stop!" came the voice of reason, the only voice that could make me stop.

I froze, fist in mid-swing. No, not a fist. My hand had opened, claws extended. I hadn't even realized it. If I had followed through with that swing...

A big hand closed around my wrist in a gentle grip. Head still in the fight, my power tried to suck his in. It couldn't. He helped me to my feet. I turned away from the three men lying barely conscious on the ground to peer up at Vidar's tall, dark form. His power flowed out and around mine, cradling it, encasing it almost. It soothed me, helped me think again. His gentle hazel eyes lacked the surprise I felt at this, almost as if he'd known he'd be able to placate my power.

Hand sliding down to take hold of mine, he led me several steps away from the groaning men. Someone cleared their throat and I realized we had an audience, a big one. Well over a dozen people had gathered in the park. They all stared at me with reverence, except for one. Kneeling on Leif's back, holding one of his arms twisted up at a painful looking angle, was the man who had set all this in motion: Raul Anderson. Strange. What in Hel's name would he be doing here?

"What happened?" Vidar asked, voice as gentle as the caress of his power.

"They challenged me, thought they could beat me and become the *uppskera*."

Vidar made a dismissive noise. "Idiots. It doesn't work that way."

"I tried to tell them that." I had hoped I'd been wrong. But then, they hadn't beat me, so that still wasn't proved or disproved in my book.

I looked at their bruised and battered bodies, at all the blood. They writhed slowly in agony. None of them would rise soon, and at least two of them wouldn't be able to do so on their own. They'd live. Werewolves are strong and heal fast. But seeing the damage I had wrought, that thought didn't bring me much comfort.

Low whispers started up around us. "Did you see that?"

Gods, I was afraid everyone had seen it.

"She beat three of our youngest, strongest wolves without breaking a sweat."

"Looked like she even held back."

Maybe a little, but I had tried not to. Wouldn't want to displease Odin if I lost and hadn't given it my all. But partway through the fight I had realized that if I had given it my all, I might have killed them. My entire life, I hadn't thought I was worthy of being the *uppskera*. Being born with a mark did not a chosen one make. Or so I had thought. But this ability to siphon energy leveled the fighting field. It meant my size didn't matter so much anymore. There might be a chance I could do this after all.

Vidar's hand slid down and tried to take hold of mine, but I pulled away.

"Let's get out of here," he said, tone hurt.

In a numb state of charged energy, I followed him to the parking lot. The awestruck gazes of all these people made me nervous. They parted for us, bowing low as they made a wide path, some exposing their throats, others the backs of their necks. I recognized each of them. Some were guys and girls I had gone to school with, but others were people from the town, even a few elders in their three and four hundreds. I had a feeling there wouldn't be any more challengers. I wasn't sure if that made me feel vindicated or disappointed.

They trailed along behind us like a pack following its leader. The skin on the back of my neck prickled in an attempt to raise hair that wasn't there. If

I were in wolf form, my hackles would have been standing on end. Sensing my displeasure, our followers stayed back fifteen feet or more. Comments whispered in awe, reverence, and even fear in a few cases, continued in hushed voices. Each one made me tense up just a little more. But what really ate at me was walking away from Raul. The trial had happened so quickly after my awakening that I hadn't had a chance to confront him.

I stopped. "You go ahead. I'll be right there," I told Vidar.

He nodded and took a step back. "I'll wait for you."

I nodded and walked off toward where Raul held Leif on the ground. Claude, who had just regained his feet, bowed his head low and took several quick, stumbling steps backwards.

"Let him up," I commanded.

Raul's disarming amber eyes gave me a questioning look. "Are you sure?"

A low growl bubbled from me. He nodded, let go of Leif, and stood. Leif jumped to his feet but froze at Raul's side. His gaze shifted from Raul to me and back to Raul. The two were more than just pack members, they had been friends since high school. They'd shared the limelight as two of our football team's brightest stars back in their day seven years ago. That made me more than a little suspicious. I leveled my glare on Leif. One problem at a time. My power slipped out past my defenses and I let it. It crackled across Leif like super-charged static electricity. He winced.

Leif held my gaze for all of half a second before dropping his eyes to the ground. His shoulders sagged.

"You understand now?" I asked him.

He nodded. It wasn't enough, not considering the audience that had gathered.

"What is it you understand?" I pressed.

"That I can't beat you." He swallowed hard. "That no one can. That I shouldn't have tried. I'm sorry, *Uppskera*," he said in a suitably humble tone.

I nodded. "Good. Leave us." I turned to the small audience gathered. "Show's over, folks. Go home." I put more than a little command into that last bit. The last thing I wanted was to have an audience for the next part.

People turned and started to leave, Raul among them. "Not you," I told him.

He stopped and turned to me with a curious look. His lack of fear made me feel a bit less like a monster while raising the hackles of my alpha side at the same time.

I waited for the others to get out of hearing range. "Did you send him?"

His eyes shot open wide. "Of course not. I'd never disrespect you with such an idiotic move. He acted without my knowledge."

The surprise on his supermodel face seemed genuine enough. I wasn't charmed by him for one minute, though. That perfect, wavy, chin-length brown hair, those captivating amber eyes, they may have charmed the seeker in the beginning, but not me. Not ever me. He had been the one to bite in Sonya Michaelson without asking her permission. That idiot move had started everything. Sonya's awakening as the seeker had triggered my own awakening as the reaper.

"This is all your fault."

He flinched. "I know. I'm truly sorry for what I did. But I didn't do it for the reason everyone thinks."

I tried not to roll my eyes. I really did. "Really? Then why did you bite some innocent woman in against her will and condemn both of us to this fate?" The arctic tone of my voice, or maybe it was the words themselves, made him flinch again. It was quite satisfying to see the pain flash across his face.

The slight bump of his Adam's apple worked before he spoke. "Bain had something over me. He blackmailed me into doing it."

The words hit me like a freight train. Bain, alpha of the Draupnir pack, the man who killed his own brother to take control of the pack, who had kicked Vidar and a score of other wolves out when they had failed to swear allegiance, had his claws in this. If Raul could be believed.

Anger moved my legs a step closer. Though he flinched from the bite of my power, Raul didn't cower or step back. It made me wonder how powerful he really was. "How did he know about the seeker?" I asked.

"I don't know, but he did. He knew about you too. But I wasn't going to just let him have her. And I was going to ask her permission to bite her in. Things just got pushed up, and I couldn't." He swallowed hard and squeezed his eyes shut for a long moment. "But I knew her family history. I talked to her about what she wanted in life. I thought she would say yes. I wouldn't have done it if I'd thought she'd say no," he answered in a steady voice free of fear.

"You bit her in with the intention of her being a potential mate so she'd have a choice and wouldn't go straight to Bain's pack."

He nodded. "But Bain found out. He made my sister his co-alpha to punish me."

"Why didn't you say all this at your trial?"

His gaze darted about the empty park before returning to me. "Because there's more going on here than just Bain wanting the seeker in his pack. I'm sure of it. I just don't know what. If I exposed him, no one would believe me, and I would have risked not being able to find out."

Understanding dawned, as did a new and surprising respect for Raul. "That's why you accepted your sentence of being a *kennari* so easily, because it would keep you here in Hemlock Hollow."

"Yes. I have to figure out what's going on and stop it before anyone else gets hurt." The determination in his tone, the defiance in his eyes and stance, it spoke of the wolf he could become. I liked it.

"I'm going after Calder. Keep me posted." I started back toward the parking lot.

"I will. But Ayra..."

I looked back over my shoulder at him through a veil of white-blond hair.

"Be careful. Your brother is dangerous," he said.

A grunt came from me. I knew that better than anyone." My gaze fixed on Vidar waiting back at my motorcycle.

He leaned against it, arms crossed over his broad, chiseled chest. I hated how he casually touched my things, like he had a right to. After how he'd left me four years ago, he had no rights to anything that had to do with me. How many nights had I lain awake, barely able to breathe from missing him? I wanted to kick his ass to the curb—literally—and leave him right there without looking back, just like he'd done to me. And I would have if I didn't need someone who knew Calder so well and who I knew would have my back. It wasn't like I could ask Elí. Not only because he was out of the state either. While he was a fighter, he didn't have it in him to kill anything, not even a spider. And killing would have to be done before this was over.

I tried to pretend Vidar wasn't there, looking like a dark, gorgeous god leaning on my motorcycle as I dug out my keys. It was wrong that someone I was so pissed at could look so good.

As I approached, he touched my arm. Heat and comfort spread from his hand deep down into me. "That was intense. How are you?" he asked in a hushed voice. The hidden meaning beneath his words came through loud and clear.

He'd seen me beating Corey, and he'd seen what I'd been about to do to him. He was afraid I was losing my grip on my temper. And I was. In fact, the desire to pummel someone still raged through me. He would do nicely if he kept pushing.

"I'm fine," I snapped.

He flinched almost imperceptibly, a twitch of his right cheek and a tightening of the skin around his eyes. His hand withdrew from my arm, leaving me feeling cold and empty, but vindicated. If I hadn't known him for so long I might have missed the pain in his eyes. All that hard muscle, and a simple tone of voice had hurt him. Something pinched inside me at knowing I had hurt him. But he had hurt me infinitely more.

He beamed a gorgeous smile at me. "Don't get me wrong, they had it coming. Those jerks have always been low-level villains. You were amazing, by the way. Is it wrong that I was imagining sound effects as I walked up?"

A smile tried to crack through my carefully placed stoic expression. "I see Iceland didn't take the comic book geek out of you," I said.

He puffed his hard chest out. "Nothing has the power to do that."

The memories that brought up were too much to handle at the moment: the two of us sitting in a tree, reading the latest edition of our favorite comics, lying on the cool grass staring at the stars together, comparing favorite superheroes. My chest tightened. I started the bike.

"Do you need a ride?" I offered, praying to Odin that he didn't. I hadn't meant to ask him. It had just slipped out. Memories were one thing, but him pressed behind me on my bike was another altogether. That would break me.

He thrust his head in the direction of a silver truck. "Nope, got my truck. I'll follow you."

I nodded and put my helmet on before he could see the emotion scribbled all over my face. Inviting him along had been a bad idea, a moment of weakness that would rear up and bite me in the ass. What had I been thinking? Looking over that tall, dark body through the safety of my mirrored helmet visor made it pretty clear I hadn't been thinking at all. I'd been feeling, something I hadn't let myself do for the four years he'd been gone.

I turned the throttle and sped away from him and our looming audience.

CHAPTER FOUR

AYRA

In obscurity lies our survival.
-Uppskera Journals

It looked like a rainbow had exploded on my tiny front lawn, flooding it with flowers and packages of every type and color. The heady smell of dying foliage and melting chocolate wasn't altogether bad. But it wasn't good, either. The sight made me cringe. Already the dumpster out back brimmed with a similar haul that I had cleaned up only last night. Where I was going to put all this, I had no idea. The worst part was, half of it probably wasn't recyclable and would end up in a dump somewhere. Foil gift bags, plastic packaging around chocolates or candy, things my kind should have known better than to buy. But even *varúlfur* were forgetting the impact they could have on the world. Such a waste.

As I draped my helmet over the handlebars of my BMW S1000RR, Vidar's silver long-bed Dodge truck pulled up in my gravel drive. His long legs practically reached the ground when he swung out of the thing. He swallowed hard, wide-eyed gaze locked on either the mess on my front lawn or the two-room hunting cabin I called home. I couldn't be sure which. Either way, it made me want to crawl back inside my helmet and hide. The cabin was a far cry from the three-thousand-square-foot home

I'd grown up in. But I'd take it any day over that sprawling prison. Green paint peeled away from the weathered wood siding, and one corner of the metal roof over the porch sagged. Vidar's expression remained neutral as he looked it all over.

"You're living in the Johnsons' old hunting shack," he observed.

"Yeah, though they haven't let me pay rent since my *uppskera* powers awoke." The depths to which that irked me showed in my tone.

Vidar swallowed hard, eyes narrowing as they turned to me. "Renting it?"

I nodded, head held high as I strode through the bright boxes, bags, and flowers. Hovel though it was, I would not be ashamed of my home. "Since I left home at eighteen."

"You've lived here two years?" he asked in a strangled voice.

Boxes and bags crunched as he rushed to follow me and failed miserably at maneuvering his way through the mess. "You didn't mention that in your letters."

One shoulder lifted in a half shrug. "Didn't seem relevant, especially considering you didn't mention much of anything in *your* infrequent letters."

He grabbed my hand and, damn it, I couldn't help but flinching. The encounter with my father was too fresh.

"Was it that bad at home?" he all but whispered. Flashes of horrible memories hit me: the frequent slaps from both Mother and Father over nothing, the insults from all three of my family members, constant harassing over being so thin and frail, Mother taking my *uppskera* journals and books on weather and storms away when I didn't work out enough or eat enough, my brother beating me bloody and bruised in the guise of combat training. Being of the *uppskera* bloodline, they had wanted to "prepare" me in case the power awoke in me. The required reading of the journals throughout my childhood had actually been one part I hadn't minded. Once they figured that out, they used it against me like everything else.

"Yeah, it was that bad," I admitted in a hard voice as I tore my hand free of his grasp.

"Oh, Ayra." The pain and helplessness in those two words made me ache.

It wasn't that I didn't want his pity. People who reject the pity of others have always puzzled me. I've had such a shortage of it in my life that I understand the value it holds. At least they feel something gentle toward me. Despite how mad I was at Vidar, my first instinct to him in pain was to try and put a stop to it. That in itself made me angry. He didn't deserve me hurting for him. I'd done enough hurting *because* of him. The shine of moisture in his eyes nearly stole my words. Fingers twitching with the desire to reach for him, I folded my arms beneath my breasts.

"Don't. Not now. Not after all this time."

He flinched both from my words and the bite of my rising power. The next part poured out before I could stop it. "I wanted you to train at the temple as much as you wanted to join it. It was your dream since you were six. Dreams are meant to be followed. When you were chosen over your two older brothers I was so excited for you..." I had to pause to swallow the lump in my throat before I could go on. "You monks are the protectors of our ways, the chosen men and women of Odin. I get that. But you disappeared, Vidar."

He took hold of my shoulders in a gentle grip, his brows scrunching together. "I am sorry. I had to. It was the only way the temple would train me. What letters I was able to send, I had to sneak out, and then I worried they would get ahold of them somehow, read them, and kick me out."

I refused to give him a response. He didn't deserve one. He went on, speaking fast and desperate. "But listen, you are a protector of our kind too. Your parents, your brother, they should have treated you that way. If others in Hemlock Hollow had known, they never would have let them be cruel to you."

The anger in his eyes was too much. It worked at the edges of my own, trying to feed it. I stepped back so his hand fell away from my shoulders.

"You know how they were. They didn't want anyone else to steal me away and use me for their own gains. Then my power wouldn't benefit them. And I didn't want people to treat me differently, to fear me. They would have if they'd known I had the *uppskera* mark. I didn't want this." I gestured to my front yard.

He looked down at the flowers and packages around his feet. "These are all gifts," he observed.

"Bribes," I corrected. "Attempts to get me to join their packs."

Understanding dawned in Vidar's pretty eyes. "You didn't choose a pack when you turned eighteen," he said, not sounding at all surprised.

As he shouldn't. Though I was born into the Arnoddr pack of Hemlock Hollow, that didn't automatically make me one of them. Not until I had been old enough to choose two years ago. It wasn't a bad pack. Isak was a good alpha, and his mother Iona a benevolent stand-in while he searched for a mate. I liked Isak a lot. He was more of a father to me than my own ever was, always so kind and encouraging. But that had been before he knew what I was. If I went back to the pack now, people would treat me differently, he would treat me differently. That was the last thing I wanted.

"I belong to the AVW. That's enough for me."

Vidar's brows pinched together. "They're great, but they're more of a club, an organization at best, meant to share information and ride motorcycles and fast cars together. They aren't a family." He wasn't wrong. The American Viking Werewolves were considered an umbrella pack—a pack with many members who belonged to other packs. They didn't govern their members.

"Which is part of why I like them. I've had my fill of family," I said.

I turned away from Vidar and worked my way through the packages on my tiny porch. These ones were brown shipping boxes, half a dozen of them, gifts sent from Elí. He sent several a week, things for the wedding mostly. I cringed and hoped Vidar didn't notice who they were from. Not that I should care. I picked one up that was directly in the way and opened my front door. "Arnoddr didn't know what I was then. Staying wouldn't have been fair to them or the other packs."

His soft steps sounded behind me on the hardwood floors of my little shack. "The pack with the *uppskera* in it would be the most powerful pack in existence," he observed.

Pausing for a moment to let my werewolf sight kick in and combat the gloomy room, I hung my keys on the little rack beside the door. The scents of cat and the diluted lemon cleaner I liked to use lingered in the air. But considering this was the first time I'd had Vidar in my home, I was glad I'd cleaned recently. Not that it took much. With only a butcher block bar top that served as both my kitchen counter space and my table, a single plush chair tucked into the nook by the window, and my bookshelves, there wasn't much to the room.

My gaze snagged on the SOARS—Significant Opportunities in Atmospheric Research and Science—pamphlet I'd left out on the counter. Adrenalin shot through me. I struggled to keep my power calm as I casually walked up to the counter and set the box I'd picked up on top of the pamphlet. The idea of Vidar seeing me pining over a NOAA program I couldn't participate in because I wasn't a college student filled me with shame. The reaction pissed me off. I shouldn't feel shame over leaving my abusive family and their money behind.

A questioning meow came from the back room, followed by the patter of tiny paws. My one-eared, orange-striped cat jogged into the room. Well, he wasn't one-eared exactly, but a big enough chunk of his right ear was missing that most would consider him so. He jumped up on the coffee table and rubbed at my hand. The moment he saw Vidar he puffed up like he'd been put in the dryer on a fluff cycle. A horrible yowl issued from between his bared teeth.

"It's all right, Heimdallr. Vidar is a...friend," I said.

Vidar's eyes widened, but he smiled and relaxed. "You named your cat after the guardian of the *Bifröst*. I like it."

"He watches over my place, so it seemed fitting. I found him here when I moved in."

He laughed. "Of course you did. You've always had a knack for finding and taking in stray cats. It's still a marvel to see," he said in a bit of a shocked tone.

"He took me in. And just because we have canine in us doesn't mean we can't get along with cats," I said.

Vidar reached a hand toward Heimdallr, who hissed, leaped down, and took off into the kitchen.

"Tell that to him," Vidar said with a laugh.

Two steps took me to the door that led into my bedroom. Shame tried to rise up in me again at Vidar seeing my place, but I forced it down, mostly. From the bedroom closet I took a backpack. When I moved to the dresser and began filling it, Vidar followed me in. Left with no other choice, he sat on my bed. It was that or get run over as I worked my way around the tiny room, gathering what I needed. Hands clasped before him, back rigid, he looked terribly uncomfortable, as if he hadn't been on my bed a million times when we were kids. But those biceps bulging from beneath the royal-blue sleeves of his clingy shirt and the way he took up half of my twin bed just sitting there, reminded me that neither of us were kids anymore.

The stirring in my lower abdomen also reminded me that I'd always seen him differently than he saw me. That rekindled my anger with him. He wasn't here for me. He was here for the *uppskera*. The way he smiled at the framed print of a dragon from one of our mutually favorite books as kids almost soothed that anger. His smile grew as his gaze took in the bookshelves lining every wall of the tiny room.

"I like what you've done with the place. Reminds me of the Cabin of Dreams," he said.

He knew just what to say to dig under my skin like a tick. I snorted. "Maybe a portion of one room in it. But thanks."

The Cabin of Dreams was a place we'd made up when we were kids. We'd imagined every room in it, down to the tiniest detail of what to hang on the walls and put on the shelves. It had been the refuge in my mind, the place I went when things got too bad at home. All I'd had to do was close my eyes and I was there. It had gotten me through the darkest of times. Not wanting him to see how deeply the memory affected me, I moved in to the tiny bathroom to gather my toiletries.

I heard Vidar swallow hard. "Are you still going to go through with the marriage now that you're the *uppskera?*"

"Of course I am. I'm an honorable wolf. I keep my vows." Even from all the way in the bathroom I felt his power surge in a way that meant he was in pain.

Good. That meant he remembered the vow he and I took, to be there for each other no matter what, a vow he broke.

It was several long moments before he spoke again. "We should talk about the lightning thing."

"What about it?" I called back, anger leaking into my words.

Last month I'd saved the life of the *leitar*—the seeker, the yin to my yang—by channeling lightning through her and turning it to a healing force that attacked her wounds. Well, I'd *helped* save her. She did her part by attracting the lightning.

"Now everyone knows," Vidar said.

He had known I could channel lightning since we were kids. He was the only one who knew. Not even Elí knew about it.

"No, they don't. They saw the seeker and I get hit by lightning, that's all. They have no idea I can channel it. They just know we both can survive getting hit by it." Recalling the moment, my brows pinched together, and I shook my head. While I was still angry with him, he was the only person I could talk to about this. "There's something else, though, Vidar. The seeker, it's like she attracted it, as though she's a lightning rod." I could channel electrical energy, but I had to have access to it. What she did was something altogether different.

Vidar cocked his head to the side and went quiet. His brow scrunched up in that adorable way it always did when he was deep in thought. An adorable deserter who condemned me to years of pain and an arranged marriage. Digging around for the things I needed, I turned my back to him.

I'd gathered the last of my essentials before he finally spoke. "That's disturbing. It has to be related to your ability."

Grabbing my three least-read *uppskera* journals off the bookshelf, I stuffed them into my pack. A quick double check of the cat door leading out onto the back porch to make sure it was open, and I was ready to go. He had enough food and water in his bowl to last a week, mostly because he rarely touched it. Heimdallr preferred hunting his meals, and he was quite efficient at it.

I started for the door. "Did you learn anything at the temple about my ability to channel lightning?" Though he'd never come out and said it in the beginning, I had suspected it was one of the reasons he'd wanted to study at the temple. The boy—no, man now—had possessed an insatiable curiosity, and my ability had taken center stage for that curiosity much of our childhood. Once he dropped off the grid, I was afraid he'd forgotten about it, and me. But I had to know.

Shaking his head, he opened the door for me. "Sadly, no. But I had to be careful. I didn't ask anyone directly because I thought it best to keep it a secret until we knew what we were dealing with."

Excuses. Just as I suspected, he forgot about me. The heat of his body and comfort of his power wrapped around me as I walked past him. It took a lot of effort to make my legs keep moving. I wanted to collapse against that hard chest of his, lose myself in the feel of his arms. I'd dreamt of it so many times since he'd been gone... But those were the silly dreams of a girl. I was an engaged woman now and the *uppskera* on top of that. And I would not allow myself to be used by someone who only wanted me because I was the *uppskera*. Surely that was the only reason he was back. Sure Elí felt that way too. But it was different with him. I'd always known our union was strategic for him. I couldn't stand the idea of Vidar possibly feeling that way.

Three new scents hit me as we stepped out into the sun. The musk within them was mild, suggesting pups who hadn't quite hit puberty yet. Another scent lay below it, a different kind of musk from some kind of small animal. My sensitive ears picked up two mocking voices over the protests and pleas of a third coming from around the side of my house. Instinct kicked in, not a territorial one, but a protective one. Thanks to my brother, I knew the sounds of bullying all too well. I couldn't just let this be. Eager to get away from Vidar, I slung the pack over my shoulder and started that direction.

A few moments passed before I heard Vidar's steps follow me.

Through the tall pine trees hugging the side of my house, I saw an all too familiar scene.

Three boys—the eldest of which couldn't be over twelve—stood beside my raised bed of orange poppies and red tulips. The two hovering over the third like vultures had at least thirty pounds on the younger boy. One boy with a messy mop of brown hair grabbed something from the clutches of the smaller boy. An angry squeak filled the air. A brown furred form writhed in the grasp of the mop-haired boy. The fear-filled eyes of a ferret caught in the bigger boy's hands rolled toward the small boy. The creature's little heart beat so hard I could hear it from here. The predatory look on mop-haired boy and his friend's faces said they heard it too.

The small boy bared his teeth at the other two. "Give him back. Now! If you hurt him I'll—"

"You'll what, pup? Bite us? Oh wait, you can't! You haven't even become yet," the mop-haired boy taunted.

The third boy bared fangs at the smaller one. "We're doing you a favor. Bringing the *uppskera* a gift like this is just stupid."

The little boy grabbed for his ferret, but mop-haired simply lifted it up out of his reach. "You're stupid, both of you!" the little boy yelled.

His tenacity made me smile. If he kept this up, he'd get pummeled, as he likely had on more than one occasion by these very boys. But he wouldn't give up. I could see it in his eyes. His fingers curled into fists.

"What is all this noise in my backyard?" I demanded as I strode out of the trees toward them.

The two bullies sucked in breaths and spun toward me with eyes so wide, they were more whites than anything else. They ducked their heads and hunched over, the human equivalent of tucking their tails. The small boy spared me only a glance before lunging in and snatching the ferret back. Stroking the creature, he clutched it to his chest and whispered words of comfort to it. The ferret's heartbeat started to return to normal almost immediately.

"*Uppskera*, we're so sorry we disturbed you. We didn't know you were home," Mop Hair said.

The other boy produced a colorful gift bag from behind his back. "W-w-we brought you a gift," he stuttered.

"I see that."

They flinched at my approach, hunching down even lower. But not the little one. He stood tall, turned slightly away from the other two, shielding his ferret from them. I took the offered bag. To my surprise, several bags of flower bulbs lay inside.

Mop-haired boy's eyes rose slowly to my face. "We thought those'd be better than cut flowers that would just die. This way you'll have flowers every year," he said with a tentative smile.

I nodded. "That was very wise of you. Thank you. This is a fine gift."

His eyes brightened, and he and the other boy straightened a bit, both smiling. After several moments of me not returning the smile, they started to reek of fear. Deciding to let them stew in it a bit, I turned to the small boy.

"What have you there?"

His throat worked hard to swallow as he turned to me. He sniffled a little, lifted his chin, and held the ferret out to me. His lips quivered as they turned up. "I brought you a gift too. I know it might not be as clever, or grand, but Simon is a good friend. I thought you could use a good friend."

Had I the ability to tear up, I definitely would have. But tears hadn't touched my cheeks for many years. It wasn't that I believed they were a weakness. I just didn't have any left. Instead, I put on a scrutinizing look as I accepted the ferret. The other two boys grinned as though they had scored some type of victory. The little creature went very still. It stared at me with large eyes, its little clawed feet tensing and relaxing as if it couldn't decide whether I was a threat. But then, wasn't everyone? The thought brought a sardonic smile to my lips, ruining the gruff ruse I was putting on.

Moving slow so as not to alarm him, I cradled the ferret in one arm and scratched his head. He snuggled into the crook of my arm, apparently deciding I wasn't a threat. If only that were true. I looked back at the small boy. The look of despair pulling his features down wiped away when my gaze touched him. His back straightened and he tried to smile. Many adults couldn't show such fearlessness around me now that my power had awoken. It was impressive, and more than a little inspiring. Maybe I wasn't the big bad monster so many feared me to be.

"He's a fine ferret, and there is no greater gift than a friend," I said.

Pain hid behind his smug expression, and his eyes kept straying to the ferret. The other two boys shot him dirty looks when they thought I couldn't see. I stared straight at the mop-haired boy, letting him realize I'd caught him in the act.

"What are your names?" I asked.

Mop-haired boy stood to his full height. "I'm Kristofer. This is Jon." He sneered in the smaller boy's direction. "And he's Emil." At the third boy's name, Kristofer's face scrunched up as if he'd tasted something fowl.

Still petting the ferret, I stared hard at Kristofer. "The strong protect the weak in the pack, Kris. Do you know why?" I asked.

Eyes darting about as if searching for an elusive answer, Kris flipped his mop of hair back and snorted. The scent of anxiety drifted from him, not as rank as that of fear, but a close second.

It was Jon who answered. "Honestly, *Uppskera*, we don't."

A look of relief came over Kris, and he shrugged and nodded at the same time. He couldn't have been more noncommittal if he'd tried. Clearly, he didn't want to displease me, but he didn't want to submit completely either. Not bad qualities in a *varúlfur*, really. Emil started to look worried, no doubt about the fallout from this encounter.

"Many don't," I said. That drew the rapt attention of all three boys.

"How do we shift in Hemlock Hollow without fear of being seen?" I asked.

Knowledge shone in Emil's eyes, but he didn't speak up. "The sat umbrella blocks us out from the satellites," Kris said, sounding quite pleased with himself.

I nodded. "Yes, it does, very good. Do you know who made it?"

Kris and Jon exchanged a confused look, and eventually looked back to me and shook their heads. When I gave Emil a questioning look, he perked up.

"Einir Gunderson," he said.

"Very good, that's right." I looked back at the other two. "And Einir is low in the pack. When he was young, he was small and weak, yet because he was protected, we can now shift anywhere in Hemlock Hollow without fear of discovery from satellites."

Their eyes widened, as did Emil's smile. I gave it a moment to sink in. "And Einir isn't the only one," I went on. "There are doctors, lawyers, scientists, pilots, and more who are all lower members of their packs. They help our kind survive and thrive. That is why we protect the weak, because while they may be weak physically, they are strong in other ways that will help the pack."

Their faces dropped into slack looks of shock as understanding lit their eyes. They looked to Emil with a new kind of interest. It was both encouraging and sad. While I might have changed the way they saw him, such a lesson was one they should have learned from their parents a long time ago. I had a feeling it was only one of many they may have failed to teach. I looked down at the bag of bulbs dangling from my arm.

"Emil's right, I could use a friend, or three. How would you boys like to do the *uppskera* a favor?" I asked.

They smiled and bounced on the balls of their feet, each nodding in turn.

"I'm going away for a while. *Uppskera* business. I need someone to watch over things for me here, otherwise stuff will continue to pile up in my yard, my plants will die, and someone might break in. It's a big job that will take all three of you," I said.

"We can do it!" Kris insisted.

"We'll work together," Jon said.

I narrowed my eyes at him, then at Kris. "Do you really think you can do that? All three of you?"

"Yes, ma'am."

"We can, honest."

I looked to Emil, who had remained quiet. "Do you think you can do that, Emil?"

He swallowed hard and nodded. "I can. I will."

Looking around, I shook my head. "I don't know. It's a big job. I'll need you three to separate out the gifts, recycle what can be recycled from them, re-use what you can, and clean up the rest. I'll also need you to plant these flowers, keep them and my grass watered, and..." I paused and looked down at the ferret. "I'll need someone to look out for him for me while I'm gone." I looked from the ferret to Emil. "Do you think you can do that, Emil?"

The young boy's shoulders went back as a smile spread across his face. "I can."

I smiled as I handed the squirming ferret back. "Thank you."

The other two boys shot envious looks Emil's way. Not a good state to leave things in. Head dipping just low enough that I could peer at them from beneath my white-blond brows, I poured a touch of my reaper power into my eyes. They collectively took a step back. I let the look fall away and replaced it with a smile. No sense in scaring them. I only wanted them to be sure of whom they were dealing with. Their cowed looks told me they were more than sure.

"And Jon and Kris, I'll need you to look after my cat. He'll feed himself, I just need you to make sure no one messes with him. If you can all work together and pull this off well, you will earn the friendship of the *uppskera*," I said.

Kris's eyes went wide. "A cat? Why do you have a cat? They hate us!"

I shook my head. "They don't hate us. They see us as superior predators, and that can make them a bit fearful. My cat, Heimdallr, keeps my place free of rats and mice. He serves a purpose, and he's my friend."

"He serves a purpose, just like the lowest in the pack," Jon observed.

A smile came easily to my lips. "Exactly."

The thump of a hand slapping against a heart drew my gaze back to Kris. "You have our word, we'll guard Heimdallr."

Their excited energy filled the air, wrapping around me like a warm summer breeze. They exchanged smiles and nods, even with Emil. In their excitement, they talked over one another, proclaiming their undying loyalty, ability, and eagerness. I handed Kris the bag of bulbs.

"Thank you, young wolves. I appreciate your help. I've got to run. You three take care and be good to one another," I said.

They called out farewells as I turned and started back around the house. Even from around the side of the house I could hear their energetic voices talking about how they couldn't believe they'd met and befriended the reaper. Then I heard Kris ask in a tentative voice, "Emil, since your family are farmers, do you think you might be able to help us with how and where to plant these flowers?"

"Yeah, I could help with that."

"Awesome! Let's find a spot where she can see them from her window!"

Their conversation made a sliver of hope cut through the darkness that always seemed to surround me now. If they could really work together, I might have done some good in their lives. And maybe helping to change the minds and intentions of two bullies would help me sleep better at night. Gods, I hoped so. Any chance to do something good that didn't involve killing was one I had to take. Soon the reaping would start, and I would need something positive to hang onto when that happened.

Vidar's smiling face waited for me at the front of the house. Leaning back against the hood of his truck, arms crossed over his broad chest, he looked all too pleased. And enticingly sexy, but I was trying to ignore that part. Calling up my anger over being abandoned helped.

"That was a good thing you did," he said softly when I approached.

I slid my sunglasses on to hide the emotion his words stirred. "I don't have to be the thing that goes bump in the night all the time," I said.

He pushed away from the truck and took a step toward me. His hand lifted as if he wanted to reach for me, but it stopped halfway from his side.

"We need to talk, Ayra," he said.

Whatever he had to say couldn't be good, not by that serious, dark look in his eyes. I didn't want to hear it. It was far too late for apologies or explanations.

"Look, Vidar, I get it. Talking about this as kids was one thing. Now it's real, it's happening. You don't owe me anything. You don't have to protect me anymore. I'm stronger, faster, better than I ever was, and you know how good I was back then. And now I'm not afraid to use it. You don't have to be a part of this. You deserve to have a pack, if not a mate, a life." I forced the words out.

I'd wanted to rage at him about how he'd left me, about how he'd only come back because I was the *uppskera* now, about how he wanted something from me like all the others. But the words wouldn't come out. Instead, I'd gone soft, like always.

A sort of strangled look came over him, like he couldn't breathe. The last part was too much. I shouldn't have said it. It insinuated things I had once wanted for him, for us. Me and my big mouth. Gods, I didn't want him to realize I had wanted him, not now. Mostly because I didn't now. I was engaged to a great guy who cared about me. And just like that, I realized I still did want Vidar. But as my brother used to say, "How's it feel to want?" *Horrible, it feels horrible, always has.* Thinking of him—and what I couldn't have with Vidar—stirred my anger back up. Not that it took much. The fury waited forever, barely beneath a surface so thin it felt transparent.

"So do you," he said softly. So much pain filled those three words that I cringed.

It almost made me forgive him, and I couldn't do that. "People would kill to be what I am. Calder did. Again and again." My voice grew as dark as my thoughts. Dammit, I hadn't meant to go down that road. I forced myself to brighten, to smile. Due to this damn superhero complex of his it would be easier to make him leave if he thought I was okay. "But, hey, I have the world at my feet, literally. There isn't a wolf out there who would challenge me and win." That did make me feel good, and I let it show. No one could bully me now.

My steps sped up as we reached my bike. I wanted to get on it and away from Vidar. The sooner I did, the better. Being nice, pretending I was all right... I couldn't keep it up for long. Agreeing to his help had been a mistake.

"Why don't we load your bike into the back of my truck, and I'll drive. That way we can catch up," he said.

I walked around my bike, putting it between us. For what I was about to say, I needed distance. The opposing fronts of what I needed and wanted threatened to pull me apart. I picked up my helmet and stared at my BMW's pearly white gas tank. The reflection of my pale face and even paler hair looked like a ghost. That's exactly what I needed to be to him— no more than a ghost from his past.

"That's a bad idea. I appreciate you wanting to help me. I really do. But you can't, you shouldn't. The reaper's job is something best done alone," I said, having to force the last words out.

It shouldn't be this hard, shouldn't hurt this bad. I'd been alone for four years. It was something I was used to, good at. And a big part of that was his fault. Cutting him out now meant I would be truly alone. But hadn't I been for the past four years? And that was a good thing, the way it should be. I forced myself to look up into that face that had grown only more attractive with the passing years.

"That's not true," he said.

He took a step closer, reaching across the bike for me. I stepped back out of his reach. "Don't, Vidar. You left me when I needed you. Now I don't. There was no reason for you to come back," I said.

Those hazel eyes turned cold. As triumphant as that felt, it hurt too.

"I'm about to become a killer. You don't need to see that." The words slipped out as a sympathetic pang shot through me.

"I'm sorry I left you, more sorry than you'll ever know. I didn't want to, but I had to. And you need me. No one left around here knows Calder like I do. I can track him." He swallowed hard. "And we're all killers, Ayra. It's our nature. But you...you are the *uppskera*, one who kills with purpose. There is no shame in that."

Damn. I had misunderstood the chill in his eyes by a mile. I couldn't tell him how much I craved the fight, the kill. And I hadn't even reaped yet. The desire had been building ever since my power had awakened. Each day it grew stronger. How bad would it be once I had killed? I couldn't tell him of all people that I was the worst monster of all. Unable to speak, I shook my head. Vidar leaped over my bike and took me by the shoulders.

"With your power, urges awoke too. To hunt, fight, kill. I learned all about it at the temple. You aren't bad, or evil. These urges help the *uppskera* do what needs to be done. But they can also be dangerous to you," he said.

I held his stare, transfixed by the acceptance in it. An acceptance I didn't deserve. Elí looked at me with awe and a touch of fear, but never acceptance. So maybe Vidar did know, but that was different than seeing me give into such urges. And he had lost the right to be by my side for that.

"So, you did learn something at the temple other than just how to be a *lögreglu*," I said.

"I did," he said in a low, breathy voice.

The warmth of his hands on my arms, the brush of his callused palms, and the heat of his hovering, muscular body all threatened to set me on fire. The green shirt featuring the Hulk that hugged his pectorals told me he would feel just as hard as he looked. Desire rushed up to feed the fire inside. But his shirt made me fear what I'd turn into once the reaping started. Here I was, always lusting after a man other than my intended. My control was slipping already. I tore away from him before he could smell my need. I didn't want to need someone who had left me behind.

"There's more you need to know. Please, hear me out. Let me at least give you a ride to wherever you're going," Vidar said. His desperate tone tugged at me.

One part of me wanted to do whatever it took to make him stop sounding like he was in pain, though a much larger part of me reveled in it. But he was right. If he knew more about what I had become, I needed to hear it. And he could track Calder objectively, without getting emotional about it. While keeping him with me was certainly a bad idea, it was also necessary. I couldn't let my emotions get in the way of capturing my brother before he did something even more stupid.

"All right. You can take me as far as Idaho. I have a cousin there I think Calder might enlist for help," I said, voice low so the boys in the backyard didn't hear.

The gorgeous smile that spread across his face tugged at my heart and libido. It reminded me of better days, days spent swimming in the river, running through the forest, days as happy kids without a care. Well, mostly without a care. There had always been my brother and my parents. But they hadn't been as bad when Vidar was around.

He grabbed my five-hundred-pound motorcycle by the frame, picked it up as if it weighed less than a bale of hay, and set it in the back of his truck. I tried not to admire the muscles in his arms flexing while he did it. I failed. Suddenly the road to Idaho seemed very, very long, and somehow not long enough.

CHAPTER FIVE

VIDAR

I rambled on about Iceland for an hour. Nervousness always raised the urge in me to talk, to fill the silence, to avoid the true issue. She would eventually figure out I was holding something back about the temple. But I couldn't tell her what it was, and she would get even madder at that point. But that wasn't the only reason I rambled. I loved Iceland, and I wanted to tell her all about it so she felt like she had been there with me instead of here being tortured by her worthless brother. Oh, the ways I wanted to hurt that son of a bitch...

Despite my dark thoughts, I kept my stories light. I told her about getting lost on the Reykjavik University grounds my first—and second, and third—time there. I told her about how on my fourth trip, someone took pity on me and told me my deplorable Icelandic made it sound like I was asking the way to the whorehouse instead of the history hall. The memory of that scorched my cheeks with embarrassment—which thankfully she couldn't see due to my dark skin. But by the way she laughed, it was clear she saw it in my eyes. I didn't mind. She laughed and that made it worth it. Gods, I had missed that carefree, bell-like sound.

I kept trying, but that was the only laugh I got out of her. Tense energy filled the space between us, making it thick, cavernous, impossible. The Order had forbidden me from telling her what she had been waiting all these years to hear. Their rules and restrictions weighed heavier on me now than ever before.

The evening grew dark enough that it forced me to turn the headlights on, not out of a need to see. My *varúlfur* eyes could see for a mile. But other cars couldn't see me, and that could put them in danger. Ayra let out a long sigh. My gaze gravitated back to her. She looked almost ethereal, her porcelain skin practically glowing in the dark, her white-blond hair draped around her like a silken cloak. The years had added a sharpness to her high cheekbones and a fullness to her lips—not to mention her petite breasts. No, never mention those, because if I did, my gaze would travel there and I couldn't allow it to do that.

She was from the *uppskera* bloodline, so far above my station that even if she wasn't engaged I wouldn't have a chance with her. Not that she was the type to care about such things. No one had known about her bloodline until recently, except for her family, which was probably the only reason it had taken as long as it had for her to get engaged.

"Thank you, V, I needed to laugh," she said.

The use of my old nickname—the one only she called me—stirred much more than just emotions. It hurt deep down, all the way to my soul. I never should have left her. Now, not only did the temporary vow of celibacy tie my hands, but she was engaged. But did she love him?

"You know I'm always good for a laugh," I said with a forced smile.

Leaning her head back against the headrest, she sighed and looked out the passenger window. "You're good for so much more than that," she said in a wistful voice. And was that a touch of desire? I could have sworn I felt it flare in her power, her scent. No, I had to be imagining it, wanting it so bad I made myself hear it, feel it. When her head rolled back in my direction, the gaze she fixed me with possessed a coldness that told me I had definitely imagined the desire. It was gone too fast for me to be sure, replaced by her ever-present tension.

"So, what besides your Bachelor of Science did you get from Iceland?" she asked in a guarded tone.

My Bachelor of Science, something I know she wanted as badly as I did, though for different reasons. My interest was in sustainable energy, hers meteorology. On the surface her reason seemed a little deeper. The whole channeling lighting thing was something she and I had struggled to understand since we were kids—alone. She'd always been terrified to tell anyone else she could do it. And I'd kept her secret. I had hoped my studies in sustainable energy might teach me more about the nature of her ability. Sadly...

"Not much when it comes to your electricity channeling, either from the university or the temple. But when it came to the *uppskera*, the temple knew a lot," I said.

Some of the darkness that clung to her left her eyes, and she sat up straighter. "Do tell," she prompted. The warning in her tone discouraged me. If I told her the whole story, would the Order find out, and more importantly, would it turn her away from me? I decided to start easy, with the history bits. That part wasn't forbidden.

"There hasn't been an *uppskera* in three hundred years because our kind used to be far more reckless with those they bit in. The practice of biting in criminals to force them to serve penance to their victims' families being outlawed played a big part."

She rolled her hand at me in a "go on" motion. "All things I learned from the journals on my own," she said in an impatient tone.

The implications of that made me swallow hard before I could go on. "Your heightened power, strength, and speed come from the ability to tap deeper into your instincts than any other *varúlfur* can. But it also makes you wilder, your power harder to control. It's why you feel the instinct to hunt, to kill, stronger than you did before." I stopped, afraid to say the rest.

Pulling her knees up beneath her, she turned sideways in her seat to face me. She was such a petite thing that she didn't even struggle with the seatbelt when she did it. Sinewy, hard muscles moved beneath her skin, and that was about it. If I didn't know better, I would have thought she didn't eat much. But she had always been rail thin and ate like a horse. Coming from sturdy ancestors, she had always considered it a curse—along with a lot of kids in middle school who had picked on her when I wasn't around.

The interest in her eyes didn't sway me, but the trust did. I had to tell her. If she was going to choose me for her *verndari*, I needed to live up to that trust. More importantly, I had to make up for the years of barely talking to her. How I could stand to be her *verndari* while she was married to another, I wasn't sure. But I would figure it out, for her. I owed her that much at the very least.

"History has shown the *uppskera* have trouble holding on to their humanity because their edge between instinct and reason is far thinner than that of any other *varúlfur*. Many have tipped over into full instinct mode all the time, losing themselves to the reaping. Though today's generations don't remember, it's part of why the packs have such a healthy fear of the *uppskera*." The anxiety pinching her delicate features into a look of something near pain stopped me. I laid a hand on her knee. "I'm sorry I didn't tell you earlier, but that isn't the kind of news someone should get in a letter, and..." I swallowed hard, fighting my training. "The temple forbade outside contact."

Blinking eyes that had misted over, she nodded. Seeing that made a million needles of pain stab into me. Dammit, that was part of why I hesitated to tell her all this. The hard look that banished the moisture worried me even more.

"I understand. It's just..." She swallowed hard before going on. "It's just that's what I was afraid of."

Oh. She didn't mean she understood about why I hadn't kept in touch. I wanted to say more, but I was too afraid they might find out. I took hold of her hand. "But you won't face it alone. Every *uppskera* has their *verndari*."

Her narrowed gaze lifted to me. She cocked her head to the side in that cute way she did any time she found something suspicious. Gods, I had missed seeing that. Face hardening, she pulled her hand from mine.

"You said that before. It doesn't make sense. But I'm guessing that's because it has a deeper meaning than someone to protect the reaper. Out with it," she demanded.

Always straight to the point. I loved and dreaded that about her. If only she weren't drawing away more by the moment. Damn their rules. I had to tell her. "The Order of the *Verndari* has trained *varúlfur* for centuries to be *verndari* to the *uppskera*. It isn't physical protection, but mental, or so they think. The *verndari* protects the *uppskera* from losing themselves to their own instincts once they begin reaping," I explained.

Her power crackled over me like embers, stinging, biting, burning. "How?" It was an order, not a question.

"By being there for them, reminding them they're still a person, still more than a killer. But I suspect there's more to it than even the Order knows. I think the *verndari* is linked, connected, essential to the reaper, and has something to do with their ability to channel lightning."

She grinned. Not exactly the reaction I'd been expecting, quite the opposite, in fact.

"What?" I asked.

The mixture of happiness and sadness in her eyes reminded me of the look in my grandmother's eyes when she'd been on her deathbed. A powerful chill rose bumps all over my body.

"It's cute that you still do that, think in threes," she said.

"What do you mean? I don't do that."

"Yeah, and I'm not a size two or a B cup."

Those words drew my eyes to her breasts. They were perfect in my opinion, just the right size to fit in my mouth. The outline of her curves made me think she wasn't wearing a bra. Heat burned up my neck to my face, making my eyes fly open. I was sure it wasn't a sacrilege to think of the *uppskera* in such a way. The Norse Gods revered sex and the power that came with it. But she wasn't just the *uppskera*, she was Ayra, the girl I'd loved my entire life. My gaze plummeted to her mostly bare legs folded beneath her. No matter how hard I tried to stop, I looked up the length of those slender legs to where her cut off jean shorts barely covered the beginning of the curve of her ass. Damn that vow of celibacy. Damn it straight to Muspelheimr.

I looked back to the dark road unfolding before the headlights. "I'm so sorry. I didn't mean to leer at you. It's just that, you grew up while I was gone."

I wanted to kick myself for being so completely inarticulate. Of all the things I could have said...

Down deep in her chest, she made an affirmative, appreciative noise. "So did you," she said.

The crotch of my jeans became painfully tight. I sat up straight in my seat, and put both hands firmly back on the wheel. Sighing, she turned in her seat and stretched her legs out beneath the dash. Then it struck me; she was distracting me to avoid the conversation.

The ticking yellow lines of the road helped me focus. "I didn't just go to Iceland to study energy." I swallowed hard, having to build up the courage to say the next part. "I didn't just join the temple to serve Odin and learn to be a *lögreglu*, either. I also did it to learn more about the *uppskera* so I could help you. I might not have learned about your ability to channel electricity, but I did learn how to help you with the rest of it. I want to help you, Ayra. It's all I've ever wanted," I said. Out of the corner of my eye I saw her stiffen and wrap her arms around herself.

Fear shot through me. Since we'd been kids that was what she had done when she was about to shut me out and close herself off. Except, this time, it wasn't an argument with her mother she didn't want to talk about, or a bruise from her brother she wanted to hide. This was her life, her future, and I couldn't let her shut me out of it. I knew she'd react this way. It was exactly why I had hesitated to tell her.

Her teeth ground together audibly. "Keeping in contact with me would have helped me." The words were cold and peppered with anger and pain.

I jumped in to try to cool her anger. "I had to see what I could learn. We knew so little about the whole situation. Let me help you now. No one should carry the weight of their entire race's fate on their shoulders alone. I'm your best friend, I should be the one to help you."

Expression guarded, she fixed her cold gaze on the road ahead. "You were, four years ago before you dropped off the face of the planet. It's best if we just remember things the way they were and move on."

"I'll never move on from you, Ayra. I can't, I won't."

Her glacial eyes locked on mine. "I am engaged. And besides, I'm going to become a killer. I don't want you to see that. It could change the way you look at me."

The dull feel to her power worried me. It flared when I put my hand on her leg, flowing over me in a tingling rush. Thankfully, this time it didn't hurt. "Nothing could change the way I look at you."

She tensed, but didn't pull her leg away. "Don't be so sure of that," she said in a flat tone. "So tell me, why would the *uppskera* be chosen by the Gods, and their *verndari* be chosen by the Order?"

I didn't want to tell her, but I had to. "It isn't, exactly. The Order only trains them and narrows it down to a final three. It's then up to the *uppskera* themselves to choose out of those three."

"Why aren't all three here at once for me to choose from?"

Despite preparing myself for those very words, I flinched at the pain they caused as much as the coldness of her tone. "We are selected in order of how we final in the trials, and we get to attempt Impression in that order."

"Again, chosen by mortals and not the Gods. Why is that different from the way the *uppskera* is chosen?"

"The Order believes it is to give the *uppskera* a choice, since they weren't given one in the matter of becoming the *uppskera*. And also, because they don't believe Odin counted on the madness that can come with being the *uppskera*."

A guarded expression came over her. "Is that why you went to the temple?"

"Yes, but there is so much about the Order that is secret."

"Yeah, I'm starting to see that," she mumbled.

Huge droplets of water started to splat on the windshield, forcing me to focus harder on driving. While neither of us could die very easily in a crash, I didn't want to ruin Ayra's motorcycle, or my truck. The smell of wet vegetation and asphalt flowed into the vents. Within moments the droplets became so numerous I had to turn on the wipers. Ayra sat up straighter, the hint of a smile starting to work at her lips. Her power surged with something close to joy. I smiled. The rain always had the opposite effect on Ayra than most people. She rolled her window down, breathed deep, and leaned out into it.

After less than half a mile, she turned to me with a radiant smile. "Pull over, I want to get out," she said.

Though I shook my head, I started keeping an eye out for side roads leading off into the trees. "You still like to dance in the rain?" I asked, knowing the answer. Memories of dancing in the rain with her as kids flooded back. Gods, how she had looked, laughing, happy, so beautiful. I shook my head. Thinking like that would lead down a path I had taken an oath not to travel. Besides, she clearly wanted nothing to do with me. Which was exactly why I had to do whatever I could to make her happy.

A half-smile broke through her carefully crafted mask. The joy in her eyes as she watched the rain streak down the windshield said volumes.

I could deny her nothing when she was like this. Helheimr, who was I kidding? I couldn't deny her anything any time. I turned down the next dirt road off to the right. The headlights reflected off tall grass that grew between the ruts. At least that was a good sign no one was likely to be down this road. But then, we were in the middle of nowhere in Montana. It wasn't likely there would be anyone anywhere out here. Such was part of the beauty and allure of Montana, especially for our kind.

After a few twists and turns, I pulled off to the left in a spot where the trees gave way to a meadow. I slid open the back window of the truck while Ayra clicked through the stations on my satellite radio. Kaleo soon bellowed through my truck's speakers about being no good, an irony I'm certain wasn't by accident. Ayra loved irony. But it was good music, so I wasn't about to fault her. Not that I ever would anyway. She cranked up the volume and leaped out of the truck. Unable to suppress a smile, I opened my door and stepped out into the pouring rain.

Before I took two steps my shirt was soaked through and my shorts were well on their way. I peeled the shirt off and draped it over the tailgate. As a *varúlfur*, I had an aversion to any more clothes than were absolutely necessary anyway. It hindered shifting. The shorts, though, those were very necessary at the moment. Being naked would be a bad idea. Watching Ayra gyrate with that natural grace of hers and sway to the music only solidified that thought.

Thankfully, my vow of celibacy only extended to the time she chose a *verndari*. A little insurance by the Order that a potential *verndari* wouldn't try to influence the *uppskera's* decision with great sex—or worse, tying them together as mates. Insurance that came with the highest cost imaginable. Anyone that broke the vow during the time of Impression would be hunted down and killed. So until she chose, I couldn't cross that bridge. And Gods, how I wanted to cross that bridge. And then there was the matter of earning her forgiveness first.

Barefoot in the grass, she moved with the grace and abandonment of one who felt completely at home in nature. Neither the dark nor the rain hindered her. By the time I reached her, her hair flew about her in wet clusters. Her blue half-shirt with the gold W symbol from one of her favorite comic book heroines had plastered against her pale skin. I loved that she still wore vintage comic book T-shirts like I did. It made the distance that had separated us for so long feel a little less solid. Even if she did cut half of the shirts off. The sight of her bare midriff made me rethink that. Especially since she cut them in half.

She looked like a creature born of moonlight, all pale, beautiful, and utterly haunting. And the way she moved, oh Gods, it made my mind go to nasty places, places it had no right going to. Odin forgive me for coveting the chosen one. But damn, I wanted to covet, caress, and please her in so many ways. More importantly, I wanted her to choose me so I would always be close to her. I wanted to help her fight back the darkness. I wanted to help her keep her sanity, her sense of self in all the crazy of being the *uppskera*. And though I knew it was a stupid instinct considering what she was, I wanted to protect her. If she married Elí, I still wanted to be her *verndari*, even if I could never be with her the way I wanted.

Smiling with the same abandon she had when we were kids, she twirled with her hands held high, delighting in the storm.

"Thank you, Thor, for this storm!" she said.

The joy in her voice grabbed at something deep in me. This was the happiest I'd seen her since I'd been back. I swayed to the music with her, trying not to focus on the enticing way her hips swayed. She didn't move away from me. I took that as progress.

"You've developed some serious skills since we were kids," I said, having to raise my voice over the patter of rain on the truck.

She shrugged and twirled away a bit. Her wet T-shirt clung to her breasts. I closed my eyes against the sight of her pert nipples and moved to the music. Her power was like a gentle pressure pulling and pushing at me, telling me where every part of her body was without needing to see. Normally smell would tell me all of that, but the rain dampened things too much. Thankfully, it also worked a bit like a cool shower. If only we could be a guy and a woman instead of the *uppskera* and her potential *verndari*. My eyes opened, a mistake considering how tremendously hot she looked with her arms above her head, her body gyrating perfectly in rhythm to the song.

"Clearly. You've developed mad skills, and here I am swaying like the geek at the junior high dance," I said with a laugh. I couldn't help it; my brain and my mouth weren't connecting. It had always been like that with her. Part of me had expected that to change after four years. But she still had that effect on me.

Laughing, she literally danced a circle around me while I swayed like an idiot. "I always thought your dancing was cute." The storm was getting to her, draining her anger, intoxicating her.

It wasn't right for me to enjoy her company like this, when she was in the throes of storm ecstasy. I hadn't earned her forgiveness yet. But if felt so good to be this close to her without the pressure of anger holding us apart.

The glow of the truck's interior lights that seeped around her motorcycle highlighted her high cheekbones and deep dimples as she smiled. My heart skipped, forcing me to delve into some serious—and no doubt hilarious—dance moves to cover it. Proving me right, Ayra laughed so hard she had to pause and bend over to hold her stomach. Hearing her bell-like laughter was worth it. A few songs later, the music slowed. Taking her hand, I spun her in and placed a hand on her hip in an old-fashioned dance position my grandmother would have approved of.

Rain and darkness combined to obscure her from me slightly, creating a mist of water bouncing back up around her that gave her an otherworldly look. My breath caught in my throat.

"Thank you. I haven't laughed like that in a long time," she said.

I drew back, giving her a wide-eyed look of mock hurt. "Wait, what are you saying? My dance moves are laughable? I beg your pardon, dear lady, but I have mad skills."

She nodded. "Mad, yes."

We both laughed as we spun in a mockery of a waltz. The cool grass beneath my feet and the warm woman in my arms felt like the closest to Valhalla I might ever get. And it was close enough. Not knowing how few moments she might get to dance and laugh, I wasn't about to cut any of them short for my own gain.

My eyes drew to where she tugged her bottom lip in between her teeth, worrying at it. Her power flared hot against me, and yet I wanted to be closer, needed to be, had to be. Though my oaths and everything I'd learned at the temple screamed at me not to, I started to bend down toward her. Eyes closing, she rose up on her toes, her chin titling up to me.

Lightning crackled overhead. The taste and scent of metal filled the air. Ayra grinned and threw her head back, eyes closing against the onslaught of rain. Her power began to pop and crackle. The sensation pulled at my own, making it flare up. My hands went to her waist as she reached her arms up to the sky. Thunder shook the ground beneath us. Lightning flashed in jagged lines across the sky not half a mile away.

"Maybe this isn't a good idea," I said.

Her radiant smile took my breath away. "The best ones never are. But maybe you should get back," she said.

She took a step back. I held tight to her waist, my hands feeling freakishly big as they all but encircled her. Again, lightning lit up the sky, closer still. The hair on the back of my neck started to rise. A prickling sensation traveled from it down my spine. Ayra's eyes widened and she tugged back harder against my arms. The strength in her little body surprised me. I got the feeling she could pull away if she really wanted to.

Ayra couldn't attract lightning like Sonya could, but the longer she stood out in the storm, the higher the chances were that it would strike her. Inevitably, it always did.

"I don't want you to get hurt," she said.

The concern in her voice got me. I smiled. "Not to worry. I've been working on my tolerance," I said.

Her pale brows rose high. "How exactly? By grabbing hold of live wires?"

I shrugged. She wasn't far off.

Eyes going wide, she smacked my chest.

Lightning crackled again, closer this time, the bolt longer, as if reaching toward us. No, not us, toward her. She pushed at me, tensing to pull away. Experience told me I should let go and step back like she suggested. But part of me wanted to test what I'd been secretly working on. I drew my power up from my core, raising it like a shield around me. Then the world exploded with a crackle. Ayra lit up like an LED, energy from within making her so bright, looking at her felt like looking at the sun. Her skin almost seemed translucent. The expression on her face became something close to euphoria.

It felt like I held a live wire in my arms, pulsing with endless energy. Pain flowed through me, working at the edges of the shield of power I had built up around myself. Like I had practiced with electricity, I worked as an insulator, helping Ayra hold the lightning. The pain started to wear thin spots in my shield. Breathing grew difficult. Just when I thought I was about to lose my shield altogether, Ayra threw her hands up in the air and directed the lightning back into the sky. It erupted from her outstretched fingers, cutting through the dark clouds in two jagged lines of ultra-white light.

My head sagged and my knees started to tremble. Ayra peeled my hands from her waist, put a shoulder under one of my arms, and started to lead me to the truck. The world swayed with each step. Though I was weak, nothing felt damaged. Before I could make any useless protests, she had the tailgate down and was pushing me back onto it.

"Are you crazy? You should have let go! What hurts? How can I help?" Questions flowed out of her in a rush.

All I could think about was how she hadn't let go of my hands yet. Gods, she looked beautiful all charged up from the lightning, like a star that was almost too bright to gaze upon. The concern pinching her features together ruined the look a little. She moved in closer, stepping between my legs.

"Vidar, talk to me! Are you all right?" she demanded. Power flowed around me, squeezing, trying to make me comply, make me submit. She didn't do it consciously. I could tell by her wide eyes and the frazzled feel of the power. If she had, I wasn't entirely sure I'd have been able to resist if I'd wanted to. She had become that powerful. That realization stirred my desire back to life.

I nodded slowly so the world didn't spin too much. "I'm fine, just weak. Nothing hurts," I said, each word a struggle to get out.

She straightened a little, eyes growing wider. "Are you really sure? The last time you did that you had internal bleeding."

Delicate fingers danced across my bare chest. If I wasn't so exhausted, I would have gotten one hell of a hard-on. As it was, my body was getting there, just much slower than it normally would have.

I smiled, for more reasons than one. "That was four years ago. Like I said, I've been working on insulating myself from electricity."

She stopped touching me to cross her arms beneath her breasts. The outline of her hard nipples beneath her thin, wet, cotton shirt distracted me.

"Why?" she asked.

Wait, what was it she was asking about? Oh yeah... "Because there has to be a reason you can channel lightning, and there has to be a reason I can withstand it better than anyone. I figured what I can do is like insulating, like helping to direct the flow. So I wanted to get better at it, just in case. I think *verndari* were meant to do more than help keep an *uppskera* from going full-on wolf," I explained.

"Can others of the Order insulate electricity like you can?"

I shook my head. "No. Resistance to electricity seems to be something unique to my family."

Her hands moved to her small hips. "You still think it's part of Odin's plan for me? Now you think maybe it's part of his plan for us?"

"More than ever. Ayra, you healed the *leitar* using the lightning."

"Helped."

I put a hand over one of hers. "That proves Odin has a greater plan for you both than just hunting down newly bitten and dealing with them."

"But you said they didn't know anything about my ability to channel lightning at the temple," she said, voice filled with doubt. "Maybe it's just a weird genetic quirk." She sounded disappointed, like maybe she liked the idea of me being part of the equation and didn't want to discount it. *Naw, that has to just be wishful thinking.*

"That combined with my ability to create a shield that insulates it would be far too big of a coincidence."

She rolled her eyes a bit and nodded. "And we don't believe in coincidences," she repeated our old saying.

Thunder shook the night again. Ayra spun away, my hand sliding right off her rain-slick skin. Arms out to her sides, palms up to catch the rain, she spun in a circle. Part of me wanted to go to her. I needed to keep working on my insulating. But I wasn't so sure I could take another hit of lightning so soon after the first. If her ability was anything like it had been when we were kids, she could do this all night. And I had a feeling her ability had grown along with her.

The minute light from the dash in the truck was more than enough for my *varúlfur* eyes to make out every sexy detail of her wet silhouette. For now, I'd just watch the show. But what shot down out of the sky at her wasn't lightning this time; it was a bird. The monstrous thing had a wingspan of easily over six feet. Ayra yelped in surprise. Pale limbs flailed as feathers pounded the air. The distinctive screech of an eagle pierced the night.

"Shit!" I exclaimed as I leaped from the tailgate and ran to her.

Careful not to use full strength so I didn't hurt it, I knocked the bird aside. It barely touched the ground before it was back in the air again, flying toward us. Wrapping Ayra in my arms, I shielded her body with my own. Talons raked down my back in hot lines. My flesh gave way enough to sting like Helheimr, but thankfully not nearly as much as a human's would have.

"Don't hurt it! Please, don't hurt it!" Ayra said. Clutching her tighter, I encompassed her body with my own as completely as I could. I'd comply with her request only so long as I could keep the raptor from harming her. If it meant taking a bit of abuse, I could deal with that. All life was precious. That, and she'd never forgive me if I hurt it. After a few more painful rakes across my back, the eagle retreated. The edges of the wounds tingled, not from rain, but from my power rising up and beginning to heal me. Already the raw pain of damaged nerve endings began to fade. Deep as some of the gouges felt, it would take until tomorrow to heal completely.

A glance over my shoulder revealed nothing but a multitude of rain droplets sparkling in the glow from the truck's interior. The night brightened momentarily as lightning crackled high up in the clouds. Suddenly I was very grateful Ayra could only channel lightning, not call it. If the eagle got hurt because of her, she'd never forgive herself. In a move too quick for me to counter, she dropped down out of my arms and dashed away. Her head turned this way and that as she searched for the bird.

The rain muted our keen sense of smell. Using some of the training I'd received at the temple, I dampened my other senses down until hearing took the forefront. The cacophony of drops on the truck and even my own skin distracted me. I focused harder, listening for any hint of rustling feathers or a small, rapid heartbeat. Ayra turned to her right, gaze going straight to a tall fir tree. It should have been impossible for her locate it before I did. The training I had undergone was like no other, making me unique even among *varúlfur*. But then, she was the *uppskera*. Not even the best training the Gods had to offer could compare to her natural ability.

Just as she tensed to walk toward the tree, I grabbed hold of her arm. I toned my hearing back down before speaking. "We should leave it be. It was probably protecting its nest. We should go," I said.

While all of that could be true, it wasn't what made me want to leave.

Something about the entire encounter with the eagle had felt off. Sure, other predators were a bit more aggressive and territorial around our kind, but only with posturing. They never attacked. Animals were too smart to pick a fight they wouldn't win. Well, most were.

Ayra's shoulders sagged as she tugged free of my hand. "You're probably right."

After one last longing look at the slowly retreating storm, she started for the truck. An urgency from deep inside told me to get her out of here. I didn't breathe easy until she climbed in and closed the door. Eyeing the shadow of the large raptor in the feathery boughs, I made my way to the driver's side.

As I got in and started the truck, she made me lean forward so she could check my back.

"You'll live," she said, voice hard once again.

"Are you sure?" I asked in a mock-serious tone.

"Despite being incredibly foolish—but brave—I think you will."

I grinned. "You think I'm brave?"

"Oh, yes, such a brave werewolf to take on a bird for me. It was quite gallant." Her sarcasm stung.

"Well, it was a very large bird." I made a gesture with my hands as to how big.

"It certainly was. And your restraint was admirable." Beneath the sarcasm I detected a hint of humor.

I scoffed. "Restraint? Me? I think he was the one restraining himself."

An eerie foreboding worked at the hairs on the back of my neck. I hid it with a smile. Maybe I'd been reading too many Dean Koontz novels in all that spare time I'd had at the temple. Something deep down told me that wasn't it at all. I put the truck in drive and took off fast enough to spin the tires on the wet grass. Even after we pulled out onto the highway, I couldn't shake the feeling of being watched.

CHAPTER SIX

AYRA

Killing for pleasure is not instinct, it is an illness, insanity. The insane must be put down lest they threaten us all.
-Uppskera Journals

Not even the comforting scents of pine trees and earth could shake the horrible feeling that woke me. My phone vibrated beneath my pillow. I dug it out and squinted against the soft glow of light as I peered at the screen.

A text from Sonya: *On my way to a newly bitten in Pinehurst, Idaho.*

Dread suddenly made my body feel like it weighed a ton. Sonya, the seeker, the yin to my reaper's yang. She found the nearly condemned and tried to help them control their wolves before the next full moon. I went in and cleaned up if they couldn't or wouldn't. Only three days remained until the full moon, not much time to teach someone to control something out of control. Swallowing hard, I sat up. My first reaping could be within a matter of days.

There would be no sleeping now.

I crawled more than stepped out of my tiny backpacking tent. Vidar had invited me to sleep in the cab or bed of his truck, but I'd refused. The near kiss in the rain almost had been a mistake of epic proportions. He wanted to kiss the reaper, not me. If that weren't true, he would have kept in touch with me, and he would have come back sooner—before I had promised to marry another.

Darkness lay heavy over the forest. I stepped out into it and stretched, trying to shake the feeling. The rain had died down to only a misty feel in the air. My souped-up *varúlfur* hearing told me Vidar still slept soundly in the bed of the truck. Deep in my gut, a terrible feeling remained, like maybe more than my phone had woke me. I listened beyond Vidar, searching for I don't know what. The dark held only the normal sounds of a forest: owls, mice, a fox. It couldn't be the eagle. We had driven over a hundred miles after that encounter. So soon after a perceived threat to its nest, it wouldn't have flown this far away. In moments the fog of sleep cleared, and I realized the feeling hadn't come from an outside source.

Deep in my soul something pulled at me, something dark. The urge to go toward it grew so powerful I took a step. With each waking breath my awareness sharpened. Two breaths later I realized it wasn't a 'what' that pulled at me, but a 'who.' Somewhere out there a newly bitten had lost control of their instincts, had become a condemned. They had done unspeakable things to people. I felt it like I'd stepped into their head for a moment. Worse, they were going to do it again, soon.

I peeled my clothes off and tossed them back into my tent. If I went for my motorcycle, Vidar would wake up. The risk wouldn't be worth it. If I was right, and the pull I felt was the reaping, I didn't want Vidar anywhere near where I was going. Or more specifically, near me when I did what had to be done. With concentration, I sharpened my sight into that of a wolf, and crept slowly away from our camp. Once I was far enough away that he wouldn't hear me if I stepped on a branch, or feel the change in my power, I reached for the ground.

A thought was all it took to make my molecules heat up and slide around to shift me into a wolf. I landed in the pine needles with two white paws. Soft fur rippled over my muscles as I moved, insulating me from the rain. All four legs pumping, I plunged into the forest at full speed. The feel of the condemned amplified, not because I grew closer, but simply because I had shifted into a wolf. The hunter instincts in me woke with a ferocity that made my breath catch. I had to get to this person before they hurt anyone else. And I knew they would, I could feel it, as though I was connected to them. I ran faster.

One mile ticked by beneath my paws, two, three. Trees whipped by. I crossed two different roads. Four miles passed. Being a daily runner, I knew the feel of each mile by the thrum in my muscles. The pull took me deeper into the forest, back the way Vidar and I had come from. My hopes of having this done and over with before he could wake and realize I'd gone fled with the fifth mile. The misty air would dampen my scent a bit, slowing him down when he did wake and try to track me. But it wouldn't stop him. I had to hurry.

The urge to kill surged inside, but it felt hollow, removed.

With a touch of relief that quickly turned to horror, I realized the urge wasn't mine. The condemned was on the hunt, and somehow, I had tapped into his mind. No, not tapped, I had been sucked in, as if by a whirlpool. He wanted to slash, rend, kill. This wouldn't be his first. He'd killed when he was human. The urge rose in him like an addict jonesing for another hit.

For a heartbeat, I saw through his eyes.

He stood at the top of a hill in a forest. Below him in a dark meadow he could just make out the outline of a cabin. Smoke rose in lazy drifts from the chimney. A sickening excitement coursed through him.

I poured all my power into my legs, using all that energy I had absorbed from the lightning strike to go faster. Trees and underbrush blurred as I flew by. My paws barely felt like they touched the ground. Time seemed to stand still regardless of how fast I moved. The power signature of the condemned continued to pull at me like a magnet. Still, it took several minutes before the terrain started to resemble what I'd seen through his eyes. As I broke through the trees at the top of a hill, I felt another power. Though similar, this one wasn't the condemned. The similar nature told me it was a shifter. The musky smell with an altogether different tang to it told me it wasn't a wolf. I knew other shifters existed, but I'd never seen one. I'd barely been out of Hemlock Hollow thanks to my controlling parents.

I had no idea what I was about to rush into, but it didn't matter. This was the place I'd seen through the eyes of the condemned. I knew it even before I heard the screams. The toxic feel of his power reached out to me stronger than ever. It wasn't just that this man had lost his battle with sanity when he'd first changed. He felt corrupt, evil. Being bitten didn't do this to people. This man had to have started out this way. The urge to end him rose in me. It tried to eat away at my reason.

Not knowing what I'd find in that cabin, I plunged down the hill. All that mattered was getting there and stopping him. Ferns and pine boughs parted before me, barely brushing my fur. Exposed roots and webs of ivy passed beneath my paws without the slightest snag. Nothing could stop me. I felt like a force of nature. Not even the stifling fear of having to kill someone could slow me. I wouldn't let it.

The smell of blood tainted the air, weighing heavy on it like an impending storm. A silence fell that was somehow worse than the screams. I tried to run faster, but I couldn't. As it was, the scenery flew by so quick the trees were only a blur. Scent alone kept me from colliding with them. Could I be knocked unconscious now that I was the reaper? I wasn't sure. Finally, my paws scraped across the steps of the cabin's porch. I dropped my head and launched into the door shoulder first. The doorjamb exploded, sending shards of wood flying, and the door blew open. Yellow light from flames in the open fireplace made the grisly scene glow. My brain took a moment to process what my wolf eyes saw. Or maybe it was just that my brain didn't want to register it.

The walls and floor looked like someone had splashed buckets of red paint everywhere. While the sliver of innocence in me wanted to believe that's what it was, my instincts new better. The smell was unmistakable and overwhelming. A mangled body reduced to meat, blue muscle, and glistening bone lay on the floor. Another draped across a couch, enough left of it for me to recognize it was a woman. Fresh as the blood smelled, I had just barely missed the slaughter. All reluctance I had to kill this condemned fled.

Something thudded toward the back of the cabin followed by a distinctly inhuman grunt of pain. Could there be someone left alive? Gods, the other shifter I had smelled! I plunged through the cabin, relieved for the open floor plan that left no question as to which way I needed to go. After a skidding turn through the kitchen, I saw a back door gaping open. A heartbeat later, I ran through it and out into the night. The growl of another of my kind made me dig my claws into the deck to halt my desperate flight.

A scent so strong and musky it stung my nose yanked my gaze to the right. Crumpled against the cabin wall not ten feet away lay a large black bear. It had to weigh more than twice what I did. Looming over it, clutching a baseball bat, was the source of that which had pulled me here. The bat looked tiny in the naked man's meaty hands. Well, naked save for some kind of chest-mounted action camera. His muscled body was so tall and broad, it was easy to see how he'd taken on a bear and won. The man was huge, and coming from someone who grew up around Icelandic descendants, that's saying a lot. Blood splattered in erratic patterns across his flesh, thick and clumpy in places, suggesting meatier bits clung. None of it looked like it belonged to him.

Wild eyes slowly made their way to me. Lips pulling back from his teeth, he dropped the bat and took a step toward me, growling. His body began to blur, the sign he was about to shift. Being a newly bitten, his transformation was slower, more like molasses pouring from one container to another, rather than water. I leaped on him before his form could turn solid again. His flesh—so like cotton candy in his in-between form—parted with ease. Despite the fact that he easily outweighed me more than the bear, I bore him to the ground with the force of my will and power. The electricity still coursing through me from last night's lightning strike added an unnecessary edge.

By the time he solidified, my muzzle was deep in his chest cavity. I gripped his rapidly beating heart in my fangs and shook my head. Hot blood sprayed down my throat and across my chest. I didn't stop shaking until his heart stopped beating.

A roar unlike anything I'd ever heard cut through the fog of my killer instincts. Fangs bared, I lifted my head from the steaming cavity of my kill. The bear had regained his feet and now stalked toward me. Part of me knew I should shift back to human form and tell him I wasn't the enemy. He wasn't the bad guy here, I could feel that in his power, his energy. I think he'd been trying to stop the condemned. But with my kill still fresh on my tongue and another threat approaching, I couldn't quell the instinct to fight.

I stalked toward him, my paws squelching in the blood that covered the deck. The sound tugged at me, trying to raise something like regret. It slowed me down. I had shed that blood. The growl vibrating in my chest faltered. Thoughts, reservations, guilt, all tried to surface through the instinct. My steps slowed even more.

The bear cocked his head and roared at me again. Aggression spiked in me, pulled a warning growl up with it. Trying to push it back down only made it worse. With a grunt, the bear hopped on its front paws, then reared up to stand on its hind legs. His huge paws swiped the air in a warning of his own. Such a show of aggression made me lose what little control remained in my grasp. My muscles bunched in preparation to leap.

From within the house came a masculine cry of surprise, then the pounding of footsteps. Both the bear and I froze and stared one another down. There was no way that man on the floor could be alive. Could there be other survivors in the house? I hadn't heard anyone, but I'd been completely focused on finding the condemned. The press of the power of one of our kind from within the house told me it probably wasn't a survivor. This power had a comforting familiarity to it.

Oh, Odin. Not him, not here, not now.

A figure darkened the doorway leading onto the deck before I could make the decision to run. Muted starlight shone on wide hazel eyes set over six feet from the ground. The shadows made his skin look like obsidian, all shiny from running and working up a sweat. He had to have been running like the fires of Muspelheimr had been chasing him to make it here so soon after me. Those eyes went from me, to the body behind me, to the bear, and back to me.

"Easy, Ayra. The *berserkr* isn't your enemy. At least I don't think he is. Are you?" Vidar asked, with a heavy threat on the last two words.

Berserkr. Gods, to hear him called that made it real. The Norwegian word for werebear, though it translated more closely to "bear skin." Iceland didn't have them, so my ancestors hadn't given them their name. Damn, I was looking at an honest-to-Odin *berserkr*. That wondrous thought brought me completely back from the edge of instinct.

The air rippled with the *berserkr*'s power as he shifted back to human form. Hairy as he was, he honestly didn't look a lot different. I kept my eyes averted from the flash of pink flesh I saw at his crotch, no easy task considering I was still in wolf form and reached exactly that level. Damn tall men. It wasn't that I was averse to seeing the reproductive parts of a man, just not this man, and certainly not now.

"No, I'm not. The question is, are you mine?" the *berserkr* asked in a gravelly voice.

Vidar held his hands up before him as he stepped out onto the deck. "Definitely not. She came here to try and stop what happened inside," he said.

The *berserkr's* bushy eyebrows pinched together like caterpillars about to do battle. His heavy gaze moved from Vidar to me. "You're the *uppskera* everyone has been talking about."

"She is," Vidar answered for me.

"Yeah, well, she needs to work on her timing."

"Easy. She's new at this and is doing her best," Vidar said through a growl.

The *berserkr* looked from me, to him, and back to me. "Starting a pack already?" He sounded as if that idea concerned him.

"No. Every reaper has their *verndari*," Vidar said.

Bushy beard pulling up into a sneer, the man shook his head. "Whatever that means. Just be careful it doesn't mean the same thing. The reaper should be reaping, not gathering others to them."

I shifted back to human form and made a scoffing noise. "People don't gather to me, they shy away. You have nothing to worry about there."

The man's eyes narrowed down to slits before he waved a hand in dismissal. "This is my town. I'll take care of this," he said over his shoulder as he strode back into the cabin.

I wanted him to fight me, yell at me for being too late, anything so he didn't leave. Facing Vidar after what I'd done was too much. Covered in blood and gore, I had to look every bit the monster some of the old stories made the reaper out to be. Hel, I felt every bit the monster. I had just torn into a man's chest cavity and shredded his heart. That he had been a bad man didn't make it much better. The ease with which I'd executed him—and the lack of remorse I felt over it—disturbed me. It should have been hard to kill a person, especially the first time. As a *varúlfur* who had grown up hunting, I had killed a lot of things. None of them had been humanoid, until now.

Light from the open door glistened across the massive pool of blood spreading over the deck. It dripped through the boards, splattering in a rhythmic pattern on the ground beneath. Bile stung the back of my throat.

I launched forward. At the edge of the deck, I had to stop to throw up. My intention had been to run into the forest as far from Vidar as I could. But running and vomiting are a bad combination, and I already had enough nasty shit on me.

The thought made me look down. Blood and thicker things covered me so thoroughly it looked like I wore a skin-tight red shirt, one that grew stickier by the moment as it coagulated. The sight and thought made me vomit until I had nothing left. Dry heaves continued to convulse my throat. My knees gave out and I hit the deck hard enough that it hurt even through the numbness trying to grip me. It felt good. I didn't want the numbness, didn't deserve it. A man lay dead because of me. That should hurt, a lot.

I was so distracted that I didn't hear Vidar approach. He bent down next to me before I knew he was there. The feel of his hand on my back made me jerk, not because he had startled me, but because I didn't deserve his gentle touch.

His skin made a peeling sound as it came away from mine, which made me dry heave a few more times.

"Ayra, are you hurt?" Vidar asked in a tone so soft it was almost a whisper.

I had to get clean. Once the heaves stopped I focused my hearing on the forest. The rush of water revealed a river not more than a long sprint away.

"I'll be right back. I have to get clean," I said.

Leaving felt wrong, but I couldn't stand another moment of being covered in blood and bits. I dropped off the deck, shifting into a wolf in mid-leap and hit the ground running.

"Wait, Ayra—"

Vidar said more, but I pinned my ears against my head and refused to hear it. I ran with everything I had, not caring that I left bloody paw prints behind. Better he see that than the horror I no doubt looked like. That was precisely what I hadn't wanted, the reason I had tried to push him away. At least he hadn't seen me kill the man. That was something, I guess. Though the sky was beginning to lighten with the coming of dawn, I didn't need it to find my way. The fresh, clean scent of the water drew me to it like a beacon. In only heartbeats the cacophony of water tumbling over rocks greeted me. The brush gave way to the most beautiful ten-foot wide silver strip of water I'd ever seen.

Not caring how deep it might be, I plunged right in. When my paws didn't reach the ground, I shifted to human form. The process of doing so in water had a cleansing effect. My toes brushed the sandy bottom. The slow-moving river carried me down a ways until my feet settled firmly and I found a large boulder to brace against. Before my stance was even stable, I began scrubbing at my skin. The blood and gore washed away easily. Too easily, really. But it left behind an impression, a horrible feeling that no amount of scrubbing could get rid of.

Taking out a killer sounded easy, necessary. Actually taking a life, no matter how dark and twisted that life was, left a stain. It didn't matter what he had done. It mattered what I had done.

Once my skin started to feel raw, I started on my hair. Getting the mess that had been the newly bitten out of that was a bit more challenging. When my fingers came across thicker bits dry heaves wracked me again. But I didn't stop until long after the water ran clean. Tears stung my eyes. I scrubbed at my face, trying to wash them away along with the guilt they carried. I was a killer now. That reverberated down deep into me, down to my soul. My mind couldn't stop repeating the thought. It was the kind of thing you couldn't wash off. The realization only made me scrub harder.

I kept smelling blood. No matter how I scrubbed, it wouldn't go away. It took a while for me to realize the scent came from my bloody paw prints on the river bank. I ducked my head under the water to escape the smell for a moment. While submerged, it occurred to me that I would need to exit the river away from the paw prints to cover my tracks, like a murderer.

But then, I guess that's what I am now.

Opening my eyes beneath the water, I watched the dark landscape of rocks as the current carried me slowly downriver. In spots it was barely deep enough to swim, but I managed. Being hardly a buck-ten at five-foot-five had its advantages. If only it had kept me from being the reaper. Drifting weightless in the cool water accentuated the numbness I felt. As a shifter, my body temp ran hot enough to keep me warm even in the snow runoff-fed rivers of Montana. Part of me wished it didn't so the numbness could work its way deep enough to stop me from feeling the pain.

But no, that would be wrong. I deserved to feel this pain. Kicking off the sandy bottom, I pushed myself to the surface. The night air brought a scent to me that I'd been dreading. Vidar was nearby. Much as I might want to, I couldn't avoid him forever. I walked from the river and found a dry boulder to sit on. While I waited for him, I wrung out my hair and started to weave it into a braid. By the time I finished, he emerged from the tree line. Though I knew the river had washed me clean, I couldn't help but look down to make sure. Only then did it occur to me that I was naked as the day I entered this world.

It shouldn't have bothered me. Vidar had seen me naked innumerable times when we were kids. Due to the need to get naked to shift, werewolves weren't shy by nature. But this was different. Vidar hadn't seen me naked in years. I was of mating age now. And he was the only person I had ever wanted to mate with. My body responded before I could stop it. Suddenly I wished I had left my hair loose so it would cover my nipples, which stood at attention. Damn traitorous body.

The tense lines of Vidar's silhouette shot a spike of guilt through me. Running away had been cowardly. But then, he should know all about that. It wasn't fair to think that, not when I knew he had gone to the temple for my sake, but I couldn't help it.

"Ayra, are you all right?" he asked.

The deep notes of his voice did naughty tingly things to me, making the muscles between my legs tighten. Dammit, there couldn't be a worse time for my sex drive to go haywire. Thinking such thoughts right now made me feel even more monstrous. Where was my damn anger when I needed it?

"I'm not hurt. I just...had to wash," I said. The memory of the blood and gore forced me to repress a shudder.

Vidar's nearly silent approach pulled my gaze back to him. The bulge of his arms, the width of his shoulders, how his dark skin helped him melt into the shadows, it all fed my desire. His confident stride and the way he held himself screamed alpha. It took an embarrassing amount of effort to keep my breathing steady. The urge to tackle him and have my way with him forced me to look down or risk doing something I'd really regret. If he wanted me and not the reaper, if I wasn't engaged, if his vow didn't stop us, it would be different.

What on Helheimr was wrong with me? How could I even be thinking about that right now?

Head turning away, gaze on the ground, Vidar approached me like I was a deer who might bolt. I couldn't blame him after the way I'd run away from the cabin. Even that cautious approach seemed sexy, like a predator closing in on its prey. The closer he got, the more my desire grew. He smelled delicious, like leather, wood, and alpha. Alpha enough even for the reaper. Though it wasn't fair to Elí, the last part excited me the most. Gods, how I wanted to roll around naked in that scent.

Something had to be seriously wrong with me. To be feeling like this right now was sick. Wasn't it? Not only did I respect myself more than to settle for a man who wanted me for what—not who—I was, but I had just killed someone.

"Here," Vidar said as he wrapped something around my shoulders.

I reached up and took hold of the collar of a canvas-style tan jacket. Well, it would have been a jacket on Vidar. On me, it was more of a trench coat that would reach my knees once I stood up. It held his amazing scent and the lingering feel of his power. I wrapped it tight around me, taking comfort in it that I wouldn't allow myself to take in him.

"Thank you," I said, the words sounding as hollow as I felt.

He started rubbing my arms. Bumps rose on my skin, shooting up my arms, to my nipples, and then straight down between my legs. A desire so powerful it felt like it might consume me, made me shiver. How could I possibly feel this way right now? It was insane.

"You don't have to face this alone," he said.

The sound of his deep voice did it to me all over again. Shaking my head, I squeezed my eyes shut and stepped back. The need didn't disappear when his hands dropped away from my arms, but it withdrew enough for me to think. "I didn't want you to see me kill someone," I said. The words made that hollow emptiness rise up in me again. While it felt more proper than desire, I thought I should feel guilt, or remorse instead. But I couldn't make those feelings stir.

Vidar took a step toward me. His closeness tugged at me, making me feel like a teenager with raging hormones. Or a wolf in heat.

"You did what you had to. That man had killed, and he would keep killing. Any future victims he would have had, you saved them," he said.

He held up a bloody mess of straps attached to a small action camera. Lips curling up from his teeth in disgust, he added, "Sicko even recorded his kills."

"I know he was a sicko, but you didn't see me do it. Vidar. It was easy, too easy."

He took another step toward me. "You've trained to be a fighter your entire life. It was muscle memory, instinct. There's nothing wrong with that."

I tried to read how he felt through his power, his stance, but he remained stoic and blocked off from me. Vidar always spoke the truth, though. He wouldn't lie to me, even to make me feel better. But then why was he hiding his emotions? Maybe he was repulsed by the aftermath of what I'd done. He should be. Hel, I should be. And I shouldn't care if he was. But I did.

"But there's something wrong with me," I whispered.

He took my hand. "What do you mean?"

The way his big, dark fingers completely encompassed my small hand renewed the tingling sensation in my stomach. Before it could spread between my legs, I pulled my hand free. I wasn't going there, for so many reasons.

"I took a life. I should be feeling guilty, remorseful, reflecting on all he could have been, some kind of crap like that. But I only feel...relief." Gods, it sounded even worse out loud. I shouldn't have said that. Now he would see the monster I had become. This was exactly why I didn't want him with me. Something about the man cut right through my filters and common sense.

Frigg save me from myself.

With an aggressive move that made both my hackles and desire rise, he took my hands in his. When I tried to pull away, he held fast. I could break the hold if I wanted to. It wasn't a matter of strength, but of leverage and speed. But I didn't want to get away from him. I wanted closer, a lot closer.

"There's nothing wrong with you. That is a coping mechanism. It's how soldiers get through battle, by focusing on survival and processing things later," he said.

On some level, his words made sense. But all I could think about was how great that deep voice would sound screaming my name at the height of passion.

"Sounds like you've been reading up on the subject," I said in a breathy voice. The reasons for my anger toward him slipped further away with each inch that closed between us.

"I have, though I first learned about that at the temple."

Was that a hint of desire in his voice? No, couldn't be.

My thumbs started making small circles on the backs of his hands, and I couldn't stop them. Unwilling to let go, but needing a bit of distance, I stepped back. My heels ran into a boulder. Pulled by our clutched hands, Vidar stepped closer. I leaned back and ended up sitting on the boulder. His legs touched my toes. I ran my feet up along his bare legs until the canvas of his shorts brushed me. All the while chanting in my head to stop, I wrapped my legs around his and locked my ankles together. I pulled his hands down onto the boulder, bending him over so his face was level with mine.

"It's more than that." I paused and licked my lips as I stared into his hazel eyes. "I want to climb up all that beautiful, dark skin of yours and ride you like a bull."

The words liberated me, but they also strengthened my growing need. It didn't help that Vidar's breathing sped up.

"Like a bull?" he asked, curiosity and desire deepening his voice. Yes, it was definitely desire. But was it desire for me, or for the *uppskera?*

I leaned in to whisper in his ear. "Yes, hard and fast, leaving you dripping wet." The image of my own words made me wet. I became acutely aware of my nakedness beneath the coat.

A deep groan filled with need rumbled through the big chest so close to mine. "Whatever you need," he said as he leaned closer. Was that a touch of pain and regret in his tone?

In that moment I knew I could have him right here, right now. The man I had wanted my entire life just offered himself to me. I had imagined this moment so often over the years. But not ever like this. Of course that was regret in his tone. He had taken a celibacy vow and to break it would be to break him. Discipline and order were Vidar's life blood. Making him break something he held so dear would only prove me to be the monster of all monsters. And didn't I deserve better than someone who had abandoned me, who wanted me only because of what I was?

Most importantly, I had made a promise of commitment to Elí. Not only would it be dishonorable to betray that, something I vowed never to be, but it would mean the Arnoddr pack would never accept me. They were the closest thing to family I'd ever had, far closer than my own blood. They might even banish Elí for a failed engagement.

I scampered backwards off the boulder, coming to stand on the other side of it. "This isn't right. How can I want to have sex after just having murdered someone? What kind of sick person am I?"

Sadness filled Vidar's eyes. He shook his head. "You're not sick, or a monster. You, the werewolf who takes in stray cats and helps pups who are being bullied. You could never be a monster." He started to work his way around the boulder. "Being in a life and death situation stimulates your most basic survival instinct, the one to mate. You're feeling it so strongly because of that. I shouldn't have offered, but I thought that might be what you need."

Something about that rubbed my fur the wrong way. "Why are you so concerned about what I need?" More like what the *uppskera* needed, but I couldn't bring myself to say that.

The way his shoulders sagged almost made me regret sounding so harsh, but the furtive way his gaze darted to the ground made me glad I had. The posture reminded me of how he'd been when we were kids and there was something he was afraid to tell me.

"Because I'm your friend. And I want to be your *verndari*," he said in a voice so quiet, if I didn't possess the heightened hearing of a werewolf, I wouldn't have heard him.

Oh Gods, the F word. He didn't want me. He wanted to placate the *uppskera*, to help fight back the murderous rage the temple had told him would grip me, a rage that had slipped away like smoke at his touch alone. It came scratching back.

"You learned a lot about the *uppskera* at the temple. Didn't they get suspicious of all the questions you asked? What aren't you telling me?" I demanded.

His head rose and the strength that filled his eyes banished the little boy who was concerned about my reaction. Power radiated out from him like a furnace. The heat pulled at the wolf within, and the woman. My legs moved me a step closer before I even realized it. It wasn't that I didn't care about what he was hiding, but if he said it naked with me riding him, all the better.

No. That was not acceptable.

Vidar was worth far more to me than just a means to scratch an itch. Even if it would mean scratching that itch really, really well. And if I was being honest with myself, I wanted him to want me, not the *uppskera*. And I would not be the reason he broke a vow for which he'd never forgive himself. To keep my head, I had to close my eyes as he strode over to me. The image of his fine body lingered behind my eyelids. I knew I should circle around to the opposite side of the boulder, but I couldn't bring myself to move away from him. This was survival instinct he'd said. I could control it. When his footsteps stopped, I opened my eyes.

He extended his hand to me. "Walk with me, please."

Even if I wanted to argue and get mad, this was Vidar. I couldn't turn away from him, especially not if seeing the remains of the man I had killed didn't scare him off. He was the one true friend I had. Pathetic, considering he had abandoned me for the past four years. But I had no one else. Ignoring his outstretched hand, I crossed my arms beneath my breasts and motioned for him to lead the way into the dark forest.

CHAPTER SEVEN

VIDAR

A n unstoppable rush of words about the aftereffects of reaping—complete with hand gestures, and sound effects—issued from me. Of all the nervous habits to have, mine had to be spewing my thoughts without filters. I couldn't blame Ayra when her fangs extended and she gritted her teeth during the first mile of our trek. She let me talk until I stopped, not interrupting to put in so much as a single word. It made it worse. I started to ramble.

If this went south, I could lose her forever. Someone else could end up her *verndari*. If that happened, I didn't know what I'd do.

She made an exasperated noise. "For four years, my best friend all but fell off the face of the planet, abandoning me, or so I thought. You couldn't have mentioned this in the sporadic letters you sent me during the first three years you were there?" Her anger burned so hot I felt it in the air. "You could have used code, or something, I don't know. You should have found a way to tell me." The edge in her voice grew sharper with each word.

She had me there. If I had told her, maybe she wouldn't be engaged to someone else. I focused hard on the brightening forest before me. "They would have found out, and I would have been kicked out of the Order.

Someone else would have ended up as your *verndari*. I couldn't stand the idea of not even having a chance." I had to swallow hard before going on.

Growling, she stopped, grabbed my arm, and yanked me around to face her. The fierce look in her eyes excited me so much my breath caught in my throat. Kink wasn't my thing, but strong women were, and she looked downright ferocious. Gods, I wanted her so bad. Before I realized it, I reached out and brushed a stray lock of pale hair from her cheek. Anger drained from her eyes when I cupped that cheek. She leaned slightly into my hand.

"I didn't want to be the one to scare you, to shatter your dreams. And I couldn't stand the idea of someone else being chosen to be by your side," I whispered.

A long sigh eased from her, the warmth of it brushing my hand with the barest touch. Heat spread out from that touch. *Helheimr!* Why did my body always take over my mind when it came to her? Now was not the time. That was not what she needed. Even if it was, she hadn't chosen me yet, so my vow of celibacy was still an issue. Then there was Elí. I forced my hand to drop away slowly.

Her eyes slid closed and she nodded. "I want to say I understand, but Vidar, we used to tell each other everything."

The tired sound of her voice worried me.

"I know. I'm so sorry." But it would have meant being left in the wings while another person stood at her side through all this, someone potentially less capable. That would have broken me.

She started walking again, this time at a slow pace. The angry crackle to her power receded a little. One glance back was all it took for me to dash to her side. "What if I don't want a *verndari*?" she asked.

My answer came slowly, having to be dredged up and forced out. "You could lose yourself and become a killing machine with one purpose and no conscience or mercy. It happened to every *uppskera* throughout history that did not have a *verndari*. At least, that's what the Order says."

Sighing, she ran a hand braid, which was now mostly dry. "The *verndari* would travel with me, see me reap."

"I don't have to be there for the reaping, no. But immediately after, yes. I would need to stay close to you. I would want to stay close to you." I hadn't meant for that last part to come out.

"Sounds like something Elí is better suited for."

The words stabbed me deep down. "It takes special training. And then there's your lightning channeling. No one is better suited to help you with that than me." I had to clear my throat before I could say the rest. "And I... shouldn't have tried to kiss you, shouldn't have offered to have sex with you. It was overstepping by a mile. I didn't mean to disrespect you or Elí. I'm sorry. It won't be an issue again."

Several long moments passed before she responded.

"You deserve a better life than being tied to a killer," she whispered.

Not wanting to be overly aggressive and grab her like my gut told me to, I stopped walking. I couldn't let the alpha in me rear up. She was the *uppskera*. A show of dominance, no matter how slight or well meaning, could be disastrous. When she stopped beside me, I almost put my hands on her arms. But I let them drop away. It would be inappropriate, and I couldn't go there again.

"We're all killers, Ayra. It's in our nature, and I don't mean as wolves, I mean as humans. You are a killer of killers. You stop them from doing any more harm, which they would certainly do, being *varúlfur*." I clasped my hands in front of me. If I didn't I was afraid I'd wrap her in my arms. "I've been tied to you since the first day we met, and I wouldn't have it any other way."

She took a step closer. Before reaching me, she stopped and pinned me with an angry glare. That look coming from anyone else would have started a fight they'd be hard pressed to win.

"You want to be close to the *uppskera*, to take advantage of the power that comes from being associated with me, just like all the others," she accused.

"Gods, no, never! I don't care about you being the *uppskera*. I don't care about power. I care about you. That's all I've ever cared about." Maybe that was going too far, revealing too much, but I couldn't take it back now.

She fussed with the tip of her braid, but didn't march off, so I took it as a good sign. Might as well go for broke. "If it were up to me, we'd be in Iceland right now, getting you registered for the fall semester at Reykjavik like you always wanted. After you got your master's we'd chase storms together." I had to swallow and take a breath before I could go on. "But Odin has other plans for you, for us."

I thought I saw the sparkle of moisture in her eyes before she turned and started walking. Whether it was a good sign or bad, I didn't like that I'd caused her pain either way. This time she kept her pace slow.

"I wanted to come to Iceland, desperately, but I couldn't. For one, I didn't think you wanted me there," she said, bitterness thick in her tone.

The hesitance of her words made me think I wasn't the only one with something to hide. "And for two?"

Gaze on the path before her, she bared her teeth, which sported sets of canine fangs. "Calder wouldn't let me. I tried, twice, almost made it to the airport once before he dragged me back, beat me, and threatened to kill me if I tried again. Then my parents arranged my engagement to Elí and everything changed."

The growl that roared through me surprised me as much as it did her. Fury built behind it. Desperate for a release, I punched a tree. Bark and bits of wood exploded as my fist blew right through the side of it. Ah, Hel, and here I was supposed to be the one helping her control her violent tendencies. In this, I couldn't help it. The thought of someone tormenting her made me want to explore all sides of my rage on that person, especially when it was her own brother.

A slight smile tugged at the corners of Ayra's lips, cooling my ire instantly. "Maybe I should be helping you with your killer instinct," she said. The teasing tone in her voice heartened me. Maybe I could be what she needed after all.

"When it comes to Calder, yes," I admitted.

Her head tilted up, gaze traveling through the trees to stare at the nearly full moon fading to a pale disk in the dawn sky. She started walking faster. "We need to get to Idaho," she said.

She had said "we." My heart soared high as a valkyrie. I nodded. "Yes, he has to be stopped." The sooner we stopped him, the sooner she could get back to pursuing her dreams, her life.

"Yeah, he does. Sonya texted me. She's on her way there now. She felt the call of a newly bitten," she said.

Concern pinched at me. Could she handle another reaping again so soon? She was stronger than I'd ever seen her. The way she held her head up despite the fathomless depth of torment in her eyes blew me away. She sped up, making it clear she was going whether I thought she was ready or not. I had to lengthen my stride to keep up with her, a lot.

"When did she text you?"

"Right before I went to the cabin. The more important question is, why didn't she feel the pull to the one here like I did?"

My brows rose. "That's how you found him, you felt a pull?"

She gave one quick nod, more a dip of her head really.

"If you felt the pull, that means he was beyond saving. 'The *uppskera* only feels the pull once the bitten starts to tip over toward madness,'" I quoted from one of the old books at the temple. Another quick nod came from her. It had been in the *uppskera* journals, of which the temple had copies.

"It was more than that, though. He'd been mad before being bitten in. I could feel it in him, like a dark stain on his soul. He'd killed before, when he was human," she said.

That hadn't been in the journal. "You could feel all that?"

"Yes."

A shiver ran through me. That made it so much worse than just having to kill the man. To see inside him down to his darkness... It was one thing to know true evil existed in the world, but to touch it like that, I couldn't even imagine how horrible that had to be. I took hold of her hand as we continued to walk, figuring it was okay considering the situation. It took a moment, but she still withdrew her hand.

My pocket vibrated, making me jump. Damn, I forgot I had stuffed Ayra's phone in there when I didn't find her in her tent. Eyes pinching into a questioning glare, she looked at my pocket, her *varúlfur* hearing easily picking up the sound. I pulled it out and handed it to her.

"I grabbed it when I didn't find you in your tent, just in case."

She accepted it without a word and looked down at the screen. Power started to crackle and snap around her, jumping and biting at my skin even though I stood a few feet away. Her eyes shone in the way predators' do in the night. But it was more than that, it was pure fury, the scary kind. Instinct told me to step back. I ignored it.

"What is it?" I asked. Part of me feared it would be Elí. My jaw clenched.

"Calder." The one word was so much of a growl that I barely

understood it. Through all that anger I heard a deep-rooted pain that made my hackles rise.

With her in so much pain, I didn't want to ask, but I had to. "What did he say?"

She handed the phone back to me with hands that shook. *I had hoped my man would fare better, but I did enjoy the video. I'm sure it will go, how do you kids say, viral, when I upload it at the end of this month.*

My fingers clenched in an involuntary spasm born of anger. I stopped myself just before I could crush the phone. The tone of the text both reminded me that Calder was nearly seventy years old, and revealed the depth of his insanity. One hand went to the camera in my pocket. I wanted to crush it too, but it could hold clues to Calder's location.

"He wouldn't," I growled.

"He will. He's gathering footage to post on a site that will out us to the world. I read it in his journal," Ayra countered in an eerily calm tone.

My skin crawled with the primal fear of discovery. "How can we be sure he didn't live stream straight to a website or social media feed?"

"We can't be. But I know he would want to wait, to draw out our fear of him doing it, torture me with it. That part is just as important to him as the reveal itself."

"But his method is insane. If people see this they'll hunt us down, not let us take our place in the world beside them."

Ayra nodded. "That's what he wants. He doesn't want to be beside them in the light, he wants to rule over them."

"Why is he drawing it out?"

"Partly, I think, to delay until he can figure out how to kill me, partly because it has something to do with this attack he's planning at the end of the month." The emotionless way she spoke made dread prickle along the back of my neck.

I hated to press her, but I had to ask. "Can we be sure he won't do it sooner?"

Her eyes flicked my way for a few steps. "I'm sure. My brother is very patient in his schemes."

"Good." Ayra looked at me with wide, surprised eyes. I went on, "His arrogance will give us plenty of time to catch him and kill him before he can carry this out."

She almost smiled. "Yes, we have to. He's planning more, a war. Maniac wants to rule over this world."

And here I'd left her alone with that son of a bitch for four years. I couldn't speak anymore, which was a bad sign for me. From high above, an owl hooted as we walked beneath its tree. Recalling the incident with the eagle, my protective instincts reared up. Silly on several levels, I knew, but knowing that didn't quell it. The sound had an eerie warning note to it that raked across my nerves. We both picked up our pace. I wasn't sure which I wanted more, to get to Idaho or to get out from beneath the all too sharp gaze of that owl. Maybe it was just nerves, or maybe it was my actions that disrespected her relationship with Elí, but now I felt like everything was watching us.

CHAPTER EIGHT

AYRA

*Instincts must be mastered by the third night of their first full moon, else the newly
bitten will be lost to insanity and turned over to the reaper.*
~Uppskera Journals

I couldn't shake the sick feeling in my stomach. It wasn't from
watching the footage, though that definitely didn't help. All that had
been on that was the condemned killing that poor couple, and then
fighting the *berserkr* and me. No hints as to where Calder might be. The
son of a bitch had covered his tracks like I knew he would.

With each hour that passed, the sick feeling grew. It felt like hunger,
but I knew that wasn't it. Vidar bought me a combo meal at the last fast
food place we'd passed. Though I had no appetite, I'd downed it so he
wouldn't worry so much.

It aggravated me that he worried about me now, after all these years. I
could have used some of that concern when my parents were pushing my
training to the point of me puking from exhaustion or my brother was
beating another lesson into me. I got why he left, I just wasn't ready to be
okay with it.

If only he had told me sooner, like years ago. I might not have agreed to marry Elí if I hadn't felt so abandoned. I couldn't think about that, though. It stirred the ever-present anger in me back to life.

The delicious smell of french fries still lingered in the cab of the truck despite our windows being down. It brought my mind back to food and to the feeling in my stomach.

No, this was something else. Hunger might not be far off, but this was not the kind that filled one's stomach. This resonated through my entire body. An hour or so before Missoula, I figured it out when I started to feel the pull. My gaze traveled out across the rolling hills of wheat and grass bathed in bright sunlight. Somewhere out there a newly bitten was very close to losing their sanity. The time for me to step in grew near. But this person felt like they were trying. Today was the last day of the full moon, the day after technically, but the last day that it forced newly bitten who couldn't control themselves to change.

The seeker had those three days to convince the newly bitten to face their wolf, to control it. If she couldn't by the end of the third day, our laws said I had to put it down. Three days of uncontrollable shifting fried the sanity right out of a newly bitten. After that, they'd never to be able to control it, and they'd keep killing. So said the old journals of past *uppskera* that I'd been reading. The likelihood that I'd have to kill again increased with each hour.

I tried to take comfort in the fact that I was a killer of killers, someone who prevented them from doing more harm to others. Vidar repeated it often enough to me that I heard it in my sleep. When I could sleep, which wasn't often. And it would have been comforting had I not wanted to kill again so badly. I wasn't sure yet if it was only for the sheer thrill of it or a desire to rid the world of another psycho. Did it make me one of them if the primary reason was the prior?

I flipped another page in Calder's journal and puzzled over what I saw there. "What the hell?" I murmured.

"What is it?" Vidar asked, glancing in my direction.

"It looks like a...schedule. Routes, roads, Department of Corrections, hmmm..." Chills bubbled across my skin like snowflakes as I realized what it was. "Oh, Odin. No."

"What?" Vidar's voice had turned urgent.

A news story I'd seen made it click into place. "It's routes for the transport of prisoners. Oh my Gods, that's where Calder is getting the condemned. He's attacking prisoner transports, freeing them, and biting in criminals."

Vidar cursed in Icelandic before saying, "That sick son of a bitch."

The pull yanked at me like a scent trail. "Take a right up there," I said, pointing to a side road.

With the impressive skill of one who drove fast often and well, he took the turn in a split second, managing to keep it smooth so it didn't jostle my bike in the back. He scored huge points for the last part. After a mile, the road turned to gravel. The rev of the truck's engine eased as Vidar let his foot off the gas a little. His gaze shot to the sun, which had nearly reached the horizon.

"How fast do I need to go?" he asked.

I reached for the pull, trying to gauge the intensity of it. While it remained just beneath the surface, telling me we were headed in the right direction, the urgency had gone out of it. Strange, considering night drew closer by the moment.

"This speed is good."

The fields soon turned to fir and aspen trees alongside the road. Vidar's stimulating deep voice filled the truck. Thankfully, he didn't broach the subject of the *verndari* or Elí again. Something like that needed processing. I was far from ready to talk about it.

He went on about Idaho. He covered everything from the terrain and climate, to the one pack known to reside not far from this location. I didn't mind. The sound of his voice soothed me. It always had. He liked to talk, and I liked to listen no matter what he talked about. I knew he was trying to take my mind off what I might have to do, and I loved him for that, but I also thought he was trying to take his mind off it.

Part of me wanted to believe what he'd said meant he wanted me as a woman. But could I really believe that? A person could change a lot in four years. Not to mention that would mean breaking his celibacy vow and my promise to Elí and his pack.

A good chance remained that I could push Vidar away, convince him to move on and find a mate. I should want that for him, but I didn't. The very thought made my skin burn with jealousy. It was wrong on many levels, but I couldn't stop feeling it.

As we approached a stop sign at an intersection of gravel roads, I reached for the pull again. It was all but gone. From my open window I caught a familiar scent. "Take a left," I told Vidar as we rolled up to the stop sign. "Should I speed up?" he asked.

"No need."

"Sonya will be safer if we get there early. You don't have to worry about your bike. I can handle this truck with ease."

"No need. I think she's succeeding," I said.

I loved that he spoke his mind and didn't abase himself to me like everyone back in Hemlock Hollow. Even Elí did it. They all either feared me or wanted me to join their pack so it would be stronger. The relief of being around someone who potentially didn't want notoriety or power from me made me breathe easier. Vidar himself made me breathe easier. And it didn't hurt that his lack of fear made him hot as Muspelheimr.

A long breath eased out of him and every muscle in his body seemed to relax until he nearly slouched in the seat. I couldn't help but wonder what bothered him so deeply, me killing or me having to kill. One could change the way he thought of me, and the other could change the way he thought of the world. I didn't like the idea of either one happening. Or was it something else entirely?

His expression lightened. "Should I stop or turn back around to the highway?"

"No. I want to talk to Sonya."

"Onward it is then," he said with false cheer.

I couldn't blame him. Going to see Sonya meant seeing a person I might have been forced to kill—and still might. But I had to ask her something that I didn't want to discuss over the phone. The pull came from a dirt road leading off into a group of aspen trees. "Take a right there," I directed.

Vidar did as I asked, slowing to maneuver down the rutted road. "You sure about this?" he asked.

"No, but I have to do it."

"Good enough for me."

Damn, he made it hard to keep him at a distance. Gaze on the side mirror, I concentrated on watching my bike, making sure it didn't jostle too much in the bed of the truck. The tie-downs we'd put on it held it securely, but I watched anyways. It was easier to watch that instead of the gorgeous man beside me. A mile or so down the road, the trees gave way and revealed a huge two-story barn, red paint flaking away from the dry boards. Just as old were the scents of horses and hay that clung to the place. Everything about it screamed "abandoned." The rutted road went on past it, leaving the barn in an untouched patch of wild grass and flowers.

"Here," I said.

He eased the truck to a stop in the grass. Through the open window drifted Sonja and Ty's faded scent trails. The soft green grass tickled at my bare feet as I stepped out. It seemed wrong to enjoy even such a simple sensation when I might be on my way to kill someone. Sure, the feeling had faded, but I was new at this. Anticipation sang through my veins, carrying me across the distance between me and the barn at a swift pace.

I shouldn't want to kill again, but I did. The world was a dark place filled with even darker people. If I could stop just one of those people from hurting others, I wanted to do it. No matter what it cost me.

I sharpened my hearing. From within the barn came soft, urgent whispers. At over fifty yards with walls in the way, I couldn't make out what they were saying, but I knew they were there. Footsteps sounded from inside, approaching. Two other sets of footsteps retreated deeper into the barn. I picked up my pace and lengthened my stride. Behind me I felt the pressure of Vidar's power as he followed. How he did so without making a sound, I had no idea. A few seconds later a tall figure darkened the gap where the sliding door stood partially open.

Arms crossed over his broad chest, the six-foot-four man leaned against the barn, his bulk blocking the opening. Chin-length blond hair framed pretty eyes and a Hollywood-like handsome face.

"Hello, Teach," I said.

Though I attended the University of Montana where Tyler Viðarsson was a professor, he had never been my teacher. I didn't take history classes. But since he had also been Sonya's *kennari*, the title fit.

He nodded, power crackling off him in delicious waves of energy. "Hello, Ayra."

"I need to speak with Sonya."

"No need, she saved this one."

I stepped closer, into the midst of that crackling energy. It stung, but in a wonderful way, like hail pounding down on me in a massive storm, a storm with the promise of lightning. The stinging turned soothing as it sank in deeper. My skin drank it in eagerly, just like in the fight with the bullies back in Hemlock Hollow.

Drawing in a sharp breath, Ty cursed in Icelandic and moved into a fighting stance. The flow of energy stopped. On instinct, I tried to reach for it, but something blocked it now. Ty. I had a feeling that if he wasn't alpha material, I might have been able to keep drawing it anyway. But he was, and for that I was thankful, because I wasn't sure I could have stopped. And I hadn't meant to do it in the first place. Gods, I really needed to get a handle on this power.

"What did you just do?" he asked through a growl. Fascinated, I stared at him.

"I don't know. But I apologize. I didn't mean to." The *uppskera* journals didn't say anything about that. Since the incident in Hemlock Hollow I had looked, hard.

"What happened? Is everything good here?" Vidar asked as he reached us.

Ty's narrowed gaze shifted from me to Vidar. "I am not sure. I think she just...siphoned energy from me," he said.

Head cocking, I shrugged. "I didn't siphon so much as absorbed the energy he was giving off. You boys chat about it. I'm going to talk to Sonya."

I took a step into the barn but Ty moved to block my access. "As I said, she saved this one."

"Yes, I can feel that. He isn't why I'm here. As *I* said, I came to talk to Sonya."

I didn't want to go through a guy who was alpha material, they tended to take things like that badly. But I would if I had to, and I thought I probably could. My confidence didn't come from arrogance, but from what I could feel of his power and how it compared to my own.

One of Ty's pale eyebrows rose. "You can feel that she saved him?"

"It's more about what I don't feel from him anymore. Now please, step aside."

Doing as I asked, Ty swept a hand toward the interior of the barn in invitation. "Since you asked so nicely. But you will not mind if I follow, I do hope."

"Not at all," I called over my shoulder as I strode inside. The two old friends exchanged greetings as they trailed behind me. They had been packmates once, before Bain had taken over the Draupnir pack and kicked them both out. That kind of bond survived a lot. Right now it served to keep Ty out of my way.

The scents of old hay and even older manure tickled at my nose, bringing up dark memories of being dragged against my will into my awakening. Anxiety reared its ugly little head in me, trying to feed on my fear so it could grow. The deep desire to turn and flee from this barn slowed my steps. But I wouldn't let it stop them. Fear gave birth to anger, which swiftly devoured its predecessor. It grew. Anger at my brother for doing this to me, anger at those he had bit for hurting people, anger at Vidar for leaving me to handle it alone, all burned within, threatening to turn into an inferno.

Two energy signatures close together drew me to the back of the barn. Down an aisle of old, empty stalls and around a corner, I found them. Light spilled through a half-open back door, bouncing off millions of dust particles, and outlining two figures. Shadows hid their faces. But I didn't need to see them. The feel of Sonya's power pushing against my own was unmistakable. Then there was the newly bitten. The taint of darkness on him made my power flare so much I grew nauseous. The way he shook with fear made my fangs extend in anticipation of a chase.

A flash stopped me in my tracks. No, not a flash, a memory.

Shouts, his shouts, punctuated the sound of flesh slapping flesh. His hands reared back again and again, connecting with the bruised face of a young woman. The final slap sent her spinning to the ground, but not before her head connected with the edge of a coffee table. After a bit of twitching, she went very still. The man's shouts turned to sobs, then he sank to the ground.

The flash ended, leaving me with even more rage. The man whimpered and took a stumbling step backward. Sonya grabbed his arm. "Don't run, or she will chase you, and I won't be able to stop what happens," she warned.

Fangs bared, I strode closer. "You killed her."

The man jerked. "You were in my head! How did you do that?" He shrank in on himself and tried to pull free from Sonya, but she held fast. It made me think of the woman who'd been cowering in fear of him.

Teeth gnashing, I growled. "Because I am the thing the monsters fear." My voice sounded nothing like a human's, and I didn't care.

Ebony hair and the beautiful brown of Native American skin moved in front of the man. Sonja's chestnut eyes glowed in the shadows. The fronts of our powers brushed against one another like the hot and cold that created a storm. In fact, that's what it felt like, a storm building.

"Ayra, stop. He mastered his instinct and gained control," Sonya said.

My gaze darted to her. "He beat a woman, then killed her," I growled.

Sonya nodded. "I know. But he can't make amends for it if you kill him."

I shifted my weight, head tilting so I could see him around her. The asshole looked like he was about to piss himself. It only made me angrier. "He won't be able to do it again either," I said.

"Killing him won't make up for what he's done. Only he can do that."

Dammit. I hated that she was right.

The man stepped out to her side, exposing himself. He kept his head bowed and his eyes at my feet. At least he wasn't entirely stupid. "And I *will* make up for it. I want to make up for it. I need to. I owe it to her and her family to try. I'll never raise a hand against anyone ever again. I swear," he said in an endless rush of words.

I forced my anger back down. Like bile, it didn't go easily or without leaving behind a terrible taste. "And how do you plan to do that?"

He ran his hands slowly through his sweat-slick hair. "Easy there," Sonya said. "He only just beat the instinct today. He hasn't had time to come up with a plan. But he will. I'll make sure of it."

Letting out a breath, I straightened up out of the fighting stance I'd automatically slid into. "All right."

Sonya drew back a bit in surprise. "Just like that?"

"Just like that. I'll know if he slips up, and if he does, I'll come for him. No discussion, no mercy."

A whimper came from the man.

Ignoring him, Sonya cocked her head at me. "So you didn't come for him now?"

"No, I came to talk to you."

"Oh." Sonya relaxed out of her fighting stance. Head turning to look over her shoulder, she said, "Stay here and the nice reaper won't kill you. I'll be back." Looking at me, she swept a hand toward the open door. "Shall we go for a walk?"

The newly bitten nodded furiously and backed up until he ran into a post. I gave him a little growl for good measure. It was wrong to enjoy the way he flinched, I knew, but I enjoyed it anyway. Shifting my attention to Sonya, I followed her out into the sunlight. I didn't need to see the man to keep tabs on him. The taint on him acted like a scent trail that would lead me straight to him if need be.

We walked out into a field of golden, thigh-high grass riddled with weeds and the occasional blue or yellow flower. The scents of growing things warming themselves worked like a palette cleanser for my nose. That building had smelled like sin and bad memories. Damn Calder for ruining the smell of a barn for me for the rest of my life. A Montana girl who couldn't stand the scent of a barn was a sad thing.

An old oak tree with gnarly limbs stretching out low to the ground cast its shade over us as we walked beneath it. Sonya leaped up ten feet straight into the air and settled onto one of the limbs as though it were a bench. The wistful grin on her face began to fade as I jumped up and joined her. Rough bark pressed into my mostly bare legs, but I didn't mind. The shade the big leaves offered felt good.

"I'll never get tired of that," Sonya said, looking down at the long drop to the ground.

"Being a werewolf does have its perks," I agreed.

Her childlike enjoyment of one of the simplest benefits of being a werewolf made me smile. She'd taken so naturally to it that I sometimes forgot she was newly bitten.

I looked out across the golden field and up into the vast blue sky. Would the sky seem smaller once we crossed over into Idaho? People said it felt that way in other states. I'd never left Montana, so I wouldn't know. Well, I guessed I would soon. I took a deep breath and stopped stalling.

"I'm sorry we didn't get to talk before I left Hemlock Hollow. I was hoping to get the jump on my brother to prevent things from going any further than they already had," I said.

Sonya's smile faded away. "Unfortunately, he has at least a month on us, probably more."

I thought back to the pictures of crime scenes plastered all over the walls in Calder's loft. "Definitely more." Anger spiked within and I had to work hard to stop it from giving me tunnel vision. "He's been doing this since before I was born."

"Do you think he had anything to do with Raul biting me in?"

"I'm sure of it. The woman Raul was engaged to was Calder's girlfriend," I said. The very idea of Calder having a girlfriend made me cringe, remembering the newly bitten back in the barn. But as far as I knew, Calder had never raised a hand to her.

Sonya's eyes narrowed. "You think Calder made Raul bite me in just so he could keep his girlfriend?"

"Not at all. Calder never cared about her. I heard him say it often enough. He used her to manipulate Raul."

"But why me, then?"

"The same reason he bit in all the others over the years, they awoke our power. But Calder might not be the only one who manipulated Raul. Did you talk to him after the trial?"

She stiffened. "No."

A deep sigh pulled from me. I couldn't blame her. "He told me Bain, Alpha of the Arnoddr pack, blackmailed him into biting you in."

Her brows rose. "The guy who took over the pack by killing his own brother? Why would he want me bitten in?"

"Raul said because he wanted you as his mate, to strengthen the Arnoddr pack and solidify his place as its alpha. It makes a bit of sense, considering how divided that pack still is."

Sonya's claws extended from her fingers, biting into the tree branch. "But Raul bit me in to be *his* mate."

"He said he did that to save you from having to be Bain's mate, said he was hoping Bain would hold up his end of the bargain before he found out."

"And what was this supposed bargain supposed to be?" I couldn't blame her for the doubt in her tone.

"I'm not sure. He didn't tell me that part, but because of it Raul thinks Bain is tied to this, that he's dangerous. That much, at least, I do believe."

Her eyes grew wide and her mouth dropped open a bit. For several long seconds, she didn't say anything. "All right, I trust you."

She swayed a bit on the branch. I prepared to grab hold of her, just in case.

"What connects your brother to all of that?"

"He's close friends with Bain. And he wanted to be the *uppskera*. He was hoping that by biting in so many people who wouldn't make it, the power would awake in him. But then I was born."

Sonya shook her head. "If that's what he wanted, why hasn't he stopped?"

"He wants to expose our kind, so they can take their rightful place as the alpha predators of the world. His words, not mine," I said.

"Idiot. There would be an all-out war."

"That's what he has planned. I found a journal of his. He mentions a battle in July. I think he's building an army to attack something, or someone."

Her eyes widened. "Shit. Any idea where, or who?"

"Not yet. But he's been tracking prisoner transports, breaking the prisoners free, and biting them in. I think they're what he plans to use for soldiers."

"That's insane. Why would he use them?"

I brushed a strand of pale hair back from my face and looked out over the meadow. "Maybe because they'd be grateful, loyal. Maybe to mess with me."

"Because you see inside their heads, experience the crimes that have pushed them over the edge."

The haunted tone of her voice made me look long and hard at her. "You see inside their heads too."

She nodded.

Silence stretched between us for a long moment until I finally filled it. "You can attract lightning."

"And you can channel it. But what does that have to do with what Calder is up to?"

"By Thor, I wish I knew."

She turned sideways on the branch to face me, pulling one leg up to her. "You healed me with it."

"No, I just used the lightning to kick start your power so it healed you faster."

"Ty tells me other *varúlfur* can't do that. How long have you been able to channel lightning?"

I didn't even have to take time to think about it. "Since I made it through the *verða*. I was eight."

Her brows shot up into her dark hair. "Wow, that's young isn't it? Ty said most go through it during puberty."

With a flourish of my hands, I pointed toward myself. "Yes, well, I decided to skip the whole puberty thing."

Laughing, Sonya tagged me in the arm with a fist that could use a bit of work. "Don't sell yourself short just because you're petite. It gives you more of an element of surprise, and you're not any less hot because you're a size zero."

"Size two, actually," I corrected her.

We shared a long laugh that felt utterly foreign, and even more amazing because of it. Maybe it was wrong, against a cosmic code of some kind, but I felt like I could count Sonya as a friend. For a short while we watched the oak leaves sway in the wind.

"I've always loved storms," Sonya said.

"Me too. It's connected with what Calder is doing, I just don't know how," I said.

"He knows you can channel lightning?"

That caught me off guard. "No, he doesn't."

"You're sure?"

"Absolutely. I hid it from him, very well." Any time I could do something he couldn't, Calder would increase my "training" until I was black and blue—and often bleeding—and so sore I could barely move the next day. If he had found out I could channel energy... What he would have done to me would have been the stuff of nightmares.

To my surprise, Sonya didn't question it. "How many people do you think are behind this?" she asked instead, surprising me yet again. I could see why Ty liked her.

"You mean aside from James and the others who have followed him around since they were pups?"

She inclined her head in a short nod.

I recalled what Raul had said that day in the park. "Initially, I had thought it was just my brother and a handful of his friends. But now I'm not so sure." I looked long and hard into her eyes. "We can't trust anyone but Ty and Vidar with our secret. This lightning thing, it means something, something important. I just don't know what yet."

"I agree."

Well, that was easier than I had thought it would be.

"There isn't anything in the *leitar* journals about it, and I'm guessing there isn't anything in the *uppskera* ones either. And we can't be the first. That means someone, or several someones, don't want us to know about what we can do, or more importantly, why we can do it," Sonya said.

Her intelligence surprised me and convinced me that Raul definitely hadn't chosen her on his own. "I think you and I could have been friends under different circumstances," I said.

Forehead wrinkling up, she smiled in contrast. "But we are friends."

Friends. I'd never had a female friend. My brother made sure I never had time for it. Couldn't have me confessing that I was of the reaper bloodline to anyone, let alone show them the mark I had been born with. Not that his influence would have mattered. I had always been a skinny, extremely pale— especially for the Norse—little girl. Hel, I still was. Kids were terribly unaccepting when it came to such things. It was part of what made me so angry that everyone wanted to be close to me now that I could offer them something.

"I don't see how. I will kill the ones you don't save. I imagine a thing like that would stress a friendship beyond its strength."

She made a sort of snorting noise. "Their salvation isn't my responsibility, it's theirs. If they aren't strong enough to want to fight the instinct to kill, and won't listen to me when I try to help them, then they're the ones that seal their fate, not me, and not you." She waved a hand. "I'm not an angel and you're not a devil. We're just two women trying to right the wrongs of a couple of idiots. And damn history and tradition if it says we can't be friends."

The left side of my lips turned upward. "You and I are going to get along great."

"Damn straight."

Swinging her legs out, she leaped down. Dandelion seeds puffed up into the air at her landing, a few snagging in all that long black hair. I jumped down and landed beside her. My insubstantial mass barely disturbed the blades of grass I landed on. Without a word between us, we started to walk back toward the barn.

After a few steps, she spoke. "We should keep in touch more than just about the newly bitten."

"I agree. If the lightning thing happens to you again, will you let me know?"

"Yeah, definitely. If I can attract it and you can channel it, I think that means we're meant to work together to do something with it." Her face crinkled up again and she shook her head. "I just wish I knew what. And I can't see what it has to do with the newly bitten."

"Me neither. But maybe together we can figure it out."

"We can. We will."

Instead of going through the barn, we skirted around it. She didn't seem to want to step inside it any more than I did. At the corner stood Ty and Vidar, bodies tense as if they were ready to sprint toward us at any sign of conflict. Sonya and I exchanged a look and a smile.

She rolled her eyes at Ty as she looped her arm through his. "I told you we'd be fine."

Ty's gaze softened when he looked down at her. "Yes, well, I am glad to see there is no blood."

Sonya slapped his chest. "Always worrying, this one."

A small flare of jealousy moved through me. Not for her relationship with Ty. Sure, the guy was smoking hot, if one was into the modern-day Viking look. But me, I preferred tall, dark, and handsome, emphasis on the dark. The jealousy was for the relationship itself. Elí and I didn't have a relationship, unless you counted a religious devotee and the object of his devotion.

"One more thing," I said. "We ran into a *berserkr*—a werebear. He said others were concerned about us gathering a pack."

"Why would they care about that?" Sonya asked.

Ty went tense. "Because they are afraid you will bring the wolves together and tip the balance, making the wolves more powerful than the other shifter races."

He and Vidar exchanged a look. "Exactly. Which means we have to be careful. They consider us a threat," Vidar said.

Ty nodded. "We will be careful. You as well. Let us know if you hear anything else. We will do the same. And Vidar..." Ty paused and gripped his shoulder. "Be careful."

Vidar gripped Ty's shoulder in return. "You too, my friend."

I nodded to Sonya. "Thanks for talking with me. We'll keep in touch."

"Definitely," she agreed.

Ty reached out a hand to Vidar and they grasped forearms. "Good to see you, Vidar. I hope we can continue to meet under good circumstances," he said.

"As do I. Take care, Ty."

Arm in arm, Ty and Sonya disappeared into the shadows of the barn. Vidar relaxed when I stepped to his side. His eyes filled with a thousand questions I knew would pour out of him the moment we got in the truck. Right now, I wouldn't be able to answer them. Not because I didn't want to tell Vidar, but because I didn't know. My gaze worked its way up his towering, hard body. The brown T-shirt proclaiming #TeamThor in gold lettering made me smile. Gods, I loved how he embraced his inner nerd and didn't care what anyone thought about it. No matter how much I told myself not to, I enjoyed the view. The concern in his hazel eyes almost broke down some of the carefully placed bricks in the wall I kept around myself. But not quite.

"I'm going to ride my bike for a few miles. I need some time to think," I said.

"I'm still a good listener. You can bounce stuff off me," he said.

I started for the truck, and he turned to walk at my side. "Yeah, I know, but I don't need to talk, just think. We'll meet up in a few miles. Nothing to worry about."

Not giving him a chance to respond, I dropped the tailgate when we reached the truck. I jumped in and started undoing the straps that held my bike down. Just smelling the metal made me long to be in the seat. It wasn't as good as an LS-218—the fastest electric bike on the market. But a girl had to go with what she could afford. And considering I lived on ramen noodles and meat from the discount counter, I was lucky to have the

BMW. As it was, I'd bought it in boxes from an old lady in Billings whose husband had died.

Part of me wanted to apologize to Vidar for brushing him off, but a bigger part wanted to scream at him. Coming this close to reaping and having to walk away took its toll. With each moment, fury built inside, rising until it felt like it would block my throat. In the barn a few yards away hid a man who had beat a woman to death. He deserved to die. I wanted him to die, preferably by my claws. That desire made me sick with self-loathing.

My breathing sped up, sweeping my heart rate along with it. I clenched my fists tight so I was forced to make my claws retract—or end up cutting myself. The tang of blood on the air revealed my failure.

"Are you okay?" Vidar asked.

"No. I mean, yes, I will be. I have to process."

I could see an argument building in his eyes, and I knew if I didn't shut him down quick this could turn ugly.

"I just need to be alone for a bit to think," I said with far more force.

For a moment his face fell into such a look of despair that I wanted to take my words back and get in the truck with him. The look disappeared in a flash, though, leaving him unreadable as stone. I hardened the shell around my heart.

"Whatever you need," he said in a flat tone.

When I freed the last strap, he grabbed hold of my bike. I almost told him I could get it, but I stopped the words before they could form. Distance I could handle, but hurting him any more than necessary, I couldn't. I leaped out of the truck.

He picked up my five-hundred pound motorcycle by the frame, lifted it over the bed rails of the truck, and set it on the ground. Admittedly, I couldn't have done it quite that well.

"Thank you," I said as I took hold of the handlebars.

He nodded and returned to the cab of the truck. Okay, maybe I'd been a little hard on him, but it was better than taking my anger out on him. The newly bitten's energy signature dragged my gaze back to the barn. That taint on his energy, like a bad spot on fruit, called out to me. My hands shook a little with the effort of holding back as I dug my keys out of my cargo shorts and straddled the bike. Calm radiated out from the bike into me. The edge of my anger wore down. Guilt tried to rear up and take its place. Starting the bike quenched that.

The anticipation of the wind against me and the white lines zipping by made everything else fade. Vidar returned with my helmet, jacket, and boots in hand. He stared at the patch on the back of my gray Cordura jacket for a long moment before handing it over. Woven in metallic blue thread was a wolf's head formed of knotted lines. Around that were two circles that held within them the Norse elder futhark runes, making it look a bit like a wheel. Above it was a rocker with the initials AVV, below it, another rocker that said Montana. I finally had to tug the jacket from his hands. "You're a member of the American Viking *Varúlfur?*" he asked in a shocked tone.

No judgment clouded his eyes, surprisingly. "Yes."

"But you said you didn't choose a pack. An umbrella pack is still a pack."

I shook my head. "It isn't the same. They have no alpha, and they have members from many different packs. They're more of a republic than a monarchy. I like that about them."

His eyes widened, and he nodded as if impressed.

I slid my jacket and boots on. One moment of silence stretched into several that quickly became uncomfortable. On top of the anger building in me, a deep concern rose. It helped clear my mind a little.

"I have Bluetooth in my helmet so I can call you if I need to," I said.

His shoulders relaxed. "There's a bar just off the highway after you cross the state line into Idaho. I'll meet you there," he replied.

It wasn't a suggestion or a question, but the decisive words of a man who had the power of an alpha behind him. The woman and wolf in me thrilled at that. Hel, even the reaper in me thrilled at the idea that he might be strong enough to stand beside me. But I couldn't indulge in thoughts like that. I put my helmet on. Behind the mirrored face shield I breathed easier.

Before those guarded, gorgeous hazel eyes of his could change my mind, I pulled the throttle back. The grass and gravel forced me to go slower than I wanted. At first, pulling away from the barn felt like trying to pull a tooth that didn't want to let go. It didn't hurt exactly, but it felt so wrong that I just wanted it to stop. I had to remind myself that the newly bitten had shifted back to human on his own. He had control, and he wanted to make up for what he did. That made him newly bitten, not condemned.

The pressure in my chest started to ease, but I figured it was more from the distance than my thoughts. When my front wheel touched the paved road, that pressure gave way completely. I could think past the anger again. I opened up the throttle and left the newly bitten—and the desire to kill—behind.

Unfortunately, I also left everything I had ever wanted in life standing at that truck as well.

CHAPTER NINE

VIDAR

Pain rooted me to the spot. She did not need me, whether to talk, vent, or just be near. She needed to be alone, probably so she could call Elí. That reverberated through me until I could feel it all the way down into my bones. Damn the Order for not letting me talk to her. Damn them and their vow of celibacy, or I would have kissed her already. Damn them straight to Muspelheimr.

Watching the cloud of dust her motorcycle kicked up into the hot July air felt like watching everything I'd ever wanted go up in smoke. No. Blame and anger wouldn't get her back. I couldn't give up. I wouldn't give up. Whether she knew it or not, she needed me. I jumped in the truck and cranked the motor to life. Gravel spun as I tore down the road after her. The truck started to bounce in and out of the ruts so badly that I was forced to slow down after only a few yards. By the time I reached the paved road, Ayra was long gone.

But I knew which way she went. I could feel her pulling at me like my true north. Turning my gaze away from the setting sun, I followed as fast as I dared. If I got pulled over, it would only make me later. Chances were she wouldn't get pulled over. I wouldn't get that lucky. I pushed my speed as fast as I dared, thankful I'd gotten more truck than I needed. The pull of her power remained within my range and that was all that mattered. It would be better if she didn't see my truck in her rearview.

In less than half an hour, the sun sank below the horizon, casting the landscape into deep shadows that forced me to turn on the headlights. Already Ayra's scent began to fade from the interior of the truck. It bothered me on a deeper level than I wanted to explore. If I thought too much about that, I'd start to press harder on the pedal. The tall evergreens flanking the road made me a bit nostalgic for the days when Ayra and I used to run through the forest near Hemlock Hollow as kids. I missed those careless days so much. Worse, I had missed the opportunity for so many more when I'd left. If she didn't choose me as her *verndari*, it was all for nothing.

My mind wouldn't shut off as I drove. I kept going over everything I should and shouldn't have done, every bad decision I'd made. All I'd ever wanted to do was make this life that she didn't get to choose easier for her. And all I seemed to be doing was making it worse. Now she was engaged to someone else and it was starting to look like I might not be able to win her back. My distraction was so complete that I didn't see the huge shape in the middle of the road until I was almost on top of it. Dark as it was, I thought it was a cow at first, not uncommon in Montana.

But cows didn't generally move much when you came across them. Dang things would stand right in the middle of the road and stare you down as you passed them by. And I'd never seen one come straight at a vehicle like this one did. At the last moment, I realized that was because this wasn't a cow. My *varúlfur* night vision kicked in and revealed a huge brown bear leaping toward the hood of my truck. Metal crunched and squealed as it landed right in the middle, struck the windshield hard enough to spider web the entire thing, and then went flying over.

The damnable ABS system fouled up my instinctual attempt to pump the brakes. Somehow I still managed to keep the truck under control and bring it to a rolling stop. Where, I had no idea, since I couldn't see out of the windshield. Not wanting to be at a disadvantage inside the cab, I flung the door open and jumped out. The soft white glow of my headlights shone off a tree trunk not ten feet from the bumper. The thick, musky scent of bear hung heavy in the air. My power stirred, making the skin along the back of my neck prickle.

Four dents on the hood the size of massive paws made me think the damn thing had jumped on it rather than rolled up there like it would have if I'd hit it. Come to think of it, the creature hadn't looked fearful like an animal about to meet a ton of hard metal usually did. It had looked... purposeful, like it had meant to run right at me. My mind flashed back to the cabin, to the *berserkr*.

Turning slowly, I scanned the area with my wolf eyes. The iron tang of blood on the air was weak, as if the bear was barely wounded. The smell came from the back of the truck on the passenger side. As I crept in that direction, I pulled my T-shirt off and tossed it in the open driver's door. No sense in ruining one of my favorite shirts. The press of power came from the trees just behind the tailgate. Definitely not a regular bear.

The strange grunting, sniffling sounds only a bear could make came from the nearby trees. Boughs rustled, sending the scent of pine wafting even stronger into the air. From out of the darkness lumbered a huge shape that looked me in the eye even though it was on four legs. My power flared more. I realized it looked so big partly because it was on a slight hill. Still, it was huge.

Instead of coming toward me, it went for the passenger door of my truck. The truck rocked as it rose up, putting its front paws on the door and its head inside.

"Hey, Yogi, get out of my truck," I yelled.

Loud sniffing noises carried to me as it shoved its head farther into the cab. The desire to go all green superhero on the intruder made my skin tingle with the beginnings of the shift. Good as I was, I'd never fought a *berserkr*, and I didn't know how it would go down. Tired of being ignored, I leaped over the bed of the truck, landing just behind the *berserkr*. I grabbed it by the mound of fat and hair between its shoulders and yanked it away from my truck. The thing had to weigh close to four hundred pounds. Air expelled from it in a loud grunt as it hit the bank several feet back. Roaring, it rose on its hind legs.

"I warned you to get out of my truck."

Huge paws clawing at the air, he roared again in answer. My fangs extended. A growl began to build in my chest.

"Why don't you shift back so we can discuss this like civilized people?

I'm going to need your insurance information," I suggested, allowing just the hint of a smile through, showing my fangs.

The *berserkr* plunged onto all fours hard enough that I swear the ground shook, though that could have just been power rolling off him. Teeth bared, growl tearing between them, I held my clawed hands out, ready to meet him. He barreled toward me. When I could smell his breath and feel the brush of his coarse fur, I stepped aside. He slammed head first into the tree that had been behind me, hard enough to make sharp pine needles rain down on us. I thrust a front kick into his side that blew the air out of his dazed body.

"How about now, Yogi? You want to shift back and talk?" I offered once again.

A paw swiped at me fast enough to catch the edge of my shorts. Claws snagged in the material, but thankfully missed my flesh. "Thor's balls! I was trying to avoid ruining my clothes, you bastard!"

Shaking his head, he stumbled toward me. Another weak swipe came at me on my right, this one missing by a mile. When I leaned back out of the way, he flung himself on me. I grabbed him by the fur between his front legs, placed my feet against his chest as I fell, and rolled us down the embankment. At the end of the roll I kicked out with all my strength. The *berserkr* went flying into the road.

I chased him down as he rolled to a stop. While I moved, I shifted into hybrid form, the between stage of wolf and man. Most *varúlfur* couldn't do it, and I was counting on the fact that the *berserkr* wouldn't expect it. My body sprouted long fur, my legs bent backwards, my head turned into that of a wolf—mostly—and claws extended from my fingers and toes. The *berserkr's* eyes widened until they looked like marbles about to pop from his head. He started to back up.

Before he could get very far, I grabbed him by the hair of one shoulder. I gripped until I felt my claws bite into flesh. Growling and snapping, I pulled him to me.

"Shift," I commanded in what could barely be called speech.

He resisted, gaining a touch of my respect. I let my power roll over him in a biting, stinging, burning flood. It pulled at his with a merciless magnetism, another trick most couldn't do. This one was reserved for alphas. I'd been able to do it since the year I came through the *verða*.

With a whimper, he shuddered in my grasp. A moment later his body flowed into that of a man. Left with no loose skin or fur to grasp, I adjusted my grip to encircle his throat. His hands wrapped around my wrist, sinking deep into the black fur. No matter how hard he pulled, he couldn't loosen my grip. I shifted back to a man as well because speaking while in hybrid form was nearly as hard as in wolf form.

"Why did you attack me?" I demanded.

"What are you? I thought the woman was the reaper, but you..." Respect tinged the awe in his tone.

"I'm one of the Order of the *Verndari*. Ayra is the reaper. And trust me, she can do much worse than just shift into a hybrid."

Wide, wild eyes darted every which way so fast it made me dizzy just watching him. Finally, his gaze settled on me. "Where is she?"

I squeezed a little harder. "I just told you she's scarier than I am. Do you really want an introduction?"

He coughed and gasped until I realized I needed to loosen my grip for him to answer. "If not me, someone will kill her. It has to be done."

I willed my claws to grow until they dug into his shoulder. "Why on Helheimr would you say that?" He only growled in response. I extended my claws more, piercing his skin. "Tell me!" I yelled, pouring power into the command.

He gasped, a ragged, pain-filled sound. "If she unites the wolves, they'll be stronger than any other group of shifters. One group can't be allowed to have that much power."

"She has no intention of joining a pack for that very reason," I said.

"Are you sure about that?"

I thought about her jacket, the AVV, an umbrella pack that encompassed half the *varúlfur* on the planet. "Yes," I lied. "Now who sent you?"

He didn't answer so I squeezed, hard. The look on his face remained obstinate. I lifted him off his feet, no easy task considering we were close to the same height and he was heavy as a mad scientist in an iron flying suit. He kicked and struggled for several seconds, hands pulling uselessly at my arm.

I lowered him enough that his feet touched the ground. Easy as flexing a muscle, I let the wolfy glow fill my eyes and made my fangs extend. "Last time I'm asking so nice. Who sent you?"

"It doesn't matter who sent me. There will be others, and not just from the *berserkrs*. The Council is concerned. That alone is enough to motivate the races to take action. We won't allow her to empower any one race more than the others, and we won't allow your race to out themselves to the world," he said.

He couldn't mean the Elder Council of Hemlock Hollow, the *Varúlfur* Council, or even the Caninus Council. He wouldn't be privy to what they discussed. "You mean the Shifter Council?" My surprise came through in my voice. So much for control.

"Oh, yeah, well I guess you weren't invited to that meeting."

I squeezed his neck again, my claws biting into the back of it. "The Shifter Council had a meeting about our *uppskera* without inviting the *varúlfur*?"

A smug smile curved up his oxygen-deprived lips. He tapped on my hand. I let go enough that he could answer. "I didn't say the *varúlfur* weren't invited. I said you weren't invited, *verndari*." He spat the last word out like it was a foul thing.

I shoved him away from me so I wouldn't punch him in the face. Not one to disappoint, he gave me another opportunity when he launched himself at me. I side-stepped and drove the instep of my foot into his solar plexus. Hands grasping his midsection, he doubled over. I threw a right hook into his jaw, rotating my hips to put a good amount of power behind it. He went down hard.

"Stay down," I warned.

The obstinate villain grabbed my leg and yanked. Tucking my chin against my chest, I managed to keep my head from slamming into the asphalt, but not the rest of me. Faster than I thought the brute capable, he straddled me before I could regain my senses. He grabbed me by the throat and started to squeeze. And damn but he was strong.

"Never! I will kill her, even if I have to go through you," he said.

My vision narrowed, and not because I couldn't breathe. Fury burned through all reason and mercy. I shifted to hybrid form. Flexing my neck muscles alone moved his hand enough away from my windpipe that I was able to scream like a Viking plunging into battle. Without hesitation, or even a thought beyond protecting Ayra, I thrust my clawed hands into his chest. They hit his breastbone and stopped. Raking down, I freed them of his flesh.

Though fear shone in his eyes, he reared his fist back. Before it could fall, I thrust forward and closed his throat in my teeth. One good shake tore open his carotid. Blood spewed into my mouth in a hot, horrible torrent. My wolf side reveled in it at the same time my human side gagged and pulled away. I threw him off me and shifted to full wolf form. Unable to move, I stood and watched while his life's blood brightened the concrete and he twitched his last.

I forced the focus that didn't want to come. The *berserkr* likely wasn't the only one with the notion that the *uppskera* had to be taken out. Not if the Shifter Council had met to discuss her. And she was out there alone. Desperation erased the scribblings of instinct from my mind, giving me a clean slate that allowed me to think.

Blood squished like thick paint beneath my paws as I rose. An iron-like scent drifted up from it, filling my nostrils and choking my throat. This was not like the comic books at all. I didn't feel heroic or dashing, only horrible. I ran off into the trees as far and fast as my paws would carry me in a matter of seconds. Then I circled back to the edge of the tree line and leaped for the bed of the truck. The entire vehicle shook with my impact. I shifted back to a man, grabbed my shirt from where it lay on the wheel well, and climbed into the cab.

One glance around and a good hard listen revealed no witnesses and no one coming for as far as I could hear—which was at least a mile. My steady hands shifted the truck into drive a second before my bare foot pressed on the gas pedal. I'd left nothing behind to tie me to the killing, save for my blood. For a human, that would be damning evidence, but not for us. *Varúlfur* blood degraded due to the shifting nature of our atoms. In tests it would show up as tainted wolf's blood. It was part of the reason our kind got away with so much killing.

The stench of his blood—rank with a bear's musk—clung to me. I pressed the button to roll down my window. Fresh, warm air blew in around me. My gaze dropped to my hand on the wheel. Already his blood was drying beneath my nails, coagulating on my face, throat, and chest. I'd have to pull over and wash soon. But first I had to put some distance between me and the body.

Though he had attacked me, had brought this on himself, the gravity of what I'd done struck me like a super villain's right hook. The air felt too cold. The cab of the truck seemed to close in on me. The classic rock blaring on the radio that I'd been enjoying so much an hour ago hurt my ears. Assassin or not, he'd still been a man. I had killed a man. The worst part was, I wasn't sorry. And to protect her, I'd do it again if I had to.

CHAPTER TEN

AYRA

"The murderous rage rides on the tail of insanity, condemning any who lose their battle with control."
-Uppskera Journals

The rock music of the roadside bar drew me into the packed parking lot. I drove around to the front where a row of Harleys stood in a neat line. A few Sportsters and Road Kings stood among mostly classic Fat Boys, Soft Tails, and genuine Choppers with Ape Hanger handlebars on some and racing bars on others. Not a windshield among them. No yuppies here. It could be a rough crowd.

Fine by me.

Rough crowds were kind of my thing.

I squeezed my BWM into a spot on the end of the row next to a beautiful 1979 Shovelhead with a ghost flame paint job. Neon blue light from the bar's sign overhead bathed the sidewalk before me. I rolled up my jacket and tucked it under the straps of my cargo holder behind my rear seat. No sense in riling up the locals with my patch and rockers. It didn't mean what they thought it meant, but the rough sort of bikers rarely listened long enough to hear that part. In my short jean shorts and blue half-shirt sporting the name of a classic metal band, I'd fit in well enough.

My phone vibrated as I rose from my bike. It was only Elí texting yet another picture of flowers for the wedding he needed my opinion on. The man was obsessed with the arrangements, as if making the ceremony beautiful could hide the ugly truth that he was marrying a monster. The business-like manner of the text stung, a lot. I shoved my phone back in my pocket. I couldn't deal with that situation right now.

Pulsing drums and screaming guitars welcomed me long before I opened the door to the packed establishment. Most people gathered around the bar and tables that framed the dance floor. A dozen or so dancers meant I'd have plenty of room but might draw a bit of attention if I wasn't careful. Oh well, I wasn't against busting a few heads if I had to. A girl should be able to go where she wanted to go, after all. The scents of sweaty bodies and sweet liquor mingled in a way that wasn't all bad. The wonderful press of energy made it oh so worth it. I needed this bit of normalcy bad enough to risk just about any crowd.

The air literally felt thick with it, almost palpable. Sexual energy, the energy raised by dancing, even a bit of hostile energy from too much testosterone, all of it felt amazing, like a well-mixed cocktail. It tingled across my skin, begging to be drunk in. So I did. They wouldn't feel it. I only soaked in what they gave off. This wasn't my reaper power, just a normal werewolf ability to feel the energy in a room. Smiling, I let the door swing shut behind me. A few gazes turned my way, mostly men leering at my legs. Before any of them could get any ideas, I strode straight to the dance floor.

The hard rock pulsing from the speakers on the stage pulled at my soul with each drumbeat. My body responded, moving to the music of its own accord. Hair swinging with each step, I gave over to the sensations of music and energy filling me. The other dancers ignored me for the most part, at first. One song turned into another. Thankfully, they kept the beat strong. With all the energy I soaked in from the other dancers around me, I needed the fast pace. By the next song I was surrounded by others, mostly men gyrating as close to me as I'd let them, but a few women too.

I allowed those giving off the most energy to surround me. Caught up by my power, they danced with abandon, giving off more and more energy. Soon I became light-headed and giddy. The press of all the bodies became very...stimulating. Though I had zero interest in the young, shirtless biker guy trying to grind against my hip, I wished he was even less clothed. I wished he was Vidar. Closing my eyes, I imagined for a moment that he was. But when I opened them to see a stranger hovering over me, it turned my stomach. While he was good looking, he was not Vidar.

Before it could get awkward, a tiny Vietnamese woman exuding an impressive amount of energy sidled between us. Shirtless biker-guy grinned like an idiot as he ground up against her for a minute until she shot him a warning look that made him step back. Hel, it would have made me step back. Her little gold dress blended with her chestnut skin tone in a way that made it hard to tell how much it covered in the dimly lit bar. Braids of the most amazing ginger and black hair that looked so natural I couldn't tell which was her true hair color bounced and swayed with every move she made. Gold eyes that had to be contacts regarded me with a mixture of mischief and interest. The only piece of jewelry she wore was a gold necklace set with a large onyx. She matched my moves with impressive skill, shadowing just close enough with every part of her body to barely avoid touching.

Whoops and hollers of encouragement sounded from the surrounding men. The song changed and a screaming guitar drowned them out. Gold eyes kept up with me easily despite the drastic uptick in the beat. As we danced, the stress of the last month melted away until all I thought about was the music and the intriguing woman beside me. While she didn't give off any more energy than the guy we'd shrugged off, there was something about her that drew me. The fearless way she stared into my eyes impressed me. No challenge sat in that gaze. It seemed more calculating than anything else.

The music slowed. She wove her body around mine until barely a breath separated us. Her arms moved about me in sinuous waves. Braids brushed against my shoulders, my breasts, as we swayed ever closer. Mild though her energy was, it still managed to be intoxicating. Her lips came close to my neck, her breath trailing across my skin. Part of me didn't mind. Maybe it was that she felt safe where the guy hadn't. I couldn't be sure. A level of aggression lay behind her full-lipped smile that was often rare in women. And those eyes... I couldn't find the edge of a contact lens no matter how hard I looked. And she let me look very, very close. Normally my werewolf sight would pick that kind of thing right up.

My stomach cramped up, not in the way that meant I was going to vomit, no, far worse than that. Tainted *varúlfur* energy approached from outside, a condemned, and one that was deep into the dark side already. All the stress I had shed rushed back in with a vengeance. My body froze as I saw inside the mind of the condemned.

Blood everywhere. An axe in my hand still had chunks of flesh and soft bits sliding off it. The messy remains of a woman and a child lay at my feet, my child. Euphoria filled me, along with the desire to do it again. Already a plan was forming in my mind.

The urge—no, the *need*—to kill him surged up and washed away the stress, the doubt. This monster had to die, right now. I forced a smile for Gold Eyes.

"Sorry, gotta go. Thanks for the save," I said.

She nodded as if she'd heard me despite the blaring music. I turned and shoved my way through the full dance floor to the tune of numerous protests from guys who didn't want the show to end. One grabbed hold of my arm with a grip strong enough it would have stopped a normal woman. I twisted up and toward his thumb, easily breaking his hold without even using my werewolf strength. Quicker than I expected, he grabbed hold of both my wrists.

"Why don't you stay? My friends and I were enjoying the show," he said.

I whipped my hands around and grabbed his wrists, squeezing hard enough to make his bones grind together. Power burned behind my eyes, which I knew would make them shine like an animal's in the dark. He gasped as he stared wide-eyed at me.

"I have business outside," I said.

The aggression left his eyes, and fear bubbled up in its place. His top lip curled into a sad mockery of a snarl. "Fine bit—Ouch!" A touch of my power pushing into him cut off his words.

He nodded. This time he didn't reach for me when I left. The door opened onto a packed parking lot aglow with neon blue light. I had to step out from under that light before I could let my werewolf night-sight kick in. Heat signatures popped up everywhere: a man propositioning a woman near the road, another man walking toward the bar, a couple in a car having sex. None of them were the person I felt. Their energy signatures lacked that extra something werewolves possessed. I focused on my sense of smell since it was the longest range of my senses. The overwhelming odors of alcohol, cigarettes, and bodily fluids overrode everything else. Finally, I had no choice but to tap into my hated sixth sense.

At the slightest urging, it uncurled within me with an eagerness that took my breath away. It was like it had been waiting. With it came that intense drive to chase and kill. Strength flooded my muscles and my senses sharpened beyond that of even a werewolf. It hit me hard and fast, like a drug that went straight into the bloodstream. I stood on the knife's edge of control, instinct just a slip in the wrong direction. The problem was, I wanted to leap in that direction. I craved that out-of-control feeling much like I craved storms and the energy they brought. Fear of that craving helped drive it back enough to allow me to think.

Like a strong magnet, my power snapped to the newly bitten. No, not newly bitten. He had seen at least six full moons. I felt it in his memories. And he had reveled in the kill each time. Unfortunately, I felt that too. He stood down wind of me, at the edge of the forest that stretched beyond the parking lot. I took one step in his direction and he bolted. Instinct propelled me after him.

Once I reached the fragrant shelter of the fir trees, I slowed a little to pick up his scent trail. It led me deeper into the trees, thankfully away from prying eyes and under cover from satellites. My prey couldn't have been more accommodating if he had meant to be. Suspicion bloomed inside me. I slowed, paying close attention to my surroundings. The scent trail led down into a hollow between two hillsides covered in trees, a perfect ambush spot.

I strode straight into the hollow. Fury clouded my mind. Like I suspected, his trail disappeared in the middle of the hollow. The clever bastard was already taking well to being a werewolf. Not good. Rays of moonlight shifted across the ground before me as the boughs they filtered through moved. It could just be the wind, but it wasn't. The pressure of his power hovering over me made that abundantly clear.

At the last moment, I stepped back. Air whooshed from him in a loud grunt as he hit the ground before me on all fours and fell to his stomach. In only a pair of pants, he was at least partially prepared to shift. Grinning, he rose slowly, like he didn't have a care in the world. That expression worked like gasoline on the fire of my anger. It took a while for him to unfold his tall body. His stiff movements revealed the fall hadn't been soft. A farmer's tan darkened his arms halfway down. White supremacy tattoos covered Farm Boy's bare chest. Calder knew how much I hated prejudiced people hiding behind Odinism. Our religion had nothing to do with prejudice, but some people liked to think it did. By turning this jerk he was just trying to piss me off.

"So this is the famous *uppskera*? Calder said you weren't no more than a little thing, but damn! This'll be too easy," he said, butchering the Icelandic word for reaper.

The images of the woman and child he had killed flashed behind my eyes when I blinked. It gave me all the motivation I needed. Hands opening, I extended my claws. "I believe the word my brother would have used would have been insignificant," I said.

He laughed. "Yeah, that's the word he used."

His eyes widened as they took in my claws. "I didn't know we could do that." A pale pink tongue darted out to wet his lips. Excitement of the sickest kind filled his eyes. "That could come in handy."

"Only the most powerful of us can. And you are definitely not that," I said as my lip curled up in disgust.

"You don't know a thing about me, little lady."

"You're a monster who is going to die for what you did and what you would continue to do. That's all I need to know."

The confusion clouding his eyes made me sad. I wanted him to know why he was dying. I wanted him to regret killing that woman and her child. But he wouldn't. I could feel that as surely as I could feel the stain of what he'd done on his soul. A snappy comment started to emerge from his smug smile, but I'd heard enough. I couldn't hold the fury back any longer.

Claws out, I launched toward him. He jumped back. Eyes widening, he tripped over a stick, which probably saved him more than his pathetic jump. Skin gave way beneath my claws. Five bright red lines appeared across his chest as he fell. I darted in, intending to follow him to the ground, but he surprised me by rolling out of the fall to his feet. A leg swung at me. I let it hit the back of my knees, using it to help propel me into a backflip that carried me over him as he shot in for another attack that missed.

When I landed, I threw a roundhouse kick into his solar plexus. He doubled over, wheezing.

"Where is my brother?" I demanded.

He flinched, lips twitching as he fought the command of my power. I wasn't his alpha, so I couldn't make him tell me, but I was his better by far, and I could at least make it hard to deny me. I dumped my power over him in a scalding rush that made him cry out.

"Idaho, last I knew," he said between gasps. What do you know, turned out I could make him tell me.

My hand drew back for the swipe that would open his throat. The feel of another energy slammed into me, halting my strike. Farm Boy drove a fist into my stomach. The second energy came up behind me, fast. I ducked and heard flesh hit flesh. The idiot hit Farm Boy instead of me. Suddenly two sets of arms were reaching for me, swinging at me. I ducked and dodged. The second man looked like he was related to the first. The stain on his soul was a match as well. Both condemned, and both killers.

While they had fighting skills, their rushed moves proved they weren't disciplined. Still, one raked claws across my forearm and the other struck me hard in the right shoulder.

They worked together, using the terrain and each other to get the upper hand and wear me down. Out of breath and bleeding, I was left with no other option. I dropped my guard and sucked in a bit of their power. It hit me like a truck, both with horrible images and the taste of corruption. But it pumped adrenalin straight through my veins and into my power.

As I dodged the punch of one, I sliced open the stomach of the other. He fell to the ground, bloody hands trying to hold the wound together. I ducked beneath a kick from the second one. Before straightening, I raked my claws across the wounded man's neck. They bit deep. Hot arterial blood shot into my palm. It wasn't enough. After what he'd done, I wanted him to suffer. But I didn't have time.

The feel of yet another's energy washed over me as I turned to fight the second guy. When I swung for him, he wasn't there. A moment before I saw her, I realized the third energy I felt wasn't a werewolf. It was a shifter, for sure, but not a werewolf. Moonlight glinted off the orange and black coat of a tiger as she bore the second man to the ground. Fury erupted in me at the sight of her stealing my kill.

My thoughts scattered in the deluge of anger. Deep down, I knew it was the rage Vidar had warned me about. But even knowing that, I couldn't fight it. I didn't want to fight it. What I wanted was to claw, bite, and kill. The weretiger tore my prey's throat out before I could stop her.

No, not my prey, the condemned. It shouldn't matter how he died, only that he did, so he couldn't kill another innocent. That thought took the tiniest bit of the edge off my rage. Still, my control was threadbare.

Golden eyes fixed on me, she held tight until he stopped twitching. She wiped her paws on his clothes in a very untiger-like manner. Gaze still on me, she trotted straight toward me, striped tail flicking behind her. Claws out, I slid into a fighting stance. An effortless-looking leap launched her straight up into the air and well out of my reach. Her body flowed like water into that of a woman. Her hands grabbed a large branch and she pulled herself up onto it. Naked as the day she was born, she sat staring at me with a familiar, inquisitive look. Long black and ginger braids swung down around her naked, chestnut-hued skin, teasing her hard nipples. An onyx pendant gleamed between her breasts.

The dancer from the bar. My anger washed out on a tide of confusion.

One of the bodies twitched on the ground near me. Before I could think, I was upon it, slashing and tearing. I couldn't stop until it was no more than an unidentifiable bloody mess beneath my claws. Panting through my fangs, I stood over it, trying to grasp a thread of my control back. So much blood and gore everywhere, on the ground, on my clothes, my hands. Disgust and shame rose to the top of the fucked-up cocktail of my emotions. I hadn't even shifted to full wolf form to do it.

Bile burned the back of my throat. I darted to a bush and emptied my stomach, all the while keeping an eye on the woman. The worst part was, I couldn't tell if it was the power of the condemned that had made me vomit, or having torn them apart. Blood covered my hands. It should have bothered me. It didn't. Spitting several times, I moved into position to try and flank the woman. She watched with obvious interest.

"Come up. It will be smarter to leave the scene through the trees," she invited, as if I hadn't just lost my shit and gone all psycho. Though she spoke impeccable English, she had a decidedly Vietnamese accent that took me a moment to place.

Her power exuded a sense of calm that puzzled me. In a way, it reminded me of the Zen-like presence Vidar possessed. But this was different, dark in a way I couldn't put my claw on. Regardless, I had to get away from these bodies. I glanced up, gauging the distance. It was at least fifteen feet straight up. I jumped, shifting in midair just as she had. The world swam in and out of focus. I cleared the branch she sat on, barely grabbing the one above her. Breathing hard, I dropped down beside her. My head pounded and my stomach lurched. Thankfully, I had nothing left to throw up.

This whole sucking werewolves' power thing was not all it was cracked up to be.

Up here the smell of death was much more subdued. Between that and her calm aura, I found I could breathe and think easier.

"This wasn't your fight. That wasn't your kill," I said after a moment.

Her brows rose. "An interesting response."

I took a deep breath, forced myself to focus. Part of me still wanted to fight. But she wasn't my prey. She was a freaking weretiger, and for that reason alone I had to control myself. Not to mention, I didn't know how I'd do with the way the power of the condemned had left me feeling. "Sorry, I just... Thank you for helping me. You didn't have to do that."

"I know."

Everything about her from the way she sat—poised, but ready to launch—to the way she kept scanning her surroundings, spoke of a predator. Or rather, of a killer. At the same time, she managed to look comfortable as could be, one leg gathered beneath her exposing more than I cared to see. How she could act so casual sitting next to me after what I'd just done, I had no idea. And she smelled...aroused. The last part disturbed me for more than one reason. I had not meant to give her the wrong impression about my intentions where she was concerned, and the fact that she was aroused by what I'd just done, ick.

"I had to see more. I had to know more about you before I made my decision," she continued.

Maybe I'd get that fight after all. I hated how that excited me. I leaned away a bit, turning toward her so I'd be in a better position to defend myself. Clearly she had no qualms against killing. It wouldn't make much sense for her to attack me after helping me, but nothing about tonight's encounter made sense.

"Your decision?" I asked.

"Whether or not to try and kill you," she said in a matter-of-fact tone that made it sound like deciding what pair of shoes to wear.

My eyes widened. But that was the only reaction I allowed myself. Two hard beats of my heart were all it managed before I got it under control. The prospect of another fight so soon sent thrills through me that felt a bit like lightning. She would not be an easy opponent. But I didn't want to fight her, or so I kept telling myself. It didn't escape me that she'd said "try and kill you." Only a confident woman could admit that it wouldn't be a sure thing, confident and smart. It made it hard not to like her a little, even if she had come to kill me.

"You've come to kill me," I said in a level tone that allowed only a touch of disappointment to come through.

It wasn't her that I was disappointed in. I barely knew her. It was whoever had sent her. What I couldn't figure out was, how did my brother know a weretiger?

She shook her head. "No. I came to *decide* if I would try."

"And what did you decide?" I asked, resisting the urge to extend my claws. No sense in getting hostile if she didn't. Or so I told the anger ready to boil just beneath the surface of my control.

A rumbling vibrated from her as she leaned in. She straddled the branch and scooted closer to me. Her bright pink tongue wetted her lips as she slowly reached a hand out toward me. I held perfectly still as she wrapped a lock of my arrow-straight white-blond hair around her finger and lifted it to her nose. The rumbling in her chest deepened. By Odin, she was purring! Her eyes fluttered closed. One hard nipple as pink as her tongue brushed against my arm.

A huge smile parted her full lips when her eyes opened. "I decided I'd rather fuck you than fight you. You're far too intriguing to try to kill."

Leaning back, I put my hands up, palms out—no claws. "Whoa. I seemed to have given you the wrong impression." Would it offend her if I told her I didn't play for her team?

Her hand trailed across my leg. "Are you sure about that?"

I moved slowly back so I didn't provoke her. It took every ounce of control I had left not to give in to the rage. It would be so easy, but so wrong. Gaze trailing across her, I let her see me appreciate how beautiful she was. She had risked her life for me. I would not allow my unjustified anger to make me do something stupid.

"I'm sure. I'm supposed to marry another."

She sighed long and deep as she stood. Brows rising, she brushed her braids over her shoulder and arched her back, poking her breasts out. She had at least a cup size on me. Running her hands up her body, she watched me closely. My reaction must not have been what she'd hoped for because her bottom lip stuck out in a pout. "The best ones are always taken. Shame, we would have had fun."

I smiled. "Of that I have no doubt. Can I ask you something?"

"Of course, gorgeous."

"Why can't I feel your shifter power, and who sent you?"

Her face smoothed out into a stoic expression that looked all business. "That's two questions, and I can only answer one." She brushed a hand over the onyx hanging between her breasts. "This disguises the true nature of my power, making me appear human."

I wanted to touch it, and I might have if she weren't naked and hot for my body. "Magic?" I asked instead, awe tinging my tone.

"No, just tech designed by a very talented wereleopard. As for the second question, I can't divulge the name of my clients. That's confidential. But I can tell you they are probably not the only one sending assassins. And my client will probably send another when I tell them I'm refusing the job."

The word "assassin" made me twitch. I couldn't help it. An assassin sent after me, it fueled the rage almost as much as the presence of a condemned. "Why?"

"The Shifter Council met to discuss you. They're scared you'll unite the *varúlfur* under one leader, making them stronger than any of the other shifters. They're afraid of what you'll do with that strength," she said.

The Shifter Council, elected officials from each territory that represented the shifters in that area. They were the closest thing we had to a democracy that oversaw us all.

Did that mean it wasn't my brother that sent her? Lengthening claws forced me to open my hands. So what if the werewolves united? Like the forests all over the world, we'd been dwindling away long enough. Much longer and we could disappear altogether. Being from one of the races who was losing their natural habitat the fastest, the weretiger knew the fear that brought all too well. Which could be why she had come here to potentially kill me. With the steadily disappearing jungles, her kind had become so rare they were close to extinct.

Fury for the dying habitats filled me nearly to overflowing. But at the moment I had nowhere to direct it. My whole body shook with the effort of containing it. I couldn't exactly take it out on her. She had decided not to try and kill me despite the threat I posed to her kind.

I thought back to my jacket, my affiliation with the AVV. An umbrella pack was already somewhat like what they feared, a uniting of my kind. But I didn't lead them, no one person did. That was the whole point of the umbrella pack.

I held her golden gaze, and my tongue. There was so much I wanted to say in response, but not to her. She wasn't the one judging me and my motives. With a head thrust, she gestured to the next tree over.

"We should jump to a few trees, try not to touch down with our human feet until we're away from the kills," she said.

Relief eased my shaking. Action would help the anger, even if it wasn't fighting. The moment I nodded, she leaped. She cleared the twenty-five or so feet to the next tree with a limb big enough to support her and landed without even stumbling. While I could jump just as far, I was no weretiger, so I didn't even attempt to follow suit. Instead, I went for a smaller branch just above hers, and grabbed it with my hands. Momentum swung me almost too far, but my iron grip held me in place. When I dropped down onto the branch she stood on, I could feel the imprint of the bark pattern in my hands.

Wide gold eyes regarded me with delight. "Pretty damn good for a *varúlfur*," she said.

Using the excuse of scanning for the next tree, I looked away from her naked body. "Being the reaper has its benefits," I said.

That purring sound came from her again. "Too bad I won't get to find out the more interesting benefits," she said.

Rather than answer, I jumped for the next tree. We continued until we ran out of trees large enough, or close enough, to jump to. It took us close to the backside of the bar. We dropped to the ground just outside of the glow of neon lights. Pine needles made for a soft, nearly silent landing. I listened hard and heard nothing but the distant sounds of music and patrons. The scent of blood hung in the air, or maybe it was just stuck in my nose. One look at my weretiger company and I realized others seeing us come from the direction of a crime wasn't our only concern, or even the most pressing one. Her skin tone helped her blend well enough into the shadows of the trees, but the moment we stepped into the parking lot, someone was bound to notice she was naked. And covered in blood as I was, I wouldn't be able to step out there at all. Maybe it was dark enough.

Before I could ask, she started walking off to the left, which was thankfully not the direction of the parking lot. The moment I followed, the pressure of another werewolf washed over me. This one felt comfortable and familiar. The warmth of that power soothed my anger until all that remained of it was a fading mist. My power flared up, reaching out for it. Not realizing the weretiger had stopped, I nearly ran right into her.

It was all I could do not to growl. Damn this unpredictable temper! It made me feel like a teenager going through her first period again. Only times that by maybe a hundred.

A tall shadow moved out of the trees just ahead of us. The energy coming off that shadow soothed me like a balm. Green eyes with yellow flaring out from the pupils glinted with a predator's shine. Again, I smelled blood.

"Vidar," I said, a bit breathless in the wake of his effect on me.

Those eyes narrowed at the naked woman standing before me. His lips parted in a bit of a snarl. His power cracked and popped with anger. And if I didn't know better, I'd swear it hid a good amount of jealousy beneath it. The fact that he glared at the naked woman in front of me rather than ogled her filled me with relief. The need to fight flowed right out of me.

"Ayra? What's going on?" he demanded.

He sure sounded jealous. I shook the thought off and stepped out from behind the weretiger. "This is..." I looked back at her, cocking my head.

"Kali," she said.

Cautious of his tense posture, I approached Vidar. Fangs bared, he stared past me at Kali. "What are you doing with her? And why does she smell like a cat?" he demanded.

Part of me thrilled at seeing his alpha side, something he usually kept hidden. It made him even sexier, if that was possible. Another part wanted to bare my fangs and challenge him for acting like that. Or better yet, throw him down on the forest floor and have my way with him. That thought stirred my desire into a raging fire that sped up my breathing. Damn, I forgot about the survival instinct of mating that liked to sneak up on me after a kill.

"She's a weretiger who helped me take down two condemned," I said.

Blinking, his expression transformed from anger to shock. He met me in two great strides and took hold of my hands. Instantly, a soothing feeling washed over me. The last lingering effects of the power of the condemned faded like a poison leaving my system. Vidar's desperate gaze flicked to her for only a second before it traveled over my bloody body.

"Two? Are you all right?" The tenderness in his voice did things to me down deep. It also softened the mortar in the walls around my heart. The concern radiating off him made me think maybe, just maybe, it was for me and not the reaper.

This close I realized it wasn't just the blood on me I smelled. He was bleeding. Panic reared up in me. Gripping his hands tight, I leaned back to get a better look at him. The darkness hid too much of him from me. The scent came from his leg.

"Not a scratch. But I smell blood on you. What happened?" I asked.

"It's not bad. I'll tell you about it in the truck," he said in a soft voice. "Do we have bodies to take care of?" The question came so easily to his lips that it stole any words I had.

From behind us Kali answered instead. "No need. I have people on standby for that kind of thing."

At the approach of soft steps, I let go of his hands and turned. While we'd been talking, Kali had found her dress and put it on. She nodded. "Now I see why." She pressed a card into my hand. "If you ever need anyone killed, or want to tumble with the fairer sex, give me a call," she said in that purring voice of hers.

Her gaze took a leisurely trip up and down my body, then she winked before turning and walking away. The need to call after her, to correct her for mistaking Vidar for my intended, rose in me. But I couldn't get the words out.

"I'm not sure which of those proposals bothers me more. Leave it to you to find one of the races of cat shifters," Vidar said when she disappeared into the thicker trees.

My phone buzzed. Cringing as blood smeared on my shorts, I dug my phone out of my pocket. Unlocking it left a swipe of crimson across the screen. I had two texts, one from Calder, and one from Raul. Dread filled me. I clicked on the one from Raul first.

We have reason to suspect someone is sending assassins after you. Be careful.

"No shit," I mumbled. Then I saw the time of the text, almost half an hour ago. It probably went off while I'd been dancing. Wait, we? Who could he be talking about? Probably his old football buddies.

Taking a deep breath, I clicked on Calder's text.

You're getting warmer, little sister. But you never were very good at catching me. Do try to make it in time or it will take all the fun out of it.

As I read it, I heard his snide, condescending voice in my head. The fury that had been smoldering erupted into an inferno that threatened to burn me up from the inside.

Vidar's hand closed over mine, dousing the flames in a deluge of compassion that took my breath away. The soothing feeling intensified when my hand instinctively clutched his in return. It felt amazing, like a nice hot bath after a long day of training. Better than that. Not only could I think through the anger, but it began receding completely as if driven away by his energy.

"Who's it from?" he asked.

When I was able to draw breath in again, I answered, "I'll explain everything in the truck. We should get out of here, fast."

I would catch him. My brother was in for several surprises if he thought I was the same little girl he had bullied throughout my childhood.

Vidar nodded, then looked down at my body again. "Agreed, but I'll get your bike. You can't be seen like that. The truck is parked in the woods just down this way a bit, minus a windshield I had to kick out."

Clinging to his hand like a lifeline, I let him lead me away from yet another gruesome homicide I was responsible for. At least this time the only bodies were those of the condemned.

CHAPTER ELEVEN

VIDAR

T he hum of the tires helped me think, but I wasn't sure that was a
good thing.

Assassins from two different shifter races were after my little white wolf. Even though I'd seen it with my own eyes, I could barely believe it. I didn't want to believe it. But I had no choice. On top of that, her villain of an older brother had gone completely super villain bent on bringing *varúlfur* into the light, even if it meant all-out war. Ayra needed me now more than ever, and I felt like she was slipping further away by the moment.

Physically, she couldn't have been farther from me and still be in the truck. She sat sideways, knees pulled up beneath her, face leaned into the breeze from the open window as she read Calder's journal. Long locks of her straight, pale hair blew back, bringing the scent of river water and moss to me. Beneath it lay that distinct spicy scent that was hers alone. It was similar to a mixture of peppers and cloves with a touch of sweetness. While in Iceland those long years that was the one thing I had longed to smell.

Deeper beneath those scents lay that of blood. River water couldn't wash that out. I feared it was a smell that would always follow her now. Being part wolf, I didn't mind it. But I knew she hated it and didn't want it, and that made it difficult. What I wouldn't give for real powers so I could take her away from all of this like a superhero. But I wasn't even sure the big man in the red cape could fix this.

I focused on the rock music playing on the radio station, enjoying the sweet and sometimes harsh voice of The Pretty Reckless lead singer. The woman had some serious pipes. The song ended before I could embarrass myself by singing along. In its place came the voice of a radio announcer reading the news.

"Another wolf attack prompts a county-wide hunt by authorities—" I hit the search button to find a new station. The next one it landed on was spewing yet another account of the same news. I tried again. Same results. I gave up and switched to satellite radio that had no news. The evidence that Calder was successfully sowing the seeds of fear and hatred couldn't be denied. For now, innocent wolves were paying the price.

"Why, Calder, why?" I mumbled.

After a long while, Ayra answered. "Because he has a superiority complex. He thinks we're better than humans, and he thinks he is the best of us. My parents doted on him far too much, insisted he was of a Gods-favored bloodline, one that was meant to rule our kind. He bought into all that crap. Then he got pissed when I was born with the mark instead of it appearing on him. Now I think he's mad at Odin for not choosing him."

Bumps rose along my skin as a thought occurred to me. "You don't think he believes in that old story about a child of Fenrir killing Thor and starting Ragnarok, do you?"

"I think that's exactly what he believes, and what he wants."

She fell silent after that and for once, I didn't push. I shouldn't have dredged up all that negativity in the first place.

When my eyes started to get blurry, I followed the signs to a campground not far off the road. The place appeared deserted, without even a camp host. Under the cover of darkness, I pulled into the most remote spot I could find that was choked with trees. Pine boughs brushed the truck as I nosed it in so no one could see the dented hood.

Ayra set the leather-bound journal in her lap and looked over at me from beneath furrowed brows. "A pay campground. Do you think that's wise?" she asked.

I thrust my head in the direction of the nearby stone building that housed pay showers. "Thought you might like an actual shower." I sniffed at my arm. "I know I certainly need one."

She looked down at her hands. "Yes, thank you." Her flat, hollow tone almost sent shivers through me, and not the kind her voice normally gave me.

She opened the door and jumped out of the truck before I could say anything. I grabbed my backpack from the back and followed her. We set up camp in a silence so tense it was hard to breathe. Or maybe that was just the fear crushing my chest. Each moment of silence, I felt her pulling further and further away. Her battle fury had receded completely, but this was almost as bad in its own way. While I built a fire in the campground-provided L-shaped steel fire pit, she set her tiny tent up. The zippered front faced the fire, not the truck where I would be sleeping.

The only thing I could hear or smell within miles of us were squirrels, owls, and a badger. The lack of people helped me breathe a little easier, but only minutely so.

As Ayra stepped inside her tent and unfurled her sleeping bag, I looked down at my hands. They were clean from an earlier visit at a river, but I could still see the blood, smell it, feel it.

"I killed a man today," I said, more to myself than to her. After the words left my mouth I realized how stupid it was to be saying that to her, of all people. She had killed three now, and would have to kill many more.

This horrible feeling of guilt and shame was one she'd already felt and would feel who knew how many times more. Or was it? I didn't know if everyone who'd killed someone felt this way.

Ayra strode over and took my hands in hers. Her intense gaze made me regret ever learning to talk. I was such an idiot. This had to be so much worse for her. "I know it smells and feels like that *berserkr's* blood is on your hands, but it isn't," she said gently.

I stared at her, dumbfounded and speechless—a rare thing for me, the speechlessness, not the dumbfounded part.

She went on. "It's on my hands. His death is my fault, not yours. If I hadn't become the reaper, you wouldn't have had to do that. If you hadn't been with me..." She dropped my hands and looked away. Her energy heated up, became something well on its way to volatile.

I stood up, stepped around her, and blocked her path before she could walk away. "Don't think that way. I shouldn't have said that. It was stupid, thoughtless. You've already been through far worse."

She crossed her arms beneath her perky breasts. "You are many things, but never stupid or thoughtless. And what you had to do was just as bad as what I have to do. That's the problem," she said.

Moisture shone in her pretty blue eyes, making them look like jewels. I hated that this hurt her. I put my fingers over hers where they rested on her arm. She tightened her grip on herself so I couldn't slip my hand into hers.

"No, it isn't a problem. It's just...you know me, I like to talk everything to death. That's all it is, just me being me."

The way she wouldn't look at me made it hard to breathe. I took her by the shoulders. "I'll do it again if I have to. I don't regret protecting you."

Finally, she met my gaze, but the sorrow and determination in her eyes almost made me wish she hadn't. "But you do regret killing, as you should. You need to stay *you,* and being anywhere near me almost guarantees that won't happen. This is why I haven't chosen you. This is why I *can't* choose you."

She stepped back out of my grasp, and I was too stunned to stop her. "Being with me will ruin your life. And you'll get nothing out of it," she whispered.

"No," I said with such vehemence that she turned back to me, eyes wide. I had to swallow the lump in my throat before I could finish. "My life would be ruined without you in it."

Her mouth dropped open and she stared at me for a long moment, struggling for the words it seemed. "V... I..." I held a hand up and she fell silent.

"My energy, my power, banishes the rage that threatens to consume you before and after reaping. Don't think I haven't felt that. I can help you. I do help you. But that isn't the only reason I stick around. I need you...in my life too. And I don't mean the reaper. I mean my storm-loving, comic book reading, crazy mad skills dancer best friend." I clamped my jaw shut before I could say too much, before it could all pour out, before I couldn't take back what she may not want to hear.

Her surprise-filled eyes widened.

I wanted to tell her that my vow of celibacy ended the moment she chose a *verndari*, but I was forbidden to do so. The Order was very strict about allowing the *uppskera* to choose with a mind clear of desire or mating instinct. The choice had to be about what was best for the *uppskera*, not the woman. And as much as I wanted to disagree, I couldn't. Even if she did choose me, we could never mate because of Elí. But I was okay with that if it meant I got to remain at her side and help her.

I waved a hand. "Enough heavy stuff for tonight. Neither of us needs that right now. You go take a shower and I'll get something cooking on the fire," I said with false cheer.

The sweet smile she gave me held more sadness than joy. She nodded, grabbed her bag, and headed for the showers. An ache started to develop deep in my chest as I watched the way her little cutoffs hugged her ass when she walked off. It took a colossal amount of effort to force myself to look away. Even looking away I could still see her, as if her silhouette was burned into my retinas. That tiny, perfect package of white-blond hair and big blue eyes was my kryptonite.

I had to find a way to control my feelings for her and make this work. This wasn't about me and what I needed. While getting food from the truck, I tried not to look at my hands, to see the blood I imagined was still there, to smell it. Yes, I had a killed a man. That left me feeling horrible and hollow inside, like a part of me had died with him. It didn't matter that he had been an assassin. But Ayra didn't need to hear how bad I felt. I had a choice. I could walk away from all of this. She never could.

By the time she returned, I had two steaks browning on the grill I had put over the fire. She sat down on the log beside me, close enough that our legs touched. Years of monk training was all that allowed me to keep my heart rate normal. Trying to think when she was this close, well that was another matter altogether.

After a while she emitted a sound somewhere between a growl and a sigh. "The Shifter Council discussed me without inviting me to speak. I can't let that go."

"I agree."

She turned wide eyes to me. "You do?"

"Of course. That surprises you?"

She shrugged. "Well, yeah. You've always been kind of a peacekeeper, and confronting the Shifter Council is going to create a bit of havoc."

"More than a bit. It's going to create a *lot* of havoc. But it needs to be done. Gotham wouldn't meet to discuss the caped crusader without inviting him. Oh wait, I think that did happen in Volume..." I trailed off as I tried to recall the number. "It doesn't matter. What matters is that the assassination attempts stop. And I think confronting the Shifter Council is the only way to do that."

"All right, *verndari*, so how do we do it?" she asked with a smile.

Could that possibly mean she was actually considering me for her *verndari*? The look on her face made me think she was. The weight of the nine worlds started to lift from my shoulders. An idea began to take form. "We convince them to meet again, then we make sure you're in attendance."

"How? Even if we get them to meet, they do it virtually since they're all over the world. They could just shut me out, deny me access."

I forced my gaze away from her long legs and back to the fire. "We know a hacker that can make sure that doesn't happen. If we can force them to meet, he can guarantee they don't shut you out."

"There's a catch. I can hear it in your voice."

She was too sharp for my own good. "There are a few catches," I admitted.

Sitting up straight, she studied me. I struggled to find the words and couldn't.

"Don't make me tickle it out of you like I did when we were kids."

The thought of her hands all over me, fingers digging into me, body straddling me, it was too much. I shut my eyes tight. Measured breaths kept my body from reacting, but just barely. She grabbed hold of my side and wiggled her fingers against my muscles. Eyes flying open wide, I gasped and squirmed. Beautiful lips smiling and open in a laugh captivated me, her other hand grabbed my other side and tickled me without mercy. Heat filled me as I laughed and squirmed, powerless to escape, and not wanting to anyway.

Caught in the throes of my ridiculous ticklishness, I fell over the log onto the pine needle-covered ground. Like I had imagined—and feared—she followed me over it and straddled me. The moment her legs landed on either side of mine I forgot how to breathe. My ticklishness overrode my self-control, leaving me helpless against her. I had to stop her.

Guilt and jealousy over Elí stabbed me in the heart. The words of my oath rang in my head. The warning of the priest of the Order replayed like a bad dream. If a potential *verndari* was discovered to have had sex with the *uppskera* before her choosing, he would be banished from the Order. Banishment didn't just mean shunning. It meant being hunted down like a dog and slaughtered. Extreme, yes, but we were Vikings. Extreme was our thing.

I grabbed her hands and pulled her down to my chest in an attempt to move her pelvis away from mine. Her hard nipples poked into my chest. It wasn't cold out tonight, and even if it had been, we were *varúlfur*, we had a resistance to cold. That meant she was aroused. Now that I thought about it, concentrated a bit, I could smell her desire, feel it in her power. It filled not only her power, but her intense eyes as well, eyes that hovered only inches above me. Her body relaxed against me. Our groins touched, the intense heat of her sex scorching my cock. A pale pink tongue darted out to lick her lips. Gods how I wanted to do the same.

Odin help me. This was a bad idea, the worst. Her eyes started to slide closed as her face descended to mine. Unable to find the will to resist, I closed my eyes as well. Her breath touched my lips, entered my mouth as I parted it. Then she was suddenly gone. Her slight weight disappeared from atop me. Eyes snapping open, I sat up. She stood on the opposite side of the fire, chest heaving with deep breaths, fists opening and closing.

"I shouldn't have done that," she said in a breathy voice.

The *verndari* blood in me wanted to help her in any way I could, while the alpha in me wanted to take her, lay claim to her. She was so willing, it was hard to resist. But that willingness was just the aftereffects of the reaping. Wasn't it? She was engaged to another man.

I forced myself to respond. "It's okay. The reaping does that to you. I understand."

I wanted to be all things to her. I wanted to steal her back from Elí. But I couldn't bring myself to say that. And I had taken an oath. Hiding behind the oath wasn't very superhero-like of me, but it was the foundation of all my training. And it was a death sentence not to.

Hands covering her face, she shook her head. Anger spiked within her power, prickling out from her to dance over me. "Gods, even I don't understand. I thought I knew what I was, and how I was going to deal with that. Now, all I know is I could never do that to you, V. I know how much your oaths and honor mean to you."

"They don't mean as much to me as you do," I said, keeping my voice soft to try and hide the vulnerability in it.

She took a few steps around the fire toward me. The gentle look she gave me hurt more than a punch to the balls would have. I knew rejection when I saw it. "You mean the *uppskera*."

"No. I mean you." The words came quick and easy, without a thought.

She squeezed her eyes shut tight for a moment. Her power went cold, as if a wall had gone up between it and me.

"I will not destroy something that is such a huge part of you by making you break your vow. You are still my friend." She bowed under the weight of more left unsaid.

Rather than argue like my heart wanted me to, I listened to my head and gave her a smile instead. "Even after my radio silence the last four years?"

She bent and pulled something out of the bag beside the small cooler. Brows rising, she slapped a spatula into my hand. "Always. But I may have to reconsider if you overcook those steaks any more than you already have."

"Oh, damn!"

I plopped down onto the log and gave the neglected steaks my full attention. The tangy, sweet scent of steak sauce filled the air as I poured it onto the meat in an attempt to return some moisture to it.

She grabbed a pop from the cooler and sat down beside me, causal as could be, as if we hadn't just been about to kiss. Fire blazed to life along my skin.

"So what are these catches to your plan?"

The words doused my desire completely. "My friend who can help us is a computer genius with his own renewable energy company," I began.

"I don't see the catch in that."

It took three deep breaths to steel myself enough for the next part. "He's a *draugr*."

Her unopened pop plummeted to the ground with a plunk that ensured it would explode upon opening. She grabbed my arm. Her eyes grew wide enough to impress a manga artist.

"A vampire? An honest to Odin vampire? For real?" The wonder in her tone made me smile.

"For real."

"I thought they were extinct!"

I stood and walked toward the cooler. She followed right on my tail. I grabbed two steel camp plates, silverware, and a bag of chips. When I handed her one set, she took it without even looking.

"They almost are," I said.

I placed a steak carefully on her plate, ensuring she felt its weight before I pulled the spatula out from under it.

"How do you know one?"

Cringing at how overdone my steak was, I put it on my plate and sat down. "I met him in Iceland last year."

Questions began to pour out of her faster than I could ever hope to answer, and that was saying something. One followed another, and another, and another, with barely a breath in between. She was beautiful when she was like this, smiling, eyes wide with wonder, voice filled with excitement. Caught up in her delight, I answered when I could. Mostly she rambled on in wonder while I listened. This was one role reversal I didn't mind at all, especially seeing how happy I had made her. For that, I would endure anything, even the bluest balls in the history of blue balls.

For the first time since I'd come back to the States, I believed things might actually work out.

Too bad taking her into the den of one of the most dangerous paranormal creatures of all time was such a horrible idea. Yes, this man was my friend, but there was no telling whether or not he would see her as the threat the shifter races did. And if he did, we might be in for the fight of our lives. So much for me protecting her.

CHAPTER TWELVE

AYRA

"From the seed of Loki we sprang, to become the warriors of Odin."
~Uppskera Journals

Even halfway through the next day I couldn't stop thinking about the vampire. I'd never imagined such a wonder still existed in this world. Thinking about it was easier than thinking about Vidar and the way my will crumbled a bit more with each sweet word he said to me. He needed me, not the reaper, me. And Odin help me, I believed him.

But if I went down that road, my family would disown me—and I didn't hate them all, just my brother and parents. I'd be dishonored, my word worth nothing. The Arnoddr pack would likely shun me, and the other packs of Hemlock Hollow might follow suit. That town was my home. Pack was life. What would I do without a home and any chance at a pack?

Traveling through the rolling fields of Idaho farmland gave me nothing but time to think. But time was running out. Dust from the dirt road rolled up off the front wheels, forcing me to put my window up. My cousin's house lay only a few miles down this road. I knew I should have been thinking about what to say to him, but my thoughts lay elsewhere.

Mostly they lay on Vidar and how scorching he looked in the clingy maroon muscle shirt he wore today. It lay across his pecs and six-pack in a way I longed to. The way he laughed, joked, and sang under his breath to the radio took me back to our childhood. The good parts of it, at least. Even if it really was me he wanted to be near instead of the reaper, could I let him live this life? Not even having to fight and kill a *berserkr* had driven the man off. He had the stones for it, that was for sure.

Was it possible to have my best friend as my *verndari*, to travel with him, fight side by side, and still stay true to the man I promised to marry? I wasn't sure. The bigger question was: was that what I wanted?

I had to turn my mind to the other fascinating distractions, or I would go mad.

"So they really don't have to drink blood," I said.

V smiled at me across the cab. "Not exclusively, but at least a little, yes. If they don't their sensitivity to light gets stronger and they get weaker and weaker until they die. It also prolongs their life and heightens their senses and strength, so most drink it regularly."

"Wow." That still blew me away. The fact that he kept answering the same questions over and over again, and not getting aggravated at me, revealed that he might actually have superpowers. I could handle having a *verndari* with superpowers. So long as it was him.

"And you're sure they're not immortal?"

"Pretty positive. Evan told me they have a similar lifespan to ours."

So many of the myths weren't true. That didn't take much of the wonder out of their existence for me, though. "Evan...what did you say his last name was?"

"McDougall."

"Not a Norse vampire, then."

"Nope, Scottish. Though the Norse did settle there, so in a roundabout way, he kind of is."

"Does he wear a kilt? What was he doing in Iceland?" Each question made him smile. His smile drove away the dark.

"He didn't wear one any time I saw him. And he was attending Reykjavik University."

Bummer about the kilt. I was dying to know if they really wore nothing under them. More questions sparked to life, so many of his answers did that. "Was he studying renewable energy as well?"

"Yep."

"An earth-conscious vampire." The idea fascinated me.

"Sure, why not?"

I shrugged. "Considering their prey, I would think an urban hunting ground would be more their style."

He cocked his head in that cute way he did when he was thinking. "Good point."

The burgundy shirt drew my eyes again. I couldn't stop thinking about how good that body had felt beneath mine last night, how beautiful his green and yellow eyes had looked gazing up at me, filled with desire. I forced myself to think of Elí's robin's egg blue eyes, the adoration that filled them when they looked at me, the gentleness of his touch. It didn't work.

So I kept asking questions. It helped to focus on something besides how much I wanted to leap across the cab of the truck and ride Vidar. I didn't realize how hard I'd been staring at him until we turned down a rutted dirt road with only a sprinkling of gravel left on it.

The scents of feathers and bird shit blew in through the window. Nose wrinkling up, I covered my face with my hand at the same time Vidar cursed in Icelandic. Another smell mixed with it that I couldn't quite place. Along the right side of the road rose a large birdhouse. The cooing and screeching of doves came from within. I'd forgotten how much of a racket the things could make. Why anyone associated them with peace, I did not know. The fear and anxiety the birds gave off left just as bad of a taste on the back of my tongue as their scent.

I scanned the cornfield behind the birdhouse. The green shoots stood no more than waist high, allowing me to see right over them and down the rows. Nothing more nefarious than an ugly scarecrow stood among them. That I could see.

"Your cousin keeps pigeons?" Vidar asked as he rolled up his window.

"He's an extreme survivalist and a conspiracy theory nut. He thinks birds with written messages are the only way to communicate safely."

The way Vidar's eyes widened made me think maybe I hadn't prepared him properly for my cousin. The reaper line wasn't exactly a stable one.

"In that case, it makes sense why he and Calder got along so well," he said.

The truck eased to a stop.

A tangled mess of willow, oak, and fir trees engulfed a ragged single-wide trailer that made my hunting cabin look like four-star accommodations in comparison. An air conditioner clung to one window like a growth, while another window had been boarded over. Tin foil covered all the others. An old, rusted Harley circa 1920 poked out from under a hill of blackberry briars to the right of the house. To the left, the frame of a '73 Fatboy sat up on blocks with various parts strewn on the dead grass around it. The sight was a stark reminder that my family didn't share the wealth among its less desirable members.

The stench of stray dog washed over me as I opened my door and stepped out into the weed-choked lawn. Well, at least that told me he still lived here, despite the deserted look of the place.

"I see he isn't in good with your parents," Vidar observed.

"Nope. He's mad as a hatter, and you know how my parents feel about imperfection."

Of all people, he knew best. Throughout our childhood my parents had done everything they could to make me stop being friends with him. His gentle mannerisms and love of comic books had convinced them he'd never amount to anything they deemed worthy. They never thought he'd actually follow in his father's footsteps and become a cop, and they definitely didn't believe he was alpha material. They were clueless idiots. If they saw him now they'd see exactly how wrong they had been.

"He sounds charming," Vidar said.

I held back a shudder. "As a cobra. Don't forget, he and Calder have always been close."

He took a step forward. I grabbed his hand and pulled him to a stop. "Careful. Smell that?"

Eyes closing, he breathed in deep through his nose. "I smell a lot of things, none of them good." His nose wrinkled up.

The scents of metal and darker things dotted my cousin's yard like the nasty little surprises they were. But then, I had experience with them. Vidar didn't as far as I knew.

"Wait, what is *that* smell?" he asked. "It's all over the yard."

"Mines."

Claws pricked the back of my hand as his control slipped ever so slightly. "How do you know what those smell like?"

"He and Calder share a fondness for things that hurt people." I tried to keep my voice flat, emotionless, but a touch of old fear came through.

Wide eyes scanning the property, Vidar muttered, "And I thought my family had problems."

"Oh, they do," I assured him with a wink.

He laughed and bent down to bump my shoulder with his. "All right, we stick together and I follow your lead."

"There will be trip wires and other nasty surprises. Stay alert," I said.

"Will do." The way his voice dropped an octave and got quieter made muscles low in my body clench tight. Telling myself it was wrong to react to him in such a way didn't stop it from happening.

That terrible wet dog scent came strongest from near the trailer. The slightest creek of metal shifting under weight told me exactly where he lay.

"Oliver, get down here, you son of a bitch, or I'll come up there and get you," I hollered.

Louder creaks of metal came from the rooftop. A spiky mess of blond hair poked above the blackberry briars that had grown up over the roof of the trailer. Over the sweet scent of overripe berries I could smell the metal and gunpowder from the rifle he held in his hands.

"*Ayra, ert petta pú?*"

Vidar made a snorting sound. "No, it's a body snatcher with her scent and voice," he mumbled beneath his breath.

Eyes wide, I drew my fingers across my throat in the universal "cut it out" motion. Vidar's top lip on one side rose along with a brow. I mouthed the words "he'll believe you."

"And leave that rifle there so it doesn't go off when you jump," I called up.

Ignoring the last part, Oliver jumped from the roof of the trailer with the rifle still in hand. He landed ten feet or so away and wove through the weed-choked yard in an erratic pattern to reach us. A pair of worn-out camouflaged cargo pants hung on his gangly, long legs, and a dirty olive-green T-shirt made his slight chest look caved in. Only my cousin could make six-foot-three inches look slight and frail. High cheekbones reached sharp points below the corner of ice blue eyes narrowed in suspicion.

He greeted me in Icelandic, which roughly translated to an insult to my mother, which meant he believed it was actually me. Our mutually terrible relationships with our parents was something we had bonded over as kids. Though I was so not the hugging type—thanks to said family issues—I hugged him back when he embraced me.

When he finally let me pull away, I told him, "English, Oliver. My Icelandic is rusty. Nothing to worry about, he's one of us." I thrust my head up at Vidar.

Oliver's gaze narrowed and he sniffed the air. "Smells like it. But Ayra, he's black, there is no way he's Norse," he said in a chiding tone.

I let a little growl slip out that snapped Oliver's attention to me. He hunched in on himself a bit and stared at my feet. "Of course he is. This is Vidar Balderson."

Submission melting away, Oliver looked back up at Vidar with wonder-filled eyes. "But he's so big. You were just a skinny little thing. How did you grow so big? You must tell me! Oh how I long to be big and strong."

And there was the crazy.

Letting his rifle drop to the ground, Oliver dashed to Vidar's side and began circling him, looking him up and down. Vidar gave me a sideways glance. I shrugged and retrieved the rifle. Even though the barrel had been facing the trailer when it fell, I said a prayer of thanks to Frigg that it hadn't gone off.

Vidar cleared his throat. "Uh, I eat a lot of protein and work out regularly."

Mumbling to himself, Oliver poked Vidar here and there. "I suppose I could try this. I suppose I *should* try this." A quiet growl sounded from Vidar. Letting out a yip, Oliver jumped back.

"Oliver, I need to find Calder," I said.

Focused as he was on Vidar, he didn't hear me. Short on patience and time, I growled long and loud, pouring a touch of my power into it. Oliver yelped as though I'd kicked him. His head whipped in my direction as he went down on one knee. He exposed his neck to me. Guilt wracked me. Though he was close to Calder, Oliver had always been nice to me. Many times he'd tried to play mediator between us.

"*Uppskera, uppskera*, I forgot you're the *uppskera* now!" he cried. "How could I forget that? My own cousin, the *uppskera*! Such an honor to belong to a bloodline blessed by Odin himself."

His mumblings turned to whimpers as I strode up and put a gentle hand on his shoulder. "Calder is in trouble. I need to find him," I said.

He nodded with manic enthusiasm. "No and yes," he said, perfectly convinced of each answer.

Arguing would get me nowhere, so I didn't bother. "Where is he?"

His answer came in a rush. "Oh I don't know. But he did say you'd come looking and that you needed to find him in due time. He said that, yes he did."

I took his hand and pulled him to his feet. "Did he tell you how I could do that?"

Grinning at me, he nodded. He took off running for the trailer in yet another erratic pattern that made him look like a headless chicken. The moment he thundered up the rickety steps to the trailer I unloaded the rifle and pocketed the bullets.

Warm energy washed over me as Vidar moved close enough that our arms touched.

"You weren't kidding about the crazy part," he whispered.

"His mom shifted when she was pregnant with him," I explained.

Vidar gasped. "Seriously? And he survived? Wow. The kid is a lot stronger than he thinks he is."

I nodded. "Yep. Too bad about the bat-shit crazy part. But he's sweet and has a good heart."

Vidar did that one brow-raise thing I never could seem to do. Tingles spread from my navel down. Gods I loved it when he did that. "And he and your brother are close?"

I shrugged as if my hormones weren't kicking the tires and lighting the fires. "He's my brother's one and only soft spot."

A harrumphing noise of disbelief came from Vidar. He opened his mouth to say something, but Oliver came sprinting back out of the trailer, screen door slamming behind him. After a jig through his maze of landmines, Oliver rejoined us. He practically bounced on the balls of his feet as he handed me a postcard.

"He said you would come, and he was right. Calder is always right. And he said to give this to you when you got here. Said it would show you where to go," he said.

The postcard had a picture of mountains and vineyards with the words *Visit Beautiful Hood River* across it. On the back fifteen words were scrawled in my brother's unmistakable sloppy writing.

Come join the fight. It would be a shame if we got started without you.

I handed the card to Vidar. "Where's Hood River?" Vidar scowled down at the card.

"In the right direction." Prickles of apprehension worked their way down my spine. Coincidences weren't something I believed in, especially not where my brother was concerned. "He's been leading me to Oregon all along." I looked to Vidar. "Is it possible he knows your friend?"

"Not likely. But there's definitely a reason." Rather than spill it, he looked pointedly from me to Oliver. Then he glanced back at the truck. "Can you carry everything you brought on your bike?"

"Always." At some point during this trip I'd expected to go it on my own, which was part of why I put the hard side luggage on my bike and brought my tent and sleeping bag. But I had a feeling that wasn't what Vidar had in mind.

He looked to Oliver. "Do you have one of those that runs?" he asked with a nod in the direction of the Harley frame up on blocks.

A sly smile worked its way onto Oliver's face. "Oh, yes. I have two and a half."

Lines of confusion formed between Vidar's eyes. I got where he was going with this and interjected. "We need one good running one, Oliver. To help us reach Calder."

Vidar pointed a thumb over his shoulder. "I'll trade you that truck for it."

Eyes narrowing at the truck with suspicion, Oliver cocked his head. "But it has electronics."

"Yes, it does. But it's worth a lot, even dented up like that. You could sell it," Vidar said.

No kidding. The thing was probably still worth a good chunk more than anything Oliver had. But Vidar was making the right call. The truck's tire tracks were at the scene of a crime.

"For the cause, Oliver," I pressed.

Letting out a long, dramatic sigh, Oliver beckoned for us to follow and started for the trailer. After exchanging a glance, we followed him carefully through the minefield that passed for his front yard. He took us around the side of the house to a large metal shed with a roll-up door secured with three different kinds of locks. I gave Vidar a long, hard look as Oliver worked on opening the locks.

I mouthed, *Are you sure?*

He nodded.

The roll-up door rattled as it opened to reveal what felt like a portal to another world, or at least another garage. Rubber coated the floor in black and white squares that made it look like a huge, spotless chessboard. Stainless steel cabinets and shelves lined one wall. Along the other stood three bikes, one in an organized state of repair with parts lined up along a nearby shelf. The other two lay hidden beneath covers. From the shelves to the floor, the place was immaculate.

A gasp and curse from Vidar made me smile. I had known what lay on the other side of the door and it still shocked me. What lay beneath those covers was anyone's guess. Oliver went through bikes too fast to ever be sure. He grabbed the gray cover on the closest bike and pulled it free. Folding the cover neatly without looking, he stepped back away from the bike, not out of reverence, but out of something that smelled like fear.

The sleek V-Rod Harley, all decked out in black, was a shock even to me. On each tank the Norse compass of knotted runes and wolf's head were painted in silver and white. Despite my distaste for the brand's tendency to leak oil wherever they sat for any extended period of time, I was impressed, so impressed I found myself walking toward it alongside Vidar. We both reached hands out to stroke it at the same time, our fingers brushing over one another.

From Oliver's wide eyes and the way he took a step back, you'd think we were touching a fiend from Muspelheimr. "Electronics for electronics. It's a good enough trade, I guess," he said.

Though I kept my expression neutral, inside I cringed. Even damaged, Vidar's truck was worth over twice what this bike was. The look of boyish joy on his face made it clear he didn't share my reservations.

He walked around it, eyes taking in every inch of it as if it were a woman. I actually found myself getting kind of jealous.

Making humming noises to himself, Oliver wandered deeper into the shop and began rummaging through the cabinets. A few moments later he returned with a set of leather saddlebags, four straps so clean they had to be brand new, and an envelope. "Here, these go with it."

When Vidar took the saddlebags and straps, Oliver opened the envelope and laid the title on the counter. He pulled a pen from his back pocket and signed it before handing it to Vidar as well. "At least the truck won't have to sit in my shop until I can sell it."

Once Vidar got the bags on the bike, he pushed it out into the afternoon sun. Oliver and I trailed along behind him, Oliver to keep distance between himself and the bike, and me to watch Vidar's fine form as he walked away. Unfortunately, Oliver only let him get a few steps before he dashed in front of him to take the lead and guide us safely back out.

"Where did you even get a bike like this?" I asked.

"Calder got it for me. Wanted me to learn to trust electronics. But there aren't electronics on Asgard."

I touched his arm as we stopped beside the truck. "It'll be a long time before you make it to Asgard."

Shoulders rolling inward, he shook his head. "That's what Calder said. But you're wrong. Ragnarok is coming. That's why you woke up."

Oh, no. If I didn't get him off this roll we'd never get out of here. I shot Vidar a desperate look. He gave me a subtle nod.

"Well, no time to waste. I'd better get you that title," Vidar said as he opened the passenger door of the truck.

My cousin prattled on about the end of the world while Vidar and I unloaded my bike from the back of the truck. In only moments we had our things loaded onto the two bikes. I was impressed by how little Vidar kept in his truck. His bulky sleeping bag took up a lot more space on his rear seat than my compact one and tent put together, but we made everything fit well enough.

Oliver's eyes widened as I hugged him goodbye. "It's not just my cousin hugging me, it's the *uppskera*. The *uppskera*!" He literally trembled with delight as he started on a tangent about me being chosen by Odin.

I held a finger against his lips. "And the *uppskera* has to get back to her mission. You take care of yourself. Stay safe. And sell that truck as fast as you can."

Eyes growing big, he nodded like a bobblehead. The moment I moved my finger he began to ramble again. Before he could build up any steam, I turned away and walked back toward the bikes.

My attention gravitated toward Vidar as he threw a leg over the Harley and sat down. That one little movement threatened to crumble the carefully built walls around my desire. Seeing him straddling the bike was too much. His biceps and triceps flexed ever so slightly as he wrapped his hands around the handlebars. In only a pair of shorts and a T-shirt, he wasn't exactly properly equipped to ride—well not a motorcycle at least. But he still looked damn fine. I had to turn away as he fired it up.

The thing was so loud we were going to have to get him a Bluetooth-ready helmet just so we could talk while riding. Laughter so delighted it seemed boyish despite its deep baritone sounded within all that motor noise. It made me look back at him against my better judgment. The smile on his face combined with the happiness oozing from his energy made it impossible to draw my next breath. How I was going to keep up my resistance to him all the way to Oregon, I had no idea. I had a feeling I was in for the toughest—and most stimulating—five hours of my life.

CHAPTER THIRTEEN

VIDAR

Riding the bike made me feel like a superhero—even if it was loud as the thunderstorms of Helheimr. It was worth it. With the wind blowing through my clothes and the yellow lines zipping by so fast they were reduced to a blur even to my eyes, it felt like I was flying. I'd forgotten how much fun riding a motorcycle could be. Four long years had passed since I'd been on one. The reason for that rode alongside me, looking like the ghost of a ninja in her gray riding gear, white helmet, and white jacket, gripping that pearly white BMW between her thighs. What I wouldn't do to be that bike...

We had grown up riding motorcycles together. When I turned sixteen, I bought a pair of Hondas from a wrecking yard and we'd fixed them up. Aside from martial arts, it was the one non-geeky thing I'd been into as a kid. But I'd always had to refer to a manual. Not Ayra. She was a natural when it came to the workings of a motorcycle. Back then she'd looked hot enough to melt titanium in her short jean shorts bent over a bike with a wrench. Now, leaning on the tank, hand gripping the open throttle tight, she made me want to explode.

No matter how fast we rode, the stench of that birdhouse at the end of Oliver's driveway stuck with me. It must have gotten into my nose. An hour later I still smelled it. Before us the tree-lined road rose up to a hilltop where the sun seemed to be hanging in wait. As we crested the hill the light hit me full on and rendered my sunglasses useless. I felt like that superhero with eyesight that cut everything it crossed like a laser, only in reverse. The squeal of brakes and rubber yanked my attention over to Ayra.

Something huge and feathered cut right in front of her. And I mean huge—far too large to be any bird I had ever heard of. Then there was the problem of the human body attached to the wings. My head couldn't wrap around what I was seeing, probably because it was too busy bringing the Harley to a screaming halt. Ayra wove her bike around the winged person, not once, but twice, as it dove toward her again. She whipped around in a tight circle and came back toward me.

The winged person—a man with brown and black hair that matched his multi-colored wings—dove for her again. Ayra swerved onto the grassy shoulder of the road. She knelt on her seat and yanked the front break so hard the bike did a reverse wheelie and launched her into the air. Claws extended, she collided with the winged man and bore him to the ground. Her helmet clattered to the concrete near my feet. Feathers and blood flew through the air.

I jumped from my bike and ran toward the chaos. Before I could get there, the winged man broke free and took to the air with two beats of his massive wings. He made it less than twenty feet off the ground when another winged person collided with him. Their screeching made me want to bury my head in the ground. Enduring the pain, I ran to Ayra's side. She stood, chest heaving, fangs bared, growling up at the two winged creatures. They started to fall—straight for us. I scooped Ayra up and dashed out of the way.

Feathers poofed up from the impact of the two hitting the ground. The newcomer knelt on the chest of the one who had attacked Ayra, talon-adorned hands around his throat. This one was a female. Long golden-brown braids hung down around a sharply featured face that was lovely in a fierce way. Golden-brown wings that had to span at least fifteen feet, attached at her shoulder blades, twitched and moved. Many of the feathers were over two feet long.

Ayra literally vibrated with tension. I kept my arms wrapped around her waist, not wanting her to leap into the fray again. Not yet.

"Move and I will end you," the female warned the male she knelt on.

Ayra growled, but thankfully didn't struggle. "Get off him and I'll end him now," she said.

The female looked at us. Her eyes were the pure blue of a completely cloudless sky. The look in those eyes was apologetic. The golden wings arched around the male like a raptor hiding its prey from other predators. "I am sorry, *Uppskera*, but I can't do that. He has to face a power even higher than yours for this."

I had half-expected her to sound otherworldly, ethereal, but she just sounded like a woman.

"You know what I am," Ayra said.

The winged female turned her head just enough to look at Ayra and me out of the corner of her eye. "Of course, but I think you know what I am as well. I apologize for this one's conduct."

The male bucked beneath her, his massive wings flexed enough to raise him a good foot off the ground. She thrust a hand onto his chest and pushed him back down.

"Don't apologize for me, Halley. If you had the sense Odin gave a raven you'd help me kill her," the male snapped.

Halley slapped the male across the face. "Blasphemous idiot. She's an agent of Odin."

He pushed himself up onto his elbows and hissed into her face. "Like Hel. She is *varúlfur*. They're born of Fenrir and by their very nature they can't be agents of Odin. The things she did, my birds saw. They showed me. She has to die."

She gripped his neck and squeezed. "You've been using the birds to watch her? You bastard. They aren't your pawns." Her wings fluttered with what might have been anger. "Retract," she commanded. Her talons dug into his flesh. Tiny lines of blood started to run down his neck. "Now."

At first his hands gripped hers, pulling at them, but in moments they fell away. He gasped until he couldn't gasp anymore. Being bigger than her, it surprised me that he couldn't overpower her. His wings drew in, flowing much like our forms did when we shifted, then they abruptly disappeared. He went limp and hit the ground with a thud. Halley rolled him over, tweaked his arm up at an awkward angle, and looked over at us.

"I don't suppose you guys have a rope?" she asked.

"I can do one better than that," I said.

I dashed back to my Harley and grabbed the handcuffs out of my saddlebags. Ayra's brows only raised a bit while the winged woman's eyes widened considerably. Donning an innocent look, I shrugged. "My dad and brothers are *lögreglu*." Her shocked expression didn't change by the time I reached her. "Cops," I clarified.

The hint of a smile pulled at her lips. "I got that. I understand a bit of Icelandic. It's just..." A full smile bloomed as she shook her head.

She took my handcuffs and slapped them on properly with ease, despite the fact they were hinged instead of chain cuffs. Most civilians struggled with the hinged cuffs since they weren't very common outside of law enforcement. "You're pretty handy with a pair of cuffs," I said, instantly regretting the words because of how dirty they sounded.

I let a sideways glance slide in Ayra's direction. Was her face red with a touch of jealousy or was it just from fighting?

"That might have come across wrong," I said.

Halley waved a hand as she hauled the now very human-looking man to his feet. She flapped her great wings once, then folded them in. As they drew in, they disappeared. The process looked similar to shifting.

"Don't sweat it. And I'm a firefighter pilot, so I've done my fair share of handcuffing. We should move this off the road," she said.

Because being a winged woman who could make her wings disappear wasn't cool enough by itself. Had it not been for Ayra, I might have fallen in love right then and there.

Ayra appeared at our sides, silent as a ghost and twice as haunting.

"And you're also a valkyrie, aren't you?" she asked.

That exact question had been burning the back of my tongue, but I hadn't been able to build up the nerve to ask. Valkyries were the stuff of bedtime stories, creatures I always hoped were real, but never imagined I'd ever really meet.

We walked off the road, Halley dragging the man with impressive ease. Firefighters had to be able to pull their own weight—literally. And I had a feeling this one could do that and much more. The fact that something as amazing as a valkyrie could have a day job blew my mind.

"I am. We both are," she said, motioning to her captive.

I rolled my Harley off the road, remembering it only because I nearly ran right into it. I couldn't stop staring at Halley's back, wondering where her wings had gone, how they worked. The handcuffed man mumbled to himself about blasphemous heathens and Ragnarok. He sounded as crazy as his wide eyes made him look. Those eyes fixed on Ayra. A protective urge swelled up in me. I stepped in between them. His hatred burned with real heat.

"She has to die. She will bring about Ragnarok. You have to kill her," he said.

Growling, I bared my four fangs at him. "Not only do I think she's undefeatable, but anyone who tries to get to her will have to go through me. And they won't make it."

Face scrunching up in frustration, the man shook his head. "Ragnarok, you idiot. The end of this world!"

Ayra got in his face. "I would never kill Thor. I'm loyal to Odin. Just because we're descended from Fenrir doesn't mean my kind are evil or all beholden to Loki."

The man flinched and tried to draw back against Halley.

"I didn't say you would do it. I said you'd cause it," he responded in a harsh whisper.

With a grunt, Halley jerked him back and turned him away from us. "I'm sorry. He's one of those extremist zealots, completely crazy. And he's going to pay for attacking you and revealing our kind to those of this world." She said the last to him, all but hissing it into his ear.

The man sneered at her. "If you think he'll side with you, you're a bigger idiot than I thought. He banished their kind here to protect his son, who is our lord, our prince! Or did you forget?"

A loud smack sounded as she backhanded him. "Shut up! The only other thing worse than letting one of this world see us is telling them about us."

The man shrugged, seemingly oblivious that the slap had been hard enough to leave a raised red print on his cheek. "Won't matter if we kill them. You care too much about this world and the creatures in it, them especially."

"You don't care enough!"

I watched in awe, taking in their sharp features, slender forms, and swift mannerisms. "Holy shit, valkyries are real," I whispered.

Ayra rolled her bike over next to where I stood. "I know. Crazy, right?" she whispered to me.

The awe in her voice, her wide eyes, took away the haunted look that had clung to her since I'd been back.

I leaned close to her. "And you kicked one's ass."

A smile lit her face up like the clouds in a lightning storm. Gods, she was beautiful. "Not quite. We were interrupted."

"But you would have."

Her smile grew. I wasn't just humoring her to see that smile. She would have kicked his ass. I could tell by the way the fight had been going and by what I knew of her skills. It didn't surprise me. She had been amazing before she became the *uppskera*. Now she was as otherworldly as these valkyrie.

Halley's head turned from side to side, her gaze scanning the tree-lined road. A moment later her wings materialized out of her back. "If you'll excuse me for a minute, I've got to turn this guy over to the authorities. There's a meadow to the northeast of here. Meet me there. We need to talk."

"Of course," Ayra answered before I could even open my mouth.

Halley nodded to Ayra and unfurled her huge wings. Two loud snaps like a tarp whipping in the wind sounded, and the valkyrie took to the air. Golden-brown wings blocked out the sun for a moment, and then they were just gone like a spaceship engaging warp drive. Nothing I had ever seen could compare to it, not the waterfalls of Iceland, not the full moon rituals of *varúlfur*, not even meeting a real vampire.

...

Finding the clearing wasn't the problem, getting the Harley there was. I had to all but carry it most of the way. The thing got heavy, even for me. I tried to imagine the valkyrie feathers we had gathered and placed in the saddlebags making it lighter. We stopped beneath a huge pine tree that had to be a hundred years old from the size of its trunk. The shade it offered from the summer heat was just as welcome as the trunk to lean on.

"Valkyries are real," Ayra said again.

Between the two of us we'd used that phrase in one form or another at least five times now. It still made me smile. "Crazy, isn't it? I thought they were just bedtime stories," I said.

Practically hopping a circle around the tree, she gestured with her hands. "I know, me too. Did you see the way they fought in the air? That was spectacular!"

I hated to ruin her carefree moment of innocent amazement, but I had to. Glancing about, I took hold of her hand and started to lead her deeper back into the trees. Red tinged her cheeks. While I wanted to think it was because I held her hand, it was more likely that it was from her excitement. Pale brows furrowing together, she looked back at the motorcycles.

"Do you think we're in the wrong spot? We can't leave the bikes," she said.

I shook my head. "It's not that. One of them was trying to kill you and we don't know much about valkyries. It could be a trap."

Her eyes widened. "You're right. Why didn't I think of that?"

I tapped my chest. "*Verndari*, remember? It's in my blood."

She gave me a bit of a shy smile. "Well, you're good at it."

"All the more reason to choose me." Though I kept my tone light, I stared straight ahead. I tried to make my words teasing, so they'd hide that I wanted her to choose me for more than just her *verndari*. She looked down at our intertwined hands, making me think I had probably failed miserably. And here I was overstepping, again. But she didn't let go.

"You really want to be around all this death?" she asked.

I looked at her. "I really want to be around you."

Her eyes squeezed shut and her face scrunched up as if my words had caused her pain. She let go of my hand. The brush of her soft skin across my palm stayed with me in the form of shivers that ran all through me.

Gods, if she would only choose me!

Her muscles stiffened until each step looked painful, robotic almost. She folded her arms tight under her breasts. It might have been wrong to enjoy the cleavage shot this gave me right down the V-neck of her shirt with a red phoenix on it, but I did it anyway. She may be the *uppskera* to everyone else, but to me she was still a woman. A damn fine one.

"Me, or the *uppskera*? Vidar, I—" Her words cut off and her head tilted back, gaze going skyward. A moment later I heard it too, huge wings beating at the air.

I opened my mouth to warn her to wait and watch, but halted the words when she stepped behind a tree. She turned sideways and the fir hid her from the clearing. I had to pick a much bigger tree.

Though the beating of wings grew louder, I didn't see anything. It sounded close, so close the valkyrie should have been landing in the clearing twenty feet from us. My nose told me some kind of winged creature was right there. I looked at Ayra. She shrugged, appearing as confused as I felt. A ripple of energy not unlike a breeze rolled out from the clearing. The form of a woman materialized in the clearing. Golden-brown hair hung down over a bare back—with no wings. But it was Halley. Even though her back was to us, I remembered her scent.

I didn't have to say anything. We waited, our gazes scanning the forest for well over a minute. After a while, Ayra tilted her chin up, nose in the breeze. She sniffed for a long time before looking at me and nodding. I nodded back. We stepped into the clearing together. Our steps were so silent Halley didn't turn toward us until we'd crossed half the distance between us.

"You can cloak yourself," Ayra said. Halley nodded.

"Is it magic?" I asked, unable to keep the hopeful tone out of my voice.

She shook her head, crushing my hopes. Oh well, I supposed it was enough that valkyries existed. "Nope, just technology."

Ayra split off from me, flanking Halley. She narrowed her eyes at the valkyrie. "Not even *varúlfur* inventors have come up with that kind of technology yet," she said.

"It isn't from this world. It's from Asgard."

Goose bumps erupted all over my body. I opened my mouth to ask one of the million questions that popped into my head, but Halley held up a hand.

"I can't say any more than that. I shouldn't even be here," she said, gaze darting around.

"Then why are you?" Ayra asked, her tone almost making it a demand.

Halley looked long and hard at her. "Because Horace was wrong. You aren't agents of Loki. Your very nature is to fight against the chaos, which is Loki's doing, to bring order back into balance. Don't you agree?"

Ayra's eyes widened, and it was like watching a lighthouse come to life within her. It both thrilled and hurt me to see her like that. How could I ever hope to possess something so ethereal?

"Wholeheartedly. I am loyal to Odin." She turned that bright gaze on me for a moment before looking back at Halley. "*We* are loyal to Odin."

Halley's tense shoulders relaxed. The lines between her brows smoothed. "Good." Her back went rigid and her eyes cold. "Very good, because Ayra, you're more than just the *uppskera*." She paused and gave her a long look that reminded me of the way a bird watched its prey before it pecked out its innards. "But you know that already, don't you?"

The look Ayra gave her back was cold enough to make the waterfalls in Iceland seem warm. "And what would you know about that?" she demanded.

I stepped up to her side and stared Halley down as well, which physically was easier than I thought. The valkyrie barely had to look up at me. She was rather tall for a woman, five-foot-eight maybe. But that wasn't what made me want to look away. She was a valkyrie, for Thor's sake, one of the chosen. Here I was just a *verndari* hopeful who hadn't even been accepted by his *uppskera* yet. Hel, I wasn't even an alpha. But I could be both. I knew it, I felt it, and because of that, I wouldn't back down.

Though she held her head high, Halley's throat worked as she swallowed hard. It was subtle, and she hid it well, but it was clear we made her a bit nervous. Good, that meant she was smart.

"I know everything about it. All valkyrie do, which is why he came after you. But you don't have to worry. We were instructed to have no contact with you," she said.

Ayra put a hand on one slender hip. "I can see that's going real well already."

Halley let out a small laugh. "I was given permission to come back to warn you."

Power spiked from Ayra, making my own leap up with it. "Warn me? Is that the beginning of a threat?" she asked.

Hands going up, Halley shook her head. "No, not at all. You misunderstand, or I said it poorly, I'm sorry. I only mean to warn you that if you misuse that other power of yours, it could lead to the death of Thor."

"But how? I would never..." Ayra's voice choked up and her words stopped.

Halley's expression softened. "No, I believe you wouldn't. But what you can do could lead to someone else being able to."

Ayra looked at me, her eyes filled with questions. I wanted to touch her, comfort her, but I knew now wasn't the time. And I also knew it might be me that needed comfort more than her because behind those questions hid an untapped well of strength any superhero would be envious of. I knew what she was thinking. What could her ability to channel lightning have to do with harming the Thunder God? Lightning couldn't hurt Thor. And wait...

"So Thor is... I mean, he can die?" I asked. I'd always thought of the Gods as immortal, despite the tales of Ragnarok. I had figured the whole end-of-the-world thing and death of the Gods was a story meant to teach us a lesson, not an actual possibility.

Shoulders sagging, Halley looked at the ground. "Your kind has been on this world so long they've forgotten the truth. Yes. Asgardians don't age and die like the people of this world, but they can be killed."

"Then this power of mine is bad?" Ayra asked.

Eyes pinching into slits, head shaking, Halley took a step toward Ayra. "No, not at all. Your power is a gift from Odin."

Ayra remained stoic, unconvinced. "Why would the Allfather give me a gift that could kill his son?"

Halley let out a frustrated sigh. "It isn't your gift that can kill Thor, but it can lead to it. That, or it could help save the nine worlds. I'm sorry, I can't explain more. And Odin gave *uppskera* that gift to reward them for being loyal to him. Only the most loyal ones of the bloodlines are chosen, and you, Ayra, are one of those."

The aggravated vibrating of Ayra's power eased. "So I should avoid using my power."

"No. Use it, you need to learn to control it." She nodded toward me. "He can help with that. You could be two of Odin's most powerful *einherjar* someday if you master it. Just don't let anyone else use it for their means. And don't ever combine it with the seeker and the key's power. That's how it could lead to Thor's death."

The heaviness of the conversation made me want to sit down, badly.

But as hard as it was for me to hear, it had to be twice as hard for Ayra. I stood tall by her side. I had to be the mountain she could rely on to shield her from the storm.

"The key?" I asked.

Halley shook her head. Feathers rustled as wings materialized out of her back. "I have to go before I say too much." She took a small leather-bound book from the back pocket of her jeans. "This should help."

Ayra accepted it from her. "An *uppskera* journal. But why wasn't this with the collection the bloodlines have?"

"Because not every *uppskera* could do what you can do. And the journals of those that could are kept in a library in Valhalla." Halley dipped her head to both of us. "Take care, *uppskera* and *verndari*. I'm glad I got to meet you."

Her huge wings swept up and on the downstroke she became airborne. In another swipe of them she disappeared, leaving us in a feathery-scented breeze. Ayra turned a wide-eyed gaze to me. The smile on her face took me completely by surprise.

"Valkyries are real," she whispered.

I put an arm around her as we both leaned our heads back into the breeze and breathed in the scent of a race that hailed from Asgard. For a moment we were two kids again, filled with wonder and hope. No matter what happened, at least we had that.

CHAPTER FOURTEEN

AYRA

The uppskera must look into the eyes of demons and not become ensnared by their gaze.
-Uppskera Journals

Turned out the not-so-sleepy town of Hood River was barely in Oregon. And while it sat on a river, it wasn't the Hood River. Under the blanket of night we cruised up I-84 along the Columbia River where it separated Oregon and Washington. Despite it being July, a misty rain enveloped everything, giving the lights of the town a blurred look. I followed my nose to the greenest smelling part of town—no easy feat with the murky scent of the river and rain overwhelming everything else. Even if Calder were here, I might not be able to smell his trail over the moisture unless I was right on top of it, so I had to go where I thought he'd go.

Two-story buildings lined a stretch of street bordering a waterfront park that had what appeared to be a sandy shore. I looked over at Vidar. He hunched on his Harley as if trying to crawl into the machine. His shorts and T-shirt clung to him like a second skin, revealing planes and valleys of muscle I hadn't noticed before. My body tried to react to the sight. With a will that was steadily fading, I stopped it. The skidlid helmet my cousin had given him covered nothing but the top of his head. He was the very picture of a hot, miserable mess. It made it increasingly difficult to stay angry at him.

I pressed the button on the front of my helmet that released the lower half and flipped the full-face shield up. I needed air. The scents of damp earth and concrete intensified. Exhaust, pungent garbage from back alley dumpsters, and the varying scents of too many humans lay beneath. Unfortunately, the rain could only do so much to wash a place clean, especially a city.

Vidar didn't say anything, and for that I was grateful. His outstanding *varúlfur* hearing had to have picked up at least part of the conversation. I'd been shouting at one point, after all.

Noses in the wind, we crawled down the mostly empty street just fast enough to keep our feet off the ground. Vidar touched his nose and pointed to the right a moment before I smelled it, not just my brother, but his blood. The scent was old, but unmistakable. Every time I'd been able to draw the asshole's blood during a sparring match had been a tiny victory to me. One never forgets what victory smells like when they were an abused little girl. We turned down the street.

The smell led me to a stop sign, or rather, the street sign posted above it. The barest traces of blood smeared across the street sign remained. The misty rain was making quick work of it. If we had arrived even a half hour later, it would have been gone. Lucky for us, last week had been hot and dry here, because by the scent of it, this clearly hadn't been left here yesterday. And I was sure it had been left, like a trail of breadcrumbs I was supposed to follow.

"I don't like this," Vidar said just loud enough for my sensitive ears to hear him over the rumble of his Harley.

"Me neither."

But as with everything in my life, I didn't have a choice. I turned down the road the bloody street sign pointed toward. Not willing to crawl into a potential ambush, I closed my helmet and pulled the throttle back. The road led us swiftly out of town. The Mount Hood National Forest soon swallowed us whole. Towering pines and spruces squeezed out all but the barest glimpse of the midnight-blue sky and two-lane road ahead.

Something deep inside told me this was exactly where Calder wanted us to end up.

I slowed to a crawl once more and lifted the lower half of my helmet. In less than a quarter of a mile I smelled more old blood. This time it came from a huge spruce standing sentinel beside an unmarked gravel road. We turned at the tree. After only a hundred feet or so it became clear the road was only a deep turnout that looped through a stand of trees and back to the road. I rolled my bike to a stop beneath feathery boughs, killed the engine, and pulled my helmet off.

My power flared a second before thunder rolled across the not-so-distant hills. I peeled my nylon jacket off, needing to be free from the constraints of the stiff, plastic armor within it. Something was coming, I could feel it deep down in my bones, and it wasn't just a storm. I focused on the feeling. Watching Vidar swing from his bike, wet cargo shorts clinging to his fine ass, didn't exactly help me concentrate. I closed my eyes.

The press of tainted power came from all sides. Four condemned approached. My eyes opened. Tall trees and hills surrounded us. We weren't exactly in a hollow, but I'd certainly call it a deep valley.

"We need to get to high ground, now," I said.

I took off at a run deeper into the forest. Vidar followed without a word of protest. The thought of him seeing me reap made my stomach churn—violently. But I couldn't make him leave. Some of the condemned might follow him. I knew he could take care of himself, but I didn't want him getting hurt because I ran him off. Especially not when the reason I wanted him to leave wasn't for his own safety, but because I was afraid of what he'd think of me if he saw me kill.

Within moments we made it to the top of a small hill. The trees covering the land didn't allow us to see very far, but I still felt better. Through gaps in the pine boughs I saw our bikes. I smelled the musk of the condemned before their wolf forms trotted into sight. Four of them surrounded our bikes, canine snouts swinging this way and that as they checked for our scents.

While they jogged around, I removed my boots. When I unbuttoned my shorts Vidar raised his brows at me. I lifted my head in the direction of the werewolves, hoping he'd get it. If we fought them in wolf form, they'd likely stay in wolf form. Four wolf corpses would bring no attention from the authorities. Four more human corpses would start to look like a trail. Vidar nodded and took his shirt off. All that muscle covered in that dark skin distracted me. I still couldn't believe how much he'd filled out in the four years he'd been gone. My skinny comic book geek was no more. The problem was, I'd wanted him even then. Now he was a mountain of perfection that distracted me to no end. And I couldn't afford a distraction right now.

I removed the rest of my clothes and dropped them in a pile. Vidar's expression didn't change when he turned my way, but his power spiked and the scent of desire rolled off him. I reached for the ground and shifted into a wolf. A heartbeat later, Vidar shifted too. The moment he did, my desire for him intensified as my wolf side recognized a suitable mate. The wolf didn't care about semantics and reasons. It only recognized that Vidar was perfect in every way that mattered. I shoved the instinct down deep and focused on the fight that was coming our way. It wasn't easy.

In the subtle body language of wolves, I told Vidar we should move to a spot a few trees down. The fir trees there had thicker, lower boughs that would help hide my blinding white-blond coat. I knew they'd find us. I wanted them to. But I had no intention of making it easy on them. And it would be on my terms, in a location of my choosing. Vidar and I took off at a jog together. I crouched behind the big, feathery boughs while Vidar chose a spot deeper in the shadows and all but disappeared.

We didn't have to wait long. The condemned panted and growled as they sniffed along our trails, all but announcing their locations. One approached from each direction. I braced myself—not for the attack, the clumsy idiots were still a hundred yards away—but for their memories.

In another few breaths they slammed into my mind with a vengeance.

Big hands around a woman's neck, squeezing harder and harder. Those same hands unzipping his pants after the life went out of the woman's eyes.

Sitting on a park bench watching children play, choosing one of them by the way the little girl's shorts clung to her behind.

Breath coming in excited gasps filled with anticipation as he stalked a jogger on a remote forest path.

Raising a knife to stab a man writhing and bleeding out from a dozen other wounds.

Each image hit me like a punch in the gut. And each one was from a different man. Rage exploded through me like a series of fireworks. It took my breath away, threatened to steal my reason. The desire to kill them for what they had done turned into a desperate need. In the cesspool that was their minds, I could feel that they would do it again. Some had killed multiple people already, some before they had been bitten in, some after.

Roar tearing from my throat, I stepped into the open.

Come for me. I wanted them to find me so I could kill them. My claws dug into the soft earth in anticipation of rending their flesh. The only thing that kept me from chasing after them was knowing by staying put they would all come to me.

Vidar's nearness soothed me and helped me think clearly. Thankfully, he stayed hidden in the shadows. It could work to our advantage, him being hidden.

The condemned felt new, months old at most, which meant they may not realize he was there until it was too late.

Two of them crested the hill at a dead run. Both were brown with white markings, though one had black running up his nose. They stumbled and tripped over their own paws like gangly pups not yet used to their bodies. Gods, they really were only a few months old.

The other two remained hidden, holding themselves back. I felt the anticipation eating away at their restraint. The press of their power told me exactly where they were. One hunkered downhill ahead of me, using the brush for cover. The other crouched behind me, hidden by a tree. I couldn't be sure that they didn't smell or see Vidar, but I didn't think they did.

The thrill of the coming fight coursed through my veins in an invigorating rush that made me flash a wolfy grin. They both leaped for me. I jumped up, clearing their furry backs. On the way down I shifted into my hybrid form. I kicked one condemned with my elongated hind legs. The other I slashed out at with my clawed hands. My claws parted the fur and flesh of Black Snout's shoulder at the same moment my feet connected with the other.

The double strikes put me in a stretched-out position that left me no choice but to hit the ground. I rolled as the pine-needle-blanketed ground met me, shifting back to a full wolf as I did. Both of the condemned rose slowly to their feet. Fear wafted off them in noxious waves. It drew me in almost as strongly as if they had turned and run. The press of more power came as the other two charged over the hill and attacked. From behind me came a surprised yelp followed by snarling and snapping. The snarling I recognized as Vidar's.

I didn't have time to worry about him because a brown wolf nearly the size of a bear barreled down on me. From the touch of his mind I recognized him as the one who liked to stab people. At the last moment, I shifted to my hybrid form when he jumped for me. I grabbed his front legs, thrust my hind legs into his stomach, and rolled with him into a judo roll that threw him past me. Before the roll completed, I raked his chest with my clawed hind legs. The steamy blood of the condemned splashed all over my fur.

Continuing the momentum of the roll, I continued all the way over and shifted back to a wolf to land on all fours. Vidar made a grunting sound of pain. The other two came at me, preventing me from turning to check on him. Fury exploded in my chest. It felt like it might consume me.

"Enough!" I roared as I shifted to human form. Maybe it wasn't the wisest choice with two wolves bearing down on me, but I didn't care. All that mattered was the righteous rage, that and the burning desire to keep Vidar safe.

Both came for me at the same time. I released the reins on my control and sucked their energy in like it was water and I was dying of thirst. Only it was more like anti-freeze with a sweet promise and a killer aftertaste. I caught both wolves in mid-leap by the throat. Holding them up was easy considering I tripled my strength by drawing their power in. They felt light as feathers, snapping, snarling, writhing feathers, but still feathers. Their hind legs caught me a few times, scratching my bare legs.

Drinking in their powers allowed their memories and thoughts to flow freely into me. One of them was the rapist, the other the child molester. The images that assaulted my mind were worse than any strike they could have landed on me. The pain and terror their victims had felt coursed through me. I squeezed their throats harder. A third wolf came at me from behind, the knife-happy guy again. Claws raked across my back. I sucked so much of his power down, so fast, that I heard him collapse to the ground with a grunt. The horrible images didn't stop. My fingers squeezed harder. My claws elongated, digging into their furry throats as their kicks slowed. Windpipes crushed with a little pop in my hands. The images stopped.

Relief washed through me, soothing my mind. I dropped the twitching wolves, needing to get to the next one. The horrible images of the dead wolves' crimes made my knees weak. Bile stung the back of my throat. I took a shaking step in Vidar's direction. His power washed over me like a summer breeze, allowing me to breathe easier.

Vidar's black furry form hurtled through the air at the fourth condemned, a monstrously big brown and white wolf. The jogger-stalker. Vidar's jaws closed around the throat of the condemned.

Between us the third wolf struggled to rise to his feet. I felt what he wanted to do to me and it made me sick to my stomach. I strode up to him and stomped on his neck so hard it snapped beneath my foot. Claws extended, I bent, preparing to eviscerate him for good measure. Vidar's gaze caught mine over the tops of the bodies as he lifted his bloody snout from the throat of the condemned. Crimson splashes and droplets marred his beautiful black fur, and it was my fault. That realization stopped me in mid-crouch.

The air around him shimmered like the desert on a hot day. A moment later he rose onto the legs of a man, a naked man. Gods he was hot as Muspelheimr. It didn't matter that he was stepping over the corpses of three wolves we had just slain. Desire rose in me, burning away both the anger and the feel of the power of the condemned. I let out a long breath as the images of what they'd done fled from my mind.

Vidar spat several times, cleared his throat, and spat twice more. "Gods, his blood tasted terrible," he mumbled.

"Their power is worse." The words poured out of me before I could think about it, or stop them.

Brows furrowing, Vidar looked me over. "You aren't hurt are you? You took out three before I even finished one. By Thor, how did you do that?"

The sight of his bare chest at my eye level distracted me, made it hard to think. Would his pecs feel as hard as they looked? My bloody hand was halfway to him before I stopped it. If he didn't get away from me, I wasn't sure I could hold myself back.

"I sucked their power in, making them weaker, and me stronger."

He stopped walking, shoulders pulling back. "You can do that?"

The surprise on his face hurt, and the rejection surely to follow would hurt even more. But I could take it. I had to.

He shook his head. "Of course you can, you just said so. Sorry, that's just...wow!"

Unable to respond in any way, I stared at him. That was the exact opposite reaction I'd been expecting. Even Vidar shouldn't be able to forgive such a thing. Stealing someone's strength rather than possessing one's own wasn't very Viking-like.

"But, I'm not strong. I just syphon strength from them. You don't think it makes me weak, unworthy?" I whispered the last.

Vidar shook his head as he closed the distance between us. He took my face in his hands. His big, callused fingers felt amazing against my cheeks. All the residual darkness left over from the power of the condemned vanished in an instant. I became acutely aware that we were both naked, so aware I had to close my eyes to hide my desire for him. I knew he was right about it being a survival instinct to want to mate after a fight, but that didn't help make it feel any less wrong, especially not with wolf corpses cooling at our feet.

"No, Ayra, don't you understand? This ability is what gives Odin the freedom to choose the right person based off their mental ability to handle the job," he began.

Intrigue drove back my desire enough that I opened my eyes.

He went on. "Being the *uppskera* is more about control and balance than it is about strength and size. If the Allfather wanted someone big and strong, he would have chosen your brother. But he wanted you because you are more capable of handling it mentally."

His words resonated deep down inside me. If he were right, then that changed everything. And it made too much sense to discount. I had far better control over my temper than my brother could ever hope to have. In fact, that thought alone burned up the last of my rage and scattered it like ashes, or maybe Vidar's touch did. His palms felt so good cradling my face, warm, and strong. Desire flared to life in the ashes of my anger.

All I had to do was take one step and our bodies would touch. The need to do so became almost overwhelming. In his eyes shone the same desire. My hands rose from my sides. The scents of blood and death stopped me. This wasn't right, not here, not now. Thunder rolled through the cloudy sky as if even the Gods were in agreement.

"I can't do this," I whispered.

"I understand. You feel obligated to the Arnoddr pack, to your family."

The depth of sadness in his eyes tore things loose inside me. "No. And yes. It's just..." A stiff breeze carried the clean scent of rain to me, along with the tang of lightning. I took a large step back from Vidar. "I have to go," I said.

He reached for me, but I took another quick step back. "Ayra, no, don't." The pleading tone in his voice tugged deep inside me.

I couldn't allow it to ensnare me. Thunder shook the dark sky again. I turned and ran.

CHAPTER FIFTEEN

AYRA

While the leitar attempts to save the individual, the uppskera attempts to save all of
our kind.
~Uppskera Journals

It would have been easier to run as a wolf, faster, but I couldn't shift. Vidar was in human form and I wanted him too badly in that moment for my body to allow me to shift. I'd read about this, but never experienced it. *Varúlfur* remained in the shape of their desired mate on instinct when aroused. I tried to fight it, to force myself to shift, but I couldn't.

My legs pumped as fast as they could, carrying me deeper into the forest. Rain pattered down on the leaves, creating a roar that covered the sound of my pounding heart. Big drops plopped on my shoulders and hair. In a half mile I was soaked, rain streaming down my naked skin, plastering my hair to my face and shoulders. But it didn't cool the fire inside that burned for Vidar. Nothing could.

A hand closed around my left biceps. I could have pulled free if I'd wanted to. The problem was, I didn't want to. For so long, I had been worried about what everyone else wanted for me. It had worn me down. Through the thunder and the rain, I hadn't even heard Vidar behind me.

But I'd felt him, and I could have run faster. My restraint melted away more and more with each step I took away from the wolves' corpses.

Chest heaving with each deep breath, I turned and faced Vidar. Rain streamed down his dark skin, catching the dim light as it surged over his muscles and ran between them. My gaze followed all that running water straight down to the V of his abdominal muscles to the hair at his groin—and the beginnings of an impressive erection. My eyes slammed shut and I forced my chin up before I opened them again. His chiseled jaw and full lips weren't any less inspiring.

I was confused, messed up. He didn't deserve to have to deal with that.

"I don't want to force you to break a vow you hold dear. I shouldn't have tempted you. It was wrong and disrespectful to the Order you serve," I gasped.

Thunder boomed, swallowing his answer. Water droplets flew from his short black hair as he shook his head. He took a step closer. "Nothing about what we feel for each other is wrong, Ayra. The most important vow to me is the one I made to you before I left. The one to help you."

My mouth opened and my jaw worked, but no words would come out. Hearing him say that was too much. It was all I'd ever wanted to hear. Elí didn't want to help me. He wanted to make everything perfect and pretty around me to hide the blood and death. He wanted the power and prestige being married to the reaper brought, but not the blood and death. He loved the reaper, but certainly not me. Vidar had faced those things more than once now and hadn't flinched. He took another step toward me, close enough to touch. I shook with the need to reach out, but I couldn't. This wasn't fair to him.

"It's too late for us," I said, barely loud enough to be heard over the patter of rain on leaves.

He stepped forward and I stepped back. "Never. I'm so sorry I left you. I'm so sorry I couldn't tell you all about the Order. But mostly, I'm sorry I never told you how I feel."

Each word exploded into the wall around my heart like a missile. "Don't be. I bring nothing but death. You deserve better than me. You deserve a wife, kids, a pack."

"Stop telling me what I deserve! I deserve the kind of love that is written about in the stars, the kind that only comes along once in your existence. I deserve to be with the woman I've loved since I was eight."

Those words immobilized me as surely as any freeze ray in his comic books could have. I craned my neck back to stare up at him. In his hazel eyes his soul was laid bare, revealing just how deeply he meant them. I couldn't move, couldn't speak, couldn't even breathe. Here I was thinking like him now, my mind working in threes. It would have made me smile if I wasn't so utterly shocked by what he'd said.

His hands slid up my slick arms until they gripped my biceps. "It's okay if you don't feel the same way. I understand if you still want to...marry Elí. I just wanted you to know. There is no place I'd rather be, no person I'd rather be with, no fate I'd rather have."

Now I did smile. I closed my eyes, swallowed hard, and reached for my calm center. I found it standing right in front of me. He went on before I could speak.

"I've always wanted to be your mate, but when you became the *uppskera*, I didn't think I was worthy. So I hoped to be your *verndari* instead, thinking it was as high as I could reach."

I shook my head. "Why would you think that?"

"My family aren't directly from the bloodlines that came to this world. You're higher than royalty. I have no pack since my alpha was killed and I was kicked out. I'm not even an alpha myself—"

I put a finger against his lips. "At first?" I asked.

His lips turned up, and I felt his hot breath against my finger. It sent tingles straight to my groin that tightened every muscle on its way down. He straightened up even taller. "We were made for each other. I would kill for you, and I would die for you. I am worthy." Strong arms slid around me. "And I think maybe you want me too, and not just because of your instincts. If I'm wrong, tell me and I'll leave and let another candidate have their shot at Impression. I will step aside and never raise a claw to Elí. But if I'm not..."

Those arms tightened until our rain-slick bodies were pressed against one another. The brush of his abs against my breasts almost drove me out of my mind. I felt the barest touch of his erection against my stomach. My eyes fluttered, but I wouldn't let them close. I had to think fast before I lost it.

"Since you were eight?" The question popped out before the protest I had prepared. Dammit, my control was slipping. How could it not? Being in his arms felt more amazing than I had imagined.

He cast a smile down at me that warmed me to my core. "Mmm hmm. Ever since that day I saw you up to your knees in the pond catching frogs, your braids brushing the water. I knew you were the one for me."

"But I... But you..." I felt like an idiot who couldn't string a sentence together. I shook my head to clear it. "But don't you want a pack, a family, the Order?"

One hand cupped my chin. He bent down, which took his hard body away from mine, but put his lips closer. "I want you. I joined the Order only to help you. You're all I've ever wanted. You are my family, my pack. That's all I need." His intense eyes held me as intimately as his arms. "What do you need?" he asked in a whisper that brushed my lips and resonated through me.

"You. I've loved you since that day too. I never knew you loved me in the same way. You never showed it." Again, the damn words poured out before I could think about them.

His smile grew. The joy in his eyes would have taken my breath away if I could have breathed in the first place. "I come from a long line of *lögreglu*, it's in our nature to protect. Being older than you, I felt like I had to protect you, even from myself. But now, you don't need protection from anyone."

I turned my head away. "But myself."

He turned my chin back. "No. You handle the fury just fine."

"Because you're close."

"Then keep me close. Make me your *verndari*."

"But I'm a killer. I've made you a killer. How could you want to be with me now?"

Laughter bowed his back and made his chest touch me again. "First, you're a killer of killers. That's a noble calling. Second, we're all killers. You didn't make me into anything. Third, how could I not? You are the most amazing woman I've ever known, with the kindest heart and most selfless attitude. And wanting to be with you has nothing to do with the reaper, and everything to do with you."

The words turned my walls to dust.

An intensity filled his eyes as he drew my body against his again. This time he didn't hold his hips back. His erection pressed against my stomach in a long, hard line. Just feeling it against my skin made me wet. Gods, I'd wanted him for so long.

He leaned down, bending his legs to keep our bodies molded together. "And now that I know you love me, you won't be able to get rid of me. Loki himself couldn't tear me from your side. I deserve you, Ayra Valdísdóttir, and you deserve me."

This alpha side of him, declaring what he wanted, it crumbled my resistance and made me dizzy with need. I smiled. "You'd fight the trickster god himself for me?"

His fingers trailed up my cheek and he brushed a lock of hair from my face. Rain dripped from his lips. I wanted to lick it off. "Him and his army," he said in a husky voice.

"It may come to that. When I break off my engagement to Elí, I don't know how bad Isak will take it. But I do know how bad my family will take it," I said.

Those delicious, full lips of his turned up. "When, not if?"

I nodded, grinning so big it hurt my cheeks. His eyes brightened with the glow of his wolf.

"I would fight your entire family. I would even fight Isak, alpha of the Arnoddr pack, and every one of his *verndari* if it came to it," he vowed.

A small laugh slid from me. "Really? Isak has like thirty *verndari*." Each alpha had a circle of *verndari*, men and women who protected their pack. They didn't belong to an Order but the pack itself, a different kind of *verndari*.

"Really."

"I chose you, Vidar Balderson, a long time ago. There has never been, and never will be, anyone but you," I breathed out. A weight as heavy as Thor's hammer lifted from me.

"As your *verndari*?"

"My *verndari*, my mate, my everything." The words freed me from an arranged marriage I'd never wanted in the first place and liberated me from the last chains of my old life.

A huge goofy smile turned up his full lips. "Then I am released from my vow."

Shock made me pull back a bit. "What?"

"The vow of celibacy ends when the *uppskera* chooses her *verndari*. It was only to make sure the potentials didn't use mating to influence you. I wasn't allowed to tell you, under threat of disqualification and death," he said.

"Let's make a new vow, right here, right now," I said, pulling him closer. He lifted a brow in question. I went on. "To each other. That nothing and no one will ever come between us again. And to never have secrets from one another."

"I vow it," he said without hesitation.

"I vow it," I responded.

I rose up on my toes and pressed my lips against his, hard. The way the motion rubbed his erection between us made me light-headed. His mouth opened and our tongues collided in a greedy battle. One of his hands cupped the back of my head, the other encircled my waist, both holding me with a reverent tenderness. But I could feel the depth of his need in his kiss. I knew it matched my own. And I had no patience for tenderness, not when I had waited my entire life for this moment.

He cradled me with one hand and began to lower me to the ground. At the last moment, I twisted and rolled us over so I ended up on top. He let out a surprised laugh as I landed on him. The laugh turned into a hungry sound as I pressed my body along the length of his and rocked up and down against his pinned erection. Something between a growl and a moan slipped from him. The sound made muscles between my legs clench and got me wet. Letting out a hungry sound of my own, I fell to kissing him again. The brush of his pecs beneath me hardened my nipples.

His hands ran down my rain-slick back, over my butt, and to my thighs. The sensation of his rough hands against my skin drove me half wild with desire, maybe more than half. I moaned into his mouth before sealing my lips against his and sucking on his tongue. One arm around my waist, he sat us both halfway up. His other hand reached around my butt to fondle my opening. When his finger slid inside me, I wanted to both rock back to it, and press forward to better feel his erection where it tickled at my pubic hair. He made the decision for me, leaning me back against his hand and pushing his finger farther into me.

I broke the kiss, threw my head back, and cried out, but distant thunder swallowed the sound. In several wonderfully long minutes, he brought me screaming in a way nothing battery powered had been able to do. Breathless, I sagged against him. He nuzzled into my neck.

Great as it was, it wasn't enough. I needed him inside me. The power of that need made me shake.

I reached between my legs and took hold of his erection. He growled against my neck, the sound filled with a need of his own. Gods, he was so hard and big. Much bigger than the vibrator in my drawer at home. I'd have to take it slow was all. The realization filled me with anticipation. I pressed him to my opening and started to work my way down on him. The slow process soon had him flat on his back, writhing in pleasure. Once I had worked him inside me, we found a perfect rhythm, his hips rising as mine descended.

He massaged my breasts, teasing my hard nipples until I leaned into his big hands. One of his hands worked its way up to cup my face. The depth of affection in his eyes washed away any doubts I'd had about him wanting to be with the woman instead of the reaper. He sat up, wrapped an arm tight around me, and kissed me. The chaste, sweet touch wasn't enough, not with him moving inside me, massaging my deepest, most intimate parts. I parted his lips with my tongue, teasing at the softness and warmth within until his tongue chased mine back into my mouth. As we kissed, he gripped my hips, helping to lift and push me down faster and faster.

An amazing pressure built inside me from somewhere deep that he touched. I pushed him down onto his back, hands moving up his chest. My fingers clenched his pectorals so tight my nails dug tiny crescent moons into his flesh. The pressure continued to build, filling every part of me with a buzz not unlike that lightning left behind. Inside me, I felt him swell. Little sparks of intense pleasure started to go off as my muscles clenched around him. As he came screaming my name, I came screaming his. A more perfect storm had never existed.

CHAPTER SIXTEEN

VIDAR

Morning sunlight filtered through the tent opening and spilled across Ayra's hair, making it shine like white-blond silk. Long, pale eyelashes fluttered against her cheeks as she slept in my arms. Her lips were curled up into a smile that suggested only good dreams visited her. While last night had been amazing in an earth-shattering way, this moment felt like perfection. Her naked body pressed against the length of mine beneath the sleeping bag had made me wake with a raging hard-on. But I wasn't about to rouse her and ruin her peace for my own needs. There would be plenty of time for more of that later.

I hoped. A small chance existed that she might change her mind when she awoke and tell me to hit the road. Her desire to protect me and what she thought I deserved and wanted in life was positively heroic. But I hadn't been kidding about her not being able to get rid of me. I'd follow her to the ends of the earth—and beyond.

A tinkling bell sounded from within our clothes where I'd hung them overhead to dry. It had to be Ayra's cell phone. She stirred against me. It chimed again and she bolted up into a sitting position.

Damn electronics.

Her head turned in my direction. One hand covered her yawning mouth while the other reached down to stroke my chest. A languid, satisfied look darkened her usually robin's-egg-blue eyes to a beautiful sapphire hue. My breath caught. For a long, fantastic moment as she stared at me like I was the center of the world, I thought everything might be all right. Well, as all right as a life hunting murderous werewolves could be. Then her phone chimed again.

She reached up into her clothes and dug the device out. Her back went rigid. I'd never hated electronics more. Her power crackled and grew like the pressure before a storm, filling the tent until I could hardly breathe. I pushed my way through it, sat up and put an arm around her.

"What's wrong?"

She didn't answer, but she didn't have to. I read her phone screen over her shoulder.

Calder: *It's not nice to break my toys.*

Calder: *You'll pay for that when I see you in Cannon Beach. Do try and make it in time for the battle this weekend. I'd hate for you to miss it, sister dearest.*

I carefully plucked the phone from Ayra's white fingers before she could crush it. "Well, I've always wanted to visit the Oregon coast," I said.

"But we have to go to Portland. I can't let him distract me from that," she all but growled.

I rubbed her back. She relaxed ever-so-slightly against my hand. Some of the tension drained from her power. "He won't. We have to go through Portland on our way to the beach."

She pulled her clothes down from where they hung. "Good. Let's get going."

Half-dressed and looking like a tiny raging goddess, she was out the tent before I could protest. Though I knew it was wrong on multiple levels, I prayed for the Gods to damn Calder to the harshest lands on Muspelheimr. Or better yet, let me send him there with my own claws.

...

We rolled into Portland before the sun was even fully up, which was a problem considering *draugar* sleep during the day. That rumor was true. He was expecting us, but I didn't want to be rude. The rain coming down in epic sheets didn't exactly allow any sunlight through the cloud-ridden sky. A *draugr* could technically walk around in these low-light conditions. But I didn't want to chance it. Instead of turning down his street, I took Ayra toward the Waterfront Park.

As we traversed the bridges and crawled through the morning commuting traffic she called Elí and told him she wasn't going through with the arranged marriage. I'd tried not to listen in, but I couldn't help it. She didn't waver and he didn't beg or ask for a reason. He sounded relieved. The moment she ended the call, her spirits had lifted. It floored me that she had been able to make such a call while driving through insane traffic, like a detached business transaction. It made me realize there really hadn't been anything between her and Elí more than a mutually beneficial arrangement. I felt relief, guilt, and sadness over it.

We stopped at a diner for a quick breakfast and she called Isak. The alpha had been surprised only about how long it had taken Ayra to break off the arrangement. He even told her she still had a place in his pack should she want it.

After eating in record time, we hit the road again.

As we drew closer to the park I called her through our Bluetooth helmets. She'd made us stop along the way before Portland so I could purchase one. Admittedly, the full face thing did help block out a lot of outside noise, helped me talk to her easier, and made me look a bit like a galactic soldier, so it wasn't all bad.

Road noise sounded as a dull roar in the background when she answered. I focused my hearing down to the device built into the helmet near my ear.

"It's early. Don't want to be rude," I said.

"But it's like nine o'clock or something."

"Yeah, but he sleeps during the day."

"For real?" Her tone rose with excitement. It made me smile.

"For real."

We wove in and out of the insane bumper-to-bumper traffic for a moment, concentrating on not getting flattened. Superhero-like powers or not, a semi at sixty miles an hour versus a motorcycle wouldn't end well for us. And ninety-nine percent of drivers didn't see motorcycles. It was part of why I liked to stick to trucks, big ones. We soon pulled under the cover of a parking garage. As we took our helmets off, the barrage of questions began.

Ayra shook out her gorgeous waist-length hair, stealing my breath.

"Well?" she prompted.

"Well what?" I asked, oblivious to anything but the sight of her.

"I asked if they burn up in the sunlight."

"No."

"In churches?"

I laughed. "No. I don't think the modern gods of this world care about their existence. And besides, they aren't evil, just different."

She hung her helmet on the nifty little lock she had on her license plate cover. Unfortunately, she left on her nylon motorcycle jacket with the AVV symbol on the back. It wasn't the symbol that bothered me. From what she said they seemed to have some pretty good ideas about the future for our kind. Rather, it was the amount of clothing covering her. Not fair, considering I wore a jacket myself now. But if she would be willing to shed clothing, I certainly would too.

"What's the plan?" she asked.

Again I had to make myself focus. "Walk to Waterfront Park, do a bit of research."

The mischievous twinkle in her eyes when she smiled made my heart pound. She took her jacket off and stuffed it into one of the hard side bags on her bike. My heart rate increased. As we started to walk from the parking garage she tucked into my side as if she'd been doing it for years, an arm going around my waist. And here I'd feared things would be awkward. The feel of her petite body against mine made me grow weak in the knees but pumped adrenalin through my veins at the same time. She was like kryptonite and steroids all at once. The aftereffects made my head spin and I loved it.

"Is there privacy to be found at this park?" she asked in a low, sultry voice that made my blood pump south. I was suddenly very grateful for the stretch ability of my cargo pants.

It struck me that I didn't have to worry about her seeing my reaction, or smelling my arousal. Finally, after all these years. I draped my arm over her shoulders and pulled her close enough that I could smell the river water in her hair.

"Definitely," I said against the long, pale locks.

She made a contented sort of growly sound. We walked faster. A misty, gray haze of a world waited for us outside of the parking garage. Constant rain streaked everything, obscuring the view beyond a few yards. Standing water splashed beneath our feet as we made our way down the sidewalk. The pavement soon dumped us onto a wider walk lined with old-style lampposts and a mixture of deciduous trees. While I couldn't see it through the haze of rain, I could smell the river not far ahead.

More people than I had expected milled about, and far fewer with umbrellas like I would have thought. Still, in a city of hundreds of thousands, the rain had reduced the foot traffic to just a few determined souls. Ayra withdrew from beneath my arm and took hold of my hand. I had to stretch out my long legs to keep up with her brisk pace down the path that turned along the river. It looked like no more than an undulating wide swath of hazy gray, unbroken by tall buildings.

"That's probably a pretty view when you can see it," Ayra said.

I shrugged one shoulder. "If you like that sort of thing, a huge body of water cutting through a city."

The smile on her face made her appear to beam with happiness despite the rain dripping down her porcelain skin. "I do. It reminds me of the indomitable power of nature. All these people are at the mercy of it."

"I love the way you see it."

I wasn't about to ruin it for her by reminding her of how people had polluted this massive river to the point you couldn't drink the water untreated, and probably didn't want to swim in it. She was happier than I'd seen her since I got back from Iceland. In fact, I didn't recall ever seeing her this happy. A fierce determination rose in me to keep her that way. Hand in hand, we walked along the paved riverfront path. Despite the rain and the horrible scents of the city, being at her side with her hand in mine felt surreal, dreamlike, and perfect.

"So why does the Order choose who gets a chance at impressing the *uppskera*?" she asked.

"What do you mean?"

She gestured to herself. "I was born with the mark of the reaper, chosen by Odin himself. Why wouldn't my *verndari* be chosen by Odin?"

I smiled, loving that her mind worked just like mine. "That was the first thing I asked the Order. They said because the *uppskera* has no choice in turning into a reaper of shifters, Frigg demanded of him that he give the *uppskera* that choice." It made sense that it would be Frigg, wife of Odin, who fought for the rights of the chosen. To our kind she was a champion of such things. When I heard the tale, it rang true in my heart and made perfect sense.

A sad, yet lovely, smile crept across her lips. "I like that." She pulled me to a bench beneath a cherry tree. I leaned close while she researched Cannon Beach on her phone. One headline in particular jumped out at me. Ayra read it aloud.

"Vice President plans to visit annual Plein Air Festival. Oh no." She read a bit more before raising wide eyes to me. "The Vice President of the United States. Oh Gods, V, he plans to kill the Vice President." She stood. "We have to go, now."

I rose and put an arm around her. "Easy, don't worry. It's only Wednesday. The festival doesn't start until Friday. Even if we get there tomorrow, that's a day early, plenty of time to kick Calder's ass all the way to Muspelheimr."

"We can't risk being late."

"We won't be. He will want to kill you before he attacks the VP. He wouldn't want to risk you stopping him during the festival. He knew you'd figure this out and rush to him, abandoning the council meeting. That way if he doesn't kill you, another assassin sent by one of them will. We'll go right after the council meeting tonight. It's less than an hour drive. Okay?"

Letting out a long breath, she nodded. "Okay."

We started walking again. Thunder boomed overhead. The few others braving the rain started to dash toward their destinations. Soon, we were the only two people on the path.

At her urging I retold her everything I knew about *draugar*. The infrequency of her questions made me think she wanted to hear my voice more than what I had to say. I was fine with that. We'd walked less than a half mile when she pulled me off the path into the grassy area thick with deciduous trees. The other pedestrians and bicyclists stuck to the paved path. Once my boots sank into the spongy grass I realized why. But the smile she gave me coupled with the bedroom eyes dark with desire made me ready to roll around in the grass no matter how wet it was. Her long hair did more to cover her curvy body than her wet gray tank top. I wanted more than anything to brush it back from her shoulders, away from where it clung to the roundness of her breasts.

She pulled me behind a red maple tree and pushed me up against the rough bark. Her body pinned me there, the feel of her curves immobilizing me in the most fantastic way. Hands around the back of my neck, she pulled me down to her lips. At the first urging, my mouth opened to her. Her tongue plunged in, exploring, seeking, devouring. The need vibrating through her infused me until I could barely breathe. Hands beneath her butt, I lifted her and spun us around until I had her up against the tree. The low growl of desire that came from her made all the blood in my body rush to my groin.

I kissed and licked a trail down her neck, to her collarbone, then to the top of her breasts where they poked out of her shirt. I shifted her so I could hold her with one hand beneath her butt and caress her breast with the other. Gods, she felt so good, even better than I had always imagined. The barest hint of lilac and soap mixed with a musk that was all hers in an intoxicating combination. But the scent of her desire as she grew wet from my attention pushed me over the top.

I wanted her so bad I ached. Literally. These pants had grown far too tight. And yet...

"Do you want to do this out here?" I asked as I looked around at the rainy park.

She deserved satin sheets in a luxurious hotel, and so far all I'd done was take her on the bare ground like we were animals. Okay, maybe she did the taking, but still.

"Hel yes," she said in a husky voice right before she pulled at my bottom lip with her teeth.

Her hands grabbed my butt and pulled my hips to hers. My erection ground against her pelvis. With a little growl, I plunged my tongue into her mouth. The wet warmth made me hungry for more, only in different ways and different places. Hands reaching for the fly of her jeans, I started to slide down her body. I had to know how she tasted.

From some distance away came a strange whistling sound that made me pause.

A horrible, searing pain like a hot poker stabbed into the back of my shoulder and burned through the front of my chest. I looked down and saw six inches of an arrow shaft jutting from my left pec. The arrowhead barely pierced Ayra in the abdomen. She pushed me back, tearing the metal from her body, and threw us both to the ground. Thankfully, she threw me on my side so it didn't move the arrow much. But it still hurt like the fires of Muspelheimr. It had to be silver. Two more arrows pierced the tree we'd been up against with loud "thunks."

The boom of thunder shook the ground beneath me. The gray world turned white as lightning crackled in the clouds overhead. Blood began to ooze out around the arrow. It soon flowed steadily. Before I could think too much on it, I broke off the part of the shaft that had emerged from my chest. Pain exploded through me. Something tore inside.

I looked at Ayra. "Get it out of me. I can't fight like this," I said.

She took hold of the shaft jutting out of my back and yanked it free. It hurt so bad all I could see for a long moment was white. Deep inside, something near my heart didn't feel right. I knew with a queasy certainty that it was bad. The feel of Ayra's hand on my shoulder brought me back from the precipice of unconsciousness. Her touch was so hot it felt like a creature of Muspelheimr had a hold of me.

"Stay down. It will draw them out," she said, the words barely more than a furious growl. The heat of her touch wasn't from my loss of blood, but from the force of her anger. Shit. We were in the middle of a city and this was about to go nuclear.

"Okay, but I'm fine. Don't let them force you to lose control. That could be what Calder wants," I whispered.

For a moment I wasn't sure if the pounding rain had covered my soft words, but then she nodded. Her shoulders relaxed slightly. Good. She needed her focus. I couldn't let her know how badly I was hurt.

From out of the gray mist a tall figure approached with bold steps, the rain a bright halo around his silhouette. The feel of his energy signature marked him as a *varúlfur*, but it wasn't Calder. I would know him anywhere. In this man's hands was a crossbow that he was in the process of reloading. Out of my peripheral vision I saw two more approaching, one on each side of us, all *varúlfur*. At least they weren't *berserkrs*. I definitely couldn't fight a bear right now.

"They're flanking us," I warned Ayra.

"I know," she said as she stood.

The one approaching us head-on let his next arrow fly. It took every ounce of control I had not to leap up and put myself between the projectile and Ayra. She snatched the arrow right out of the air—a foot from my face. He had been shooting at me. Ayra snapped the arrow in half with one hand and thrust it to the ground. A growl tore from her as she launched herself at the man. So much for not letting her anger get the better of her. Double shit.

The other two closed in on me. Thunder boomed overhead as if in protest, warning, I don't know. But unless Thor himself stepped down from Asgard, I was afraid this wasn't going to go well for me. The first to reach me—a bald guy with Norse tattoos all over his head—raised a knife high. I smelled the silver of the blade. They were here to kill me. The realization brought a sense of calm. If I was their target, Ayra might be safe, even if I didn't make it.

At the last moment, I grabbed Baldy's wrists, stopping the silver knife a foot from my chest. I thrust my legs up, wrapping them around his neck before he could react. With a pop of my hips, I threw him to the ground. The knife came loose in the struggle. Where it ended up, I couldn't say. Pain erupted through my chest from my wound, but I shoved it aside.

I ended up on top long enough to get in two good punches before Baldy sneaked in an uppercut and bucked me off. We rolled about on the ground, each trying our best to get a good wrestler's hold on the other. Then a booted foot slammed into my side. Stunned by the pain it drove into my liver, and reignited in my chest, I froze, gasping for breath. Another knife glinted in the muted light shed by a nearby street lamp.

Ayra roared, sounding every bit the supernatural queen of monsters that she was. Both of my attackers paused long enough to look her way. How could they not? She looked like the very fury of Odin, hair whipping about her in the wind, clenched fists held out at her sides, rain outlining her as if it couldn't quite reach her. Her eyes burned sapphire with rage. Lips that I had been kissing only moments before moved in prayer. I knew what she wanted, standing out there like that in the open, praying to Odin, or Thor, or both.

An arrow struck her in the arm. She didn't even flinch or miss a word of her prayer.

Thunder shook the ground.

I launched to my feet and ran to her. The pain in my chest tried to make my muscles seize up. My vision went black. But I ignored both and kept moving toward her by the sheer feel of her immense power. I forced the pain down. My muscles moved me and my vision came back. Just as lightning tore open the sky, I wrapped both my arms and my power around her. White, crackling light enveloped us both. Electricity pumped through her body, brushing against mine, wearing me down like a conduit exposed to more than it could handle. My chest felt like it couldn't decide if it wanted to implode or explode. But I held fast. The Gods had answered her prayers; I wasn't about to let her down.

The lightning coursing through her was so strong, I didn't know if we could do it. It pushed against my power as she started to direct it out to the three men. I reached out to them with my power, opening up tunnels that would allow the lightning to travel to them. Each rope of my power drained my energy, increased the pain in my chest, and threatened to make me collapse. I held Ayra now out of sheer necessity to stay on my feet.

She let down her dams and channeled the lightning out the three tunnels. Our would-be-assassins screamed as lightning enveloped them at nearly the same time. The horrible stench of burning flesh filled the night. They collapsed to the ground in steaming heaps of flesh so charred, DNA samples would have to identify them.

As the last crackles of electricity left her eyes, I smiled down at Ayra. She looked like the greatest superheroes all wrapped up in one petite, blonde package. Even knowing what she was, I still had the overwhelming urge to protect her, because she was mine. I kissed her forehead. Little aftershocks of static electricity snapped along my lips.

With the lightning and the threat went the adrenaline that had been holding me upright. Pain slammed back into me with a vengeance. My vision went and I fell like a red-caped man hit by a kryptonite meteor.

CHAPTER SEVENTEEN

AYRA

Rage against the darkness without so it does not become the darkness within.
-Uppskera Journals

Vidar lay bleeding out in my arms, and there was nothing I could do. I prayed and prayed for another bolt of lightning to hit me. Maybe I could use it to heal him like I had the seeker. By her very nature, she had helped. But Vidar was special too. He could insulate against it. I didn't know if it would work for him, but I was willing to try. I would have tried to do it while frying the assassins if I had known how bad V was hurt. But he had hid it from me.

When Odin and Thor didn't answer, I begged to Freya, Frigg, Tyr, and even Heimdallr. Lightning lit up the clouds, unable—or unwilling—to break through. I couldn't stay near the bodies of our enemies any longer. People were bound to come. I hauled Vidar to a sitting position. He moaned so quietly I almost didn't hear it over the rain.

"V?" I asked.

His eyes opened slowly, as if a great weight held them shut.

A sob of relief worked its way up my throat. "V! Oh thank Thor. Can you stand?"

He nodded very slowly. I ducked under his arm and pulled him to his feet. He teetered but my arm around his back kept him upright. If it weren't for my werewolf strength, he would already be back on the ground. He took a stumbling step forward, falling into it more than walking. Clinging tight to him, I all but carried him through the park at a blinding speed. At the edge of the grass, near where we had first entered the park, he went limp against me. I eased him to the ground and propped him up against a cherry tree.

"V? Wake up. Talk to me," I demanded.

His eyelids fluttered, but they wouldn't open. Panic tightened my chest until it felt like it was squeezing my heart. He needed medical help and we were states away from any *varúlfur* doctor I knew of. A normal hospital was out of the question. Our kind healed too fast. It raised suspicions. But there were things even we couldn't heal from. The hitch in his breathing as he lay unconscious told me this might be one of those things. That arrow had come close to his heart. If he hadn't been in the process of going down on me at the time, it would have probably hit him *in* the heart.

Which meant these sons of bitches had been trying to kill him. *Him*, not me. I wanted to kill them all over again. Anger started coming in a determined tide but I shoved it down. I had to get Vidar somewhere safe. I could sling him over my shoulder and carry him, but anyone who saw would no doubt call the police thinking I was on PCP or something. Besides, even if I could get him to our bikes, he couldn't hold on, let alone drive. There remained only one option. I dug around in his pockets and pulled out his cell phone. He was so weak and out of it, he couldn't help.

With a shaking hand, I searched through his contacts until I found Evan McDougall. I pushed the call button, fully expecting either voicemail or Egor to answer. When a sleepy voice with a thick, sexy, Scottish accent answered instead, I nearly jumped out of my skin.

"Hello, Vidar."

"Actually, it's Ayra."

"What's wrong?" he asked, suddenly sounding alert and fully awake.

"He's hurt. We need help." My voice shook.

"I'll send people right now. Where are you?"

I told him and then clicked the end-call button. Shoving the phone in my pocket, I scooted up against Vidar's side. His bare, rain-slick arm felt almost cold. Our kind didn't get cold. It was a very bad sign. The dark blood seeping from the wound in his chest was even more disturbing. We were hard to kill, but not impossible, especially if someone knew how to do it. Clearly these bastards had. It had been our own kind this time.

Coming after me was one thing. But whoever sent them had come after the one person in the world I cared about most. It wouldn't be Elí. When I broke things off with him, he had sounded relieved. Besides, he was too gentle for such a thing. His alphas, Isak and Iona, would never do something so dishonorable. Only my brother could be that cruel. He would pay for this, and everything else he had done, with his life.

I snuggled up to Vidar's side, trying to will my warmth into him by wrapping as much of my body around him as I could. It wasn't very effective, considering he was twice my size in every way. I pressed a hand against his wound. His heart beat faintly against my fingers. I felt useless. Without access to lightning, or electricity of some kind, I couldn't do anything for him. If I could get his energy a significant enough jolt, I could possibly give his healing abilities the boost they needed to catch up to the damage his body had taken. But the sound of thunder had already become distant, the lightning nonexistent.

We lay wrapped together in the drizzling rain for what felt like forever. A few people walked by, but they didn't see us, ignoring us in the almost instinctual way people ignore the homeless. It was for the best. They couldn't help us. I lay there willing Vidar to hang on and praying no police would happen by.

In minutes that seemed like hours I felt the approach of an interesting new power. It pulsed with a strength and vibrancy similar to that of shifters, but it possessed very distinctive differences. Two men and one woman emerged from the misty rain. Each wore a long hooded trench coat that obscured anything beyond their basic shape. They came straight for us, as if they could feel our energy as easily as I could theirs. Hand still pressed against the wound in Vidar's chest, I prepared for a fight in case these people weren't who I thought they were.

The shorter, smaller of the three stepped forward, hands held up, palms out toward me.

"We're here to help," said a woman's voice in a thick Scottish accent that took me a moment to process.

"You'd better be or you're dead," I warned.

Beneath the hood, bright green eyes and blood red hair flashed. "I'm Emilia McDougall."

"Evan's wife?"

The huge hood turned slightly as she shook her head. "His sister."

That didn't exactly put me at ease. In my experience, siblings were just dangerous enemies forced to live under the same roof.

"That smells like a nicked artery. We'd better hurry," she pressed.

At a look from her, the two men with her moved in to either side of Vidar. They knelt down but hesitated, looking to me for permission.

"I don't want to release the pressure," I said.

One of them removed a few items from his trench coat and handed one over to me. It was a roll of gauze.

"Press this against it. I'll wrap it and hold it in place," he said as he started to unroll something that resembled athletic tape.

I accepted the gauze and pressed it against the small hole in Vidar's chest. It turned red in seconds. Both men worked fast to wrap the bandage around Vidar's entire chest, pulling tight enough to press the roll of gauze hard against him. I had no choice but to step back when they lifted him to his feet. He hung limp between them as they each draped one of his big arms over their shoulders.

The moment I lost physical contact with him, fury reared up within me strong enough to take my breath away. My vision went red around the edges. The misty night took on an ominous, bloody look, or maybe that was just my imagination conjuring up its deepest desire. I wanted to see blood in that moment, rivers of it. No, not wanted to, needed to. That fury became an ocean, one with an undertow I couldn't fight if I wanted to, and I didn't want to.

"Easy there, *Uppskera*. There will be time for vengeance later. Right now Vidar needs your help," Emilia said in a soothing tone.

Her power rolled over me, attempting to calm me. But the undertow was pulling me out faster by the moment.

"Ayra..." came Vidar's weak voice.

Before the ocean could sweep me away completely, I grabbed his hand where it lay against one of the men's shoulders. His power hit me like a jolt of lightning. The fury receded in an instant. I could think again. Though his eyelids fluttered, they didn't open. I moved up alongside the men carrying him so I could keep hold of his hand.

Before I knew it, they had us loaded into the back of a gray Tesla X with windows tinted dark enough to hide the president in. Vidar lay unconscious across the seats, his head on my lap. Though I murmured useless words of comfort and stroked his tight black curls, he didn't say another word. His eyes didn't even flutter. I took the scent of coagulating blood as a good sign, mostly because I desperately needed a good sign. The world narrowed down to the slow beat of his heart beneath my hand.

Emilia drove.

At the end of each beat of Vidar's heart, I begged the Gods that the next would come. Time ceased to have meaning save for those heartbeats. Blood soaked my clothes and made me stick to the seat. The scent filled my nose, threatening to choke me with despair.

The car came to a stop. "We're here," Emilia said.

She leaped out and opened the back door nearly all in the same moment. A gurney rolled up to the side of the vehicle, making me wonder where we were. But it wasn't a hospital like I feared. We were at the end of a long cobbled drive before a huge two-story house of windows and stone siding. A massive deck wrapped around the second story that no doubt overlooked the river I could smell not far behind us. Pine and fir trees to either side of the house gave the air a fresh, soothing scent. The scents of half a dozen different flowers in raised beds all around the house mixed with it.

The guy pushing the gurney was one of the men who'd arrived at the park. He helped Emilia and me lift Vidar onto the hard surface. I walked alongside him, hand still pressed against the wound in his chest. Around the back of the house a servant's door stood open. Awaiting our arrival in the doorway was a tall man with unruly curls of red hair thrusting up from his head like fire. Eyes such a dark green they looked black at first regarded me with concern. Ginger scruff peppered a handsome face. He grabbed the end of the gurney and lifted it to ease our entrance into the house.

"Ah, Vidar, what kind of trouble have you gotten up to now?" the man said in a thick Scottish accent. He shook his head as he looked down at Vidar. It had to be Evan.

"We were attacked by assassins," I said.

His gaze shot to mine as we wheeled Vidar into a huge kitchen. "Has it really come to all that, then?" he asked. "Fools," he grumbled. "A doctor is on the way."

"No doctors."

"No worries. The doctor is a *draugr*. He treats those of our kind."

I shook my head. "I don't need a doctor, just electricity."

Ginger brows rose. "Electricity?" Evan looked at the man pushing the end of the gurney.

"Thank you, Bruce. Would you be so kind as to see to Miss Valdísdóttir's motorcycle?"

Bruce dipped his head to Evan and backed out of the room. Once the door clicked shut, Evan gave me a gentle smile. "You can trust my sister. I do, explicitly."

A snorting sound of derision escaped me before I could stop it. "You sure about that? I wouldn't trust my sibling as far as I could throw him."

"I'm sure." He took hold of the gurney near Vidar's head. Emilia moved toward his feet.

I stared ahead at the granite countertops, keeping both people in my peripheral. With one hand pressed to Vidar's chest, I wondered how well I'd be able to fight if I had to.

"No worries, *Uppskera*. You're among friends now. We can take Vidar to my workshop. I have what you need there," Evan assured me.

I gave him my full attention, putting a heavy dose of my power behind my gaze. "If you're lying, I'll kill you all."

He nodded once, looking as if he believed me and accepted my terms. Gaze questioning, he waited until I nodded to start pulling the gurney along. The wheels clicked across the tiled floor, making it hard for me to hear Vidar's heartbeat. Come to think of it, it was getting harder to feel too. We stopped at a stainless steel door with a keypad and screen on it. Evan moved in front of the keypad. Minute clicks sounded, buttons without any tone being pushed. Smart. I liked it. He bent down to the screen, putting his eye to it. A blue light flashed around him as it moved down the screen. Retinal scanner. Damn. But then, I guess I should have expected that from a guy who owned stock in so many renewable energy companies.

The metal door opened with a slight whoosh, revealing an elevator compartment. Turning sideways, I slipped through and managed to stay at Vidar's side. Like the doors, the interior was all brushed stainless steel. It smelled mildly like cleaner and metal. Emelia turned to push the floor number and I realized they were in Roman numerals. The skin on the back of my neck prickled as the doors closed us in. The elevator whirred into action, carrying us down. Gaze shifting up to the roof access panel, I tried to breathe a little easier. At least there was one other way out.

"Why electricity?" Evan asked.

My gaze shot back to him. Blue silk pajamas hugged what looked like the body of a runner. Pale as he was, he was still sexy in a disheveled, rich boy kind of way. My mind filled with questions about his kind, but I couldn't grasp any of them. I was too worried about Vidar.

"Because I think I can use it to jump start his healing ability," I said.

The siblings exchanged a look. When Evan's gaze came back to me his dark green eyes were a bit wider. "I didn't know *varúlfur* could do that."

"They can't, just me."

"Ah, it's an *uppskera* trait, then."

I gave him a hard look, pushing a touch of power into it. It rolled over him like a wave, coating him, but not soaking in. *Interesting.* He had to be quite powerful to keep my energy out. "Yes, but the others don't know and we need to keep it that way."

"Are you sure they don't know?" he asked.

"I'm sure. They never would have attacked me during a storm if they knew."

"Unless they were testing you."

Horrible prickles of dread skittered down my spine and settled in my gut. "I killed them all so it doesn't matter." Just talking about it brought back the nasty scent of their scorched flesh. I suppressed a shudder. "Besides, they were after Vidar, not me."

Evan nodded. "Ah, I see."

I tensed. "What do you see?"

"They either seek to eliminate a rival suitor, or they want Vidar out of the way for another reason."

My first instinct was to shrug off the idea. "Assassins have come after me when Vidar wasn't around. And I spoke to one who said a hit was put on me."

"Have you considered there may be more than one person who put out a contract on your lives? And that they may have different agendas?"

I hadn't, but... The guys in Hemlock Hollow that had attacked me, the *berserkr* that had attacked Vidar, the weretiger, the werewolves at the waterfront, they were too many and too random to have been sent by the same person. Why hadn't I thought of that before?

"Shit."

"The more power you have, the more enemies you have," Evan said.

The truth of the words made me sick to my stomach. "All this time, I had thought it was just my brother. Now the entire world hates me," I said, the last part coming out as a soft murmur.

Evan's ginger brows rose into his curls. "Your own brother? Vidar told me the man was villainous, but I had no idea it was that bad."

I looked back down at Vidar's still form. His breathing came ragged and slow. "Yeah, neither did Vidar until he got back and saw."

"I don't think he would have stayed away if he had known your brother was that bad," Evan said.

"He talked about me?" I couldn't stop myself from asking.

Evan smiled so big I saw the hint of very sharp canines. They were short, somewhere between ours and a human's, but definitely more pronounced than a human's, and he only had one set of fangs where we had two. "Incessantly," he said with a chuckle.

Warmth spread throughout me. It intensified my dread. All this time we'd had feelings for each other and hadn't acted on them. So many wasted opportunities and moments. If he survived this, I would never make that mistake again.

The elevator eased to a stop and the door opened. A wide hall yawned before us, walls with a beige adobe-style finish seeming to stretch out forever. Taking the end of Vidar's gurney, Emilia propelled us into that hall at a jog. She passed up a fork with halls extending in both directions and continued straight. A huge metal door similar to what one might see on a ship waited at the end. When we reached it, she punched a code into the panel beside it and lowered her eye to the retina scanner. That Evan had given his sister access to his workshop revealed a lot about how he felt about this family.

We rolled into a large room dominated by what looked like a car chassis. Not just any car, but an electric one. The entire top half of the car was missing, exposing the enormous battery. Once I got a closer look, I realized it wasn't one battery, but hundreds, thousands, all packed together in a compartment that stretched the entire length of the car from wheel well to wheel well. An L-shaped glass desk, easily twenty feet total in length, took up one corner of the room. Shelves of books, glass containers filled with fluids of various and sometimes bright colors, batteries, and wires covered every wall. But it was the batteries of the electric car the held my attention. The fat cord extending from the wall to the car chassis looked like it would do nicely.

"What do you need?" Evan asked.

I pointed. "That."

Evan's brows rose so high they disappeared into his ginger curls. "I don't think that's a good idea. Two-hundred and twenty volts run through that cord."

I stared at him. "I channel lightning."

He let go of the gurney and stepped back as I rolled Vidar over next to the chassis. "But can Vidar survive that?" he asked in a quiet voice.

A sad smile came to my lips as I looked down at Vidar. "He's my insulator."

"Your insulator?" Emelia asked.

"He can hold onto me when I channel it. He can help me direct it."

Emilia drew in a sharp breath and straightened. Her eyes flicked from Evan, to the door, and back to me. "You're like *Gungnir*," she whispered in a reverent tone.

Chills ran through me at the comparison. The valkyrie had told me that coupled with Sonya—the seeker—I had the potential to be one of Odin's greatest weapons. Hearing it said like this, though, put it into a new perspective. I wasn't sure I liked being compared to *Gungnir*, the mighty spear of Odin, one of the greatest weapons of the Gods. But it made a sort of sense I couldn't deny.

Claws extended, I picked up the power cord. "You may want to step back."

Not even my keen werewolf hearing picked up on their footsteps, but I felt their energy withdraw, so I knew they moved away. I stripped the insulation from the wires with a swipe of a sharp claw. The electricity jumped into me. I drew it in as hard as I could, inviting that wild, pulsing power to fill my body. It was more than the 120 volts I had played with as a kid, but it was like a glass of water where lightning was the incoming tide. I prayed it would be enough. The wound in my arm from the arrow I'd taken burned, but I ignored it. Vidar was all that mattered.

The lights started to flicker after what felt like only a small jolt that didn't even come close to filling me. As the power went out and plunged us all into total darkness, I let go of the now useless cord and lay my hands on Vidar. Coagulating blood squelched between my fingers. The renewed scent tried to drive a sliver of panic into me. I forced it aside and focused. Using my own power as a propellant, I channeled the electricity into Vidar.

The different parts of his power stuck out to me like different scents. His healing ability wasn't easy to find. It was fading by the moment. While perusing inside him I felt that the arrow had nicked his heart and damaged one of his valves. His werewolf strength was all that was keeping him alive, and it was failing. I directed the mixture of my power and electricity toward the part of his power that amplified his healing. My willpower helped direct it, funneling it down so all of it flowed where it needed to go. The nick in his heart repaired itself in an instant. The shredded valve knitted together a bit slower.

He jolted beneath my hands and sucked in a deep gasp of air. "Ayra!" His hands found my arms, one moved up to my face. "Are you hurt?" he asked.

A generator whirred to life and the lights came back on. Relieved laughter bubbled from me. "Am *I* hurt? You're insane, V, you know that?"

I leaned down and carefully placed a long kiss on his pale pink lips. When I drew away color had already begun to return to them. The jolt hadn't been able to heal him completely, but it did enough that he'd survive so his own healing could finish the job. Vidar smiled and my heart melted into a puddle I wasn't sure would ever solidify.

"It's the superhero in me. Seriously, though, are you hurt?" he said.

I put my hand against his where it cupped my cheek. "No, not at all, thanks to you."

Relief smoothed out his features, erasing the wrinkles between his brows and around his eyes. "Well, superhero and all, you know."

I kissed him again. His hand moved to cradle the back of my head. I clung to him, but gently, knowing he had a lot more healing to do. He felt so amazing, warm, and alive beneath my lips that I wasn't about to try and draw back. The world narrowed to just him for a wonderful moment. Then someone cleared their throat.

"I do beg your pardon, but you should take care not to overexert yourself too much just yet," Evan said.

"Now Evan, they've just reunited after Ayra feared she might lose him. Give them a moment, or ten. I've always wanted to see werewolves mate," Emelia said, mumbling the last bit beneath her breath.

Evan made an exasperated sound and said something sharply in Gaelic to Emelia. "Please forgive my sister. She grew up in the sixties and seventies," he said to us.

"Don't be such a prude, Evan. Surely you're curious too," she countered.

Vidar chuckled, the sound ending in a wince that left him clutching his chest. I put a hand on his shoulder and focused my power into my sense of hearing. His heart beat strong and steady. I let a long breath out.

"Your sister is every bit as spunky as you described her," Vidar said.

The *draugr's* lips curved up, exposing one very pointy fang. "I did warn you." He crossed the room to Vidar's gurney. "It's good to see you, my friend. I'm only sorry it's under such circumstances."

"Yeah, me too," Vidar grumbled.

Evan dipped his head in my direction. "Your lady here is every bit as marvelous as *you* described."

Fingers wove through mine. I looked down to find Vidar gazing up at me not with the adoration or worship I feared, but love. The shock of it stole away the snappy response I had to Evan's words.

"Yes she is," Vidar agreed.

His eyes trapped me, holding me like something precious and priceless. The world narrowed down to only the two of us again. I heard the others in the room, but it didn't matter. Emotion choked me until I couldn't draw another breath. Vidar had almost died. If that had happened, I would have lost my mind.

"The doctor is still on his way. If you'd like, he can take a look at you. And I hate to press, but the council is meeting at five o'clock," Evan said.

Feeling the resistance building in him, I gave Vidar a hard look. He finally sighed and broke from my gaze to look at Evan. "Yeah, the doc can take a look at me. Just so long as he gets here before the meeting. I'm not missing that."

I dipped my head in compromise. "She, and fair enough."

"In that case, we're going to give you two a moment alone while we go prepare to hack the unhackable," Evan said. He bowed his head low to both of us and made his way to the door.

A profound look of disappointment came over Emelia. "We? But shouldn't one of us stay close in case—"

"No, Emelia, come along." He grabbed her arm as he walked past and dragged her along behind him.

She walked backwards, her eyes glued to us. "But I have so many questions, as I'm sure they do about us!"

"There will be time for that later," Evan insisted. Emelia's eyes locked onto mine. "Later then?"

Her curiosity made me smile. I would have felt exactly the same were I not so distracted. "Later," I promised.

The door closed on her eager face, leaving Vidar and I alone at last. The woman in me and the reaper in me went to war. One part of me wanted to collapse into his arms and let the tears of relief fall that I'd been holding back. The other part wanted to kill everyone who threatened us.

"This is—"

"Not your fault, don't you even say it," Vidar interrupted. Unable to hold his gaze, I looked down at our clasped hands, his big, dark hand enveloped my tiny pale one. He seemed so strong, so untouchable. But today had proved he was anything but. His free hand lifted my chin, forcing me to look at him. The fierce look burning in his eyes took my breath away.

"If I hadn't been in the process of going down on you, that shot wouldn't have missed my heart. So the way I see it, you saved me twice over," he said.

"I let myself get distracted while I knew we had enemies out there. And now I'm not so sure Calder is our only enemy."

His brows rose. "Please, Ayra, don't let this change your mind. You're my soul mate. I would fight off all the assassins in the nine worlds to be with you."

I batted my eyelashes at him. "That's the sweetest thing anyone has ever said to me." I let the playfulness melt away and expose my determination. "But you won't have to, V, because I'm going to show them all that they don't want to fuck with us ever again."

CHAPTER EIGHTEEN

VIDAR

E van's conference room wouldn't stop spinning. Even with Ayra at
my side, hand clutching mine like a lifeline, I felt like I might
topple at any moment. It didn't help that on each facet of the
hexagon-shaped room a TV with revolving pictures of the hills of Scotland
took up the wall. It took a good amount of my training to keep me
standing tall and steady. Each beat of my heart sent a thud of pain
reverberating through my body. Each breath fanned the coals of a fire
smoldering in my chest. Each movement threatened to sap the last of my
energy. My body wanted me to rest so it could finish healing me, and I
desperately wanted to comply.

But I couldn't. Hel, I couldn't even show the slightest weakness. The
villains needed to think they had failed utterly, not realize they'd come so
close to success. I would not be the reason they renewed their efforts
against us. And if Ayra was right and they were sending assassins after me
now, they needed to be taught why that was a really bad idea.

Gazing up at me with a heavy look, Ayra frowned. "You sure you're up
for this?" she asked.

I grinned and leaned closer. "Darling, I'm up for anything you can
imagine."

She grimaced, which was exactly the opposite effect I'd been going for. "Is that going to be a thing now?" she asked.

"A thing?" I tried not to sound too disappointed and failed.

Her arms wrapped around my waist and she narrowed her eyes as she looked up at me. "The hometown charm thing. I'll take my comic book geek over a cowboy any day." A smile broke through as she said the last part.

Raising my arms up, I flexed one bicep, then the other. "Can a comic book geek do this?"

A huge, beautiful grin broke over her face as she pulled me closer with a little more care than I liked. "Mine can," she whispered.

That lithe little body pressed against mine made blood rush hot through my veins. My heart ached from pumping overtime, but I didn't care. She rose up on her toes and pressed her lips to mine. Her hands went around my neck. The rest of the world fell away, almost literally, as I started to sway on my feet. In an instant, her hands were back around my waist, steadying me.

The worry in her eyes worried *me*. "Easy there. Why don't you stand behind me for this, with your arms around my waist. It will remove any question as to my choice of mates," she said.

What she didn't say hung over us like the threat of an anvil. *And it will help keep you steady on your feet.* She didn't have to voice it. I could see it in her eyes. We couldn't afford to have our enemies see either of us as weak. But that didn't worry me as much as how long healing would take. Time was a luxury we didn't have at the moment. She was right, and I couldn't let my ego get in the way of that.

"Going live in five," Evan warned from the podium in the center of the room.

I nodded to Ayra and slid my arms around her waist. She turned her back to me and rested her hands atop mine. I tried to pull my hands away with the intention of putting them on her shoulders, but she held strong. My back straightened so fast I felt a vertebrae pop. Mating with me in private was one thing, but this display could give people an entirely different idea, a more formal one. She couldn't possibly be considering...

The TV screens came to life with sound and live images. Several of them divided into two images to accommodate all ten members of the

Shifter Council. One representative of each of the known races were present: a male lion shifter, female leopard shifter, female tiger shifter, male cheetah shifter, female brown bear shifter, a male black bear shifter, a female polar bear, a male panda bear, a female coyote shifter, a male fox shifter, a male jackal shifter, and a female wolf shifter. Each were of course in their human forms, but I knew who they were, and what they were. Despite an aversion to politics, I kept up on them.

The *varúlfur* councilor, Brigid Thomasdóttir, flicked her wide blue eyes from Evan, to Ayra and I, and back again. Her cheeks flushed a brilliant red and she bowed her head low to Ayra.

"*Uppskera*, you honor us with your presence," she said.

The male lion shifter snarled and bared his fangs. "Like hell! No one has the right to interrupt a council meeting. And who the hell are you?" he directed the last to Evan.

The black bear shifter answered. "He's Evan McDougall, a *draugr*. What is the meaning of this?"

"Why can't I log out?" another asked.

"How did you get past our firewalls?" demanded another.

Ayra cleared her throat. "There is something each of you needs to know about me," she said in a cold tone that commanded every eye in the room, virtual or actual.

I couldn't have stopped the crooked grin that worked its way onto my face if I had wanted to, and I didn't. She sounded hot as Muspelheimr when she took command like that. It stirred my alpha side into a nearly uncontrollable frenzy of need. Even with a healing tear in my heart, I wanted her bad. I didn't try to hide that either. It was time these people knew she was mine, and I was hers.

The questions and demands from the council members stopped. Some eyes revealed anticipation, others interest, and even some, hostility. But all remained silent.

Ayra lifted her chin and stretched to her full height. Her head still only came to my throat but her size didn't diminish her presence. If anything, it accentuated it.

"I do not belong to any pack." She stepped away from me far enough to remove her jacket.

Hands going to the back of a chair we had placed nearby for such a purpose, I leaned my weight on it as casually as I could. The world didn't try to sway away from me, yet.

She turned her jacket around, showing the councilors the AVV symbol of a roaring wolf's head on the back. "I relinquish my membership to the American Viking *Varúlfur*. While I still believe strongly in the democracy they stand for, I can't belong to any faction of any kind."

She dropped the jacket on the floor. Hard gaze moving to each gaping face on each monitor, she circled the room slowly. "Because I am I not just the *uppskera* for the *varúlfur*, nor am I even just the *uppskera* for the canine shifters. I am the *uppskera* for all of shifter kind." The *berserkr* who had been glaring hard at her flinched when she stopped at his monitor. "I am death, chosen by Odin himself to reap those who threaten our kind and break our creeds, and I do not care what kind of shifter that person turns out to be."

Council members started to look to the side, the ceiling, even the floor, anywhere but at her. Power and confidence radiated out from her, reaching them even through the monitors. And they didn't even get the half of it. Standing in the same room with her felt like sunbathing naked on a triple digit day in the desert.

After a moment of silence, she went on. "Some idiots think they can take my place, as if being the *uppskera* is a position or a title to steal. Their assassins are dead, and I will discover who sent them, and they soon will be dead too. To threaten me is to threaten the will of Odin. Anyone who does so will be shown no mercy."

She looked down, then to the side at me, a beckoning look. Stealing myself for the pain that came with excessive movement, I pushed away from the chair. My hard gaze scanned the faces on the monitors. Not a single one offered any look of challenge. I stopped just behind Ayra, resting my hands on her shoulders. When she didn't speak, I took my cue to do so.

"The assassins who came after me are dead as well. I will kill any and all who threaten the *uppskera* or my place at her side."

She reached up and placed a hand atop mine. "Vidar Balderson is not only my *verndari*, we are now mates. He is the only allegiance I have. Any who threaten him, threaten me. And we will kill any threats to us."

Warmth spread throughout me. Despite the throbbing pain in my chest, a smile came easily to my lips. That made it official, not just to our kind, but to the entire world. Like full wolves, we mated for life. By proclaiming us mates, she told them all that she wouldn't take another if I died. Rivals had no reason to try and kill me now.

I looked from one monitor, to the next, and the next, doing my best not to sway on my feet as I did so. Ayra's grip on my hand tightened. She leaned back against me, steadying me. I tried to channel all my old comic book heroes as I told them, "Do you understand what your *uppskera* is telling you? These threats against us stop now. We will not tip the balance by choosing any side, be it *varúlfur* or otherwise. Our duty is to stave off chaos and keep the balance to protect all of shifter kind."

The eyes I met looked away in submission. Several of the councilors nodded, appearing satisfied, others looked relieved. The *varúlfur* councilor dropped her eyes for a moment, then looked back up at Ayra and I.

"Thank you for your words, *Uppskera* Ayra Valdísdóttir and Vidar Balderson of the Order of the *Verndari*. I'm glad you came forward to speak to us. I will take this to the Alpha Council. We will ensure our kind understand that to go against you is to go against the entire Alpha Council," she said.

Both Ayra and I nodded to her. I thrust my chin in Evan's direction and gave him a look. The monitors went blank as he cut the feed. The vacuum of sound and energy it left in the room pulled me under. Or maybe it was just my body finally demanding I rest like a sane person and let it heal. Either way, darkness rushed in and swallowed me. Not even the fact that I was now an alpha to all the combined shifter races could stop it.

CHAPTER NINETEEN

AYRA

Beads of rain ran up my visor in a steady flow. Passing headlights sent little sparks reflecting off them out into the night. The scent of wet pavement and exhaust permeated my helmet, nauseating me slightly. There could be no avoiding it, though. Even at barely four hours past the witching hour Highway 26 was busy. Traffic lessened with each mile I got outside of Portland. Only once I passed a small town called Banks was I finally able to maintain the speed limit without passing people left and right.

The anxiety of leaving Vidar at Evan's place eased with each mile I put between us. I couldn't have him following me. He needed to heal. My brother would recognize Vidar's weakened state in an instant, and he would use it against him, and me. I could handle this without him. I had to. Emelia had given Vidar something to help him sleep, and I had slipped out the moment he lost consciousness. I would only have an hour before his werewolf metabolism burned through the drug and he woke up. But, according to my GPS, an hour was all I needed to reach Cannon Beach.

Just as the highway turned into a seemingly abandoned road winding its way through a thick forest of beautiful fir and pine that reached the sky, my Bluetooth told me I had an incoming call. It was from my brother. I let it ring for a few moments before deciding.

"Answer."

His snide, condescending voice came through the speakers in my helmet. "Little sister, you have proved far more resilient than I thought you would be. Of course, you have me to thank for that."

"Like hell I do."

"What was that? The road noise must have garbled your thank you."

My fangs extended, forcing my jaw open slightly. I knew damn well I had come through crystal clear. With speakers and microphones in all the right places, this helmet was more than adequate.

"What do you want, Calder? You had better not be running from me," I warned.

An angry growl came through my speakers. "As if. I've never run from you."

"If that were true we would have had this conversation weeks ago in Hemlock Hollow."

Calder laughed. "Clueless as always, little sister." He snarled the word "little" as if it were a bad thing. He had always tried to make me feel like less than nothing because of my size. But now it just made me realize he was the small one.

I had several more miles to go, might as well play along. "Why did you leave Hemlock Hollow then?"

"The pieces had to be moved into place. I had to do my part. Now you and me can finally get the reckoning we deserve."

The words sent a chill through me that surpassed any the rainy weather could cause. Though I knew Vidar was safe with Evan and Emelia, my thoughts still turned to him. There could be no safer place for him than in the company of two of Portland's most powerful *draugar*. It felt too much like I was trying to convince myself. The chills multiplied. I shifted down and started to pull on the front brakes.

Then memories that weren't mine barreled into me.

It wasn't just one condemned, but dozens upon dozens. All manner of crimes from the mundane to the horrific flashed in the back of my mind. I had to forcibly shut them out so I could see the road.

"I'm guessing by your stunned silence that you've felt the condemned waiting for you here in Cannon Beach."

When I didn't answer, Calder laughed long and hard. "I have them locked away from the town for the moment, but if you don't arrive within the hour, I'm going to let them loose. To get to me, you'll have to go to Wheeler Marina. Because I'm generous, I'll give you an extra eighteen minutes to travel the extra eighteen miles south."

Just as I suspected, he wanted our confrontation to take place before the festival. The idiot thought he could still defeat me like he had when we were kids.

A roar tore from me. "I'm coming for them, and you."

I let go of the brakes and pulled the throttle back. The bike roared to life beneath me. I let it nearly redline before shifting. Fifteen minutes remained in the hour and I still had fifty miles to go. I might make it, if I could avoid any speed traps. For the sake of the town of Cannon Beach and Wheeler, I had to try.

...

When my headlights hit the sign welcoming me to Wheeler, my phone rang again. The electronic voice told me it was Vidar. I gave it the command to ignore the call. The scythe of guilt dug into me. But I couldn't risk giving him the chance to delay me. If this worked out right, it would all be over by the time he could get here.

All that time I had wasted being mad at him... No. I couldn't think about that now.

I followed my GPS instructions through the sleeping town to the marina. All throughout the deserted streets I felt for the presence of other werewolves, but there weren't any. But that sense could only detect so far. The constant rain faded any scent trails over a day old that would have lingered, so that was no help either. The crisp smells of salt water and juniper permeated through my helmet. It made me anxious for action. Finally, after so many days of hunting the asshole, I would get the chance to confront him.

He had a world of hurt coming for all the horrible things he had done, the least of which were to me. If Raul was right, and Calder wasn't the only one behind all of this, I'd deal with that later. Ridding the world of my brother would be a huge step in the right direction. And it was a step I alone had to take.

The overwhelming scent of fish told me I had reached the marina before I turned the corner. It unfolded in a dark blue swath that stretched out toward the horizon. A dozen or so ships sat at the docks, their shapes dark against the slowly brightening sky. I chose a parking spot in the middle of the empty lot and shut my bike off.

I took my helmet off and hung it on my handlebars. My jacket soon followed. The rain began to soak through my T-shirt almost instantly. But it would be better to get wet than to deal with the constricting fit of the nylon and armor padding. The roaring knotwork wolf patch sewn on the back seemed to stare me down with a look of betrayal. Loneliness snagged at my willpower. By stepping out of the American Viking *Varúlfur*, I had left behind the only pack I'd ever chosen. But I wasn't alone. I had Vidar, if I made it out of this alive.

I didn't feel any other werewolves, but I could smell them. Their scents lingered like an old trail. The only fresh scent among them was Calder's. He had been through here within the hour. Unfortunately, his scent trail led down one of the docks with boats lining each side. So his plan was to ambush me. *Fine.*

I removed my boots and placed them upside down next to my bike. The less I wore, the less I had to deal with if I needed to shift fast. Gaze and senses trying to check every direction at once, I walked down to the docks. It bothered me deeply that I couldn't feel the condemned anymore. Where had they gone? Wet asphalt gripped my feet, unable to harm my tough werewolf skin, but still uncomfortable by its nature alone. Each ship I passed made me tense in preparation. No lights, no laughter, no music, no scents of humans or food being prepared, nor any other evidence of people.

Not a soul even wandered around on this rainy night. Of course, that could be in part because of the metallic tang of lightning I tasted in the air. I hoped it was all that was keeping people inside, and not the murderous tendencies of my brother. Thunder rolled in the distance out over the choppy ocean. I said a quick prayer to Aegir, guardian of the seas, in hopes that he might be kind to the chosen of Odin. From the roil of his waters, it didn't seem he was in a good mood.

At the end of the dock sat a small fishing boat, the kind with a motor on the back that doubled as a steering mechanism. Lightning flashed up in the clouds, brightening the sky just enough that I saw something in the boat. After another quick look and feel around, I jumped down into the boat. One of those white, waterproof message boards a person can place at a pool or in their shower sat on the wooden bench.

Due North, it read in Calder's handwriting.

Dark, rain-heavy clouds concealed anything beyond a hundred feet out in the ocean. I turned to the motor and looked it over. It had a pull cord like a chain saw. Fingers around the handle, I drew in a deep breath through my nose. Nothing strange that might indicate a bomb tainted the air. I couldn't be sure, exactly, but I felt sure enough to pull the cord and start the engine. It rumbled to life after two pulls. Tapping into my werewolf sense of direction, I pointed the boat due north and pulled the throttle.

The little boat broke through the water with enough speed to make the nose bounce off the surface. Waves undulated around me, looking like they wanted to swallow my boat and me with it. Wind whipped the rain against me, soaking my clothes through and leaving me with a chill that had more to do with the ominous air than the temperature. Any semblance of dawn disappeared as the sky darkened with thickening clouds. Thunder rolled across the sky like the wheels of Odin's chariot. I wasn't sure if I should take it as a warning or just as typical Oregon coastal weather.

Either way, I couldn't turn back. Twenty yards out I felt the press of my brother's power. It drew my gaze to a huge, dark shape out near the horizon in the middle of the ocean. As I grew closer, I realized it was a container ship. Metal box containers big enough to house a small RV sat here and there across the large deck. Normally those things didn't ship out until the entire deck was lined with metal boxes. It was as if someone had set sail without waiting for it to be fully loaded.

Great. Calder stole a container ship. Who knew how many people he had killed in the process? The thought made me shudder.

He had stacked up far more bodies than I had, either directly or through the new werewolves he bit in. My resolve hardened. Rather than pull the throttle back harder, I eased off it and slowed my approach. I dropped my walls a bit as I grew closer. Calder's power remained the only one on the ship. But I knew he wouldn't be alone for long. Fighting his own battles wasn't his way, not without seriously stacking the odds in his favor.

Drums of thunder sounded again. The clouds flashed bright with the evidence of lightning just above them. Both the sound and sight soothed me. If I was lucky, Calder hadn't been the one to send those last assassins after Vidar, and so hadn't seen me channel lightning. What he didn't know could hurt him. While I had to rely on luck for it to strike, a ship with metal containers scattered on its deck helped tip the odds in my favor. I hoped.

Part of me respected Calder's choice of ships. Considering these behemoths lost altogether up to 10,000 containers a year at sea, they were an environmental threat all their own. Removing one from circulation for even a day was a win. But then, Calder always had cared about the environment. It was the one thing—besides parents—that we had in common.

I shifted only my eyes to those of a wolf, allowing me to see clearly in the dark as I approached the side of the ship. The hull came alive with the tiny glow of barnacles. Calder's energy signature was somewhere near the center of the deck. Twenty feet or so away from the ship, I killed the motor and floated in on momentum. He'd know what side I approached from because he would have heard me coming, but I was hoping by drifting along the ship a bit, he couldn't pinpoint my exact spot. A flash of the old anxiety I always felt around my brother tried to rear up. But I wasn't that fearful little girl anymore.

Anger replaced my anxiety. The face of each werewolf I'd had to kill because of Calder flashed in my memory. They fanned the flames of that anger. Each memory of what those men had done, both as werewolves and before, worked like the squeeze of a bellows. The anger burned on the edge of mindless fury. I focused on my breathing, my control. I pushed away the thoughts of my brother and his progeny. Instead, I focused on Vidar, all I felt for him, all he felt for me. Calm slowly began to set in.

I leaped up to the deck of the container ship. Due to the sway of the boat I jumped from, I landed off balance. I tucked and rolled across the wet, steel deck. The roll took me back up onto my feet. Fists before me, I prepared for an attack, but it didn't come. Instead, my brother stood in plain sight, leaning up against a tall, steel container. The strangeness of his casual manner froze me in place.

He made a scoffing laugh sort of noise. "Ayra, graceful as always." The derision in his tone was meant to make me feel small, useless. For the first time, it didn't work. It only made him sound insecure. I'd never thought of him that way, and it made me a little sad.

But only a little. That sadness faded when I saw the depth of disgust and loathing in the shine of his eyes. "Calder, insecure as always," I said.

Lightning above the clouds lit the deck in an eerie glow long enough for me to see the stupefied surprise on my brother's face. Little tingles of victory worked through me. I'd never talked back to him before. It felt *good*. The look disappeared before the light could fade completely.

"Someone is feeling overconfident," he said.

"I'm not the same little girl you used to beat up," I warned him. "What makes you think you can do what your assassins couldn't?"

He emitted a scoffing sort of laugh. "You can't honestly tell me you think I'm not better than a bunch of newly bitten or a weretiger that turned out to like cunts better than cocks."

I shrugged. "Maybe you are. But a *berserkr*, then four werewolf assassins at once, not even you can think you're better than all of them. You're arrogant, but you're not stupid."

Though he recovered quickly enough, the surprise that left his face slack for a heartbeat confirmed what I'd been fishing for. Not only did he not send the *berserkr* or werewolf assassins, he didn't know about them. Raul was right, someone else was involved here. But Calder was in the dark about it. It also meant my brother didn't know about the lightning.

He laughed again, but this time it sounded forced. "Yeah, well, the black mongrel you had isn't here to help you now. From what I hear, he may be dead."

I took a step toward him before I could stop myself. A growl vibrated my chest. "Vidar is from a long, proud line of *varúlfur* who trace their lineage back to *verndari* to the king of Iceland. Trash talking him because of the color of his skin is antiquated and stupid."

Another flash of lightning up in the clouds revealed fangs gleaming in Calder's smile. "Ah, there are those nerves I love to cut open so much."

Laughing, he pushed away from the steel container and began to pace a circle around me. The misty rain became steady drops that shimmered between us like silver threads. I shook my head, sending droplets flying from my pale locks as I started to circle him as well.

I ignored the dig. "A war, Calder, really? I didn't think you were that stupid."

Wagging a finger at me, he shook his head. "Naïve as always, little sister. Humans are polluting the world, destroying it. They need to be stopped. What better way to do that than take over and rule it ourselves?"

The point was hard to argue, but his methods were another matter. "You bit people in against their will for decades. And why? All because you wanted the power to awaken in you," I said.

Calder smacked his chest. "I should lead our people. It should have worked. I should have been the one chosen. I was born first. I'm bigger, stronger, and better than you in every way."

"Clearly not in the way that matters."

Thunder swallowed his growl as he launched himself at me. Seeing him coming at me, face twisted in fury, eyes filled with hatred, looking like every traumatic incident of my childhood, made me freeze. It took me back to a life of abuse and fear. Mired in the memories, I could only dodge and block his attacks. Instinct brought some of my old habits back. I flinched and cowered, tricks that used to make him ease up for fear of hurting me so bad a teacher might notice at school. At first, I didn't even realize I was doing it.

Calder's kicks and strikes flew so fast and hard it took all of my concentration to keep up with them. It wasn't the pretty flow of martial arts, but the all-out attempts of one person to kill another. The man had scary skills. He clipped me with a right hook that sent me stumbling back a few steps. The reaper in me woke, uncoiling with a furious righteousness that coursed through my entire body. My fangs and claws extended, forcing my mouth and fists open. White-hot fury threatened to burn away all reason.

Getting hit always made me mad, but getting hit by my brother used to make me feel weak and small. Not today. Not anymore. The crack in my fear became a fissure that yawned into a canyon. The shell of fear shattered, freeing me.

I exploded in a flurry of kicks and strikes, spinning and flying at him with all the anger that had built up inside me over the years. A punch broke through his defenses and struck him in the chest, a kick tagged him on the thigh, an uppercut knocked his teeth together so hard it would have broken bones in a human. He remained on his feet, eyes wide with shock, suddenly on the defensive. My strikes forced him back one step, another, and another. I splashed through the deepening rainwater that stood on the deck, following him step for step.

Blood shone brightly at the corner of his mouth. It was a small victory compared to the surprise on his face. A mixture of anger and triumph fueled my strikes, making them faster and harder. Calder couldn't keep up. Punch after kick after jab broke through his defenses. Each one boosted my confidence higher, repairing a little of the scars of my childhood.

As I landed a punch in his solar plexus, I yelled over the storm, "I'm not weak."

After driving a kick into his midsection, I yelled, "I'm not useless."

I slammed a hammer fist across his face that drove him to a knee. "And I am not your victim anymore!" I roared. Thunder boomed as if to accentuate my words.

Rather than crumble in defeat like I hoped he would, he rolled into a somersault and came to his feet over a yard away. He threw his head back and shook with laughter that the storm tried in vain to swallow.

"You'll never be anything more than my victim!" he yelled.

Then I felt it, the press of the power of dozens upon dozens of newly bitten in werewolves. They approached from every direction in boats small enough that the storm almost devoured the sound of their engines. Right after I felt their power, the images from their minds hit me. Violence and bloodshed of every imaginable horror flashed before me. It stole both my breath and my focus.

Through the haze of a murderous memory, I felt more than saw my brother approach. By luck alone I blocked his first strike. The second hit me like a war hammer in the gut. I blocked the follow-up strike to the side of my head, but just barely. The distraction of the horrible memories of the condemned was too much. Dozens of different minds bombarded my own. In that moment I realized what a *verndari's* true purpose was: to shield the *uppskera* from the memories and minds of the condemned. And Calder had succeeded in stripping me of my shield.

The boats carrying the condemned toward me from every direction grew closer. Their proximity drove away all cognitive thought. Calder's fist slammed into the side of my head. His bare foot connected with my solar plexus as I went down. Air left my body in a rush so fast it burned. Another punch connected with the side of my face. My vision went a little white around the edges. Wait, was it my own vision, or that of the person whose memory of murdering a child replayed in my head? Or could it be the memory of the pyromaniac setting a church ablaze during Sunday worship? Maybe it was the man peeling the skin from a woman, laughing as she screamed and begged.

I held my arms up to fend off further attacks and barely felt impact after impact. Water cooled one side of me. It didn't feel like the memory of one of the condemned. I realized distantly I had fallen and now lay on the deck curled into a fetal position. My brother laughed as he drove kick after kick into me.

My brother. The reason behind all of this. If I didn't stop him, Vidar would try, and probably die. I slammed the door on the wall I kept up around my ability to sense other werewolves. The memories of the condemned shut off like a switch had been flipped. Light, scent, sound, and feeling came back to me in a rush.

I grabbed Calder's foot as he drove it into my stomach again. His eyes shot open wide with surprise right before I flew to my feet, shoving that foot back at him so hard it sent him flying. Metal rang as he slammed into the wall of one of the containers then slid to the deck. I tried to jump to my feet but things inside hurt too much. Instead, I ended up stumbling until I reached the same container Calder was against. The metal siding cooled my palm, helped me focus. Blood scented the air thickly, too much of it mine.

Roaring, Calder came at me again. I had no choice but to crack the door to my power back open and suck some of his in. Energy poured into me. It felt tainted, vile, but it helped me stand on my own. As much as I wanted nothing to do with my brother's power, I needed it. I was hurt too badly to fight all of the condemned and survive. I sucked his energy down until I felt the internal bleeding in my body stop.

With his power came his memories. I lived through him as an unwilling participant while he bit in victim after victim, choosing the darkest souls he could find, ones he knew would wreak havoc and bring chaos. Years and years of victims flashed before my eyes as if Calder were forcing the memories down my throat. But I also felt his deep love for this world, its forests, rivers, and fields. I felt his anguish over the destruction of more and more forest land, his helplessness regarding islands of plastic clogging the ocean, the toxins pouring into the rivers of Asia, and the smog hanging over the major cities of every country.

Faltering, I stumbled back.

Though he knelt in the rain, barely able to lift his head, laughter hiccupped from him.

I stopped pulling in his power. Even my bruises had healed.

While I sympathized with his pain over the pollution of the world, I couldn't turn a blind eye to what he had done. "You find your own impending death funny?" I asked.

He lifted his head just enough to fix his heavy-lidded eyes on me. "I won't be the one dying today, you stupid bitch." He laughed again, but it was shorter, forced, as if it took too much energy. "When you kept surviving the attacks, I figured out how your power worked. But it comes with a nasty catch, doesn't it? You can't steal power without feeling the dark souls of your victims. It distracts you, makes you vulnerable."

Chills raced through me, raising bumps along my skin. My distraction allowed him to force himself up on one foot. "Why do you think I kept choosing murderers and rapists?" More laughter spewed from him, sounding maniacal in its delight. "It certainly wasn't to make killing them easier on you."

Part of me had hoped it was, because if so, it meant some portion of my brother might be good and merciful. That thread of hope had been short and thin, but it still hurt when it burned away. I swallowed hard.

"And now all my hard work is about to pay off," Calder said in a downright gleeful tone.

The energy of the others scratched and scurried against the wall I kept my power behind. They were closer now, too close. While Calder had been talking, they had reached the ship. Their footfalls splashed onto the deck. Like drawing from a straw, heedless of brain freeze, I sucked enough of my brother's power to slam him face-first onto the deck. I wasn't sure if he was unconscious or not, and I didn't have time to check. The first of the condemned leaped out of the darkness at me, right over my prone brother.

A second came from my left, a third from my right, and a fourth from behind me. Two of them collided as I used the standing water on the deck to slip out of the way. More came at me. Gods, there were dozens. Claws raking and tearing, I fought them with my bare hands. I couldn't afford to drop my barriers and suck in their power, not with so many of them. Their memories and darkness would overwhelm me. Calder would eventually recover and be waiting for any moment of weakness. My gaze flicked to his body, which still lay unmoving in the semi-darkness.

The air pressure built and built, until finally crashing with a mighty boom of thunder that rattled everything on the ship. Many of the condemned stumbled. For the thunder to be that loud and powerful meant the storm now hovered directly overhead. I could both feel the prickle of electricity and taste its metallic flavor. If only I could call it down like the seeker could. While that wasn't an option, I could make myself a more attractive target for it.

Near the prow of the ship stood some sort of tower. What I hoped was a metal rod stuck out of the top of it, rising up into the misty rain. It was my best chance. Unfortunately, it was at the opposite end of the ship. I ran and leaped into the air—right over the heads of several snarling condemned werewolves. The distance was less than I thought. My feet scrambled across the top of one of the nine-foot-tall containers. The slick surface sent me skidding almost right over the other side. My low center of gravity served me well and kept me from falling.

My senses tingled. I tasted metal. The clouds above lit up in a flash with the promise of the lightning they contained. A quick scan of the area showed the next container in the direction of the prow of the ship to be about ten feet away. Praying to Freya for good footing, I ran and jumped. When I landed, I slid to my knees and skidded across the corrugated metal, stopping well short of the end. Ahead lay an opening with no containers within a distance even my werewolf power could manage to help me reach. Worse, the deck of the ship was lower, contoured into sections meant to hold the containers, like the bottom of a Lego.

Before I could decide, several of the condemned poured into the open space. Some had shifted to wolf form. I stripped my clothes off in record time. As I ran for the edge of the container, I shifted into a wolf. The flow of my atoms from one form into another gave me an extra boost of adrenalin as I hit the deck on four white-blond paws. I opened the door to my power a crack and sucked in enough of their power to weaken them and add speed to my own legs. After a wave of nausea brought on by their seedy energy, I plunged forward.

The boost their power gave me came at a cost heavier than *Mjölnir*. Murderous thoughts and memories flooded my mind. My power raged, not only at what these condemned had done, but what I felt they would do if given the chance. They each thrilled at the thought of attacking me, hurting me, violating me, and eventually killing me. And they wanted to do it to countless others.

The horrors in my mind made me slow down, hesitate when I shouldn't have. Claws and fingers reached for me. Pain burned along my left leg and right thigh as a few attacks connected. I jumped out of the container hold back up to where the deck stretched out again. In a few more yards, I reached the next container. Without hesitation, I leaped in mid-stride. Just as the edge of the container passed under my paws, I shifted back into a woman. I fell on top of the container hard enough to knock the air from my lungs. The press of energy from behind told me the condemned still pursued me. I had to stop them or I'd never reach my destination.

I would have given anything in that moment not to have to experience those horrible images again, anything but risk Vidar's life. And if he showed up before I had the upper hand, that was exactly what would happen.

Alone atop the container, I took a risk and flung open the door to my power. Their seedy darkness filled me. Images of death, murder, and so much worse gyrated behind my eyelids with each blink. But I didn't let it stop me. I pulled in more and more. Those that still could jumped up after me. I changed the nature of the way I pulled at their energy. It was easy, like flipping a switch. I forced them to shift into their wolf forms. Normally shifting came to our kind easily, like water flowing out of one form and into another. This was anything but. Many screamed as they collapsed to the deck, writhing until they finally rose on all fours as wolves.

The two that had made it on the top of the container turned glares onto me that glowed with fury. They growled as they held their ground.

Thunder swallowed the sound of their anger. I spun, preparing to take off running, but I pulled up short when a wave of dizziness made the night lurch. Claws scrambled across metal behind me. In mid-turn, I caught the first wolf that launched at me. The surface fell out from beneath me and I realized he had knocked us off the container. He bore me to the deck, jaws snapping for my throat the entire way. On our way down I managed to turn us so he cushioned my landing.

Air expelled from him in a pained grunt. Halfway to my feet, something slammed into my side. I flew through the air again, and this time nothing softened my landing when I collided with the side of a container. Pain exploded up my back and pinched deep into my side. My hand sank into a warm wetness when I touched the area below my ribs. Calder stood glowering over me, claws extended from his human hands. My blood dripped from those claws.

I pulled at his power, but even the slightest bit of it made me so dizzy I could barely stay on my feet. Worse, the taint of it made bile work its way up my throat. I'd drained too much from the others. If I took any more, I was afraid I'd pass out. Sure, he would too, but who would recover first? I slammed the door on my power. Gasping for air and pressing a hand to my leaking side, I did my best to look indignant instead of worried. Not an easy thing to do when naked and bleeding.

"Why are you running, little sister? Isn't the *uppskera* all-powerful?" Calder said over the pounding rain. "Looks like you still bleed like the rest of us."

I decided to lie. "You're my brother. Is it so hard to believe that I don't want to kill you?"

He started to say something but had to wait for a boom of thunder before he could go on. The sound made my gaze flick skyward in time to see a flash of lightning streak across the sky. It lit a wick of hope inside me. I had to get to that tower or I might die here.

"Not hard to believe—impossible," Calder said. He shook his head as he took a step closer, claws still brandished. "But you can't do it because you're weak. Just like you're too weak to be able to absorb the power of condemned *varúlfur* and not get sick, sick with your morals and your good nature. It holds you back, makes you unable to do what needs to be done—"

I had no idea what else he said, because another deck-shaking boom of thunder crashed in the skies overhead. Fangs and claws out, I launched at my brother with all the speed I had. My claws sank into his chest, but only a few inches. He caught me and turned, using my momentum to try and fling me away. Unable to reach his neck with my fangs, I clamped onto his arm. As he threw me past him, I took a good-size chunk of his forearm with me. He screamed and howled in pain, music to my ears.

I went with the fall, somersaulting and rolling to my feet. The world spun so much, I almost kept rolling. I fell to a knee. As much as I wanted to blame it on the heaving ship, it was far more than that. The dark energy I had taken in was making me sick and trying to stir up my anger. My fight to stop it left me feeling like I was stuck in a whirlpool that was swiftly pulling me under.

Calder was on me before I could regain my feet. Instead of trying to get up, I swept a leg out and caught him behind the knees. He went down, his head slamming against the deck with a metallic thud. Claws splayed, I lurched forward. He rolled out of my path with ease. A foot slammed into my side. Pain tore through me. The asshole had kicked the same side he'd managed to stab. His foot came toward me again. I grabbed it and yanked it to me as hard as I could. Calder's other foot slipped in the standing water and he went down. His head hit the deck with a resounding thud again. Unfortunately, his leg came free of my grasp.

He scampered backwards slowly, almost drunkenly, as I rose to my feet. The blows to that hard head of his must finally be doing some good.

The scent of a dozen wet wolves surrounded us. Eyes flashed in the dark, teeth gnashed, and growls rose up. But they didn't approach. A pained yelp came from the mass. Suddenly a wolf flew through the air as if launched. It collided with the nearest container and slid down the metal. More yelps sounded. Another wolf flew, and another. Calder and I stopped circling one another to turn toward the condemned.

Among them strode a huge black wolf, hackles raised, claws swiping, and fangs tearing anything that came close enough. Just in the heartbeat I watched, three fell to his wraith. The seven remaining began to back away, tails tucked between their legs.

"V, no," I whispered.

He shouldn't be strong enough to fight like that yet. But the sight before me proved me wrong. Another wolf fell to him, and another. Seeing him fight against odds that should have been insurmountable, and winning, renewed my strength and gave me faith in his ability to stand at my side—a faith I should have had all along.

"What in Hel's name?" Calder yelled.

While he was distracted, I sprinted into the fray. I tore out the throat of one condemned as he cowered back from Vidar. I cut the hamstrings of another. The five left scurried back, a few disappearing around containers. Vidar ran to me, shifting into a man in mid-stride. He caught me in his arms and hugged me tight. The steady beat of his heart against my ear made me relieved beyond measure. The warmth of his power banished the darkness and nausea the energy of the condemned had left me with. Before I could fully enjoy the feel of his arms around me, he pulled away and gave me a push in the direction of the tower.

"Go. I'll take care of him," he said.

I shook my head. He may have just taken out half a dozen werewolves, but I still wasn't convinced he was at one-hundred percent.

"We'll do it together," I said. With Vidar's help, I wouldn't need lightning.

Then I heard the growls and the claws scraping against the deck. Eyes shone in the darkness, several sets, then more, and more, another dozen at least. Dammit, they were still coming. How many of these monsters did my brother create? He must have knocked over an entire prison. With all the hate-filled news about wolves, I had been avoiding the reports, so he could have done that very thing and I wouldn't have known. They were keeping their distance for the moment as they gathered their new force together.

"We can't take them all. You have to go. Trust me to do this for you," Vidar insisted.

At full power, I did trust he could do it. But now...

I looked at Calder, swaying as he struggled to push himself to his knees. No time remained to contemplate this.

Dashing in, I touched Vidar's cheek. "I love you, V. Survive this, because I wouldn't survive losing you."

He swallowed hard and nodded. "I love you too. And I will. Now go!"

Before I could lose my nerve, I did as he said. Rain pounding against my bare skin, I ran as fast as I could and leaped over the heads of the wolves gathering by the closest container. They snapped and snarled at me. Atop the container, I paused to growl back at them, ensuring I held their attention. So many eyes looked up at me. Only a few of them were the eyes of wolves. The newcomers were still in human form, and they didn't know to fear me yet. I could use that. They looked up at me, some with anger, hatred, others with hungry eyes that made me acutely aware of my nakedness. Uncomfortable as it was, it was worth it, because they followed me when I started running. The less Vidar had to worry about, the better. He would have his hands full with my brother.

The next container was a close leap away. As I ran across the top of the second one, the sky lit up with a strike of lightning. The hair on my arms stood up, feeling like a thousand crawling ants. A smile pulled at my lips as I dropped to the deck and pushed my legs faster. Paws and bare feet pounded after me, their rhythm music to my ears. Any attention I could take away from Vidar was welcome. I wanted to turn around and check on him so badly, but I didn't dare. If I looked at him, I wouldn't be able to resist the urge to return to his side.

Two more leaps and I made it to the tower of metal at the fore of the ship. It was a cabin of sorts with windows that overlooked the cargo area. The thing thrusting out of it like a tall, metal phallic symbol looked like it might be a crane. I started climbing it. Now and then I had to jump from ledges to outcroppings, but my progress continued. Those in human form followed, scrambling up after me with a speed born of desperation. Thunder reverberated through the sky, encouraging me to climb faster. I reached the base of the crane.

Finally, I allowed myself to turn and look for Vidar. Werewolves in both wolf and human form surged over the deck toward me from every direction. Lightning lit up the night. My hair danced from the proximity. The light nature's electricity gave off allowed me to count thirty werewolves, at least, all hungry for my blood. They were too spread out. Even if I could manage to get struck by lightning, I could never direct it to all of them, not alone.

"Vidar!" I yelled, calling out to him with everything I had, willing him to me.

After a punch that sent Calder to a knee, Vidar's head whipped in my direction.

"I need you!" I called out.

He abandoned the fight without looking back. He took the least obstructed route to the tower. Four werewolves fell to his claws on his way. Two of them he threw from the tower. Their bodies landed on the deck with a resounding metallic thud. While I watched, I grabbed hold of one of the steel cross supports of the crane, just in case lightning chose to strike earlier than I hoped. Though it felt like forever, Vidar reached me in only a few moments. Blood ran from two scratches on his chest, four across his left biceps, and another across his thigh.

He wrapped me in his arms, careful not to pull my hand free of the metal. His heart beat strong and steady against my ear. For a breath, I let myself relax against him.

Thunder clapped so loud it left my ears ringing. Vidar's arms wrapped tighter around me. I looked first to him, then to the churning sky above. But the lightning didn't come. The metallic taste of it hung in the pounding rain, and the tingling feel of it thickened the air. Power began to rush toward us from all directions, and it wasn't lightning; it was the condemned. From the press of their energy, I knew they'd be on us in only seconds. I started to pray to Odin. Vidar's voice soon joined mine. The condemned grew closer and closer.

As the first scrambled atop the platform we stood on, I dropped my walls and pulled at his power. With Vidar holding me, I didn't see the terrible things the condemned had done, but its power still tasted like poison. He collapsed to the platform. The others faltered, slowed, some fell, but they kept coming. Even with Vidar blocking the visions, I wouldn't be able to take much more. They would overwhelm us. A quick glance over my shoulder revealed that it wasn't one of the condemned after all; it was Calder. He raised one hand high. In it glinted a huge blade.

Then I tasted metal. All concern over Calder melted away. I stood between him and Vidar and that was good enough for me. It had to be. Leaning back as far as Vidar's arms would allow, I threw my hands out and looked up at the sky. A brilliant, jagged bolt of lightning streaked right toward us. Pure, raw electricity filled me to overflowing in an instant, and it kept coming. I felt Vidar's power around me like the walls of a massive dam. Together we held it, but just barely.

I concentrated on the feel of the pin lights of the condemned power all around us. There were so many. Doubt tried to itch at me. The lightning became too much to hold in. Together, Vidar and I made pathways to each of the condemned. The closest target stood only feet away. Pain pierced my back, but it was dull, distant, as though it were happening in a dream.

"Now!" I yelled.

Vidar and I dropped our shields. Lightning poured down the tunnels, straight into the condemned, and Calder. Screams filled the early morning, the loudest of which was my brother's. Even if I had wanted to stop, I couldn't. Once released, the lightning couldn't be called back or even cut off. His screams brought up the memory of every time he had made me cry out in pain throughout my childhood, every cruel word he had said to me, and every person he had killed or caused the death of over the decades.

When his screams finally stopped, a mixture of sadness and relief filled the void left by the lightning. Then I felt the pain of the knife buried in my back.

CHAPTER TWENTY

VIDAR

My long strides ate up the porch outside of Evan's great room. Back and forth, back and forth, past the hot tub, down to the fancy water feature, and back to make the rounds again. His people had offered me food, drink, a comfortable place to sit and wait, but I couldn't accept any of it. I wanted to be in the room with Ayra. The doc wouldn't allow it. Something about a sterile environment for surgery. His words were a blur of nonsense.

An hour had passed since they'd taken her into surgery. Each minute that ticked away pushed my restraint closer and closer to its limit until I felt like a mad villain full of riddled questions. I respected the doc's procedures, I really did. *But what if she needs me with her? What if she can draw on my power, use it to help heal herself?* But the doc insisted she wasn't to the stage where she could do that yet.

She'd been too badly wounded. How sterile could a room in Evan's house really be anyways? Even if it was dedicated for this purpose, as Evan said it was, how could I be sure since I hadn't seen it?

I sat down hard on the handcrafted juniper bench near the water feature. My leg bounced in time with my rapid heartbeat. Flakes of dried blood fell as I twisted my hands together. My claws extended. Wood splintered beneath my toes as my feet clenched the deck. Fangs pushed my jaws apart. I leaped up and renewed my pacing. How much of the blood on my hands belonged to the condemned, and how much was Ayra's? She had been bleeding so much...

I wanted to kill Calder all over again. It took a particularly dark son of a bitch to stab their own sibling in the back. My brothers and I were thick as thieves for the most part, if a bit competitive. To even think about hurting one of them made my stomach revolt. The memory of cutting the throat of Calder's charred, still-smoking body with my own claws both comforted and horrified me. That was one villain who would not be rising again on the last page. But if he had managed to hurt her beyond repair, then he would win after all.

Gods, an hour was long enough, wasn't it? When they cut off her anesthesia, she'd snap awake immediately. If I wasn't there... At the same time I reached for the huge French doors, Evan approached them from within the room on the other side. He opened a door for me and stepped aside.

"If I'm not there when she wakes up, she might kill someone," I said.

Evan smiled. "I figured as much, which is why I came to retrieve you."

His smile looked genuinely happy, and relief shone in his eyes. My legs nearly gave out at the sight. "She's all right?" I could tell by his expression that she was, but I needed to hear it.

He inclined his head. "The doctor expects she will make a full recovery."

I enveloped Evan in such an abrupt hug that air expelled from him in a surprised grunt. When he could breathe again, he laughed and patted me on the back.

"Come along, I'll take you to her," he said.

Thankfully, we didn't have to weave very far through the huge house before arriving at an oak door in the basement level. The room inside reminded me of a recovery room rather than an operating room, making me think they had moved her in here after surgery. She lay disturbingly still in a hospital bed. A thin blanket covered her but didn't hide the tubes coming out of her arm. Beside the bed stood Emelia, clothed in scrubs, her long red hair pulled back beneath a cap. She worked at removing the IV from Ayra's arm. The moment the needle left her skin, Ayra started to stir. I rushed to her side.

When her beautiful dark-blue eyes opened and fixed on me, I remembered how to breathe again. Our hands found each other and intertwined tightly. I leaned down and placed a chaste kiss on her lips. Her other hand found its way to the back of my head and held me in place, deepening the kiss and awakening a ravenous desire. After a while I remembered where we were and drew back.

"Did we get them?" she asked.

"Every last one."

A long, ragged breath pulled out of her, leaving her sunken into the bedding. With my free hand I stroked her hair and trailed my fingers along her cheek. "I guess these superheroes get their happy ending," I said.

Her features lit up with a determined joy. "We didn't get it, we earned it, and we took it, just as Odin would have it," she said. I loved when she did my thinking in threes thing. It sounded so much cleverer coming from her.

"Yes, we did," I said through a perma-smile that felt like it would never go away.

"What will you do now that you've saved supernatural kind from exposure and war?" Emelia's voice came from the other side of the room. She sounded delighted, and a bit saucy, as if she were suggesting something carnal.

I liked her suggestion.

"These two superheroes are going back to their lair," I said. At Ayra's brow-raise, I added, "I'm taking you home, at least for a little while. We've earned a bit of R&R."

The smile that turned up her pale pink lips did all kinds of good and dirty things to me. She pulled me down for a kiss, one that I would have felt in my toes if it had made it past my groin. I crawled onto the bed beside her and took her in my arms. Everything faded away but her. Before our clothes started to come off, I thought I heard the door open and close, but I wasn't sure. And I didn't care.

...

Ayra

The July sun shone down on us with a fierce determination that almost had me sweating. Another mile up this forested mountainside and I might actually start to glisten. The healing scar in my back pinched a little, but it wasn't anything that would slow me down. Evan's doc had done a great job and the sex and sharing of energy with Vidar afterward had completed the healing, of my body, at least. The rest was going to take a while.

My brother had been a horrible son of a bitch who earned his fate ten times over, but he had still been my brother. Being back in Hemlock Hollow stung less than I had expected. There were no good memories of him waiting around any corner of the town or the surrounding forests, only bad ones. Calder had hated me from the moment I'd been born. In contrast, the people of Hemlock Hollow had welcomed Vidar and me back like heroes, complete with a parade and an upcoming festival.

My family was another matter. When I had delivered Calder's body to them, they told me I was disowned and disinherited. It hurt, but it had also felt good, like cleaning a wound out so it could finally heal. I wouldn't miss them, their land, or their millions.

Vidar's hand reached down to me from where he stood atop a steep shelf of granite. While I could have easily jumped up beside him, I accepted his hand. The feel of his skin against mine not only drove away my demons, but it felt so good and so right that I took any opportunity I could to touch him. Some sort of blue ribbon in his other hand caught my eye. He unfurled it and gave me a mischievous grin. My brows rose.

"You'll have to wear this the rest of the way," he said.

"This is getting more promising by the second," I teased. Grinning like a dog with a bone, he lifted the ribbon toward my eyes. My gaze moved down along his body and discovered the effect my words had on him. My hopes of this leading to mating increased. The world went dark as he tied the ribbon around my head. The scents of pine, hemlock, and wildflowers gave me a rough idea of the layout of the land. Birds singing in the trees and lizards skittering over the rocks added another layer to everything.

Something about the awakening of my other senses made everything more exciting, more sensual.

Vidar's hand took hold of mine, his big fingers weaving into the spaces between my own. With gentle pushes and tugs of my hand, he guided me skillfully through the rocky, tree-covered landscape. If an obstacle arose, he warned me of it and helped me maneuver over or around it.

"You're good at this. But I was really hoping it would lead to a different kind of climb," I said.

His laughter had a sexy bedroom sound to it that made things low in my abdomen tingle. "Maybe it will, after your surprise."

"What kind of surprise?"

"Well..."

We stopped and he moved behind me, placing his hands on my shoulders. Excitement rose from my abdomen to infect all of me. His fingers worked at the knot of the ribbon. As the blue material fell away from my eyes, Vidar said, "I present to you, the Wolf's Den."

Atop the rocky hillside a big, beautiful log cabin sat nestled in the hemlock and fir trees. Massive windows on both the first and second floor overlooked the stunning footbridge the people of Hemlock Hollow had built over a deep hollow that cut through the dense forest. It was meant to be a replica of the *Bifröst*, a way to honor our old ways and our Gods. Not far below the bridge, the first building of the town poked up through the trees. Across the hollow, light bounced off the multitude of windows belonging to Raul's house. His seemed to be the closest at over two thousand yards away.

I wanted to say something, but I couldn't. This place was the safe home Vidar had helped me create in my mind during my rough childhood. Imagining it room by room had helped me sleep at night as a child. Neither my parents arguing in another room, nor my brother whispering threats, insults, and telling me to kill myself had bothered me while I imagined this cabin. It had helped me get through my childhood.

Though I didn't remember giving them the command to move, my legs carried me toward the cabin. A three-tiered raised bed of newly planted flowers and bushes led up to the covered front porch. The solid oak door with a masterful carving of a roaring wolf's head done in knotwork caught my eye. Below it sat a one-eared, orange striped cat. Upon seeing me, the cat meowed and launched itself down the steps.

"Heimdallr!" I bent and petted him as he wove through my legs, meowing an endless stream of what was no doubt cat obscenities at me for being gone so long. "I missed you so much! But how did you get here?" I looked to Vidar at the last.

The sheepish expression on his face made me want to ask him a multitude of questions. But I waited.

"I had the boys bring him and your things over once construction was done. I knew you'd want to see him right away, and this is the first place I wanted to bring you."

"The boys?" I asked, trying not to laugh as I pictured a construction crew of werewolves trying to wrangle my cat.

Vidar ran a hand along the top of the stones that made up one of the raised beds. "The ones that planted all these flowers for you. You remember them, don't you?"

Emotion choked me up, so I just nodded in answer. It was a sensation I wasn't used to. Both to hide the unexpected reaction, and because I couldn't wait any longer, I scooped up Heimdallr and climbed the stairs. I hesitated with my hand on the doorknob—a beautiful bronze thing that looked like it belonged in a castle. The anticipation of seeing our dream house warred with the fear that it couldn't possibly be everything I'd always imagined. Vidar's hand settled over mine, and we turned the knob together.

My breath caught. From the floor plan of the yawning great room leading into the kitchen, to the open loft overlooking it all, every detail we had dreamed up and talked about—and more—had been worked into the design. Light poured in through a wall of windows that reached the height of both floors of the house. From the stair railing to the walls and cabinets, log accents were everywhere.

I must have squeezed too hard because Heimdallr jumped from my arms and sauntered toward the kitchen. He already seemed perfectly at home here, and it was obvious why.

"This place is amazing!" I exclaimed.

Eyes wide, trying to take it all in at once, I grabbed Vidar's hand. "Show me. I want to see everything!"

Oozing enthusiasm, he took me from room to room, pointing out all the traditional log cabin details and special touches we'd talked about. At the top of the stairs to the loft I stopped and stared in awe. A huge four poster bed that looked like four trees growing up from the floor and disappearing into the peaked roof dominated the large space. Across from it a gorgeous stone fireplace took up most of a wall. I couldn't help but imagine all the things Vidar and I could do on such a bed.

"This wasn't in our design," I said a bit breathlessly.

He came up behind me and wrapped his arms around me. "Well, we never actually talked about the bedroom. I hope you like it." The deep, sultry way he said "bedroom" made me tingle all over.

Again, my breath had been stolen so thoroughly that I couldn't speak. Silence stretched out and I couldn't break it. Vidar's arms went stiff.

"It's too much, too soon," he said in a defeated tone.

I turned and faced him, arms slipping around his waist. "No, not at all. It's perfect down to every detail, just like you."

His shoulders relaxed and his smile began to return. Those hazel eyes, gazing down at me with more love in them than I thought any person could contain, began to melt my heart. I had to get out the rest of what I needed to say before I lost my resolve.

"But there will be more condemned. I'll always be the reaper."

To my complete and utter shock, his eyes sparkled. "Oh I know. That's why I put in a training room downstairs complete with a hidden weapon room and a massive metal tree sculpture as tall as a hundred year old lodgepole pine in the backyard."

I couldn't contain my smile. "That wasn't in our design, either."

Tenderness smoothed out the laugh lines on Vidar's face. My heart thudded faster. I'd never thought anyone could feel such tenderness for me, the reaper, not even Vidar. It had been too much to hope for.

"My designs are all about you, all on you. They always have been," Vidar said, his voice that sexy, deeper octave it sometimes got.

I ran my hands down the hard, dark planes of his bare chest. "I love you, Vidar Balderson."

"I love you too."

And just like that, every dark thing I'd endured in my life was worth it.

My fingers slipped under the waistband of his cargo shorts. "What do you say we break that bed in?"

With a growl of desire that rumbled down to my center, he bent and scooped me up in his arms. There I found peace and happiness so powerful it was euphoric. Since it came with this gift, being the chosen one of the Gods didn't seem quite so bad.

EPILOGUE

G rabbing a sprouted grain bagel off the tray beside the coffee pot,
I nodded a greeting to Officer Jorgenson who's blond head I
could just see above the monitor he labored behind.

"How's it going Gilmerson? Dad in his office?"

"Not much V—Vidar. And yep, he just got back in." The last part came
out a bit strangled, as if he had almost kicked a hornet's nest and was still
afraid it might be the death of him.

Our gazes met over the top of his monitor—his eyes wide and worried,
mine narrowed in warning. We both knew what he'd been about to call me
on accident—VD, the jocks old nickname for me in high school. Comic
books geeks and jocks didn't exactly mix, even among *varúlfur*. I let the
fact show in my gaze that now I was so much more than the little kid he'd
teased in school. Slowly, he scrunched down until I couldn't see him any
more. I could have lashed out with my power, taught him a lesson, but I
wasn't that kind of guy. Besides, he was sitting here filling out paperwork
when I had just saved us from world war three.

Taking a bite out of my bagel, I made my way down the hall to Dad's
office. I rounded the corner to find the glass door open wide and Dad
smiling up at me from a mess of open files spread out behind the name
plate that read 'Chief Balderson'.

"Son! Come in, come in!" He beckoned through a grin so huge it flashed all thirty two of his ultra-white teeth at me. "Why is it the superhero of all *varúlfur* kind deigns to visit an old man in his place of work when he could be spending time with that beautiful mate of his?"

I grinned at Dad's teasing and sank into the sturdy leather chair he motioned to. "Hey, even a superhero wants to visit his dad. Can't that be enough?"

"Of course!" He frowned at my bagel. "Of all the wonders in that box from Crescent Coffee you chose one of Anderson's multigrain bagels?" he asked through a grimace.

"Not just multi, but sprouted grain," I said after swallowing a mouthful. "Anderson's huh?"

Dad ran a hand over his smoothly shaved ebony head. "He is the only one who eats those things."

I cocked my head. "In that case, I'll take the last one with me when I leave."

Dad's belly deep laughter filled the room, warming it and making me want to join in. But I couldn't, not with such heavy thoughts on my mind.

"I know that look. What's eating you?"

Breathing out a long sigh, I glanced back at the open door behind me. It wouldn't do any good if I closed it, not considering werewolves sense of hearing. My dad gave me a nod.

"Gilmerson, why don't you grab us lunch from Mike's. Two number three combos for Vidar and me, and grab yourself whatever you want. Tell them to put it on my bill," Dad called down the hall.

"Sweet, thanks Chief," Gilmerson called back.

His chair rolled over the wood floor and a moment later the back door to the police department opened and closed. Both Dad and I breathed in deep through our noses to check for the man's scent. It struck me as odd that Dad didn't even trust him well enough to have believed he really left. But, he had.

"Something is bothering you," Dad observed.

"That obvious?"

He nodded. "That you came here instead of waiting to talk to me at dinner made it so. You and Ayra are still coming over for dinner, aren't you?"

"Yeah, of course. We're looking forward to it." I let out a long sigh. "It's this whole thing with Calder biting others in against their will, and then Anderson biting in the seeker..." I let my voice trail off along with my thoughts.

"You think they're connected."

I met his calculating gaze. "Yeah, I do. Calder isn't smart enough to do it on his own and Anderson..."

"You don't think he bit Sonja of his own free will."

Dad and I shared a long look. "I don't. Raul is a lot of things, but he would never do that to anyone, Hel, to himself. It ruined his standing in his pack."

The pen in Dad's hand began to tap on an open file as he got lost in thought. "You would have made a great detective."

"Thanks, Dad. But Odin had other plans for me."

The pride that shone in Dad's eyes at that filled me with warmth. "He did indeed. So you're wondering what I'm going to do about our rogue problem."

"I was hoping you had a plan," I admitted.

The pen tapping became more prominent. "I do." The tapping stopped and I realized he was using the pen to point at the file before him.

I leaned in for a better look. A woman with shoulder length black hair sprinkled with dark blue streaks stared up at me from the page as if in challenge. Piercing blue eyes that matched the highlights gazed out of a lovely but hard face.

"Who is this?" I asked.

"Detective Sandalius. Should she accept, she'll be coming to Hemlock Hollow to help investigate the bitings and get to the bottom of who is really involved."

I couldn't help but shoot him a wide-eyed look. "You're bringing in an outsider?"

"She's a newly bitten who needs relocating, and I'll be partnering her with someone local."

The air of mystery in his tone piqued my curiosity. "And who might that be?"

"Raul Anderson."

***

Thank you for reading! Did you enjoy? Please Add Your Review! Every review helps authors and encourages readers to take a chance on a book.

And don't miss more in the Children of Fenrir series with book three, BARED & BETRAYED, available now! Turn the page for a sneak peek!

You can also sign up for the City Owl Press newsletter to receive notice of all book releases!

SNEAK PEEK OF BARED & BETRAYED

RAUL

The acrid stench of recent gunfire made my fangs extend. My lips drew back out of a self-preservation instinct. Nose scrunched up in distaste, I crept through the thick pine trees. My atoms quivered with the urge to shift to wolf form and go into track-and-attack. I resisted. I needed to keep my head in the game for this.

Through the tree line ahead I spotted sunlight gleaming off the red hood of a truck. The breeze carried something else to my nose—blood, death, and the musk of wolves. Not werewolves, but the kind natural to this world. The knowledge of their deaths still pissed me off. As I moved, I drew my duty weapon, keeping it in a low-ready position. The grips of the Glock .40 felt slick and light in my hands. A man walked around from the other side of the truck. A brown, furry shape hung over his shoulder. He flung it onto the open tailgate. It landed softly, on top of other carcasses from the sound of it.

Anger-spiked adrenalin focused my already sharp gaze. Fit but middle-aged, the man posed little threat to my life, especially considering the outline of his rifle on the rack in the window of his truck. The only weapon on him appeared to be a knife belted at his waist. I checked the air but didn't smell any other people.

The snap of a twig sounded beneath the heal of my Danner's. The man made no indication he heard the sound. I slid through the underbrush and out into the small clearing.

As I leveled the gun on him, I commanded, "Hands above your head, right now!"

The man flinched and moved like he was going to dart around the other side of the truck.

"Don't give me a reason!" I warned.

He froze, which proved him to be smarter than most criminals. The threat in my voice must have revealed how ready and eager I was to shoot his ass. I gave him a series of commands that he followed to the letter. Once he was prone face-first in the dirt with his hands out to his sides, I holstered my gun and moved in.

"Don't move!" I commanded as I put a knee on his shoulder.

In a matter of seconds, I had him cuffed and was hauling him to his feet. I patted him down in a search for weapons. Considering I'd be able to smell whatever he was packing, it was more of a routine precautionary thing than anything else. But muscle memory habits acquired at the academy died hard. Before turning him around, I found my cool and made my canine fangs retract.

"What the hell, man? Since when do the forestry po-po arrest guys at gunpoint for hunting?" the man complained.

"Poaching," I corrected.

He spat a hunk of chew onto the ground. "Like hell. I was protecting my employer's cattle. Damn wolves have been taking out the calves lately."

"Bullshit," I called him out. He scoffed at me but didn't respond. "There isn't a cattle ranch within two hundred miles of here, and you are on private land set aside as a wolf preserve. Let's cut the shit and stop wasting each other's time."

The man stared at my mouth. A hint of fear widened his eyes. Shit.

"What the fuck man? You got two sets of incisors? That's some weird crap. And what the hell, do you sharpen those things?"

I turned him around and started marching him toward my Forestry

Department Cherokee. Down the overgrown road, a dark Ford Explorer with a light bar on top bounced in my direction—Hemlock Hollow PD.

When the poacher stumbled, I dragged him, one of my hands beneath his arm, the other on one of his wrists. His complaints of pain were music to my ears, especially when we passed the tailgate of the truck and I saw how many wolf carcasses were piled in it. Half a dozen. He'd slaughtered the entire South Fork pack. And because they were normal wolves and not shifters, all I could do was arrest him.

He must have picked up on how pissed off I was because he started to try to justify himself. "Come on man, you've heard about all the wolf attacks. People are being killed, people!"

I had no comeback for that. I couldn't tell him normal wolves weren't doing it.

"You can't arrest me for protecting American citizens. It ain't right," he went on.

"I'm not."

He relaxed and stood up a bit taller, walking on his own now. We reached the back of my Cherokee. The Hemlock Hollow Police truck rolled to a stop not far from us. The tall, broad, blond cop who got out nodded to me, then opened the back door. He stood there waiting, face stoic, pale eyes staring straight ahead, prepared like the good ex-fullback he was.

The poacher started to protest as I walked him toward the truck. "What, no, but you said you weren't arresting me for protecting American citizens. You said!"

"I'm not. I'm arresting you for poaching and for trespassing on private property."

The man's murky eyes widened as they took in the name on the side of the police Explorer. The police officer grinned at him. "You're lucky one of the owners of this private property didn't shoot your hick ass," he said in a voice so mirthful it was downright disturbing. It made me smile in return.

"I didn't know I was that close to Hemlock Hollow, I swear! I must have got turned around. I'm so sorry. I'm so sorry!" he said, voice rising with each word.

I shoved him into the Cherokee and slammed the door. He pressed his wide-eyed face to the glass and continued to scream out apologies. Ignoring him, I turned to the officer.

"Thanks, Jörgensson. Another minute and I wouldn't have been able to resist tearing him apart," I said.

"Welcome, Captain." His nose sniffed the air and his blond brows pulled together. "That the South Fork pack?"

I nodded.

"Dammit. Thanks for catching him." One wouldn't think a person could pack so much sincerity into so few words, but Jörgensson was like that. "You gonna drop by to fill out the paperwork, or you want me to?"

I patted his shoulder. "No reason for you to stay late. You have a new baby at home. I'll be by. But I am going to go for a run first, see if he left any survivors behind, make sure he was the only one out here."

Jörgensson gave me his tight-lipped version of a smile. "In that case, I'll take the long, bumpy way back to town."

I laughed and he joined in. "Kiss that baby for me," I called as he walked around and got into the driver's seat of his rig.

He nodded. "Will do, Captain."

The old nickname drove away a bit of the chill of death that clung to this place, but only for a second. I put my duty weapon and radio in my rig, locked it, then walked back into the forest. Once I got deep enough into the thick, fragrant pines, I stripped down. I placed my folded clothing on top of my boots beneath a low-growing pine bough. A late summer breeze flitted across my bare skin. It felt better than good, stimulating almost. The damn, unnatural polyester blend of the uniform itched. But that's what I got for working for the forestry instead of Hemlock Hollow PD. Like most of the world, the majority of the forestry department was oblivious to the existence of my kind.

I exhaled and let my human form go. My paws brushed the pine needle-covered ground a second later. I shook out my brown and white fur, starting at my nose and ending at my tail. The movement left me feeling charged, ready to go. Thoughts focused down to the comforting state of need and instinct. The scents of the forest stretched before me into dozens of different trails. But only one interested me today.

I picked up the hunter's scent immediately. It tainted everything around it with the stench of gun oil and spent powder. Nose to it, I settled into a fast trot, eating up the ground at a speed that would make a human dizzy. About two miles later, the scent trail led me to a small cave in a rocky hillside. The darkness yawning from within it was thick with bad vibes. The place wreaked of death, recently spilled blood, and the musk of wolves—normal wolves who had been slaughtered because one of my kind had murdered people and made it look like an animal attack.

Mind stuck in a haze of anger instead of being in the game where it should have been, I almost missed the soft sound of a whine. The high-pitched sound wasn't one an adult could make So much sorrow filled the pitiful little voice it pinched at me. Not wanting to scare it, I crept slowly inside. The whine turned to the low growl of one still figuring out how to make the sound. The fact it even tried impressed me. My werewolf eyes adjusted quickly to the dim light of the cave. In the back, a ball of brown and white fluff growled at me through tiny, bared fangs. A male from the scent. It was barely bigger than my front paws put together. To its right lay the still body of an adult wolf. The scent of congealing blood surrounded the carcass.

As I approached, the pup took a step toward me. He gnashed his teeth. I made a chuffing sort of bark at him. The sound wasn't unfriendly, exactly, more disciplinary. His head perked up, then cocked to the side. I lowered my snout to his level and half-closed my eyes. Little claws clicked on stone as he trotted up to me without hesitation. He rubbed his face along the side of mine, let out one whine, and then trotted over to the carcass. When I didn't follow, he let out a bark.

Sympathy overrode impatience. I walked over to him. For good measure—and mostly to appease him—I nudged the dead wolf with my nose. A gunshot wound had made a mess of her stomach, and yet she had managed to drag herself all the way back here. This had to be her pup. I let out a short whine, took a step back, and turned from the carcass. The pup let out a series of pitiful cries that sounded eerily like human weeping. He ran over and rubbed against my leg. Careful as I could, I picked him up in my jaws by the scruff of his neck. His whimpering faded away and he relaxed in my grip.

Leaving him here wasn't an option, he'd just die. I trotted back toward my truck. Lucky for this one, we had a new mom in town, kind of a rare thing for us. He remained still and quiet the entire way back. A mixture of bravery and sorrow wafted from him—part scent, part a feeling I picked up on.

I stopped at my clothes and sat him down. He sniffed at the two piles of material, then backed away until he bumped into my leg. A startled yip popped from him. The sound turned into a growl as he stared my clothes down like they were some kind of threat. I licked the top of his head and he fell silent. A quiet chuff got his attention fully on me. I hated to put him through this, but there was no other way. To minimize alarming him, I sat down on my haunches before I shifted to human form. Eyes popping wide open, the pup growled and scampered backwards until he had climbed halfway up onto my shirt. I chuffed at him again. He froze, head cocking to the side. Staring me down, little growl still rumbling through him, he hiked his leg and peed on my shirt.

Moving too quick for him to react, I snatched him up and moved him away from my stuff. He growled and snapped at me, squirming in an attempt to get some part of me in his jaws. I held him up and gently blew into his face. He immediately stilled. Another breath and he had my scent. His fan-like tail swept to the side once, then twice. This time, when I sat him down, he stayed put.

I grabbed my clothes—the dry ones, at least. "I don't like it much either, but you didn't have to pee on it."

Lips curling up from his teeth, he watched me with suspicion. The growl-bark noise I emitted made him plop down on his butt. I put my pants and boots on and picked him up by the scruff of the neck. He didn't struggle, but I put an arm beneath him anyway. This close he would notice the scent of my skin wasn't much different than the scent of my fur. He relaxed against me, nuzzling his head into my abs. Cradling him in one arm, I picked up my offending shirt, holding it well away from us both.

As I walked from the trees, I repositioned him so he could bury his nose in the crook of my arm. No sense in him seeing the poacher's truck and the grisly remains of his pack in the bed. He had suffered enough for a lifetime, let alone for today.

Don't stop now. Keep reading and grab your copy of BARED & BETRAYED today! And find more from Heather McCorkle at www.heathermccorkle.com

NOTES & GLOSSARY

PACK BREAKDOWN:

Reinhard Pack: Five-hundred-sixty members strong. Located in Hemlock Hollow, Montana. Alphas: Ander Argeirson and Gyda Björnsdöttir (parents of Raul Anderson).

Draupnir Pack: Two-hundred-fifty members strong. Located in Hemlock Hollow, Montana. Alphas: Bain Robertson and Morene Andersdöttir as his first *verndari*, standing in as the ruling female until he finds a mate.

Arnoddr Pack: Five-hundred-twelve members strong. Located in Hemlock Hollow, Montana. Alphas: Isak Gunnarsson and Iona Hákonsdöttir (his mother) as ruling female until he finds a mate.

NEW CHARACTERS:

Kali: A weretiger assassin born in Vietnam.

Evan McDougall: Scottish *draugr* who lives in Portland, Oregon.

Emelia McDougall: Scottish *draugr* who lives in Portland, Oregon. Evan's younger sister.

GLOSSARY:

Aegir: Norse god of the seas.
Asni: donkey, ass
Berserkr: Werebear.
Draugr (*draugar*, plural): Norse for "again walker"; vampire.
Frelsari: liberator
Gungnir: The spear of Odin.
Kennari: Teacher.
Konunglegur: Royalty among Hemlock Hollow werewolves.
Leitar: Seeker of the near-mad.
Landsvæði: Territory. To shifters, once it has been invoked it means they will kill any trespassers that come into their territory.
Lögreglu: Police.
Mjölnir: Thor's hammer.
Ráðið: Council.
Uppskera: Reaper of shifters.
Varúlfur: Werewolf.
Verða: "Becoming," the change into a shifter.
Verndari: Protector.

Want even more paranormal romance? Try RED ALERT by City Owl Author, Tina Moss, and find more from Heather McCorkle at www.heathermccorkle.com

Special Agent Jame Bradshaw has five dead senators on her hands... and a pack of trouble between her claws.

As the newest team leader for the Paranormal Crimes Division, this feisty shifter is smack in the middle of a political hornet's nest waiting to implode. With the mass murder at the Capitol building and the city under a red alert, paranoia spreads like wildfire. She must solve this mystery before the higher-ups call for her head.

When former vampire vigilante and newly minted PCD agent, Drake, shows up to the scene, the case heats up and so does the tension.

Fighting off the charms of a lethal hundred-and-fifty-year-old vamp may prove Jame's final undoing...in the most delicious ways. But if this alpha shifter doesn't learn to let down her defenses and channel the passion into a true partnership, she'll risk losing more than her badge.

Please sign up for the City Owl Press newsletter for chances to win special subscriber-only contests and giveaways as well as receiving information on upcoming releases and special excerpts.

All reviews are **welcome** and **appreciated**. Please consider leaving one on your favorite social media and book buying sites.

For books in the world of romance and speculative fiction that embody

Innovation, Creativity, and Affordability, check out City Owl Press at www.cityowlpress.com.

ACKNOWLEDGMENTS

To readers old and new, thank you for choosing my book out of all the amazing books out there! I appreciate you more than I can ever say. And of course I owe a huge thank you to my amazing publishing team all the way from cover design to content and copy editing. You ladies have been amazing in helping to make Tempered & Turned the very best it can be. You are my dream team! My better half deserves all the lemon cake and mac & cheese (Just not together. Ick.) in the world for putting up with the endless hours of chatting about this plot thread or that character arc.

ABOUT THE AUTHOR

HEATHER McCORKLE is an Amazon
bestselling author of paranormal
romance, historical romances, urban
fantasy, and steampunk. She lives in the
Great Northwest with her amazing
husband and horizontally challenged
cat. As a Native Oregonian, she enjoys
the outdoors as much as the worlds she
creates on the pages. When she isn't
writing, reading, or editing, you can find
her on the ski slopes, or prepping for ski
season by hiking, mountain biking, and paddleboarding. She has been
known to play an excessive amount of disc golf, but still claims to be
mediocre at it.

www.heathermccorkle.com

 twitter.com/HeatherMcCorkle

instagram.com/heathermccorkle

facebook.com/authorHeatherMcCorkle

pinterest.com/heathermccorkle

ABOUT THE PUBLISHER

City Owl Press is a cutting edge indie publishing company, bringing the world of romance and speculative fiction to discerning readers.

Escape Your World. Get Lost in Ours!

www.cityowlpress.com

f facebook.com/YourCityOwlPress
🐦 twitter.com/cityowlpress
📷 instagram.com/cityowlbooks
📌 pinterest.com/cityowlpress